A POROUS BORDER

A NOVEL OF CANADA
AND THE
AMERICAN CIVIL WAR

Al McGregor (signature)

Al McGregor

Library and Archives Canada Cataloguing in Publication

McGregor, Al
A porous border : a novel of Canada and the American Civil War / Al McGregor.

Issued also in electronic format.
ISBN 978-0-9689207-4-9

1. United States--History--Civil War, 1861-1865--Fiction.
I. Al McGregor Communications (Firm) II. Title.

PS8625.G735P67 2012 C813'.6 C2012-903877-6

Cover design by Quantum Communications

Published by Al McGregor Communications
www.almcgregor.com

FOR SUZANNE

INTRODUCTION

The Civil War was a shared experience across North America, yet few American realize the role played by Canadians, and few Canadians understand how the turmoil affected their country.

When the first shot was fired at Fort Sumter, the British colonies in what is now Canada were a loose group of fractious provinces. By the time General Robert E. Lee surrendered at Appomattox, a new nation was taking shape.

In the early stages, the American War was a distant distraction as the Union attempted to quell rebellion in the Southern states. As the conflict grew in intensity, thousands of young Canadians flaunted or ignored neutrality laws and joined the fight. British and Canadian officials were powerless to stop the flow.

For former slaves who found sanctuary in British territory, the cause was freedom. For others, with family or commercial ties to the South, the cause would be lost. Still others had no cause but sought money or adventure. More than a few, on both sides of the border, were swept forward by events beyond their control.

For a brief period during the Trent crisis in 1861, Great Britain and the United States were on the verge of war, and even when the tension eased, the fear remained. If the South won independence, would the Americans turn land-hungry eyes to the north?

In the British provinces, John A. Macdonald, George Brown, George Etienne Cartier, and Thomas D'Arcy McGee saw stalemate in the legislature and faced decisions clouded by language, race, and religion. Only a new vision could break the political deadlock, and the effort was hastened by the fear of invasion.

In 1864, the Southern Confederacy added to the pressure with a campaign aimed at terror and revolution. Confederate agents, based in Canada, crossed into the Northern states with plans to attack Federal prison camps, burn cities, incite riots, and arm a ship as a Great Lakes raider. Their efforts would expand to political kidnapping with a link to the Lincoln assassination.

Canadian authorities ordered militia to the border in an attempt to thwart the rebel attacks and to placate the growing anger of Washington. A once peaceful frontier was on a knife's edge.

A Porous Border, A Novel of Canada and the American Civil War is based on actual events; from the vantage point of spies and generals, clerks and politicians, Southern belles and faithful servants, farmers and sailors, friends and lovers. The lives of historic figures and the fictional characters are complicated by war. Their journeys carry them across eastern North America as key participants or as witnesses. A few will meet. Others will only pass in the night.

On the Ohio River: July 1863

"Yah! Git!"

The young man dug the spurs into his horse. Only the gray hat tied to his head identified him as a Confederate. His pants were blue. His shirt was a faded white. A fully cooked ham liberated from an Ohio kitchen bounced behind his saddle.

"A bunch of the men are already across, General Morgan."

He shouted his message before pulling the animal to a halt. "I saw Lightning swimming along, pulling his horse behind him. Everybody is going to be glad to be back in Kentucky!"

The boy was rewarded with a tired smile from John Hunt Morgan. Through a month of raids and skirmishes, Morgan had managed to keep the gray linen suit clean, but today the thigh-high leather boots were water stained and covered with flecks of mud. He had gone halfway across the Ohio River with the first of his cavalry before returning to guide the remainder forward.

Only about three hundred men of the 2,500 who began the great raid in early July were left. Some had deserted; more than a few—including his own brother—had been killed; and more, he suspected, simply had collapsed from twenty-hour days in the saddle. They had fought their way across a thousand miles of Northern territory in Tennessee, Kentucky, Indiana, and Ohio.

He lifted his black slouch hat to wipe the sweat from his forehead. It was early but the day promised more steaming heat.

"Thank you, Mr. Bradley!"

The boy beamed, pleased that Morgan remembered his name, but his face fell in disappointment as his commander continued.

"Make your way back to the river and cross with the next company."

"I should stay with you, General. You may need a messenger."

Morgan considered the request. The boy was brave enough. He had first signed on as a horse holder while other men dismounted to fight, and as the ranks thinned, Bradley had been promoted. After two years of service, he was barely sixteen.

"No," Morgan lied, "We'll need you on the other side."

As Bradley reluctantly turned his horse toward the river, a loud shriek cut through the air. Boy and horse vanished in a pink swirl.

For Morgan, there was silence, but he saw another explosion to his right and a third on the road ahead. He slammed his hands against his ears, hoping to restore a semblance of hearing.

Another rider showing no military insignia galloped toward him.

"You'll have to shout, Tom," Morgan called. "That shell has affected my hearing."

Another shell burst close to his left, and just as suddenly, his hearing returned.

"The shells are from Federal gunboats," Tom Hines yelled. "They've worked up the river and are cutting off the fords. Duke is pulling the men back but there's another Federal column moving up to our right."

"And there's been dust rising in the east all morning," Morgan told him. "More Yankees are coming."

He tried to avoid looking at where Bradley had been. There had been too many others like him.

"I'm going to take the rest of the men north. If we can reach Lake Erie we might be able to commandeer boats and make our way to Canada."

Hines produced a wry grin. "It feels like we've drawn all the Federal armies into Ohio. I hope our work is appreciated."

"We've given them a scare. With all the Yankees chasing us, General Lee will have an easier time with the invasion of Pennsylvania and we're further north than any Confederate force has been," Morgan said, returning the smile but growing serious as another shell exploded on the road. "Go back and tell General Duke what's happening."

Hines had already wheeled his horse when Morgan reached across and grabbed the reins.

"Tell him. I'll regroup and collect the stragglers at the crossroads about an hour up the road. And Tom, tell him we've lost enough. No more men should have to die. If he's surrounded, he should surrender."

Hines nodded as Morgan released his grip on the reins.

"And Tom, requisition a hat or a tunic, something that makes you look like a real Confederate soldier. We don't want you captured and hanged as a spy. We need you for what's ahead."

CHAPTER 1

Journal of Paul Forsey, government clerk, summer 1862

I would have preferred India or the China Station but find myself in the temporary capital of the Canadian provinces; quaint perhaps, but far from the frenzy of London and the more likely paths to promotion.

Canada is two separate provinces under one common government. Canada East is the old French section. Canada West is said to be thoroughly English and growing rapidly. I am expected to understand the provincial concerns but already find that attention is focused on the American War.

The prominent old Loyalist families remember the American Revolution, their flight from another civil war, and cheer each Southern victory. However, other larger segments of the population admire the Union and all that it represents.

Of course, the future is well beyond the control of smalltime politicians and businessmen. If the South wins independence, Washington may seek new lands and only a thin red British line stands between the Union army and these Crown colonies.

* * *

LONDON, CANADA WEST: JULY 1862

The light from the row of torches washed across the platform, bathing the speaker in a flickering glow. His stooped shoulders made him appear shorter than he actually was, and the voice was high and thin, but the audience listened in rapt attention.

"The American war may well bring an era of standing armies, of passports, of espionage; of fluctuating boundaries and border raids. Are we prepared to welcome a state of permanent and increasing armaments for North America?"

Several voices shouted "No!" and another yelled, "Tell us what to do!"

The speaker dropped his voice as if sharing a secret with the two hundred souls in his audience. "We have the potential to create a great new nation, one that could unite the British colonies across North America, Canada East and West, the Maritime Provinces, the Hudson's Bay Company lands, and faraway British Columbia."

On the edge of the crowd, a young man snickered for no apparent reason.

"Shush," an older man glared. "We came to listen to D'Arcy McGee and not some ignorant youngster."

The young man turned to a friend of about the same age and tugged on his shirtsleeve. "Owen! Let's go!"

"Yes, go!" the older man hissed. "McGee doesn't come this way often. It's a shame to see his speech ruined by young pups."

The young man readied a retort but his friend caught his eye and shrugged his head to the rear. "Let it go, Jimmy," he cautioned before edging from the crowd.

On the platform McGee continued. "We'll need to create more business ties and expand the railroads, but the first issue is defense."

"Ah, who cares," Jimmy muttered as they retreated into the dusk falling over the fair grounds. "I expected to see more than an Irish politician at this Great Western exhibition, and I can see all the cows and pigs and horses I want back home."

"And where is home?" The voice came from behind them.

The pair hadn't noticed the man who followed them from the crowd. They turned to speak. "Port Burwell area," Jimmy declared.

A thick growth of beard snaked around the man's lower jaw, and despite the fading light, they saw he was tanned and weathered by the sun. But it was the clean, well-pressed suit that made him stand out.

"Port Burwell?" the man asked. "That's on Lake Erie, isn't it?"

"Yes," Jimmy answered, "although, we don't live right in the town. Our farms are a few miles north."

"Farms?" The man showed surprise. "You look too young to be property owners."

"Yeah, well," Jimmy confessed, "they're not really ours. My parents died a few years ago and my brother runs the place. Owen is pretty much in the same boat, except he lives with an uncle that he doesn't get along with. So, as they say, we are the last of the litter. There's no inheritance for us."

The fair vendors had begun to close their tents for the night as the three made their way back toward the entrance.

"Fair like this wouldn't be shutting down at dusk in my country," the older man volunteered. "They go well into the night with shows and contests to keep a person amused. I'm from southern Ohio."

"Well, aren't you a long way from home." Jimmy offered his hand. "I'm Jimmy Hampstead and this is Owen McFeeters."

The American appraised the two young men. Probably in their late teens or early twenties, both looked strong and used to hard work. The one named Jimmy was obviously a talker. The other was silent but took in everything around him.

"Names aren't really important," he told them. "I noticed you in the crowd and was reminded of myself a few years ago."

"Looks like you did all right," Jimmy replied.

Owen stopped to run his hands over a harness displayed by a local dealer, but stayed close enough to listen.

"Yeah, I moved around but I made real money when the war came."

The American glanced back to where Owen was hefting a harness and pulling gently on the straps. "You can buy it," the dealer told him gruffly. "But I'm closing and I'm not going to dicker."

Owen merely nodded, dropped the straps, and moved on.

3

"I'm not in the regular army right now," the American resumed. "I served my time. But I'm going back. They're offering bounties, big rewards to sign up, a hundred dollars or maybe more. That can buy a man a good time."

Jimmy whistled and then announced, "That's big money."

"Well, if I was you, I would think of heading south and joining the Union army."

The American moved closer. "I could help you through the process. Let's go down the street; I'll buy you supper and something to drink."

"Ah, sorry, we can't." Owen broke his silence. "We'll be leaving shortly."

"I sure wish we had the time," Jimmy apologized. "I'd like to hear more."

"I wish you did, too."

Disappointed, the American began to scan the crowd.

"If you change your mind, I'll be in the bar at the Tecumseh House."

"A hundred dollars bounty money," Jimmy repeated.

"We might end up in our own army," Owen suggested. "When we were coming into town, those soldiers were setting up cannons on the Wharncliffe road." He stopped suddenly, wondering if the American could be a Yankee spy.

The American only smiled. "We got enough on our hands without thinking of invading this flyspeck—but listen, boys. Forget about the British army or local militia. There's no money and you'd be bossed by some English bastard. Did you know men are whipped in the British army? If you want to join a real army, where the soldiers are treated well and are well paid, come to the States."

"Well, thanks for the advice," Jimmy began, but the American was already moving toward another group of young men.

"We should go," Jimmy said.

"Yeah, we have a long ride ahead," Owen agreed. "And I'm not looking forward to bouncing around in that wagon."

"No, no! That's not what I mean," Jimmy snorted. "We should go south, collect that bounty money and see the world. What do we do with winter coming on? Hire out again to fell trees for damn poor pay, watch the ships carry the lumber across the lake and return with all that cash for the mill owners—and we get squat?"

"A person can get killed in the army," Owen reminded him.

"We can get killed in the bush, too. Drop a tree the wrong way or have some moron make a mistake and you're dead! Remember last year when the head flew off the axe and just missed me? There's nothing to hold us here. You heard what that American called us: a flyspeck. You stay if you want. But I'm going."

"Let me think about it," Owen answered quietly.

"Don't think too long," Jimmy warned. "I'm going and going soon."

* * *

QUEBEC CITY, CANADA EAST: AUGUST 1862

"And you would be the new clerk?"

"Yes, Mr. Macdonald, I'm Paul Forsey, only at the legislature for a week."

"Well then you have a lot to learn and we're the people to teach you." John A. Macdonald spoke with a slight chuckle and while his Scottish roots were clear, his tone caught the junior clerk's attention.

Macdonald, the best-known politician in British North America, appeared tired. His coat was tossed across a nearby chair and his shirt was soiled, and crushed as if it had been slept in.

"Did Bernard send the file?" Macdonald asked, running his hands through curly but dirty hair.

"Yes, sir, the chief secretary said you wanted the latest on the American recruiting in Canada West but he said there wasn't much."

Forsey set the file in front of the minister, but it was several moments before Macdonald began to focus on the papers. The clerk was left to shift awkwardly.

"What's that number?" Macdonald abruptly shoved a page across the desk and pointed with a smudged fingernail.

Forsey reached for the paper before removing his spectacles and holding the page close to his eyes. The glasses were useless. They were supposed to make him look more mature but were of no value for reading.

"It's a five, sir," he finally announced and passed the page back.

"Ah, yes!" Macdonald agreed. "And let that be another lesson. Handwriting must be precise, neat, and easy to read."

The silence returned as he thumbed the pages.

"Take a note to Bernard," Macdonald suddenly ordered. "Tell him we need more on these crimps. They dash across the border, tell lies to our young men, and entice them to join their Union army. We need more information before we send a formal complaint. Thousands of our young men are being lured away."

"I heard fifty thousand," Forsey blurted out. "Men from Canada West and Canada East and some of the French can't speak English but the Americans take them!"

Macdonald stared across the desk, his eyes bloodshot but intense. "And where did you hear that?"

Forsey was taken aback. "Well, I...I just heard it somewhere. I'm not sure where."

"Then let that be another lesson," Macdonald scowled. "Here in the ministry we need precise information and we need to know where it comes from. Not hearsay, not rumor, not some trifle heard on the street, real facts. British men in the Union army are breaking the Queen's neutrality laws, but I can't deal with it until I am certain."

"Yes sir."

"We have to be precise. The American army is making a hash of their war. They've yet to stop the Confederacy and if they don't soon, Britain may have no choice but to step in. Each Southern victory is one more step on their road to independence. British recognition of the South will be seen as a declaration of war in Washington and that will bring us in. So facts are what we need: good hard facts."

Macdonald returned to the papers, leaving a chastised clerk to stand shifting uncomfortably in front of the desk.

A clock in a nearby office chimed the hour before the attorney general again raised his head. "Tell me," he asked. "What brings you to government?"

Forsey shifted again. The facts would show a desperate need for steady work.

"In the family, Mr. Macdonald," he said instead. "My father was a clerk in London and he suggested I spend time in a colonial administration."

His late father had gambled away the family fortune. Immigration on a one-way ticket was the only option.

"And he always taught me that working for the good of the people was an honorable calling."

Macdonald merely stared across the desk.

"Do you come from a big family?" he finally asked.

"I'm the only one left."

"Yes, well, I see." Macdonald began to shuffle the papers into order. "Family is important," he said quietly. "I have a son in Kingston. My sister has cared for him since my wife died, and of late, I've been thinking I should spend more time there. Perhaps it's time to give up politics and return to law."

He paused, lost in his thoughts, before shoving the papers across the desk. "One more thing." Macdonald stretched back in the chair but fixed his gaze on the younger man. "Nothing that is said, written, or discussed goes beyond this office. I must make that clear. Any indiscretion in that regard is cause for immediate dismissal."

"I understand."

"See that you remember it."

CHAPTER 2

Washington: September 1862

The distant pounding of hooves woke Festus Stephens, and it was only as the horse and rider thundered down the dirt track beside the tent that he remembered he was in the Union army.

It was four weeks since he had signed up in Pittsburgh, where he was ordered to a rudimentary military training camp and on to the units defending Washington. The army had moved faster than he'd expected.

The horseman reined in to answer a picket's challenge. The horse nervously stamped the ground. Then, what seemed only seconds later, Stephens heard the shout, "Bugler! Boots and saddles!"

A tall soldier rose from the rear of the tent and shook Festus as he passed.

"Might as well get up, Stephens. They'll call for us next; I've seen this before. Courier comes in with a message and wakes the whole damn camp. Sometimes nothing happens, but when they move the horse soldiers out, we're sure to follow."

Stephens knew only that the man was called Langton and unlike the recent volunteers, he had served in the regular army.

"What do you think?" another young soldier called. "Are they sending us to Bull Run—again?"

"Do I look like General McClellan? How the hell would I know?" Langton snarled.

"Keep your bloody mouths shut," another voice interrupted. This time it was a corporal who had joined the unit only a few hours after Stephens did.

"Corporal!" an officer called as he hurried through the camp. "Get your men together. No food, basic kit only. We'll be moving fast."

"Any word of what's up?"

The officer hesitated before he answered. "There's a fight brewing at a place called Antietam. All I know is that they want reinforcements as fast as they can get them."

The short, stumpy figure of Festus Stephens caught the officer's eye.

"Corporal! Men like that one—the fat one—there's no way he can keep up. Leave him behind."

"I can make him move," the corporal asserted.

"No! He'll slow us down. I don't want stragglers."

As the officer moved off, the corporal pushed up to Stephens.

"Lucky little bastard," he spat violently. "The rest of us are facing God knows what, and you get to stay and sleep."

Stephens tried to defend himself. "But I'm ready to go," he said. "I can keep up."

"Oh and I'd like to make you keep up, but that officer has made the choice. You stay. Maybe you can dig a latrine while the rest of us are winning the war."

* * *

ANTIETAM, MARYLAND: SEPTEMBER 17, 1862

"I can't really see much," the boy soldier called over the din. "All this smoke, I can't see where we're going. They said we was going to something called Anti-um Creek. But I don't see no water."

"Don't you fret over that," Langton reassured him. "Do as you are told and keep that line straight."

"I don't like it much," the soldier yelled back. He slapped at his side as something pinged off the canteen strapped on his belt. "There's supposed to be thousands of Union boys here but in this smoke I can't see them nowhere."

"Watch your step." Langton suddenly jerked him to the left. "Those men are ours." The young soldier had almost stepped on a man, one of several who had fallen in a perfectly straight line.

"Be they dead?" the youth asked, stopping in his tracks only to be propelled forward by the flat of a sword swatted sharply across his back.

"Worry about them later," a voice said. Langton glanced back to see an officer holding a revolver in one hand and the sword in the other.

"A little further, men," the officer said. "Keep moving forward."

The soldier drew abreast of Langton, eager to be with anyone who could guide him through the thick smoke and screaming projectiles.

"Just a little further," the young soldier shouted, largely for his own benefit.

Langton twisted sideways to say something but instead crumpled silently to the ground.

"Keep moving!" the officer ordered. "Keep moving!"

A few steps later, a breeze cut a clearing in the smoke to reveal a sunken laneway. Men dressed in butternut and gray lay prone with rifles resting on the grade, their attention focused to the front, unaware of the Union force approaching from the side.

"We've done it!" the Union officer screamed. "We've flanked them. First rank! Take aim!"

Fifty rifles pointed toward the unsuspecting rebels.

"Fire!"

His command came as an explosion of joy followed by a chorus of lead.

The smoke settled back in.

"Reload!" he screamed.

The boy soldier stood with his weapon still pointed forward, peering into the smoke.

The officer slapped the boy's back.

"Reload!"

Instead, there was a shot and the rifle recoiled sharply against the boy's shoulder. "I thought I could see one still wiggling," he told the officer. "I think I got him."

A second later, the boy pitched forward, cut down by a rebel bullet.

* * *

WASHINGTON: SEPTEMBER 19, 1862

Stephens didn't draw the latrine duty but was assigned as a messenger. Two days later, after delivering a note to the War Department, he slipped into a hotel dining room.

Distant screams began as he sat down. Another diner offered an explanation as he set his plate at an empty seat. "The first of the ambulances," the man said. He nonchalantly began to dip a biscuit into the gravy that drenched his food. "Poor devils have been bouncing and shaking for two days. The surgeons patch them at Antietam and send them on to the Washington hospitals but I doubt there's room for them all."

The man wore a dust-covered jacket over a checked shirt, and had plopped a small travelling bag on the table beside him.

"You must be privy to more information than the rest of Washington," Stephens told him.

The sounds continued to drift from the street. Stephens toyed with his knife and fork, avoiding the slab of rare beef on his plate.

"I suspect I am," the man answered. He patted the bag. "I have the full story of the battle right here, and in a day or so the rest of the world will know. I'm Bartlett, a reporter—well, a stringer for now, for the *New York Tribune*, but when my story goes out, I'll get a full-time reporter's job. I'm the first back, but the War Department is refusing to allow me to use the telegraph. Soon as I finish eating, I'll take a train to New York. The *Tribune* will publish without the blessing of Washington."

"So what's happened?" Stephens asked. He leaned forward, his plate forgotten.

Another shriek of pain pierced the din of the dining room and produced a brief silence. Bartlett was undisturbed and attacked a chicken breast. He took three quick bites and swallowed before brushing his sleeve across his mouth. "I won't tell you everything," he began. "If too many people know, I'll lose my exclusive or be arrested. It's happened before. The War Department likes to put a stamp on the news."

"Is the fight that bad?" Stephens wanted to know.

"It depends what you mean by bad." Bartlett reached for the bread. "For a change, the Union army didn't lose. Lee and his Confederates fought hard then slipped back south of the Potomac. So I suppose the army will claim a Union victory, but it's not much of one. And I'm guessing if our generals moved faster, they could have wiped out the Southern army."

"Well, that doesn't sound so bad." The noise from the street had lessened. Stephens began to work the knife through the beef, exposing the pink meat.

"Oh, it's bad," Bartlett corrected him. "A bloodbath with thousands dead on both sides. And thousands more wounded. This was the worst fight yet."

The door to the street opened to reveal a line of wagons filled with wounded men. Stephens averted his eyes and wondered if his former company had arrived at Antietam before the shooting started.

"Be days before we know the full numbers," Bartlett continued. "But the dead in some places are stacked on top of one another, so like I said, thousands of them."

He made short work of the rest of the chicken breast and reached for the coffee. "I'd rather have something stronger but I don't trust myself. There will be time for liquor when the story is in print."

Bartlett swirled the coffee in his mouth as he studied Stephens. "And you, my portly friend," he inquired. "You must be headquarters— or perhaps you have a political connection to keep you safe."

"No, no..." Stephens was angered by Bartlett's suggestion. "I'm going to be in action. I signed up to save the Union, and that's what I'm going to do."

Bartlett dipped a biscuit into the last of the gravy. "Save the Union, eh? I hear the war aim may be changing. Mr. Lincoln may be ready to deal with the Negroes."

"But I'm fighting to keep the country together," Stephens told him. "We can settle the Negro issue later."

"Yeah, I suppose."

Bartlett reached for a napkin and slowly wiped his mouth. "That's what you and a whole bunch of people think, but Mr. Lincoln may have another idea."

The entire dining room went silent at a piercing shriek from the street.

The reporter rose and collected his bag. "Wonder what that soldier thought he was fighting for?"

* * *

CHATHAM, CANADA WEST: SEPTEMBER 24, 1862

"Mary Ann, I found one."

The black woman stood in the door of the printing office waiting for a response. "Is you here?"

"Yes, in the back. I'll be right out."

Mary Ann Shadd Carey emerged a moment later and removed the ink-stained smock that covered her dress. "I was fiddling with the press," she explained. "All it took was to tighten one gear. It will handle a couple of hundred copies."

"Well, here's the Toronto newspaper," the woman said. She was a dark shade of black, almost blue, a striking contrast to the olive-skinned woman in front of her. "I found it whiles I was cleaning at the hotel."

The newspaper was quickly spread on a desk. "Yes, this is it. I really should have a subscription to the *Globe*, but everything costs money."

She pointed to a seat. "Sit down, Loretta. I suspect you've been on your feet all day."

"Well, I have," Loretta smiled. "But I pays the bills. The hotel boss wants another woman to clean. Would you be interested?"

If the printer heard, she didn't let on. Instead, she scanned the pages. The column titled "The American Revolution" had the latest telegrams from the battlefronts, but wasn't what she was looking for.

"Here it is!" Her fingers were pointing mid-way down the page, to the headline, PRESIDENT'S PROCLAMATION. "Give me a moment, Loretta. I've heard about this emancipation measure, but I'd like to see it in black and white."

Loretta sank into a chair.

"Oh, so it *is* here." Mary Ann's voice revealed her disappointment. "There is a reference to colonization either on this continent or some-where else. But," and she began to brighten, "the rest is as I heard. Mr. Lincoln is finally moving to free the slaves."

Loretta sat forward. "So family down in Tennessee and Kentucky be free? They can come to Canada?"

"Well, no, I don't think so," Mary hesitated. "This proclamation applies to the states in the Confederacy. Kentucky and Tennessee are considered part of the Union."

"But theys still fighting down there. You told me that before. If theys fighting, theys must be part of the war."

"Well…" She tried to think of a simple way to explain the confu-sion that existed in the states caught between the Union and the Con-federacy. "First of all, he's giving the slave states the chance to mend their ways, and—"

"It don't matter none," Loretta interrupted. "It's beyond me."

"Oh, it does matter!" The voice rang through the little shop. "It's a first step. He may be ready to accept black fighting men. Not men to care for horses or dig ditches, actual fighting men."

"You wants to send our men off to fight," Loretta grimaced, "Might be best to just let the white folks fight it out."

"I'm sorry, Loretta. I'm not being clear. I have to think about how to say this and how to write it."

Loretta scoffed. "Are you still thinking about your paper?"

"Yes, I've been thinking about it since I heard this news. It would be a special edition of the *Provincial Freeman*. We haven't published regularly in several years, but our people remember the *Freeman* and they should be told how this will change things."

"But you told me there was no money in making a newspaper," Loretta said. "You said when money was tight, nobody wanted to advertise, and especially in a paper for black people."

"I know," Mary nodded.

"And you said the *Provincial Freeman* worked best when peoples knew it was coming regular—and you ain't done one in years."

"Yes, I said that."

"And you said men, black or white, don't like a woman writing and printing, and you use the initials M.S. Carey, so they wouldn't know you are a woman. Maybe it would be best if you just find a man and get married again."

"No, I don't need a man—but yes, everything else you say is true. But this Emancipation Proclamation is so important. I'd only have to print a couple of hundred copies. It could be a one-page edition."

"Are you listening to yourself?" Loretta asked. "You are a woman, a black woman. You don't have money to waste on printing. Cleaning rooms may not be as important as the *Provincial Freeman*, but it honest work and a woman knows she be paid. But you ain't going to listen."

Loretta rose and stomped to the door. "You're going print the fool paper, aren't you?"

Mary Ann looked toward her friend. "Yes."

"Well, I think you are a damn fool," Loretta told her. "But I'll ask that hotel keeper if he might take out an ad."

CHAPTER 3

Maryland: October 1862

Owen let his eyes rove across the station platform while he rubbed at the neckline of his tight-fitting blue uniform.

The itch was still there along with a patch of ugly red skin. Jimmy, he saw, was struggling under the heavy backpack, grasping the handrail on the train car with one hand and carefully guiding his rifle with the other.

The train depot was small, once just a country stop, now transformed into a major terminal.

For a moment, he allowed himself to think of how far they had come. The harbor in the village of Port Burwell in Canada West was one of the natural breaks in the cliffs on the north shore of Lake Erie. Across the lake was a ready American market for any amount of lumber—for all the ash, oak, hickory, and maple the region could supply.

The Queen's Proclamation of Neutrality was well advertised. Any British subject who joined the American army was the next thing to a traitor.

Still, the lumber mill owners saw no problem with American money, and boats were piled high with lumber, and barges filled with horses, or cattle, or other provisions for the Northern war machine. Cold hard cash was a neutral currency.

The boats returned with American newspapers and details of the bounty offered for a live recruit. The incentive rose to $150 plus thirteen dollars a month in pay, with food and clothing provided.

By mid September 1862, Jimmy Hampstead had convinced Owen McFeeters that their future lay in the American army. The enlistment records showed them as brothers: Jimmy and Owen Burwell, twenty-two and twenty-one years of age. Place of birth: Erie, Pennsylvania. If the British should decide to look, the pair would be harder to find, and instead of crossing the lake, they'd moved west to Michigan.

The first weeks were spent in the camp at Fort Wayne, near Detroit. A time to learn to march and drill and drill and march, and care for the weapons—but most of all to learn to obey.

In their few hours of freedom, they gravitated to the small building up the road, the house of Mother Morris. A birdhouse, they joked, because Mother Morris watched over "the soiled doves."

At the tavern, there was little time for talk. Mother Morris told each guest that time was money: "No more money, no more time." And fifteen minutes, she said, was plenty of time for a young soldier to spend with a woman.

When the orders came to send the unit south, the officers grumbled and said the troops needed more training, but the men didn't care. Most of their money was gone, and Mother Morris had gathered her flock to move on.

A harsh shout brought Owen back to Maryland.

"I've got orders for fresh meat," a sergeant bellowed as he scanned the platform.

"You and you," he pointed to Jimmy and Owen. "Move over there." He pointed to two wagons drawn up to the boxcars on a nearby siding.

"Don't ask any questions—just git over there. And if anyone asks, tell them Hurley has gone to find an officer."

The sergeant was back within minutes, hustling eight confused recruits and a scowling captain.

"You men are being transferred," the captain announced. "Sergeant Hurley has orders for ten men, and that's what he's getting. Take them, Sergeant!"

"Thank you…sirrrrr!" Hurley snapped off a salute as the officer hurried off.

The waiting troop studied the new commander.

Hurley was six feet tall. His blue tunic covered a muscular frame. His forage cap had faded in the sun, and his uniform showed obvious signs of wear. Everything about him suggested tough, hard service.

"Tennn…shun!" he barked.

Twenty eyes focused to the front and twenty shoulders squared.

"Fresh meat," he growled and walked through the formation.

"Fresh meat means straight from training camp! And you will do what I say—when I say it! You are marked for special duty under Sgt. Levitus Hurley…and God help the man who crosses me."

His eyes came to rest on Jimmy. Their height and build were similar. The sergeant ran his eyes slowly down the young man's frame, from the fresh blue uniform to the boots buffed on the train.

"I have a special need," he almost whispered before suddenly remembering the other nine men.

"The rest of you, throw your gear in the front wagon and start unloading those rail cars. Bags and boxes first. Get moving!"

He scowled at Jimmy. "What's your name?"

"Jimmy Hamp…" he began before catching his mistake. "Uh… Jimmy Burwell."

"No it's not!" Hurley snarled. "It's Private Burwell! Now! Start with the boots. Get them off."

Sergeant Hurley had been among the first to answer the call for volunteers when the war began. With his experience, he developed a healthy disgust for officers, political appointees, and incompetent quartermasters—but a grudging respect for the suppliers, who filled lucrative orders with shoddy material and grew rich.

The Northern newspapers told of barefoot rebels and scant supplies in the South, but Hurley knew the Union also suffered from an inefficient supply chain. He had seen men in the rain in leaking tents and squads march in bare feet.

Hurley had decided to take care of himself, and he wanted new boots and a fresh uniform. The young soldier could have the castoffs.

* * *

They were eleven men, two wagons, and three days on the road. The sergeant offered no explanations, simply a series of orders.

Hurley rode in the front wagon with three men. Five other men followed in the second wagon, two of them dangling their feet from the tailgate. For no reason, he ordered the Burwells to march behind.

A fair Indian summer had left the roads hard, dry, and covered with a fine, ankle-deep powder, with each wagon creating a cloud of choking dust. Owen and Jimmy slowed their pace, but the sergeant would have none of it. At a brief rest stop, he threatened to tie them to the wagon if they lagged. By the end of the day, both were weighed down by a thick layer of dirt and Jimmy was limping badly. The boots exchanged with Hurley were ragged pieces of leather.

The dry weather was breaking. On the afternoon of the third day, a line of clouds began to build, and by evening thunderstorms washed over the tiny caravan.

With morning, the wind direction changed. The air was cooler, but the soldiers noticed something more. The smell of coffee, frying pork, and wood smoke could not overcome the stench of rotting flesh. No one seemed hungry, except one man. The sergeant ate well and as he finished, he pointed at Jimmy.

"Bring the horses and hook up the wagons. The rest of you, pry those lids off the long boxes. There are shovels inside; nice new shovels that need breaking in."

The sergeant rarely spoke other than to issue brusque orders, but this time was different.

"You see, ladies, we're a couple of miles from Sharpsburg and the Antietam Creek. A month ago, Bobby Lee tried to come through with his rebel army. But your gallant brothers stopped him."

"They buried our dead in shallow graves," Hurley continued. "But now they think the boys would be more comfortable if they were sleeping deeper."

The men exchanged quick glances but the sergeant wasn't finished.

"I was here a week ago. It will be worse now. So, ladies, tie a bandana around your nose if the smell offends you."

Hurley scowled at the squad before he resumed.

"We're really only interested in the Union blue. Turn up a gray back, leave him. But if the uniform is blue, do more digging. You call me when you spot stripes or officer insignia. I have to go through pockets looking for any letters or such. And," he paused, "on second thought, you better call me if you find any rebel officers."

The heat of Indian summer returned and the stench never left the air, hanging over the camp and the cook fires. Finding clean water was a challenge. One enterprising farmer had collected a dollar for each Confederate body dumped into his well. Dead horses and mules contaminated other supplies.

Only the sergeant enjoyed the work. He found the remnants of a tree damaged by cannon fire, ordered the men to clear a small shaded area, and sat humming as he watched.

He left his post only when an officer was found. The inspection was cursory, a quick glance, a pat of the pockets, and a demand that the troops lift and shake the body. Any coins or watches went into his knapsack. In a few cases, he worked the rings from a stiffened hand, or used a shovel to sever and smash a finger to obtain his prize. Greenbacks, coins, and Confederate currency went into his knapsack. Other papers were allowed to blow across the Maryland fields.

* * *

SOUTHERN KENTUCKY: OCTOBER 1862

"I'm coming down," Lightning announced, the months of experience allowing him to quickly descend a telegraph pole. A Canadian by birth, Ellsworth had mastered the telegraph and used his knowledge to find work across the South.

"All done as ordered, General Morgan," he said as he touched the ground. "The Federals think you have two thousand men on the way to Lexington, and they're sending Union regiments in pursuit."

As he spoke, he placed his telegraph apparatus safely in a protective bag.

"And they believed all that you sent?" John Morgan smiled.

"Took it all in," George Ellsworth assured him. Ellsworth listened to Federal messages and by imitating other operators, sent bogus reports to confuse Union forces.

"And with you so far away, the payroll train is moving again. It should be along in a few minutes."

"We're ready," Morgan smiled, and motioned the men to the wooded hillside. Felled trees already blocked the track.

"Would you tell Colonel Grenfell that all is ready, and then you can just sit back and relax."

Morgan watched from the trees as the train approached.

The single engine labored on the slight grade despite the fact it pulled only a single boxcar and five flatcars. Four men sat on top of the boxcar, each with a rifle in hand.

The squeal of the brakes began as the engineer spotted the obstruction and the train was barely slowing when gunshots dropped the guards. Seconds later, the rebel yell echoed from the hills. Col. George St. Leger Grenfell led charging Confederates on horseback.

Grenfell's long white hair streamed down his back, and his bright red shirt offered an inviting target; but he and his men surrounded the train before any defender could fire a shot.

Morgan watched Tom Hines ride to the closed boxcar and bang on the door.

"Morgan's cavalry," he yelled. "Unlock the doors and step out, or we'll burn you out."

As Morgan navigated the hillside to reach the train, Union soldiers began to emerge with their arms in the air.

Hines swung into the boxcar with an armful of empty saddlebags. In minutes, he was back, lashing the loaded bags onto a packhorse.

"Looks like the payroll shipment to me," he smiled at Morgan.

"Anything else of value?" Morgan asked.

"Not that I want," Hines told him. "But these other scavengers could find something."

Morgan laughed and raised his voice: "Two men to watch the prisoners! The rest, take what you want."

The rebel yell sounded again as men raced for the train.

Morgan saw a scowl grow on Grenfell's face as the older man worked his horse toward the commander. "This is not right. The men lack discipline. Looting should be discouraged."

The stiff English accent added to the reprimand.

"Let them have their way, Colonel," Morgan replied. "They may find things we can't provide."

The Union rifles, he knew, would quickly replace the older firearms.

But Grenfell wasn't finished. He pointed down the track, where Hines was disappearing. "And the payroll should go to General Bragg's headquarters."

"No, not this time. Tom has friends in the North who need funds, and we have approval from authorities higher than General Bragg. Now, as to the train…" Morgan took a moment to think. "First, that fodder on the flatcars," he decided. "Let our animals feed."

This time Grenfell nodded his approval. He beamed at Morgan's next suggestion.

"Ahead, there's a long tunnel. Move the train inside and set it afire. There are coal seams running through the hills. With a good, hot fire, the coal will catch and it will take the Yankees weeks to put the fire out."

* * *

WASHINGTON: NOVEMBER 1862

"We'll miss you in the House, Mr. Vallandigham."

Clement Vallandigham couldn't remember the name, but he recognized the face of the young representative from Iowa, another of his former colleagues offering condolence.

"Democracy is a wonderful thing," the representative was saying, "but sometimes the voters make mistakes. The people of Ohio will rue the day."

"Well, I will be back. And when I return, I'll need men like you."

"I'll be at your beck and call," the congressman said before retreating into the US Capitol building.

Vallandigham peered from the top steps, searching for the driver and carriage that would take him from his humiliation. An electoral defeat was one thing, but to have an election stolen was another matter. The extra county added to his district had been packed with Republicans, and he suspected the electoral map had been redrawn with the knowledge of the White House.

The capital was busy with the Congress reaching the end of the term. Politicians mixed with army officers; the gold braid reflecting from uniforms of ranking officers and what he considered their flock of lackeys. If Vallandigham had his way, army officers would be out of work. The Southern states would be allowed to leave the Union peacefully and no army would force them to stay.

A bump from behind almost made him lose his balance but there was no apology from the officer who brushed by.

Vallandigham found his footing and began the descent. In the past, officers had shown respect. Robert E. Lee and Jeb Stuart were models of decorum after John Brown was rooted from the arsenal at Harper's Ferry. Vallandigham had been part of the official inquiry into the attack. Senator Mason had been another, and now Mason, Lee, and Stuart were fighting for the Confederacy.

Frustrated, he pushed against the crowd. Everything had to change. Men who opposed Lincoln were arrested silently in the night. Opposition newspapers were suppressed, with the presses sometimes destroyed by mobs.

A trusted friend had whispered of a secret society forming in the North to oppose the war. The movement needed a leader and Vallandigham was ready for the challenge.

CHAPTER 4

Journal of Paul Forsey, government clerk, January 1863

*T*be cold months have arrived in Quebec City but winter brings the social season. Anything will help to ease the boredom. The war to the south continues to amaze. Thousands of men were killed or wounded in great battles at Antietam and Shiloh. The vaunted American army is unable to bring the upstart rebels to hand while the South finds new heroes. The latest goes by the unlikely name of "Stonewall" Jackson. The North has yet to find a winning general and their fall elections, with a few notable exceptions, indicate Mr. Lincoln is losing popular support, except perhaps among our men. More are joining the American army and our leaders seem powerless to stop them.

Our government teeters on the brink of defeat. I have tried to impress the powers that be, especially the attorney general, but so far, no sign of promotion. Only months ago, John A. Macdonald considered retirement, but now seems determined to stay in government. It may be for no other reason than to thwart his political opponents. The man is a skilled politician, at times outgoing, but at other times moody, silent, and secretive.

* * *

FORT ERIE, CANADA WEST: JANUARY 1863

Another icy blast of snow whipped by the depot.

Gilbert McMicken lost no time in entering the waiting room to huddle by the stove.

"The train will be delayed," the stationmaster announced. "Waiting for the plow engine. The snow lets up past Ridgeway and the engineer should be able to make up the lost time before the Welland Canal."

McMicken removed the overcoat. Time was of no concern. He wasn't expected in Windsor for two days. As he shifted, he felt the letter in his jacket pocket, the catalyst for this journey. It was a private message, a very private message, from the attorney general.

McMicken had served a single term in the legislature before accepting a job on the Niagara Peninsula. The position came on the recommendation of John A. Macdonald and all because of the trouble he didn't cause.

Macdonald had been under political fire over allegations of personal profit from the sale of surplus army lands. McMicken could have joined the uproar; could have raised more embarrassing questions and prolonged the debate. Instead, he remained silent. Macdonald didn't forget.

The letter congratulated the customs agent for his work along the Niagara, his attention to detail, and his ability to "work quietly without causing a great fuss."

Macdonald wrote of the growing American community at Windsor, the private contractors acting as recruiters for the Union army, and the Southerners who had moved to British North America.

"Our relations with the Americans have reached a sensitive stage. It is my desire to learn what may be afoot, without official government involvement. Conduct these inquiries as you see fit."

A train whistle sounded as the plow engine steamed by, barely visible in the churning snow. "We'll load now," the stationmaster called. "Move quickly. The drifts will soon cover the tracks again."

The train crawled from Fort Erie but picked up speed only twenty miles down the track. The ride would have been pleasant except for the youngster who ran back and forth and echoed each blast of the locomotive whistle. It was two hours before his mother switched him to a siding beside her.

25

While the boy fidgeted, McMicken studied the woman. Pleasant features, black hair tied in a neat bun, but while she appeared to be only in her thirties, deep worry lines creased her face. She was dressed in black so she probably was in mourning. The world could be cruel, he thought, as he drifted off to sleep.

He shouted as he woke to metal banging sharply on metal but he was relieved to see it was the conductor adding fuel to the stove. The woman watched, too. The boy was fast asleep.

"I nodded off," McMicken leaned across the aisle to apologize. "I didn't mean to startle."

She managed a faint smile. "I should apologize. Nathaniel is so rambunctious. He's been cooped up too long."

"Travelled far?"

The woman considered how much to say. The man wore a rumpled black suit and a plaid vest that stretched to cover a broad stomach. The veins in his face were enlarged and red and he dabbed constantly at a running nose. His green eyes were locked on her.

"Yes," she finally answered. "From Virginia."

"Oh, a long, long, trip for you and the boy."

She had been warned to watch for the Union agents, men who could make travel uncomfortable for Southerners.

"And you've had a recent loss?" he asked.

"Yes, my husband…" She hesitated, fearing the mere mention of his name might bring tears. "Virgil. Virgil Tunks"—saying his name brought him closer—"was with Stonewall Jackson and he…he…he died at Sharpsburg."

"I'm sorry. I don't mean to intrude."

The train rounded a sharp curve and she leaned with the tilt of the car.

"It's all right." She straightened. "I must mind my manners. I'm Elizabeth Tunks and this is our son, Nathaniel."

"A pleasure. I'm Gilbert McMicken, customs agent at Niagara."

"So you are British. I have been warned that Yankees travel here and they can't be trusted."

"This is neutral territory. People from both sides are here."

"Oh, I know. My sister is at London in Canada West. She says many of our people are there. But not skedaddlers," she continued. "Mostly women and children. Yankee men may slink across the border but men like Virgil stayed and fought."

She looked through the window to the snow-covered fields.

"Where is home?" McMicken asked a moment later.

"Near Fredericksburg. Yankees took our house, wrecked everything, and tried to burn it. But they couldn't even do that right. It's only half gone but we couldn't stay."

"You've had a rough go," he told her.

"But, I can handle it." Her voice choked. "I'm sorry, I'm going to have to talk but it's hard. When Virgil died…" her voice trailed off as she fought emotions. "When Virgil died, we went to recover his body. The men told us he fell right along Antietam Creek but they couldn't bring him along…" A tear trickled down her face.

"The Yankees wouldn't let us look," the tears were flowing freely now. "And so we don't know if he had a Christian burial."

"My God, that's cruel. It's not right," McMicken shook his head.

She removed a cloth from a handbag to wipe her eyes.

"Virgil's brother was with General Longstreet. He was captured and sent to a Northern prison camp but Southern boys don't give up. If he escapes, he'll come here."

McMicken shifted on the armrest. "How will he do that?"

"Oh, I don't really know," she confessed. "The letter said something about a hotel in Windsor where they go after they cross the border."

He tried not to show undue interest, "A lot of hotels will be looking for that business."

"No," she said absently, "there's only one our boys use."

"Mommy!" the boy was waking. "Are we almost there?"

"Hmm, I wonder which hotel?" McMicken prodded gently. But Nathaniel was rising with a full head of steam.

———

CHAPTER 5

Virginia: February 1863

The sound of a locomotive reached him well before the engine rounded the bend. Owen relaxed as the whistle sounded two long shrieks. The code had changed only yesterday and the signal was right.

He stepped a few feet from the track as the train came into view. A flatcar was first, protected by a cannon with the barrel wedged between railway ties; then the engine; five boxcars; and finally a detachment of bored but well-armed troops on another flatcar. Only their heads were visible over the ties formed in a boxlike shield. A few weeks earlier, the army had experimented with a steel boxcar and a small opening for the cannon snout. He shuddered to think of the explosive noise inside what amounted to a can. The men could go deaf but there were plenty of men and the army engineers planned more experiments.

A fireman leaned from the window for a brief nod. In seconds, the train clattered past the temporary outpost and down the Baltimore and Ohio main line toward Harper's Ferry.

Hurley had brought them to the main camp after the week at Antietam but then he disappeared with two bulging knapsacks. He was gone for a week but never said where he went or why and the men knew better than to ask.

They were moved to guard a bridge in early January. The soldiers spent the first week's building block houses at each end of the span. The river below ran through a deep rock gorge. Access from the river, the sergeant pronounced, was impossible. Trees that lined the track were cut. The logs were notched and raised until the block houses were twenty feet high. The sergeant made them rig timbers over the top as well.

"Bloody engineers think logs will keep a cannonball from dropping through," he told them, "but they won't. The logs are to keep the engineers off my back and to keep a dry roof over my head."

The three soldiers, Festus Stephens, Jimmy, and Owen, were glad to leave the construction project and patrol the track. The trio checked small bridges and watched for obstructions on the rails or other signs of Confederate activity.

Stephens was a stout little man with plans as large as his stomach. "Festus Stephens for the Senate," he would say with a sly giggle. In his mind, he wore a suit and climbed the platform to inspire voters.

In the late 1850s, Stephens had been a Democrat, shaken the hand of John C. Breckenridge, the vice president of the United States, and voted for Breckenridge in the presidential election of 1860. He rejected Lincoln. He had heard the president speak and Lincoln's high squeaky voice and gangly appearance, were just not "presidential" in Stephens's view. "I'm fighting for the Union," Stephens would practice a stump speech. "Keep the Negro issue out of it. We can settle that later."

Stephens was shocked by the Emancipation Proclamation.

"It's trouble for Democrats," he explained, kicking at the stones on the railbed. "This track is a lifeline and the people at the end of the line up north are worried. If the slave is set free and comes looking for work and works cheaper than the white man, he might get the job. The white folks will be out of work. Now, I don't believe in slavery but there has to be another way around this."

Stephens never found the answer.

Owen didn't really care about the big picture but he broached another subject. "Festus, what's to be done about the sergeant? What he did with those bodies at Antietam, and who knows what he's up to now."

"Owen, my boy." This was to be no stump speech but something for a private audience. "Keep your head down and stay out of his way.

I've got to worry about rebels in front of me and won't spend time watching my back."

They came to know each inch of track. March from the bridge, amble along the rails when out of sight of the post, snap to attention as trains passed, amble to the end of the route, light a fire and spend the night. Reverse the process in the morning. Reverse the process again the following morning and on it went for two months. Festus finally broke the routine.

A rough, dirt road crossed the line about six miles from the bridge. Stephens wanted to investigate. Like a dog on a rope, he pressed to see how far he could go. Finally, he broke the leash.

"No one is going to know. The sergeant won't leave the comfort of the blockhouse." And with that he walked up the path and was lost in the trees. He didn't return that night but as Jimmy reminded Owen, "He's a big boy."

The Burwells huddled by a small fire thirty feet from the track. A rough shelter of pine boughs brought protection from the elements and in front of the fire was a broad, six-foot high stack of limbs and branches. The branches sheltered the glow of the fire from the night trains. The precaution was taken after nervous train guards had sent a volley into the camp. Now, one soldier stood by the track to reassure the train crews while the others slept.

The rail traffic had been light when they first arrived but recently a locomotive wheezed past once an hour. The freight cars might be full of supplies for the war effort, passenger cars packed with men, or horses stamping and kicking at the wooden restraints. A few hours later, the locomotive would return with a line of empty cars.

This was light duty, the sergeant had told them. Confederates like Turner Ashby might strike with hit-and-run attacks, using boulders or rocks to block the rails, and a few bullets to frighten the crews before looting and burning a train. The rebels hadn't come close in recent weeks but in the words of the sergeant, "They're watching."

Owen felt the welcome rays of the sun as a caboose clattered by at the end of a long line of freight cars. He raised his hand to wave but the rear guard was fast asleep. He allowed the sounds to fade before waking Jimmy. "Time to go." The first kick was a gentle tap. The second produced an angry grunt. Jimmy pushed into a crouch as Owen kicked loose sand over the embers of the fire.

"No sign of Festus?" Jimmy could move from deep sleep to full consciousness in seconds.

"Nothing. We'll check that trail on the way back."

In the distance, another locomotive whistled. With the experience of weeks by the track, they knew the train was a few minutes off.

"There will be all hell to pay if we go back without him."

"He's probably sitting at the path waiting, so let's get going."

The train was drawing closer.

"Must be a new engineer," he told Jimmy, "They usually slow for those curves."

"Maybe he has a lady waiting in Harper's Ferry and can't wait to blow off a load of steam or lubricate his driving wheel." Jimmy rocked forward and back and chuckled at his own joke. The smile disappeared as the train rolled into view.

The locomotive was moving fast, but there was no sign of the crew. Instead, a limp figure was tied spread-eagle on the cowcatcher. The head lurched with the motion of the train and the sightless eyes of Festus Stephens flashed over the campsite to rest on his two friends. The shock was followed by the shriek of tearing metal as the locomotive flew from the track, dragging the freight cars into a steep gorge.

* * *

With the line blocked, extra troops were sent to clear the rails. The sergeant arrived on a pump car powered by four sweating black men.

"Good thing these gentlemen were working the line," he remarked to no one in particular. "Good strong backs on these black beasts. My and ain't this a dainty little cottage." He appraised the shelter and two grim soldiers.

"Been having a good time when out on these patrols, haven't ya? The Burwell Boys' Plantation Home. Where's the other scum bag?"

Owen decided that the less Hurley knew, the better.

"Festus—Private Stephens, sir—was hit by the train. He's dead."

Jimmy remained silent. He'd been sick several times as they probed the wreckage. The bodies from the locomotive were scalded by the exploding boiler. Their closest relatives wouldn't recognize the men. The sergeant scowled, kicked at a broken railway tie, and looked down the track.

"Good place for it, a few new rails, ties, and the line can be open tonight."

* * *

TORONTO, CANADA WEST: MARCH 1863

George Brown slipped his top coat over a peg as he summoned the *Globe* editor. The streets had been packed as he made his way to the office. The St. Patrick's Day parade, the bishop's mass, speeches on the glory of Ireland, and the carousing would all be news for tomorrow's paper.

"We'll have the latest telegraphic report from the states late tonight," the editor reminded him. "But there are only isolated incidents, a train wreck in Virginia, that sort of thing. In Toronto, a normal day so far; big crowds but no trouble. One speech caused a stir. A fellow named Murphy, who claims to be part of the Hibernian Society, laid into the British. He's obviously a Fenian."

"Ah, hot air," Brown told him. "Fenians trying to fire up the crowd. Include it—briefly—in the main column."

"And, uh, two printers didn't show up today."

"Then fire them! Don't let them back in the building. We need steady men to publish a daily paper."

The *Globe* was read across Canada West. The editions were printed to coincide with the train schedules so Brown's paper would be on sale alongside the local newspapers each morning.

"No stabbings today?" he asked hopefully.

"No," the editor smiled. "It's not like 1858. No St Paddy's riot."

"See what happens when the liquor takes hold. Are there any temperance meetings tonight?" Brown's strong opinions and pet causes colored the pages of his paper.

"No sir." The editor was prepared and offered something to whet Brown's news appetite. "But there's a lecture tomorrow night on the origins of Protestantism."

The Presbyterian in Brown was intrigued. "That should be worthwhile. Maybe the speaker will have something to say about schools. The damn papists think we should pay the priests to educate their children. I hope the speaker sounds the right notes and the legislature pays attention."

"Speaking of the legislature, Sandfield Macdonald has threatened to resign."

"We don't want to lose him." Brown the politician emerged. "If we lose him, that drunken John A. will push forward, the worst of the rotten Tories. We've got to keep Sandfield in power."

"Any more on that Detroit business?" Brown asked. Two blacks had been killed and thirty buildings burned when a white mob turned on the black community.

"The whites claimed a black attacked a white woman. He didn't, but tell that to a mob."

"The bloody fools," Brown growled. His involvement in the anti-slavery society won friends in the abolitionist community and unlike many competitors, the *Globe* was decidedly pro Union.

The editor cocked his head as music sounded in the distance. "That will be the parade."

"I can hear. I don't know the music but it's almost certainly seditious. Irish papists are one step from treason. If our attorney general, Mr. John A. Macdonald, had any guts he'd arrest them but the only thing he cares about is his own grasping drive for power."

The music faded as the band turned onto another street. "Where are they going?" Brown listened intently before answering his own question. "They turned to march past the Orange lodge. They're trying to cause trouble."

"That's all I have." The editor was anxious to get away. There were only a few hours before the presses would begin to roll.

"Wait. Those printers? Were they Irish?"

"No, both were Englishmen."

"I don't suppose they were the ones grousing and calling for a nine-hour day?"

"No, it wasn't them."

"Well, they're gone," Brown decided. "And if anyone talks about the rights of the working man or the nine-hour day, fire him immediately. I won't coddle them."

V

CHAPTER 6

Virginia: April 1863

The Burwells felt the death of Festus Stephens but the army didn't notice. Another soldier took his place. Spring brought more men to guard the Baltimore and Ohio line and to explore the path where Stephens was last seen him alive. The Burwells were among twenty men who climbed the twisting track to a neighboring valley.

The first stop was a small cabin surrounded by freshly planted fields. A wisp of smoke rose from the chimney but there was no other sign of life.

The officer in command, Captain Darby, dismounted and sent two men up the lane. He leaned on a rail fence while the pair approached the cabin, pounded on the door, and then, after only a moment, smashed the door into splinters with vicious kicks. Within seconds, one man called to the captain, "Better take a look at this."

Darby mounted the horse and urged the animal into a trot. The horse stumbled before they heard the gunfire. As Darby went down, the animal panicked, charging through a fence and into the neighboring fields. A second burst of gunfire echoed through the valley and a soldier collapsed with blood streaming down his face.

"Get down! Get down!" Jimmy knocked Owen to the grass. A corporal scanned the hills for the source of the fire but with the next shot, his head snapped back to expose a neat hole in his forage cap. The sergeant dashed for the banks of a stream. A splash and swearing competed with the sound of gunfire as three more men went down.

"Surrounded," Owen shouted as the buzz of bullets forced them tight to the valley floor.

"We surrender! We surrender." The voice filled with abject terror came from the stream.

"You have us, Johnny! We're giving up!"

But another volley of gunfire ranged across the valley.

"We surrender!" The sergeant's hand emerged above the stream bank to frantically wave a bandana. "We're giving up! Come and get us." The hand and bandana continued to wave until rebel horsemen arrived.

* * *

The remnants of the detail were herded into the barn under guard of four scruffy men in gray. The Burwells waited, their backs resting against the barn wall. The sergeant sat on the dirt floor, wringing water from his jacket, and swearing. Two men were wounded, one in the arm. The other groaned loudly, his hands clasped across a bleeding stomach. The moans angered the sergeant. "Keep that bastard quiet!"

The order was aimed at no one in particular and no one moved to obey. Jimmy and Owen exchanged glances. The wounded soldier groaned again.

"I'll shut him up!" Hurley lurched to his feet but a bullet ripped into the ground beside his boot.

"Next one will be closer, Yank, and the third one goes in your gut."

The guards trained their weapons on the muddy figure and then stiffened at the sound of running feet and the appearance of a panting rebel officer.

"It's all right, Chaplain," a guard sang out. "That brave blue coat sergeant, the one who surrendered after he wet hisself, was thinking of causing trouble, and we," he pointed to his rifle, "talked him out of it". The chaplain caught his breath and cast a withering glance at the sergeant. "If he makes any more noise, shut him up him!"

"Malone," the chaplain called to a bearded solider. "Pick two men for a burial detail. We'll do right by the enemy even if," he pointed at the sergeant, "this particular breed has no decency."

The Confederate's name was Paul Malone, he explained, as the two Canadians began to dig a shallow trench.

"Don't need to go deep but make it wide. Besides your men, we've got a man and a woman from the cabin. Damn shame! Whoever did this ransacked the house but I doubt they got much. These folks didn't have much to begin with."

Jimmy paused and leaned on his shovel.

"Don't stop, Yank," Malone warned. "We ain't got all day. Three or four feet be deep enough."

"Where you fellows from?" Malone asked eventually.

"Can—", Jimmy began but Owen gave him a quick warning glance. "Uh, Canandaigua," Jimmy continued, "Up near Erie in Pennsylvania." He hoped the rebel had a poor grasp of Northern geography.

"Never heard of it." Malone pointed to the grave. "Trim that edge a bit. Make it neat."

"I haven't travelled much," Malone admitted. "I worked in the county clerk's office until First Manassas and figured if I didn't join soon, the war would be over. I didn't count on all of you. Every time we destroy a company, a regiment takes its place. But eventually you'll run out of men."

He motioned the Burwells out of the trench and directed them to move the bodies. The farmer and his wife were the last to be placed in the grave.

"War does funny things to people," Malone said, glancing down at the victims. "This area is split between Union and Confederate, plus a few who have no allegiance."

"Was this was the work of Mosby?" Jimmy had picked up the name of a prominent raider and Malone considered the question.

"Probably not," he finally answered. "John Mosby is a gentleman. He's a strong Southern partisan, smart, and tough in a fight, but he wouldn't do something like this. No, it's more likely the work of another fellow named Mobley. People get them confused. Mobley is simple; he's not all there. But he's ruthless, bloodthirsty. He claims to have destroyed a Yankee train near Harper's Ferry a few days back. Know anything about that?"

Jimmy glanced to catch a warning in Owen's eyes.

"Trains run off the track all the time," he told Malone. "We fix the track and more trains come."

Malone considered the answer. "Maybe Mobley is exaggerating his importance, but if I was a lone Yankee soldier, I wouldn't want him near me."

The rebel chaplain did his best for the departed enemy. After a lengthy prayer and two long scripture passages, he closed the burial service.

"Man that is born of woman hath but a short time to live. His life is full of misery. He cometh up and is a cut down like a flower."

He gazed at the men around the grave and delivered an emphatic, *"Lord, have mercy. Amen!"*

"The chaplain is a real religious man," Malone whispered. "Ain't easy being a military man and a preacher."

Jimmy and Owen began to gently drop earth on the bodies.

"We do the best we can with religion," Malone told them. "General Jackson, old Stonewall, believes in the good book. Why, there was a fuss about whether we'd fight on Sundays, a fuss that continued right up to the Sabbath morning when we run into Yankees. I suspect the good Lord will understand and besides, General Jackson talks to him every day."

In the distance, a rider appeared.

"Get that grave finished. There's a dispatch rider on his way."

The chaplain walked to meet the rider and listened briefly. He pointed to the captain's horse and helped the messenger move his saddle to the new mount before returning to the prisoners.

"I have orders," he drawled. "I won't be held back by the likes of you. If you were real soldiers," he looked directly at the sergeant, "I'd send you to a prison but your kind will do us more good causing trouble among your own."

"Malone," he called, "Gather up those guns. The rest of you, help yourself to Federal supplies. We have to move."

38

* * *

VIRGINIA: MAY 1863

Somehow, the sergeant kept his stripes. It was a combination, the Burwells agreed, of outright lies, intimidation, and his superiors' benign neglect. The fiasco in the valley was overshadowed by the larger war and the humiliation of a small Federal unit was quickly forgotten. The fate of the railway was another matter. Within days, two hundred men were dispatched to the valley.

Houses, barns, and fences were burned, the livestock confiscated or killed. The residents were ordered to move north or south. There would be nothing left to live on. The Union army wanted no one near the vital railway line.

The sergeant took particular delight in setting fires but only after scouring each house. He commandeered a farm wagon and by the end of the three days, he had an odd collection of valuables. The owner of one cabin was ready to fight but bare fists were no match for a revolver. The body was left inside to burn. Owen arrived as flames licked through the roof. Jimmy told him what had happened but showed no remorse or compassion.

Matilde Shellenburg entered their lives in a line of refugees snaking up the pass toward the railway line. A few families managed to stay together but Matilde walked alone, a few possessions wrapped in a blanket slung over her shoulder. The sergeant described her as European peasant stock, the type who could pull a plow all day and satisfy a man at night. She was taller than average, well built, and strong. The work on the valley farm made her as muscular as a man but close inspection of the rugged beauty revealed a strange, far off look in her eyes.

At the railway line, the force divided. Twenty men returned to the bridge but the sergeant directed his unit into the stream of refugees. That night, Matilde joined the Burwells by their campfire and in the morning it seemed only natural she would follow the troop. The men paid her for washing, for mending, and other chores requiring a female touch. Veterans said women always followed the armies. Camp following was a noble tradition, they said, often with a wink.

Matilde was summoned to the sergeant's tent late one evening. The lantern showed the silhouettes of two figures and those outside saw Hurley reach for Matilde while extinguishing the light. Seconds later, there was a loud meaty thump and a string of oaths. Matilde emerged from the tent and walked regally to her shelter. The gasping sergeant staggered from the tent doubled in pain.

In the following weeks, soldiers tried in vain to win her attention but only Jimmy was able to break through. At first a tight smile, later grudging conversation, and then one night, a burst of laughter shocked the campground.

* * *

The spring of 1863 was full of alarms. The squad continued to protect the Baltimore and Ohio track and the flow of the war supplies. Each day brought more news or rumors.

A new Federal commander was ready to move south. Gen. Joe Hooker had his sights on Richmond but the invasion ended at a tiny outpost in a wilderness, called Chancellorsville. Hooker was soon in retreat. The good news for the Federals came with word that rebel Gen. Stonewall Jackson was dead, shot by mistake, by his own men.

"See boys," a jaded Union veteran joked, "Think about it. It's a great way to get rid of an officer."

"Shows the rebels are as screwed up as we are," said another to nods of agreement.

* * *

CINCINNATI, OHIO: MAY 25, 1863

"Bring the political prisoner down!"

"Huh. Who?" The eyes cracked open and tilted up to the shoulder emblems of a captain.

"Vallandigham! Valiant Val. Bring him down!"

"But I can't do anything without proper orders," the jailor said, struggling to his feet. "Then try these!" The captain shoved a sheet in the jailor's face and raised a lantern to throw light.

"Ah yes, now I understand." The jailor ran his finger under the words.

"It was the political business that threw me. I've got thieves, con men, murderers, and traitors but I don't have anyone serving time for playing politics."

"How would you describe Vallandigham?" the captain wanted to know.

The jailor rubbed the sleep from his eyes. "Traitor, I guess. Ain't that what he's in for?"

"Good. All settled. Bring the traitor down."

The clank of chains announced the arrival of the former congressman.

"Clement Vallandigham," the captain read, "at the order of the president of the United States, the sentence has been commuted."

Vallandigham watched in shock as a guard unlocked the shackles. Were they planning to claim he tried to escape and shoot him?

"What's going on? What do you mean commuted?"

"Oh, come now," the captain laughed. "An educated man, a lawyer, should know what commuted means. You won't be spending the next two years as a guest of the United States. I don't agree. General Burnside doesn't agree. But that's the way it is."

"Burnside," Vallandigham fumed. "Burnside! What a terrible example for the army."

"Call him General Burnside," the captain stabbed his finger at the prisoner's chest, "or those shackles will go back on. The commanding officer of the Department of Ohio deserves respect."

"Respect? The man is a despot, a dictator who abuses his authority."

"You were found guilty of disobeying an order from General Burnside," the captain reminded him and glanced again at the paper. "General order number 38."

"General Order 38 was rubbish," Vallandigham interrupted. "A direct assault on the constitutional right to free speech."

"I can gag him, shut him up real fast," the jailor suggested.

"Oh, I don't think that will be necessary." The captain eyed the prisoner and began to read again. "A military tribunal found you guilty of declaring sympathy for the enemy."

Vallandigham could not contain himself.

"The military tribunal was a kangaroo court. I did not declare sympathy for the so-called enemy. I did—understand this, Captain. There is a difference—I did say King Abraham was no longer fighting to save the Union but rather to free the slave. I did warn that those who survive Lincoln's war will face a ruinous combination of defeat, debts, and taxation, but I did *not* express sympathy for the South. I know what I said and so do the hundreds of Dayton residents who heard my speech. Do they know that Burnside sent troops to break down my door in the middle of the night and take me to prison?"

"Oh, they know," the captain said. "They didn't have the guts to try to free you. No, instead they burned part of Dayton."

Vallandigham was stunned. His lawyer had mentioned a small disturbance but said nothing of a riot.

In the shocked silence, the captain resumed. "Uh, so," he struggled to find his place. "The sentence is commuted from two years in military prison to banishment and exile. See how you like spending time with the rebels!"

"I'm not a Southern sympathizer. This is another outrage!"

"I can still order the gag," his captor told him. "Don't tempt me."

"Old Abe must be going soft," the jailor remarked as Vallandigham was forced into a wagon. "Why not leave that one to rot in the cells? A couple of years behind bars might do him good; make him less mouthy."

"Because too many people share his opinion," the captain explained sadly. "He would become a martyr behind bars. This way, he is out of sight and out of mind. Let the rebels deal with him."

ᐯ

Gettysburg, Pennsylvania: July 3, 1863

"Hurry them along," Owen heard an officer shout. "We need fresh men."

Ambulances and wagons of wounded moving in the opposite direction began to compete for the narrow roadway. Any noise from the battle was drowned by the turmoil around them.

As night fell, the fresh troops reached the Federal camps, passing figures slumped or stretched on soggy ground, medical tents and orderlies, and crude corrals filled with men in gray, butternut, or homespun clothes. The urgency of the march dissipated with the halt for the night.

By some unwritten rule, men fanned out each night for unofficial but usually reliable reports of the action. They learned of three days of hell, a victory for the Union if only because it wasn't a loss. Lee was a few miles away but his army was battered. Union Gen. George Meade was holding the high ground but his army, too, had taken a beating. The Confederate attacks of the past three days had been repulsed but no one wanted to bet the fighting was over. Try to sleep, they said, but few could.

The unit turned out at first light, with extra ammunition and weapons checked. Mounted couriers spurred up and down the lines but each message brought more delay. Finally, at mid morning, the whispers spread. Lee was withdrawing to the safety of Virginia. Would Mead follow and attempt to crush the rebel army? Orders to prepare a noon meal suggested the general would fight another day.

Two weeks earlier, Jimmy had jogged off with most of the unit, Owen remaining with the rear guard on the rail line until it, too, was hurried into Pennsylvania.

The first to arrive had been attached to Gen. Dan Sickles and on the hot afternoon of the second day at Gettysburg were ordered forward, toward a peach orchard, a wheat field and two rocky summits—ten thousand men in formation, drums beating and flags flying, until the Confederate attack.

Matilde had cared for the lightly wounded. The more seriously injured were sent to the rear, and many were missing. Jimmy had last been seen near what the soldiers described as the devil's den or the slaughter pen. Countless bodies still lay on the field and Matilde was planning another search when Owen found her. Federal units tried to reach the wounded and pioneer regiments had been told to drop their tools and scour the grounds for any still alive but the cries for help faded with the dawn.

First light found them among large rocks that might once have offered hope for protection. Bodies told the story of one of the desperate fights that would be forever obscured inside the larger story of Gettysburg. Owen read the signs as he picked his way through the bodies.

Carl Stueben, a twenty-year-old from Ohio, must have poked his head around the edge of a rock when a bullet struck him between the eyes.

Stephen Doyle had enlivened the nights on the railway with music. Now a stiff hand clutched a ramrod and the harmonica poked from his pocket.

Hiram Oster had carried whiskey in his canteen. Owen found a battered canteen with the scent of alcohol beside a body missing a face.

Owen found something familiar in a man in gray leaning against a rock as if catching overdue rest. A closer look identified Malone, the talkative Confederate from the valley skirmish. Nearby, with sword in hand, was the chaplain, hit so many times that the Bible in his pocket was shredded.

Owen willed himself to steady legs and stomach. Only at the sound of a muffled sniffle did he remember Matilde. But as he turned, he saw no tears. Instead, she scanned the rocks with grim determination. The sound came again like the whimper of a small, frightened animal.

Matilde heard it, too. Together they rounded a corner to face another mass of rock. Only a trickle of small stones gave the location away as a boot was pulled tighter into a small crevasse.

"Jimmy!" Matilde sprang forward.

He was wedged in the rocks, knees tight to his body, arms clasped across his chest as if fighting a chill. His eyes seemed frozen, yet he took in deep ragged breaths. Tears washed down his powder-blackened face, accenting two pools of sheer terror.

His hands and fingers threatened to rip their faces, thwarting attempts to pry him from the hole. In desperation, Owen grabbed Jimmy's ankles and wrenched him forward. His head slapped hard against the rock and a shudder passed through his body. But he was breathing and minutes later they lifted him to his feet.

* * *

GETTYSBURG: JULY 5, 1863

The surgeons turned them away, too busy to look at a man with no sign of wounds. "Shirkers" would be dealt with later. The left side of Jimmy's face was in constant motion with a nervous twitch. He responded to the gentle commands and suggestions from Matilde or Owen but tensed and showed anger at any sharp noise. They took turns watching through the night.

The next morning, the Union surgeons were still too busy but an orderly took pity, and directed them to where Confederate prisoners were treated.

A broken rail fence ringed a two-story farmhouse and a collection of tents pitched in ragged rows stretched to a barn in the rear. Paths already soggy from recent storms were cut to six-inch-deep muck by passing feet.

A weary Confederate doctor leaned against the open door of the barn. He agreed to look at Jimmy.

"So, he has no obvious wound," he said, wiping his hands against a bloody apron. The accent was Northern, not the expected Southern drawl.

"Ladies might not like to look at the private parts." The surgeon turned from Matilde to Owen. "But any kind of wound can set off a reaction."

"There are no wounds!" Matilde interjected. "I took him to the stream and washed him all over last night." She saw Owen's surprise. "While you were asleep."

"Don't need the details." The surgeon ran his fingers through Jimmy's hair to feel the scalp. "Where's home, son?" He looked into Jimmy's eyes. "Sometimes a reference from home will help; or something pleasant from the past."

Owen saw a blush on Matilde's face.

"What's your name, son?" The surgeon was lightly tapping on his chest.

"Jimmy," Owen prompted.

"Jimmy from?" the surgeon turned his attention to Jimmy's back.

There was no answer. Owen waited before he spoke. "Jimmy Hampstead from Port Burwell."

"Port Burwell in Canada West?"

Owen nodded.

"Well, isn't this a strange little world. I'm Dr. Solomon Secord, late of Kincardine, Canada West. It's nice to see someone from home even if under unpleasant conditions. Let me guess. Bounty money, three squares a day, eleven dollars a month, and nothing to hold you at home?"

"That's how it started," Owen admitted. "What about you? Is it the same story only Confederate script?"

Secord finished his examination of Jimmy and slumped on a small stool in the doorway of the barn. "Not quite the same. I had relatives in Georgia. The Southern firebrands don't like abolitionists but saw a need for doctors. Medical aid might be needed for the sick. They didn't think their people would be wounded, unless perhaps by the prick of a sabre. It was to be a brief, civilized little war. One thing led to another and I was forced into the Confederate army."

Owen considered the story.

"And now a prisoner, no longer under reb control, you can go home."

"Not that simple." Secord gestured to the tents. "These soldiers need help and I've grown to respect them. The Northerners aren't lily white. When they write the history of this war, I hope the historians consider the role of the moderates on both sides. A bit more spunk from them and this thing would have never started."

"And by lily white, I guess you mean the Negro emancipation?" Owen asked.

"I don't like slavery," Secord snorted. "Never have and never will, but you don't make men free by saying it's so. Slavery is doomed. The next step I'm not sure about."

"Doctor, they need you!" No one had noticed the young soldier approach.

Secord slowly rose from the stool. "Enough politics. If we survive we'll have years to argue." He put a hand on Owen's shoulder and motioned Matilde closer. "He has what we call melancholia or nostalgia. Some doctors call it homesickness. The mind is gone—from shock, from noise, we don't know. Where was he in the fight?"

Owen was baffled by the diagnosis and the question.

"We found him in the devil's den."

"Some of the worst of the worst," Secord shuddered. "I was with Bennings' Brigade on the other side. So he would have been out there through the next day, through Pickett's charge and the artillery barrage. That alone was enough to leave people deaf. He appears to have retreated." Secord touched knuckles against his head. "He's gone where medical science can't reach him."

"Doctor, they said to hurry!" the young Confederate soldier interrupted, his broad shoulders beginning to shake with impatience.

"All right, Lewis. Tell them I'm coming," Secord said, watching as the tall, muscular figure hurried off toward the house.

"He's another one. His name is Lewis Powell or Lewis Payne, even he isn't sure. There's a streak of brutal violence inside that frame and we don't know when it may come out. He's a confused and dangerous man."

"Jimmy," Matilde had listened long enough. "Will Jimmy come back?"

Secord stuffed his tools into a small black bag. "He may. We really don't know. Keep him quiet and he may recover. And, watch carefully, in these cases, an innocent thing or a sound can set them off. I can't predict what he might do."

He started across the yard but stopped and turned back. "The best thing may be to get him home, get him away from all this."

"Thank you, Doctor!" Owen reached to shake Secord's hand. "Good luck. I suppose it's a prison camp?"

"Yes, Fort McHenry, famous because some Yankee wrote "The Star Spangled Banner" there during the war of 1812." He smiled broadly. "And I tell them my Aunt Laura is famous for helping beat the Yankees in the same war, but of course, being Yankees, they didn't understand."

* * *

OHIO: MID JULY 1863

Getting away—he preferred not to call it deserting—was easier than expected. Meade's army moved to pursue the Southern force but no orders came for the remnants of the railway pickets. No orders and no officers. Hurley was missing, although, another private told Owen he had seen the sergeant as the fight began. "And a fine figure he made," the private said, "ordering the men forward as he slunk to the rear."

A neighboring unit, Ohio volunteers, provided food and when fresh uniforms and kit arrived, Owen made certain that he and Jimmy were in line. The quartermaster gave them nothing more than a quick glance. The fact that a private walked off with a sergeant's stripes was the least of his worries.

Owen and Matilde decided to take the doctor's advice and the men from Ohio suggested the route to follow. Owen prided himself on his ingenuity as he scratched out orders to find transportation and accompany trooper Jimmy Burrell to Cleveland. He wrote the signature of Sgt. Levitus Hurley at the bottom of the page.

Jimmy began to recognize Owen and Matilde and the frantic pacing eased but his face twitched and he maintained a moody silence. Once, in passing a blacksmith tent, the sound of the hammer striking metal triggered a reaction. He dropped to a crouch and with wide eyes scanned the horizon. Owen bent to touch his shoulder, only to have Jimmy spring to his feet, snarling and flailing his arms. Three men held his arms and legs until the resistance abruptly ended and a blank stare returned to his face.

For over a week, the trio moved north and west. People at farms and the villages rarely gave them a second glance. The requisitioned buckboard was stamped with US Army on the wooden tailgate; the canvas cover was new and doubled as a tent at night. The heavy workhorses were the best he could find without the army brand. They might have to sell the animals later near the border.

On the fifth night, they stopped well before sunset. The sun was hot, the road dusty, and the horses tired. Owen looked for a secluded area and found a small pasture surrounded by a rail fence. The weeds and high grass added to a feeling of desolation. He removed a section of fence wide enough for the wagon and then replaced the rails. The horses would have a night of grazing without a tether. At one end of the pasture was the blackened shell of a barn and below, in a ravine, a running stream.

Their evening routine was well established. While Matilde started a small cook fire, Owen scavenged for wood. A few dry boards from the barn ruins, a five-foot chunk of scorched beam, and then a search for more limbs or branches.

Jimmy was fast asleep when he returned and a small fire was burning. The distant sound of a splash brought his attention to the stream. He picked his way down the ravine, all of his senses on edge, until he spotted her through a break in the underbrush.

He watched silently as she paddled a few feet from shore. Her face was tanned, matching hands and lower arms, but the rest of her body and kicking legs were a stark white. He moved closer, embarrassed and intrigued. Minutes later, she emerged from the stream with the same confidence demonstrated in the army camp, her naked body backlit by the setting sun, drops of water gently falling to the ground. For a few seconds, she paused, and then she strode past the pile of clothing and continued up the bank to where Owen stood frozen. A smile played across her face as she extended her hand. "Just this once," she said. "We've earned it."

---

* * *

SOUTHERN OHIO: JULY 1863

The horses wore out quickly. Owen slowed the pace to allow more time for grazing and requisitioned grain with promises of payment over the signature of Sergeant Hurley. His revolver and a light tap on the holster were enough to arrange a settlement with any reluctant farmer.

To ease the strain on the animals, they walked beside the wagon and were near Dayton when another wagon rolled by, throwing up a cloud of dust. The dust settled to show the wagon stopped and the lone occupant, a rotund figure, twisting for a better view. Two beady eyes peered from a face covered by an unkempt beard and sideburns, all wedged under a wide straw hat. He wheeled the team and returned to stop by their side.

"Trouble?" he asked, taking in the two soldiers, the faltering horses, and finally the woman.

"Looks like you need a place to rest. I'm Paul Vogel. Got a farm up the road. Think you can get those critters that far?"

"We can make it," Owen told him.

"But the lady?" Vogel patted the seat beside him and smiled as Matilde raised her skirt to step up.

Paul Vogel was a horse trader. The first glimpse of his farm revealed a herd of perhaps fifty horses on pasture, a small house, and a barn.

Vogel pulled to a halt in the yard and helped Matilde to the ground. He lived alone, he told them, unless you counted the slaves, and he didn't.

Jimmy was showing more signs of a recovery and moved closer to Matilde as if to shelter her from the appraising eyes.

"Slaves?" he asked. "Don't you mean free people of color? The slaves have been freed."

Vogel spat in the dust.

"You ain't from Boston. I can tell by the accent. So you weren't raised an abolitionist. I guess it's what they teach you." He stared hard at Jimmy. "Let me set you straight. One, they are my slaves until I say they're free, and I ain't said it. Two, read the Black Republican propaganda, but remember the slaves are free only in the states in rebellion and Ohio ain't in rebellion, or at least not yet. And three, politics can change in a hurry. So don't give me any lecture."

He spat again, aiming in front of Jimmy's boots. Owen tensed but Jimmy stood quietly.

"Mr. Vogel," Owen began, "I have orders to escort Mr. Burwell and his companion and I have authority to requisition transportation as needed."

He produced the creased orders. Vogel held the paper close to his eyes for a full minute.

"Strangest looking orders I ever seen and I've seen some in the last few months. The army stops by regular like, looking for deserters, or rebel stragglers from Morgan's raid, and Copperheads, too, and that's anybody that opposes this war or asks any questions, I guess."

He spat again.

"Bunch of boys have been slipping away, disgusted, or maybe scared after Gettysburg. We had Mr. Vallandigham up in Dayton talking about peace and that may have encouraged more to go. So everybody is worried about a civil war within a civil war."

Vogel waited for a moment, training his eyes on Owen.

"So anyone who is suspicious or whose orders don't pass muster can be arrested just like that." He slapped his hands together.

"Men," he continued, "might get by in a prison." He pointed to Jimmy. "Or maybe an asylum. But the lady wouldn't be happy in either place."

"Mr. Vogel, I have my orders." Owen added an edge to his voice and patted the revolver. "I'll have to ask you to comply."

"Ah, shit!" Vogel said in disgust. He turned toward the barn and called, "Charlie! Jack!"

Two large black men appeared in the doorway. Each carried a rifle. Vogel ripped the orders into tiny pieces.

"Now fer Christ sakes, wake up!"

He pulled the revolver from Owen's holster. "It doesn't have to be prison. Maybe you disappear."

The black men made their way across the yard, rifles leveled at Owen and Jimmy. At a nod from Vogel, one stepped forward and ran his hands roughly over the two soldiers before turning to Matilde. This time, the hands moved slower, repeating the process two and three times.

"Got your jollies, Jack?" Vogel spat as the black man stepped aside.

Matilde maintained a stoic calm. Jimmy appeared confused.

"You don't have a choice," Vogel spoke again. "You can wait until the next officer comes by or skedaddle! Dayton is five miles away. Disappear from there. Because there's a lady involved, I'll have Charlie take you to town."

Under the watchful eyes of the black men, Jimmy and Owen unhooked the team and led the horses to the pasture.

At another shout from Vogel, a young black boy emerged from the barn with a bucket and a paintbrush. The white USA on the tailgate faded under a fresh coat of paint.

Vogel bent for a closer look.

"Give her another coat, and then a third. We'll sell it, maybe even to the US army," he chortled.

The black called Charlie climbed onto the seat of Vogel's buckboard and waited patiently for the passengers. Vogel held up his hand, a combination of command and benediction.

"Don't get any ideas about turning me in. Skedaddle and keep your mouths shut! If Charlie isn't back by sunset, I'll send for a provost marshal and tell him about two deserters. Sometimes he don't bother with a trial. I've seen deserters with holes in the back."

He spat again as Charlie clucked to the horses and the wagon moved down the lane.

Charlie became more talkative and friendly when they were out sight of the farm.

"I sure am sorry to see that hppen, especially since you are wearing my favorite color. Ol' Vogel always looks out for number one, but don't fret. I'll be back by sunset and he'll forget you by tomorrow."

Charlie shared more surprises, telling of helping slaves to escape on the underground railway to Canada. Vogel would have been shocked to learn of the traffic that had moved through his barn.

The route to the railway station took them past a long stretch of burned buildings. The result of a riot, Charlie told them. Copperheads who backed the former Congressman Vallandigham had gone wild. Charlie didn't know what to think of the Copperheads. Some of them were Democrats who didn't like Lincoln; a fair number were Southern sympathizers; and he guessed, a fair number went along for sport, because, he said, "White folks do strange things."

Charlie dropped them at the depot and disappeared into the night.

The fake orders that had carried them from Gettysburg lay in tiny pieces in Vogel's yard and Owen had no cash for tickets. But Matilde produced another surprise. She walked to the darkest part of the platform, turned her back, and bent forward to run her hand beneath the dress. The hem slipped back down and she turned to face them with a wad of bills in her hand.

Part of the money went for new civilian clothes. The blue jackets, hats, and anything connected with the army were left on a garbage heap behind the station. When the train arrived, two civilian men and one woman presented tickets for a journey north.

CHAPTER 8

Kingston, Canada West: August 1863

A few lamps burned in the upper offices of the Kingston City Hall while below, a bonfire and torches illuminated the limestone walls and the voters gathered for a campaign meeting.

"Is it fair?" the Reform candidate asked, his voice hoarse from days of campaigning.

"Canada West is growing. Our population rises each year. The Tories and the French prevent us from reaching our potential. Reform is the answer! Representation by population is the answer! Canada West deserves more seats in the legislature. It's the only way to break the deadlock."

"Well said!" A supporter cheered and waved a handmade sign above his shoulders. It read simply "Rep by Pop." The outburst brought a smattering of applause from other Reformers and catcalls from the Tory supporters but the candidate ignored the opposition.

"Let us take our rightful place in the empire. Let Canada West and Kingston grow. My friends, the riding has been short changed. Remember this magnificent hall was built as the legislature for the Canadas. The Tories and their friends decided that first Toronto, and then the French of Quebec City would host the members. Think of the thousands of dollars spent by the government officials, money that could have been spent in Kingston!"

"Damn right!" another supporter called. "Give them hell!"

The candidate drew strength from the reaction and pointed to a steamboat at the entrance to the Rideau Canal.

"And we have been overlooked again with the new capital up the canal in Ottawa…in Bytown. What a sad joke!"

"Shame! Shame!" the Reformers chanted until the candidate waved his arms for quiet, "But with the Reform proposals, Kingston will gain. We need a school to train the militia officers and what better place than here?"

He waited until the cheers faded.

"The last parliament and our local member failed us. I look across the harbor and see the British standard flying over Fort Henry…"

"Must have damn good eyes to see in the dark," a man shouted from the Tory ranks.

"My eyes are at least clear," the candidate fired back. "And not bloodshot like my opponent's. And where is John A. tonight? Why doesn't he appear?"

"Ah, shut your mouth. He's here now." Frenzied applause erupted from the friends of Macdonald.

The late arrival weaved through the audience, staggered onto the stage, tipped his hat to the crowd, and then to his opponent before almost falling into an empty seat. A moment later, he rose again and bent over the back of the platform. Tories and Reformers watched his shoulders heave. The scene silenced the audience but not the Reform candidate.

"Look at the respect he shows you. John A. Macdonald is sick from drink, again!"

"Ah, no!" Macdonald objected, his back still to the crowd. He fought to catch his breath before he turned.

"I'm not sick from drink. I'm sick from the ranting of my opponent. Stay the course, my friends. Elect John A."

* * *

INGERSOLL, CANADA WEST: AUGUST 1863

George Brown smiled and waved.

55

"Congratulations, Mr. Brown. You have a handy lead in the voting," his local agent greeted him.

"Then I must thank you for your work, Mr. Underhill. The party wouldn't be a success without the enthusiasm of the local workers."

"Call me Tim." The agent smiled at the rare praise. "I have done this before."

"Yes, and I must confess, this election will likely bring the same result. The parties are splitting the vote. It took a rebellion back in '37 to produce a government responsible to the electors. We don't need a rebellion but maybe it's time for outright separation. If we can't get our needs met thru the united province, we may have to go it alone, but we'll give the system one more chance."

"We should have no problems in South Oxford," Underhill told him. "I've only challenged one voter. The son of a well known Tory farmer tried to vote but the father owns the property, so the son won't qualify."

"It's why we need the local workers," Brown smiled. "Outsiders might have missed that one." His eyes flashed to the low platform where the voters stood.

"I'll vote for the Conservatives," a well-dressed man declared to a chorus of cheers from one section of the crowd.

"We'll have more electors today," Underhill explained. "The thunderstorm last night means farmers can't work and most of them like to come on the second day, anyway. They see who is winning and go with him."

"Brown-Reform," a man in a straw hat declared proudly.

"I do enjoy this," Brown beamed, "It's a manly act to stand and declare. One of the Maritime colonies has moved to the secret ballot. A voter writes the name of the candidate and stuffs it in a box. That's too open to abuse for my liking."

"Hey, did your wife tell you how to vote?" The shout went up as a well-dressed man pushed through the crowd.

"Yeah, she wears the pants at your house," another voter groused but the man was determined and elbowing his way forward. Someone gave him a rough shove as he reached the platform and he stumbled to the podium.

"Brown-Reform," he said meekly.

"Oh, the little woman won't like that," another man called. "You'll sleep in the barn tonight!"

"It's really pretty quiet," Underhill laughed. "I've got a few tough men up front but they haven't been needed. Ah, here's one to watch."

A young man in rough farm garb approached the stage, a half-empty bottle clutched in his hand. "I want to vote..." he snickered and surveyed the crowd.

"You're a Tory! Always have been, always will be!" a neighbor shouted.

"I want to vote for...Brrownnnn." The young man swayed before staggering from the stage.

"I don't approve of that," Brown told Underhill. "No man should sell his vote for a bottle."

"Oh, he didn't," Underhill smiled. "The Tories gave him the bottle today thinking it would swing him but I got to him last week. He was having a problem over a land dispute and I got it fixed."

"Well, that's different," Brown expounded. "The privilege of the vote should not be bought or abused."

"You keep a list of supporters, don't you?" Brown asked.

"Oh, yes," Underhill smiled. "I keep track of them all."

"Keep it up to date," Brown urged. "Unless we find new common ground, there will be another vote shortly."

* * *

JOHNSON'S ISLAND, OHIO: OCTOBER 1863

"Hey, Tom! The guard is looking for you."

"Tell him I escaped," Hines called from the prison bunk.

Basil Duke laughed from the next bunk. "The guard will have a heart attack."

Hines swung his body and placed his feet on the floor to face Duke. "We need a boat to make Canada, or we could disappear in Ohio."

"Do we go alone or stage a mass escape?" Duke asked absently.

57

"I'm serious," Hines told him. "I don't want to spend the winter."

"How do we get past the wall and the guard towers?" Duke asked. "The wall is too high to jump."

"Damn it! I'm serious."

"And so am I."

The two had surrendered on the banks of the Ohio in July. Their captors were more interested in the mere captain, Hines, than in the general, Duke. The stories of work behind enemy lines made Hines a wartime celebrity.

"We've got some of the smartest officers in the Confederacy and we can't figure a way out,"` said the frustrated rebel.

"It would be suicide to storm the walls," Duke told him, "and if we reach the water, we can't fend off their gunboat. Even I won't take on a ship like the *Michigan*."

"Maybe we could—" Hines began but was interrupted by the guards.

"That's Hines," one called, "and the one beside him is Duke. On your feet."

The men were barely off the bunks before handcuffs and leg irons were snapped in place.

"What's going on?" Hines demanded.

"You are going to visit your old companion, General Morgan," the guard sneered. "War Department says Morgan's brigands will no longer be treated as prisoners of war. You are nothing but common criminals like burglars and thieves. And if escape from Johnson's Island is tough, wait till you see the walls of the Ohio penitentiary."

ν

Journal of Paul Forsey,
government clerk, January 1864

Another year begins with stalemate in the legislature. The latest election accomplished nothing, save to stoke the fires of dissent. George Brown, a Toronto newspaper publisher, was elected, a fact that drives John A. Macdonald to distraction. The two are at loggerheads and carry their parties with them.

To the south, the Union armies are finally gathering steam. Gettysburg was seen as a Northern victory and Federal forces have regained control of the Mississippi River with the capture of Vicksburg. But the Union at times appears hapless. The rebel general, John Hunt Morgan, was confined in a formidable prison but he and a few of his men tunnelled to a courtyard and escaped over a high wall. How embarrassing for the Union. It's laughable—an odd occasion for a smile in what is becoming a very uncivil war.

* * *

RICHMOND, VIRGINIA: FEBRUARY 1864

The youngster cringed as the two men entered the tiny room at the Richmond jail. One was a sheriff's deputy and the other wore the uniform of a Confederate officer.

"Boy, we going to ask once more. Where did you get that leg?"

"I done told you. Found it on the road. It must have fallen off a wagon when they was hauling the dead to the cemetery."

The two men towered over him. The manufactured prosthesis of a lower leg and foot stood erect on the table beside them.

"Which cemetery?" the deputy demanded. The boy couldn't be much more than ten, he thought, skinny, short, and sneaky.

"I don't know, uh Hollywood, I guess."

"But you weren't anywhere near Hollywood cemetery when we grabbed you. And this here leg…" The deputy tapped the wooden ankle, "Wasn't made in Richmond. It's got the name of a fellow from the North written on it. Now tell us the truth or get whupped."

"I already told you." The boy stared at the floor and his patched shoes.

"OK, I'm going to get that wooden slave paddle." The deputy turned to leave.

"No!" The boy bolted but the officer grabbed his shoulders and forced him down.

"OK," the boy capitulated. "I took it off a dead Yankee."

"Where?" The hands on his shoulders tightened.

"Out where them raiders was last night. I heard they hanged the black fellow who was guiding 'em and I ain't never seen a hanged man, black or white. But when I was heading out, I come across this dead Yankee and his leg was turned funny and so I kicked it and…well…off she came."

The deputy glanced at the officer, who slowly loosened his grip.

"And that's it?" the deputy prompted. "You just grabbed the leg and run off?"

"Yeah," the boy stammered, "Well, I looked at some other dead Yankees, too."

"You just looked?" the deputy asked.

"Yeah." Again, fingers dug into his shoulder.

"Well, I checked them over. I wanted to be sure they was dead." The fingers tightened.

"Ow! You're hurting me real bad, mister." The fingers loosened and boy rubbed his shoulder.

"Did you take anything from the bodies?" the officer asked quietly.

"Well, they didn't have nothing but a few coins, and a couple of Yankee dollars."

He paused until he felt the fingers again,

"Ow. Don't do that. It hurts real bad."

"Tell us. Did you find anything else?"

"Well yeah. But you got to let go of me." The boy rubbed where the fingers had been.

"A pouch but I ain't had time to open it."

"Where is it?"

The boy squirmed but unbuttoned a ragged shirt and removed a small, black leather pouch. The officer seized it, pulled it open, and saw the name Ulric Dahlgren stitched inside.

"Can you read?" he asked.

"No, I ain't had no book learning."

"Deputy," the officer asked, "do you know how to find this young man in the future?"

"Yes, I could find him real fast."

"Then let him go but next time, arrest him and throw away the key."

The boy turned pale.

"Now get out of here!"

The deputy snickered as the door slammed behind the youngster.

"I wish they were all that easy. You got what you wanted? It's the first time I've worked alongside a member of the Confederate special service."

Col. Dan Mcgruder sifted through the papers, glancing at each document.

"This should do. Dahlgren led one wing of the raid and Kilpatrick, the other. It was a bid to free the Federals from the Richmond prisons. As to Dahlgren, we have his body, and we have his leg, so we can send all of him back to his family. His father is an admiral with the US Navy, apparently a close friend of Lincoln, so out of courtesy we'll want to take extra care…"

Mcgruder stopped abruptly to stare at a page. The deputy watched in silence until he closed the pouch.

"I'll need a carriage. Tell the driver I will be going directly to the office of President Davis."

* * *

TORONTO, CANADA WEST: APRIL 1864

From habit, Tom Hines glanced behind. Teamsters forced horses and wagons through the confusion of traffic. He saw well-dressed men, women on shopping expeditions, and young boys on the prowl for mischief, but nothing that suggested immediate danger, and no one who had been there when he'd checked minutes before.

Richmond in early April had been warm with the smell of the blossoms, but three weeks later, Toronto shivered in an icy breeze from Lake Ontario. The trees were bare and the city stank from a winter's worth of horse droppings tramped in the mud.

A young girl, perhaps ten years old, sprang into his path.

"Buy a flower, sir?" The lilt was gentle and she raised her hand to show a clutch of blossoms. In the crowd he noticed a brown bowler hat. A man at the station had worn a brown bowler. He fished for a coin and moved so the girl was between him and mystery man.

"They're early wood phlox," she told him proudly before moving to another customer.

The bowler hat turned down a busy side street. Hines moved the other way, sinking into the muck of the street and gently releasing the flower as he reached the plank sidewalk.

At the hotel, the desk clerk was in a talkative mood as he glanced at the signature and address on the register.

"Welcome to the Queens, Mr. Preston. From St. Louis? I thought I detected a Southern accent. We get a lot of Southrons. It's been a steady stream since '61 and picked up again of late."

The man in front of the counter had long experience with false identities and Preston was his latest.

"I suppose it's because of the war," he responded absently.

"Oh, not to worry about that." The clerk reached for a key. "We had scares. It looked like the British would lock horns with the Americans over those Confederates seized off the *Trent* but cooler heads prevailed and we're still at peace…er…We're neutral, sir. It's Room 342."

As Hines made his way to the room, his mind flashed to Richmond. The papers found on the body of Ulric Dahlgren showed the full implications of the raid. The freed prisoners were to kill President Jefferson Davis and other cabinet members. The South was shocked. Gen. Robert E. Lee sent a message through the lines questioning the source of Dahlgren's orders. The Federals replied that the papers were forged but confidential contacts hinted at more than Washington cared to admit.

Hines was one of the Confederates summoned to Richmond in the wake of the raid, men and women with experience behind enemy lines.

"Take the war to Africa," they were told. "Take the war to the North!"

* * *

RICHMOND, VIRGINIA: MAY 1864

Judah Benjamin reflected on his guest and their days in Washington. In the American capital, in 1858, Benjamin was a senator from New Orleans and Jacob Thompson, the secretary of the interior. Now, in five short years, both men were in a different capital. Benjamin was the Confederate secretary of state and Thompson was preparing for a special role.

"We call it our Canadian cabinet," Benjamin said, offering a smile. "Will you be glad to be back in the cabinet?"

On another day, Jacob Thompson might have joined in good-natured banter but there was something in the air, perhaps spring pollen or dust. He wanted to keep the meeting short.

"I'm ready to go where Mr. Davis sends me and I'd like to be on my way." He took a deep breath, grabbed for his handkerchief, and smothered a cough.

"And you shall, Mr. Thompson! A blockade runner is off to Halifax as soon as the last minor details are in place. The president wanted to talk to you again in person but we won't press him for a few days. It's the strain of the war and now the death of his son…tragic, tragic."

Thompson won control of his breathing, and returned the handkerchief to his pocket.

"And Mrs. Davis…Varina…how is she?" he managed to ask.

"Blames herself. What mother wouldn't?" Benjamin glanced up as a shadow fell across the window. The light faded as a line of clouds raced across the Richmond sky.

"She thought the servant was watching the boy. It was an open door, on a second-floor balcony, a natural lure for a toddler. At least after the fall it was over quickly. Did you see the funeral cortege for the poor little Joe? School children from across Richmond followed the procession."

Benjamin glanced absently through the window before he continued. "Odd, isn't it. All the trappings of power and the leaders can't protect their own. Oh, from war perhaps…but not from disease and accident. Lincoln lost his son, Willie, to disease, what was it? Back in '62, and now this tragedy at our executive mansion."

Thompson again felt the constriction in his chest.

"Perhaps we should just review the file and I'll be on my way."

"Very well, then." Benjamin pulled a sheet from the papers on his desk. "You already have verbal orders from the president…thank God that was done before the accident. The written orders will show that you, Mr. Clay, and staff will proceed to Canada. From there, make contact with our friends in the North, and do all in your power to encourage them. You will have access to a million dollars in Federal currency. The money represents over 20 percent of the total Secret Service budget, another sign of how important we think this is."

Benjamin stared into space as if trying to remember some important fact. Finally, he resumed. "As secretary of state, it is my duty to point out British-Canadian neutrality." A frown crossed his face, "But we'll deal with events as they occur."

Thompson rose to leave but Benjamin held up his hand. "One more thing! Keep your hands clean. Other men are already in the Canadas. One of them is named Hines. He rode with Morgan and was with the general in the famous escape from the Ohio Penitentiary. I've met him. He's a slight fellow but he can be dangerous. Rely on him for any dirty work."

* * *

NEAR TORONTO, CANADA WEST: MAY 1864

The appearance of the farm showed there was little physical difference between Canada West and the hill country of Kentucky. A single-story house was built from rough-hewn logs felled on the property. The only luxuries appeared to be the glass in two small front windows and a small overhang that sheltered a woodpile and provided space for a bench. This was farm country, a world away from the great houses and estates on the edge of the city. The nearby barn, however, was large, easily one hundred feet long and two stories high. A larger, modern house would wait. That, too, was like the hill country of the South.

Tom Hines walked his horse to the corral. The heads of several large draft horses rose from behind a feed bin.

"Are you the buyer?" The voice came from the upper level of the barn. Hines couldn't see the speaker—and by reflex his hand moved to his waist.

"I said, are you the buyer?" The voice came from behind a small door in the hayloft.

"You look too dandy to be a buyer. Stay where you are. I'll come down."

Two minutes later, a figure appeared in the shadows of the back of the barn and made his way slowly to the open door. The man walked with a distinct limp. He carried a pitchfork as a soldier on the attack would carry a rifle.

"What do you want?"

Despite the fork, the man looked harmless.

"I'm looking for Fletcher," Hines answered.

"Ain't here. What do you want with him?"

"We have business." Hines decided to take the risk. "He ordered some Bibles."

This time, the farmer hesitated before limping forward. "Well, the Lord's will be done." He offered a tough, calloused hand.

The farmer was Homer Linslow and his friend Fletcher, he promised, would be back directly.

Linslow led the way to the cabin. The ground floor was a single large room with a rough staircase leading to the half-story sleeping area above. The only light came through the two dirty windows and in the darkest corner was an unmade cot with a rumpled blanket. On a table was a two-week-old copy of the *New York Tribune*, the first hint the occupants cared for anything beyond the property line.

Hines leafed through the paper.

"It's not unusual," Linslow explained. "We can pick it up in Toronto along with all the other papers. We could buy the *Globe*, or the *Leader* but we do like those personal ads from New York." He paused for a moment to study his guest. "So we knew someone was coming."

Hines pulled a chair from the table and sat. "More company is coming but I'll wait for Fletcher to explain."

Linslow lifted a battered coffee pot from the stove and touched it with his fingers. "Still warm…only a few hours old. Coffee?" He limped to a sideboard to remove a china cup.

"What did you do to your leg?" Hines asked.

"More like what the doctors didn't do. I limp but at least I have two of them."

Hines waited as the cup was filled and the pot returned to the stove.

"My family had relatives in Kentucky," Linslow explained, "and I was visiting after the war broke out so I went along as a lark. Everything was fine until they sent us to Pittsburgh Landing. Folks up here know it better as Shiloh. I took a bullet before I could fire a shot. The army don't need cripples, so I came back here. Fletcher was one of the people who helped me, so when he showed up I couldn't turn him away."

The conversation was interrupted by a shout. "Hello, the house… Homer Linslow?"

The farmer glanced out the window.

"Stay put," he warned Hines. "This must be my buyer. It's a fellow pays in American dollars. This shouldn't take long."

The buyer had wheeled his buckboard to the corral and the horse Hines had left tied by the gate.

"That one's not for sale." Linslow limped across the yard. "That's my personal beast. Just got back and haven't taken the saddle off. The ones for sale are in the corral."

Twenty minutes later, the buckboard rolled back down the lane toward the main road and a smiling Linslow returned to the house.

"Sold them. Someone will pick them up tomorrow and in two weeks they'll be down in your country. Hey what the…" He scanned the room until he saw the figure on the cot, deep in the shadows. Hines sat with his back was against the wall, a revolver in his hand.

"Are you playing both sides of this game? Are you in the pay of the Yankees?"

Linslow was shocked. "The horses, you mean?"

The question was answered with a cold stare.

"We've got to live! A lot of neighbors went broke in the depression in the '50s, but with the war, the Yankees are buying pretty near anything and with hard money. So we sell 'em!"

There was no response from the man on the cot.

"It helps to know the beasts," Linslow continued. "Those horses are maybe fifteen years old but a little feed and care and they look younger. A week of hard work will turn them into nags. They won't pull a Yankee wagon very far."

The slate blue eyes lost none of their menace, but the revolver disappeared under the coat.

* * *

A mile down the road, the buyer stopped beside a small wood lot. Another man sauntered from the shadows.

"The horse was there," said the buyer. "But no sign of the rider. I'll keep my eyes open when I come for the animals."

The man by the trees could have passed for any local farmer. He stuck his hand in his pocket and produced three coins.

"There's more of that," he promised. "Let me know if you see anything."

The buyer tugged on his hat—almost a salute—then flicked the reins and drove off.

* * *

WASHINGTON: MAY 1864

For weeks, the capital watched passing troops, the long lines of marching men, wagons, supplies, and artillery were all moving south. The spring campaign was about to begin as it had for the last three years but this time with Gen. Ulysses Grant in command and with new hope for victory.

Lafayette Baker turned from the window before he spoke.

"I hope Grant has more success with the Army of the Potomac. An advance of fifty miles in three years is not much to brag about. Is there any late word from the front?"

His companion shrugged. If the chief of the National Detective Service didn't know, who would? Baker claimed access to the most reliable military information compiled from the reports from a network of operatives. "Get to it Baker. What do you want?"

Baker pulled a chair closer to the desk and sat. "Mr. Secretary, or I guess Mr. Assistant Secretary," he put extra emphasis on the assistant and half sneered the title.

"Get to it!" Peter Watson was impatient. Almost two years of meetings and briefings had created a growing animosity between the two men.

Baker settled into the chair and threw his leg over the arm. "I want money to send men to your old stomping ground."

"We have operatives in Philadelphia. We're covered."

"Not Philly...Toronto and Montreal."

Peter Watson was appointed to help Edwin M. Stanton reorganize an inefficient and corrupt War Department in 1862. By trade, he was a patent lawyer, and he was a well-connected Republican. He had acted as a liaison between the Buchanan White House and the incoming Lincoln Administration in the treacherous period just before the war. Now he was trusted with the secrets of the War Department. Only a few people knew that he fled Canada after taking part in the rebellion of 1837. Lafayette Baker made it his business to be one of the few.

Watson spoke softly. "I haven't been there for twenty-five years."

"It's grown since your day," Baker told him. "But still very British. The leaders like to think of themselves as aristocrats and they do seem to sympathize with the South."

"Get on with it. I don't have all day." The last thing Watson wanted was a lesson in parliamentary democracy and North American society.

"Trouble is brewing." Baker lifted his leg off the arm of the chair and settled both feet back on the floor. "Remember last year? When their governor—governor general, I guess they call him, got word of the plans to attack our prison camp at Johnson's Island?"

As Watson recalled, the Confederates planned to seize a ship, attack the American island in Lake Erie, and free the rebel prisoners.

"Go on," he ordered.

"My men—the ones that I can afford to send—say more rebels are turning up. They may have two ships on the Canadian side of Lake Erie. One near Long Point, across the lake from Erie in Pennsylvania, and the other at Rondeau, closer to Detroit. I think the rebels are waiting for arms."

Baker's intelligence operation turned in an impressive performance, even if Federal detectives were often guilty of exaggeration.

"One ship is called the *Montreal* and the other the *Saratoga*... apparently, they are fast schooners. If they get cannon, we have a problem. Here's another thing. My man in Toronto is watching a whole nest of rebels. We could ask the Canadians to help but I'm not sure we can trust them to do the job."

"Do it." Watson made up his mind. "Move a few men up."

Baker's face fell as Watson continued. "Not an army, a few men. We'll send more if there's something to it."

* * *

CANADA WEST: MAY 1864

Homer Linslow was uncomfortable and nervous. Hines had waited silently at the farmhouse until John Fletcher returned late in the afternoon.

"I'll be damned...Captain Hines."

"Hello Fletch!" The cold guest suddenly became warm and friendly. "We meet again."

"Wasn't sure when I'd see you, but figured Tom Hines could take care of himself."

Linslow was absorbing every word.

"Oh, Homer's all right," Fletcher assured Hines. "Trust him."

"I have to take your word, Fletch. But we should have a private conversation?"

Linslow took the cue and limped off to the barn. Within an hour, he was called back.

"We had some catching up to do," Fletcher said, pointing to an empty chair. "And now we'll tell you what we can."

Linslow sat but glanced at the packet of cigars on the table.

"Have one, Homer," Hines offered. "They're Cuban. A friend passed through Havana."

Linslow didn't need a second invitation and lit the cigar as Fletcher began to speak.

"Tom and I met on Morgan's Ohio raid. I got back to Kentucky, but some of the men were captured and sent to the Ohio Penitentiary."

Linslow nodded and sucked deeply on the cigar.

"Remember the fuss when Morgan escaped? Tom was with him. Meet Capt. Thomas Hines, Morgan's cavalry."

Linslow choked.

"That was you? There was a story that Morgan came to Canada, signed his own name in the register at a hotel down in Windsor. Were you with him?"

"Don't believe everything you read or hear, Homer." Hines was a different man as the hard shell fell away.

"Windsor was just a small diversion."

"Tom's going to be passing through every now and again," Fletcher continued. "And we're going to have other guests."

Linslow was struck by the contrast between the two men. Fletcher was over six feet tall, strong and packed with muscle. Hines was slight, thin, and several inches shorter with an unkempt moustache.

"What sort of things can I help you with?" Linslow asked.

"For a start, directions," Hines said. "Like the quickest routes to St. Catherines, Guelph, London, and Windsor. I can ride the Great Western and Grand Trunk but I need to know the back country."

"I can draw a good map. Or, I've got time. I can come with you." Linslow stopped abruptly at a cool glare from Hines.

"No. A map will do. And Homer," Hines's icy tone was back. "I haven't been here and you don't know me."

CHAPTER 10

Richmond, Virginia: May 1864

Soldiers in the field might be in tattered uniforms and the people of Richmond might be threadbare after three years of darning and patching, but Sarah Slater could have been dressed for a pre-war ball.

A few inches of ankle showed as she stepped from the carriage. Her long blue dress was spread over an expanse of crinolines, a matching blouse was buttoned tight to the neck, and luxurious blonde hair peeked from around a small hat and veil. The white glove of one hand balanced a Parisian parasol while the other grasped a small black case.

"That's all, Jacob," she dismissed the driver. "I'll walk back."

"Thank you, Miss Sarah," answered the smiling black man. He too was dressed in immaculate pre-war livery and drew admiring glances from those who knew the value of a well-trained slave.

"I'm to see Mr. Benjamin," she told the officer who hurried to her side.

"He's waiting and I will guide you."

"Why, thank you, is it Captain?"

"Colonel, ma'am. Colonel Mcgruder at your service."

"Do forgive me. I get so confused by the military."

"No problem, ma'am."

"I'll remember in the future," she assured him. "I am a quick learner but we must not keep the secretary waiting."

Sarah Slater had won a new admirer and moments later in a second-floor office, she collected a second.

Judah Benjamin knew the women of the South. His experience in Washington and travels in Europe added to his appreciation of the female shape and mind. Sarah Slater had all of qualities a gentleman preferred.

There was, for example, a disarming smile that emerged as the veil was lifted. He wondered if the skin might wear out over the high cheekbones as a smile washed up her face, danced over a perfect nose, and came to rest in the depths of blue eyes. It was Mrs. Slater, he learned, but the husband was dead in battle or from disease. It didn't matter. She was beyond mourning and ready for duty.

"Mrs. Slater, I am delighted. We needed a woman of refinement, someone who can move easily in the highest social circles."

Benjamin was rewarded with another smile.

"I am only too happy to help. But there is a small problem. My late husband's affairs were severely damaged by the war and I find myself in economic distress."

"That will be no problem." Benjamin scratched a note. "Give this to Colonel Mcgruder and he'll make the arrangements."

"Mr. Benjamin, you are so kind and so efficient! It makes me think this cruel war will soon be over and probably before I can do much."

Another thought crossed her mind as she prepared to leave. "That Colonel Mcgruder looks so handsome and healthy. I'm surprised he's not in the field."

Benjamin caught her meaning. The army needed every man but he didn't like the implication of shirkers in his department. "He's more valuable to us in Richmond, as you will no doubt soon discover."

A radiant smile dashed any hint of disagreement.

That night at the Spotswood Hotel she began to discover more about Col. Dan Mcgruder.

He was in his early thirties and dressed in a clean, well-pressed Confederate uniform, but he was a man, she suspected, who had never seen a shot fired in anger. His type was drawn to her like moths to a flame. Most expected her to deliver heirs to propagate white society but when they discovered her lack of funds, the interest waned. Rich, attractive widows were desirable; poor attractive widows were useful for other purposes. Sarah Slater wanted desperately to rejoin the ranks of the rich and desirable.

"From Secretary Benjamin," Mcgruder said, removing an envelope from a small black bag.

"Five thousand dollars is on deposit in the Bank of Ontario in Montreal. Present this authorization and open an account."

Mcgruder spoke with abrupt urgency. She wondered if he was one of those overbearing types aiming for constant advancement.

"I don't really like this, Mrs. Slater, but several of our male couriers have been arrested so we've opted for the fairer sex."

She stared at the envelope. The money was welcome but it was in Montreal and not in Richmond. Mcgruder sensed disappointment.

"Five thousand is more than we usually provide. Surely, it's enough?"

"It's not that. I have no money to get there. I'll be hard pressed to pay for this hotel."

Men loved these scenes, she decided. For a small loan, they expected eternal gratitude.

"I should have explained." Mcgruder pointed to the bag. "Confederate script will cover immediate expenses and get you through our lines, and there's enough Yankee currency to cover Northern lodging and travel."

Despite the danger, she felt relief.

"And if the Yankees find the bank documents?"

With a slow smile, his eyes passed up and down her body.

"Hide them. Once through the lines, go by train from Washington to New York, stay one night, and continue to Montreal. You do speak French?"

"I do."

She would be forever grateful to a former tutor. She had been an impressionable seventeen and learned many things from the gentleman who spent the summer at the family home. The proper Southern colonel would be shocked.

"Of course," Mcgruder continued, "the good people of Quebec have their own dialect."

Part of his mission was to build confidence in any new courier, but Mrs. Slater didn't lack confidence.

"Most of the work will be in English but there may be an occasion that calls for French."

"Pourquoi?" she interrupted brightly.

"If things go bad, there is a special contact. His name is Father Raymond Le Jean, and you can reach him at the Notre Dame Cathedral. But, let me stress this," Mcgruder's voice was stern, "go only to *him*. Not all of the priests share his passion for our cause."

"Oh, and the good father can hear my confession?" she teased.

The response was not what he expected.

"Don't worry," she said. "My French will be adequate. Secretary Benjamin suggested I stop by the French consulate in Montreal. He thinks at some point they might be helpful."

"Be careful in everything you say and do." Mcgruder's voice again showed concern. "This is no ladies game."

"I can take care of myself, Colonel. Trust me." She walked to a sideboard. "Perhaps a glass of brandy?" She poured one glass, glanced to see his nod, and filled another. "Colonel, I told you I'm a fast learner."

She passed him the glass. "I've got it all so far. What else do I need?"

"The dispatches," he said, sipping the brandy. "I'll bring them tomorrow. Good choice of liquor. Excellent taste!"

"I have expensive tastes, Colonel, and the Confederacy is willing to pay. Tell me about the dispatches."

Mcgruder took a deep drink and rolled the glass in his palm.

"The documents will be sealed. If you fall into the wrong hands, you can claim honestly that you didn't know the contents. There is, however, an oral message for Jacob Thompson. Tell him Richmond is in the oil business."

Her eyes brows rose.

"That's it? Richmond is in the oil business."

"Simple isn't it?" Mcgruder drained the glass and looked again at the bottle on the cabinet.

"Go ahead. I'm not paying."

Mcgruder poured a refill.

"One more thing. You will have company. Someone to protect you and assure us you are doing the job."

She spun to face him. The legendary smile was gone.

"What company? I go alone, Colonel! Jacob and I have travelled across the South with no difficulty."

"Jacob won't be there. We know about him. You purchased Jacob six months ago but neglected to pay. I wouldn't have known if you hadn't made a show arriving at the office. While you and Mr. Benjamin were talking, I had a visit from a Carolina slave catcher."

For the first time, he saw a hint of vulnerability.

"Jacob is going south, and if wasn't for me, you would go with him—Jacob to the fields and you to debtors' prison. I told the slave catcher that I couldn't remember the name of the owner and suggested that unless he wanted to join the army, he forget he even saw you. With that strong persuasion, and with Jacob in hand, he agreed."

She stood frozen for a moment, and then began to choke back tears.

"Hold the performance, Mrs. Slater. Jacob would have been sold for the right offer."

He saw the anger blaze in her eyes. "Besides you will still have a servant."

The anger turned to surprise.

"Her name is Sillery Fraser and, like you, she needs money. She is black—well, actually mulatto—and quite attractive! She's free but needs cash to buy her daughter's freedom. She won't get the money unless she cooperates. In the meantime, we protect her daughter."

CHAPTER 11

Canada West: May 1864

The train car was crowded and Hines was forced to wedge into a seat beside a corpulent traveller. There were no signs of war. Two British officers, the only passengers in uniform, boarded in Toronto and disembarked in London. Hines would eventually reach Windsor or Detroit but first planned a stop in Chatham.

The train slowed to meet another lumbering locomotive. His seatmate stirred and Hines heard a faint pop as the smell of a partly digested dinner wafted into the air.

"Komoka already." The man wore a full bushy beard and spoke with a British accent. "Making good time. I feared a delay, what with the problems of the working class."

He gave Hines a once over and decided the little fellow was his sort. "Lazy buggers want better hours and more money. If this country had more British troops we'd show them—toss them out on their keisters when they threaten strike."

He shifted and Hines braced for another blast of foul air but there was nothing.

"Bertram. Nigel Bertram," the Brit introduced himself.

"Paul Preston," Hines replied grasping a well-manicured and very soft hand.

"Strikes may spread from the American side," Bertram explained. "The engineers on the Great Western walked out last year and threaten to strike again. Their betters put up the money for the railroad, millions of pounds. These roads wouldn't have been built without English investment."

Hines looked through the window to a team of horses with a farmer walking behind. The planting season had begun. The countryside was a mix of farm fields and forest.

"There," Bertram also spotted the man at work. "A yeoman farmer. That's what the country needs. Grow enough food here to feed the Empire. I arrange transportation for the wheat for England, although right now the Americans are gobbling up all we produce. These are good days for the farmer. And you, what's your line?"

Hines was ready.

"I'm considering business opportunities. Once the war is over and the Indians gone, the farmers will move west, a big market for the right products."

"Good show! Like an entrepreneur, I do."

"Glencoe." A weary conductor walked through the car. "Glencoe, change for Petrolia and the oil fields."

The train slowed for the small station and Hines felt his hat knocked roughly as passenger hurried for the door.

"A mere hamlet," Bertram explained. "I stopped once to look at land. Good soil but population is Highland Scot. Don't know anything but Gaelic and can't or won't speak English! And that name comes from some Scottish massacre."

Hines knew the name for another reason—the horse used by General Morgan on the great raid. Hines had been sent to find Southern sympathizers but found no more than verbal support. He thought of Morgan, seated on Glencoe, and his disappointment.

"The Glencoe plow, ever heard of it?" Bertram's question brought him back to the train. "Little outfit makes a great plow. Maybe you could sell it to American farmers, or represent other implement dealers. The Massey family is doing well near Toronto."

"Interesting idea. I'll have to consider it." But the last thing he'd consider would be haggling over plows or reapers. Instead, he thought of the men who would soon join him. Safe houses in the larger cities would be best. A stranger in a small community would attract too much attention.

"Best to confine any business dealings east of here," Bertram confided. "A bit too much Yankee stock in this region. You'd be better to deal with the true English, the loyalist settlements east of Toronto."

Bertrand pointed to huge trees standing close to the track.

"George Brown, the publisher, actually made his fortune around here. He sold lumber and land before the paper was successful and now people read about democratic government in the *Globe* or listen to his Clear Grits theories and think all the government posts should be filled by election. I'm in favor of a fair break for the lower classes but leave governing to the people bred for it, the British upper class."

The train lurched over a rougher section of track. Bertram seemed to have lost himself for a moment before returning to the starting point.

"At any rate, a lot of Americans live in this area. Just came and squatted and have more dealings with Detroit than with Toronto. They're not like the pure British stock in the East."

Hines was more interested in the geography than local character.

"I can travel from Chatham by train or by boat?"

"Oh, take the steamer." Bertram grew almost lyrical. "The Thames's is a small river but it is a pleasant voyage. The breeze off Lake St. Clair is refreshing and there's always something interesting on the Detroit River."

* * *

CHATHAM, CANADA WEST: 1864

Chatham was like the other towns in Canada West with one major exception and Hines saw it immediately. The number of black faces almost equalled the white. The town felt Southern except for shops where white and black appeared to mingle on equal terms.

He peered in the window of a shop with the words "Gunsmith Jones" painted above the door. A black man handed a weapon to a white customer who laid several bills on the counter. He showed no feigned subservience but accepted the cash and smiled as the customer left.

"Gunsmith Jones makes fine revolvers," said a voice from behind.

Hines spun to face another black man.

"Ease up, Captain. You'll draw attention."

He was a few inches taller than Hines was and wore a heavy woollen shirt and a light smock. Rings of dried sweat showed beneath his arms. He wiped the perspiration from his face with a sleeve and said quietly, "I was sent for you. The horse and buggy are up the next street."

Hines noted the broad shoulders and the calloused hands.

"Captain, if I had a hat," the black man said, raising his hand to his head, "I'd take it off and curtsy. But I don't and Mr. Willis is waiting. Are you coming?" And with that, he lumbered down the street.

The buggy had seen better days but the horses suggested good breeding and an expert groom. The two men rode silently until the city gave way to countryside.

"In case you wondered," the black man announced, "Mr. Willis gave me the description of a fellow to pick up. And you were the only one that came close."

"So why didn't you introduce yourself sooner?"

"I never did introduce myself but I'm Amos Baker and even here in Canada West, there are whites who take offense when approached by black folks. Willis also said you wanted to keep your business quiet."

He urged the horses to the left to pass a wagon heavily laden with burlap sacks.

"Planting time." He pointed to the bags before pulling his team back to the right. "Farmers working all the ground they can, what with good prices and all."

Hines read "seed corn" on the bags.

"They must be prosperous if they buy seed. Back home, a farmer grows it."

"Back in your home," Baker corrected Hines, "they have to. Then they hide seed and hope the soldiers don't raid the grain bins. Up here, there's no worry of raids and last year these farmers sold every bushel. The grain merchants are so confident of good prices, they offer credit."

Baker slowed the team to meet an oncoming wagon and waved as it passed.

"Where did you come from, Amos?"

"I was done found under a cabbage leaf, or so my mammy say." Baker produced a toothy grin. "And suh, she hadn't jumped over a broomstick."

"You're a chameleon, Amos, a leopard changing spots."

Baker flashed another wide smile. "Reckon it takes one to know one." He paused. "Suh."

The road ran straight over flat country and Hines could see no other traffic ahead. Baker, too, noted the isolation.

"Actually, Captain, I am free black, born and raised in Kent County. I have papers that make me the envy of my Southern cousins, and I can read what those papers say. I read so well that Mr. Willis has hired me for American trips. Sometimes I'm a servant and sometimes I'm the one served. Depends which side of the border I'm on."

Baker turned to question Hines. "Now what about you? I'm betting you're a states' rights Confederate, who wants decisions made close to home. Or you could be a planter preserving a way of life and the value of the livestock in the slave quarters?"

The question was asked with enough impertinence to justify a whipping but Hines found himself smiling. "Where did you get those ideas?"

"Right up ahead, Captain." Baker pointed to a cluster of cabins.

Each was identical, well kept, with gardens sprouting small picket fences.

"This is Buxton." Baker pointed to a building surrounded by a large group of children. "And that is one of the first schools for black and white."

The buggy rolled by the schoolhouse and a black hand waved to Baker from a garden.

"Hello, hello," he called.

One house was larger than the others, and only a few yards from a church and a bell tower.

"Massa's house?" Hines asked.

"Massa of the heavens, Captain." Baker slipped into the drawl and as easily slipped out of it. "Bell on the church used to ring when an escaped slave arrived but there haven't been many since the war started. The tide is flowing the other way. The boys from Buxton drilled in the Kent militia and so they knew all that fancy spinning and wheeling and turning and as soon as the Federals would accept the Negro, off they went. And if that don't beat all, Mr. Lincoln is sending a delegation to see how Buxton is run. He may handle the sable hordes by following the Buxton model."

Hines paid closer attention. The South would have to come to grips with slavery either during this war, or after. Southern emancipation might bring recognition from Britain and France. Both countries were willing to deal privately on arms and munitions, but recognition of the Confederacy would come only when slavery ended. Like it not, he knew, the days of slavery were numbered.

"How did all this come about?" he asked, glancing past neat houses to the surrounding fields.

"The big house," Baker jerked his head to the rear, "is the home of the Reverend William King." Then he realized that the name meant nothing to his passenger.

"Rev. King married into a Louisiana family and inherited slaves when his wife died. He shipped the slaves North to freedom." He almost sang the word and again flashed a toothy smile.

"Now," he continued, "I was born free but colored folks like to be with colored folks and my family moved here when I was a boy. I've seen the slave pens in the South, but I don't get worked up. I guess when you grow up free, it's different."

Hines continued to stare at the houses. "They're all the same."

"All part of King's plan and makes everyone equal, I guess." Baker turned to wave to a woman. "Got some pretty strict rules. Have to pay for the land, won't abide drinking, and expects people in church on the Lord's Day."

"Too many rules, Amos?"

"I think so, Captain." Baker slipped back into his patter, "Ol' Amos likes the town life and women and not having to grub in the ground to make hisself a living. Old Amos prefers the good life. If he gets on with the white man, the white man cross his palm with silver...yes, indeed."

"So you're not impressed." Hines waved his hand to indicate the settlement.

"Don't get me wrong. These folks have been through a lot and deserve credit for what they achieved. That school was built for their children but white folks liked the education and now the school is black and white. Little white farm boys framed by rows of black and so successful the pure white schools suffer for lack of attendance."

Hines wasn't sure if he should feel disgust or if he had seen the future.

"What about King? Is he still around?"

The buggy picked up speed as they left the settlement.

"The good reverend is still with us," Baker answered. "He's not as spry but the people take care of him. A few years ago, a bunch of white rowdies wanted to teach him a lesson but word got out and pretty near every black man in Chatham closed shop and went fishing for the day."

He smiled at the recollection. "Course, they weren't fishing. They formed the nicest perimeter defensive line around the settlement you'll ever see. The Rebel army might take a lesson. Captain, no white man got anywhere near Buxton with black folks out patrolling the roads, fields, and swamps."

"You call all whites Captain?" Hines asked.

"No suh! I's don't. I only says Captain to those Ol' Amos ain't sure about." He pointed to a line of clouds on the sky ahead. "Them are clouds over da lake, da Lake Erie. Ol' Amos getting you close to where you going! Glory be, we almost there!"

It was another two hours before the carriage swung off the main road and up the lane to a prosperous farm. The field on one side was filled with fat cattle grazing on the lush spring growth while across the lane, behind a neat rail fence, the first shoots of a new crop poked above the ground.

The house was silhouetted against the blue green of the lake. The large, two-story, red brick home was framed by verandas offering shade at any hour and as in New England, a widow's walk, at the peak of the roof allowed a view in every direction.

Baker pulled the horses to a stop at steps that rose six feet to a massive, double front door.

"Willis must be doing well." Hines stepped from the carriage and flexed his knees to relieve the stiffness.

"Wouldn't know, Captain. He's private about his business." Baker remained seated. "He asked me to make a delivery and that's what I've done. I don't know how you are getting back."

"I'll find a way." Hines was more abrupt than he intended but the black was intelligent and probably knew more than he should.

"Thank you, Amos. Appreciate the ride."

"No thanks necessary, Captain. I get paid." Baker produced another full smile, clicked his teeth, and started the return journey.

Hines began to climb the steps but stopped at the sound of running feet and shrill voices. "Get him! Don't let him get away!"

A boy burst past the corner of the house pursued by three other ragged, dirty youngsters. When he tripped, the pack descended in murderous fury. All four rolled in a kicking, punching, and biting frenzy.

"Enough!" A voice rose above grunts and screams,

"I said enough!" The words were reinforced with the sharp crack of a whip. The whip cracked again, and closer, before the fury subsided.

"Stand up!"

A man strode across the grass and pulled sharply on the closest ear, lifting a body along with it.

"I've warned you, now git back to work!"

Fear spread from face to face.

"No more." He released the ear but gave the boy a sharp kick.

"Go!" The whip snapped again. "Get out of here!"

The first three backed away as the fourth rose to his feet. Tears streamed down his face but there was no sympathy.

"Back to work or no supper! Jesus, harder to handle than damn slaves!"

The man rapped the handle of the whip against his palm before he acknowledged the visitor.

"You might have helped, Tom. It was three against one."

Hines shrugged and smiled. "Did I catch you at a bad time?"

Eramosa Willis was about five feet eight, heavy set. A set of red suspenders crossed bare shoulders to hold his pants in place. "Not all that bad but inconvenient. Damned urchins cause more trouble than their worth." Willis gingerly lifted bare feet on the stairs.

"This was supposed to be sanded down," he said, pointing to the rough surface on the boards. "Something else the urchins haven't done." He pushed the door open and motioned for Hines to follow.

The house was bright and clean but sparsely furnished. A broom and dustpan lay on the floor next to what appeared to be a heap of rags.

"Erin!"

Willis shoved another door open and Hines saw the end of a bed and a flash of skin as a leg disappeared under a blanket.

"Erin, we have company. Get presentable."

Hines heard the murmur of a woman's voice. A grinning Willis returned to collect the rags. He lifted a cloth shook it and as if by magic, a dress appeared. He tossed it through the bedroom door.

"When you are ready, Erin, we'll be on the veranda."

Hines didn't catch the reply but recognized an Irish brogue.

Willis had drifted in and out of Kentucky and the life of Tom Hines for almost ten years. First as a youngster from the North who came to visit distant cousins, and then a few years later as a hellion who led other boys into trouble. The last time, with war approaching, Willis arrived with a collection of rifles. Good weapons were scarce so no one questioned the British army markings or the price. Later, Hines was only slightly surprised when Willis was identified as a contact by the Confederate Special Service.

The Willis house was perched on a low cliff, overlooking a ravine and a rough but sturdy pier. The pier ran fifty feet into the lake and ended where the lake color changed to promise deeper water. At the top of the ravine was a large shed. A set of stairs and a rope pulley system connected the shed with the pier.

"Like the setup?" Willis, now wearing a shirt under the suspenders, carried a bottle. "Besides the farm, three men are out with the boat and should be back at nightfall, hopefully with a fine catch. We clean the fish, give them a sprinkling of salt, the urchins pack them in barrels, and tomorrow we'll take them to a railway connection. Our catch can be for sale in Toronto tomorrow night or Montreal the next morning. If we go to Cleveland, we can ship to the East Coast."

Willis took a moment to gaze over the lake before focusing on the guest. "The only other industry I've considered is the oil business."

He waited a moment. "Of course, oil smells and you can get pretty dirty."

Hines remained silent and Willis continued, "Or there's the book business, selling Bibles and spreading the good word."

Hines took a deep drink and sloshed the liquor around in his mouth before spitting it over the veranda rail. "Drive was kind of dusty. I can taste it. By the way, what's your favorite Bible passage?"

"God damn it! They changed the passwords." Willis showed the streak of anger that Hines remembered.

"No, you were all right on oil. I wanted to shake you up. But I don't have much time. Maybe we should sort a few things out?"

"At your service. What do you need to know?" Willis propped his body against the railing.

The Willis family had been split by an earlier war. His father, a native Kentuckian, had joined the militia during the war of 1812 and had fallen, not for a local girl, but for the land on the southern peninsula of British territory. He returned to Kentucky only to say good-bye and leave for the Canadian frontier. A few years later, he was back with a wife and children. Eramosa, the youngest, spent summers in America with his cousins. When a typhoid fever outbreak decimated the northern family, the Americans suggested a move to Kentucky. But Willis had his own life.

"The boys yours?" Hines asked.

Willis leaned against the veranda and swung his legs to straddle the railing. "In a manner of speaking. I needed help and had to pay the Negroes when I hired them from Buxton. Why spend money when you can get something for free? An orphan train stopped in Detroit. You ever see one?"

"Never heard of it," Hines admitted.

"Damndest thing," Willis began. "A trainload of squealing, squawking brats. The streets of the big cities, New York, Philadelphia are swept to corral the urchins. Cost too much to put them in an orphanage. So they collect these kids—some of them have parents, but no one looks too close—load them on a train and send them west. Pickings were pretty slim. I got the best and they don't amount to much, but I have free labor."

He swung a leg over the railing and slammed his foot down as if to punctuate his business success.

"And that's it?" Hines was used to slaves but the urchins were white.

"Ah, they're supposed to be fed and educated and I'm giving them an education, by gawd! Eventually, they'll drift away or run off but when that happens, I'll be back to Detroit to meet another train."

He saw a frown cross Hines's face.

"Ah, come on. I know you taught orphans before the war. This is not that bad. The whip is for effect. They get food and lodging, and Erin washes up after them, tries to talk to them. Funny, you know the one that was running when you came in? The others don't like him. Know why?"

Willis waited for only an instant before he continued. "He can't talk. I don't mean he's mute. He won't talk English and jabbers in another language—Dutch or maybe Italian. He's learning though and he's gonna learn more."

His guest had another question. "The woman?"

Willis stood.

"She'll have a meal ready. She doesn't know all of my business so let's talk more tomorrow. No one will hear on the boat."

Hines nodded agreement but curiosity got the best of him. "The woman," he repeated.

"You always had a good eye, Tom, for women and horses. She was a girl when I picked her off the street in Toronto. Her name is Erin. She was seventeen and that was about four years ago. I needed someone to clean the house and, well, break the monotony. It gets quiet, especially in the winter. She gets food and lodging and the pleasure of my company. As I said, why pay when you can get it for free?"

Willis was drawn by the scents from kitchen but Hines had another question.

"What about that African? He seems smart. How much does he know?"

"Amos knows where his bread is buttered," Willis assured him. "I hire him as my black servant when I need to make an appearance and he comes in real handy down South. Funny, the things people will say in front of a black man; things they wouldn't say among their own. Amos is my second set of ears."

"And you trust him?" Hines wasn't convinced.

"Money buys trust." Willis stepped again toward the kitchen. "And, so, like I said, Amos knows where his bread is buttered."

* * *

A few miles away, Amos Baker blew the foam from a glass of beer and studied another white man.

"Captain, he wanted to buy fish, so I took him to Mr. Willis. Man was pretty quiet. Asked a lot of questions about how black folks were doing but didn't say much."

He ran his sleeve across his mouth. "Course, that's the same with you, ain't it, Captain? You asking questions and not telling Ol' Amos much! What you looking for?"

The white man dropped a handful of coins on the table.

"I'll be around. Maybe we can do business."

Baker watched him roughly shove a black man from this path as he walked toward the tavern door.

"Doubtful, Captain," he said quietly. "Doubtful."

CHAPTER 12

Quebec City, Canada East: May 1864

Paul Forsey ripped fresh newsprint to toss on the embers and hoped the blaze would ease the chill of the Canadian spring. The latest issue of the *Quebec City Mercury* began to curl from the heat. The paper, considered the mouthpiece of Sandfield Macdonald, was losing influence. With George Brown playing a more active role, his *Globe* would rise in popularity and he placed the latest edition on a growing stack by his desk.

Forsey stirred the logs, rubbed his hands, and held them to the flames before sorting the files. The legislature would meet at three. A few noncontroversial items might be open for debate but the legislature suffered from a North American disease and remained another house divided. The parties were deadlocked.

Only senior ministers would see the latest dispatch on the American war. The British government had predicted the latest drive on Confederate territory. The attacks had started in early May and opened another season of bloodletting. The rest of the dispatch appeared routine except for one request. London asked for a special watch on the activities of the Confederate commissioners. Jacob Thompson and Clement Clay could be seen socially but the Colonial office warned against anything that might be construed as recognition. The British government was determined to remain officially neutral.

A chorus of voices erupted from the hall. He reached the door to see most of the cabinet and major opposition leaders entering a nearby room. The Macdonalds, John A. and Sandfield, Georges Cartier, a leader in Canada East, and D'Arcy McGee argued as they walked. The tall frame of George Brown brought up the rear, like a shepherd guiding a flock. As Brown drew the door closed, he warned, "I have the key and no one is leaving until we have an agreement."

Brown would unlock the door before an agreement was reached but only after persuading the others the work was too important to delay. For two weeks, the men continued closed-door meetings. On the tenth day, Forsey was summoned to deliver a fresh supply of paper. He rapped softly, pushed the door open, and witnessed a rare display of anger from D'Arcy McGee.

"You think our defense is adequate. I say you are a fool." McGee waved his finger. "You think we don't need a stronger militia and the British army. Look to Virginia, the ruined homesteads..." he trailed off when he saw Forsey in the doorway. "Perhaps we should take a break."

"Oh, that won't be necessary," Brown said.

The men were sitting around a long table but Forsey could see no indication of who was in charge.

"Set the paper on the table," Brown ordered. "We won't need anything else."

Forsey quietly departed but left the door ajar.

"Leave defense for now," he heard Brown suggest. "Look at the other unresolved issues. We have to decide on the report to the House. I feel the recommendations must be unanimous. What about it, Macdonald? Do we have enough to win the support of the member from Kingston?"

But as Forsey listened, he heard the footsteps of someone crossing the room to slam the door.

* * *

ON LAKE ERIE: MAY 1864

The first rays of the sun burned the mist from the Lake Erie shore. From the boat, Tom Hines saw the pier built in a break in the shoreline. Cliffs on either side rose a hundred feet above the water. Below was a meandering strip of beach, where sand and gravel jutted twenty feet into the lake or vanished under water. The cliffs were almost yellow, a sheer wall of sand and clay, and honeycombed with fissures where runoff threatened to erode thousands of pounds of earth.

Hines fought the boat motion to focus on a figure on the widow's walk high above. The woman, Erin, was hanging out a wash. The brightly colored sheet flapped in the breeze and he realized that it was not a sheet but a British flag. Willis saw him watching.

"Confederates aren't the only ones with signals. I ordered the flag after the sheriff came last fall. I don't like surprises, so if the flag is up everything is fine. If it's not, there's a problem or an uninvited guest."

Hines saw the woman wave but Willis ignored her. He glanced above as a sail snapped and filled. The boat picked up speed and tilted as it came closer to the wind.

"Rufus, cleat her down," Willis yelled. The boy, the center of yesterday's brawl, jumped to obey.

"See. He's learning English," Willis said as the boy tied off a rope. Rufus walked to the stern and dropped unto a pile of canvas where the breeze was broken by the barrels of fish. He pulled the brim of his hat over the eyes and settled in.

"The sheriff came shortly after your associates were about." Willis beckoned Hines into a cabin just large enough to shelter three or four men. A chart was spread on a desk bolted to the rear wall.

"The sheriff didn't stay long. Just looked around and said he'd heard I had Southern friends. His superiors didn't want trouble. I think he said we shouldn't piss in our own bed. Or maybe it was foul our own nest. He said the last thing we needed was an excuse for Americans to come thundering north. I assured him that was my view and he left. The authorities are already on edge. Some one claimed a couple of ships near here were under rebel control. They weren't. But too many people are talking."

Hines knew it was true. Too many Confederates who escaped to Canada were common soldiers, brave yet eager to boast of their achievements.

"The information is coming through our people?"

"I don't think there are enough locals to cause problems," Willis replied, "And we're not fully trusted. Here's a good example. Why are you here?"

The rocking boat was having an effect but Hines forced a shy smile. "I'm looking things over. There are a few things I need to know before we can make definite plans."

"Could the plans involve Johnson's Island?"

"It's a possibility," Hines admitted. "One of several. I have no personal reason to want to return there."

Hines remembered the island prison. The barracks were built with green wood and the rough boards had shrunk, allowing rain to enter through the cracks. Even after patching with mud and leaves, the wind blew through. The Federals who scrimped on construction costs weren't about to spend on repairs.

An escape from the compound was possible but beyond the walls was three hundred acres of bush and rock, and the island was too far from the mainland to swim. Any escape would require cunning, careful planning, and sheer luck. Hines remembered it all as he rocked on a small fishing boat, only about sixty miles across the lake from the prison.

Willis called his attention to a small collection of buildings on the Canadian shore. "That's Morpeth and the Federals are even watching it. They claim a trade counsellor is needed but it's really an attempt to place another spy. The other ports along the north shore are the same size or smaller, so if you organize anything out of the ordinary, people notice, and talk. A man or two gets through but an operation of any size is sure to be noticed."

Hines was no sailor. He concentrated on the shoreline, willing his mind to overcome the queasy feeling in his stomach.

"Where are the charts?" He moved toward the desk and chair at the rear of the cabin.

"On the table," Willis replied. "Erin made a copy. She's got a fine hand."

The concentration helped Hines to control the feeling that rose from his stomach to his throat. Willis took one glance at him and pointed to the door. "Get out! No wretching in my cabin, especially near the charts. Get out on deck."

Hines moved slowly trying to maintain his dignity but a larger wave washed under the boat and sent him staggering. His breakfast soon floated on the lake. Rufus stirred as wet droplets flew by his makeshift bed. His nose told him all he had to know and he rolled to the other side of the deck.

Willis laughed. "Stay out there. After the next point, we'll make a small course correction for an easier ride. All of the Great Lakes could hear you puke, landlubber. Don't plan any lake action. Keep to dry land."

When the lake chop eased, Hines gingerly returned to the cabin and gazed at the chart. North American maps showed Erie as a large blue mass. The local edition dotted with islands was a surprise.

Willis glanced from the wheel to see him bent over the table. "You ain't gonna be sick again, are you? You upchuck and Erie will look like the thousand islands."

"No, I feel much better."

"General Meade did the original charts," Willis said.

"George Meade, hero of Gettysburg, is a much better sailor than Thomas Hines, the pasty-faced rebel." Willis snickered and saw the pasty-faced rebel scowl.

"Meade was on the lake survey based out of Detroit when the war began. We better hope the bastard knew what he was doing. The charts were made for the United States Navy but a few dollars in the right hands and any sailor from Montreal to Chicago can own a set. Locals know the lake but there are shoals off Point Pelee, and the islands have doomed many a ship."

Another large wave rolled under the boat.

"And the weather can change in flash from a light chop to a full-blown gale in minutes. But don't worry this is a lovely day for sailing." Willis offered another large smile.

Hines walked across the cabin, took a tin cup from a nail above a water bucket, and filled it half full. The gentle motion of the water in the cup produced a now familiar feeling but he swallowed.

Willis was still smiling as Hines dropped into a chair and closed his eyes.

Two hours later, Willis woke him. "Tom, we have company."

A large ship dwarfed the fishing boat, side paddle wheels pounding the water as she cut through the waves. Black smoke poured from the stack and three masts carried furled sails. Snouts of cannon lined the deck. At the stern, the breeze whipped the American flag.

"The *Michigan*," Willis announced, returning a wave from a blue-uniformed officer on the gunboat's bridge.

"Oh, for the money of the United States Navy. A fine day for sailing and the ship burns coal." Willis relaxed with the gunboat showing only passing interest.

"The first iron-hulled vessel built on the Great Lakes, twenty years old but still the biggest, almost a hundred and sixty-four feet long and about twenty-seven feet wide. Intimidating, isn't she? They're always nosy. They took a good look. Must be a training day; don't often see the cannons run out."

Rufus waved his hat at the figures on the deck of the larger ship.

Willis fought the wheel and the wake from the paddle wheels while continuing a running commentary.

"She's limited in cannon and mortar by what was called the Rush-Bagot agreement. It was supposed to prevent either the British or the Americans from developing war fleets on the lakes. Neither side wanted the expense, especially the British. She's only supposed to carry sixteen guns, but no one is sure. The Americans aren't saying and the British don't ask. But there's nothing on the lakes to match her."

Two figures emerged on the *Michigan* deck to dump the contents of a large barrel over the side. The fishing boat was soon running through a stream of eggshells, small bones, and kitchen waste.

"Bastards own the lake and know it," Willis growled, trying to avoid the debris and watching the distance grow between the ships.

"So you can't attack her directly," Hines murmured.

"Last year's plan might have worked," Willis told him and then asked, "Did you meet Minor?"

Hines stared after the *Michigan* until Willis again broke the silence.

"Lieutenant Minor was a good man. He booked passage for twenty-five souls on the daily steamer from Ogdensburg and had more men waiting at the Welland Canal between Lake Erie and Lake Ontario. Once on Erie, they would commandeer the steamer, find the *Michigan* and arrange a collision. With control of the gunboat, they'd attack Johnson's Island."

"But something went wrong?" Hines prompted and Willis spoke with disgust.

"Someone in Windsor spilled the story. The governor general sent a warning to Lord Lyons, the British ambassador in Washington, and Lyons tipped off the Federal War Department. The Americans beefed up security and Minor had to back off. Damn shame. Minor knew ships. He was wounded on the *Virginia*, on the *Merrimac*. That first clash of the ironclads—even landlubbers must have heard of that one."

Only the top of the *Michigan's* stack and smoke were visible on the horizon.

"Will they try again? Is that why you are here?" Willis asked.

Hines looked to where he supposed Johnson's Island would be.

"I'm a landlubber, remember? How much longer before we unload the fish?"

* * *

The two friends parted a few hours later at another small Lake Erie hamlet. The harbor at Port Stanley was one of the few with a rail link to the major inland lines. Hines could move to London, and from there to Detroit or Chicago or Toronto or, as Willis told him, "Wherever he damned well pleased."

"Better you don't know," Hines advised. "Go back to Erin and educate the urchins. We may need you later. I'll make sure the right people know you helped."

He patted the pocket of his single piece of luggage and the charts of Lake Erie. "Life's too short, especially in war. We'll be in touch."

CHAPTER 13

Richmond, Virginia: May 1864

Sarah Slater began to notice the change in Richmond. The Spotswood Hotel was clean and only four years old but the carpets and curtains were ragged. In the dining room, was more evidence. The guests wore clothing that before the war would have been sent to the slave quarters. The breakfast menu added to her misgivings. Robin on toast might be a culinary delight in a café in Paris but in Richmond, she expected something more substantial.

Mcgruder was pacing in the lobby and followed Sarah silently to her rooms. It was only when the door was closed that he spoke.

"A slight change of plan. You will be leaving today. The dispatches will arrive from the War Department in the next hour. Travel light—a single trunk and only small personal luggage."

He raised his hand before she could object.

"We'll see to the rest of your possessions."

His eyes roamed over half a dozen battered trunks.

"This won't do! A woman of substance needs her essentials."

"Not this time," he interrupted. "Time is of the essence. Grant's army is moving. In the confusion, another Southern lady fleeing the fighting won't be suspected."

Slater's anger gave way to excitement. "I'll need an hour, Captain. Better crack the whip over that servant. A lady needs assistance when she packs."

"Crack your own whip. You know the master/slave relationship."

* * *

A day later, two women on a small cart were caught in a tangle of wagons, horses, and men. The sound of cannon fire grew louder as they moved north but Mcgruder's pass, a wide smile and a beckoning wave eased the passage. When they encountered the first scouts of the Union army the pass disappeared under the garter on Sarah's thigh.

If the jumble on the road was any indication, the Northern army was large and clumsy. Wagons rolled off one road while a line of horse-drawn gun carriages tried vainly to push through the intersection from another. A draft horse, worn out by the exertion, dropped to the ground. The teammate reared and fought to be free of the added burden.

A swearing Union officer tried to clear a track and the two women added to his frustration. "What the hell, are you doing here?"

He seized the bridle of their horse and roughly pulled it onto the road facing a stalled wagon train.

"That way," he pointed and gave a vicious slap on the animal's rear. The horse reared and stumbled before Sarah regained control.

Ahead were miles of wagons, loaded until axels sagged with the weight of ammunition and food. Teamsters whistled as she passed, a woman in Southern finery, doggedly hauling on the reins; what must be a servant cowering beside her; and both perched on the high seat of a two-wheeled cart. A single trunk extended a foot over the rear of the cart.

Mixed with the wagon train were units of Federal infantry and a few troopers resting by the roadside. A mounted soldier trotted along-side the cart before suddenly wrenching the reins from her hands. He urged his mount forward and led them toward a stand of trees. As he stopped, Sarah saw other men partially hidden by brush.

"Major, have a look," the man shouted. He was short but wiry and in a matter of seconds had the cart horse snugged to a limb.

97

"What is it, Henry?"

Sarah spun at the sound of the wheezing voice and felt Sillery begin to shake.

"Contraband!"

The left shoulder of the major's blue tunic was torn to expose an ugly stained bandage.

"Followed them up the road. Wasn't sure what they were up to."

"Ladies, climb down."

The major began to work a knife over the ropes holding the trunk.

"Down," he repeated and pulled the trunk free to smash against the ground. The lid popped open to expose women's clothing.

"Henry!" He bent to run his hands through the garments. "Get those bitches on the ground."

The short man's leer was the final prod.

"Over there!" A soldier grabbed Sillery and pushed her to where the major rifled through the trunk.

"You too, Mistress." Henry shoved the white women.

The major finished his search with a final grope of the clothing. The breathing grew louder as he bent closer.

"What's this?"

He shook a small, fabric-covered box.

"Please, it's all I have," Sarah's voice quavered. "My family jewellery...a few pieces...nothing worth much but it has great sentimental value."

"Secesh family, reb to the core, I'll bet." Henry watched as the major opened the box.

"Pretty things, I guess. I don't know about jewels but we'll keep it," he said and tossed the box to another soldier. The minor exertion was too much. He coughed painfully for a few seconds reached into the trunk for a dress and began to wipe his face.

"Feels real smooth, Mistress. I like the smell of a woman."

A series of shouts carried to the trees and the line of wagons began to move.

"We have nothing else." Sarah's bravado returned. "No money. We're trying to reach family in Maryland."

"Yaller belong to you?" Henry joined the interrogation. "High yellow, almost white, that Negro with the white blood. What we call Contraband?"

He moved to give Sillery a closer inspection.

"Maybe her pappy spent too much time in the slave quarters but she is pretty."

A nearby bugle call curtailed further inspection.

He turned to Sarah. "I don't like your people. Like them even less since I got this," he said, pointing to the bandage and widening red tinge. "So when you leave, don't come back."

He had more advice for Sillery. "If you want freedom, you got it. This is Union territory and whether we like it or not, slaves are free. You want to go, you can go."

"On no, Mr. Sodjer sir, I wants to stay with my mistress."

The major shook his head in amazement.

"These people are stupid, dumb as an ox! Henry, bring the troop along. I want to talk to a doctor before sunset."

* * *

MONTREAL, CANADA EAST: MAY 1864

"I'm not sure I like this. We are to return to Richmond tomorrow. But we finally have a few hours of privacy and can finally really talk. I want to know more about you." Sarah Slater turned from the window of her rooms in Montreal's St. Lawrence Hall to face the servant. Sillery Fraser had proved to be a valuable asset on the first perilous journey though the war zone. Behind the mask of a Southern servant was a bright, intelligent woman.

"You are part white?"

"That Union soldier was right," Sillery explained. "My daddy did like the slave quarters. I have my mother's black hair and eyes but the rest comes from the white side."

"Did your father…" Sarah tried to think of the proper words. "Did he acknowledge you? Did he admit you were his?"

"What do you think?" Sillery's eyes flashed. "How many men will admit to that? Oh, he moved me to the plantation house and trained me as a house servant. But he didn't care when his white cousins began to toy with me. Or maybe he did, because as soon as I was grown I was sold."

Variations on her story were whispered in drawing rooms across the South. Sillery's slim but full body would attract a hot-blooded Southern gentleman and Sarah often wondered if her late husband had sampled African delights.

"Where did you learn to read and write?"

"From a widow woman." Sillery's face relaxed in a tired smile. "Mrs. Teasdale had mixed feelings on slavery. She taught me to read and write, and when she died, the will set me free. But she wanted control. I got pregnant and she sold my man south. I don't know where he is."

Her voice fell to almost a whisper. "And as soon as my baby was weaned, she sold her, too."

Sarah waited silently.

"But I found her," Sillery continued. "I can buy her freedom and the Confederate colonel agreed to pay me if I travel with you. He also promised to keep her safe. That's why I'm here." She was quiet for only a moment. "And if we are really to work as a team, I need to know what he sees in you."

Sarah smiled before she answered. "He sees a woman who gets what she wants."

Sarah was a child of the genteel South, favored with beauty and a thirst for the finer things in life. Sillery Fraser was a child of the slave quarters, favored with beauty, a paper that said she was free, and an urgent need for cash. Mcgruder had found the weakness to draw them together.

"I've met again with Mr. Holcombe," Sarah said, returning to their travel plans. "And they don't know when Jacob Thompson will arrive. In the meantime, Holcombe has a dispatch that must go to Richmond."

She took an envelope from her pocket, waved it in the air, and said brightly, "Guess where this goes?"

The women reached for the trunk lid at the same time, a friendly competition to find the pressure point and open the secret compartment.

"I wonder if that union officer has found a market for my jewels. He won't be very happy when he finds how little they are worth."

CHAPTER 14

Toronto, Canada West: June 1864

Tom Hines sat alone in the bar room of the Queens Hotel listening as conversations swirled around him.

A man stabbed his finger at the newspaper.

"A blood bath, a butcher's bill, the Wilderness, Spotsylvania, and now Cold Harbor. Grant wouldn't even agree to a truce to remove the dead and injured. But his army is twice the size and he can't win."

"Lee's stopped him," a second man agreed, "And I know more big doings are coming."

Hines studied the second man. Charles Cole was short and red-haired, with a bushy moustache and sideburns. He told of capture at Gettysburg and escape from a Union prison camp. But there was something suspicious, something that didn't ring true.

"Grant's going to run out of men," the first man was explaining.

"And if Lincoln drafts more, we'll whip them, too," Cole predicted. "Bring 'em on. We'll show them Southern steel."

* * *

Hines recalled the conversation as he stood face to face with Jacob Thompson for the first time.

"Richmond has a high regard for your ability, Captain Hines, and I'm prepared to be equally impressed."

"If I may, let me begin with a warning." Hines waited for a nod before he continued, "Federal agents and Canadian constables are on the prowl. This hotel may be dangerous. It's known as a Confederate base and is being watched."

"They know I'm here," Thompson countered. "I am an official representative of the Confederate States and I have so informed the governor general. The fact he hasn't replied is a diplomatic game. I must impress the proper people and the Queens is the best place for me. But do you have another site for your men?"

"There's a farm a few miles west. As far as you and I are concerned, the fewer meetings the better."

Thompson nodded in agreement but added, "Be sure to keep me posted. I know more of the big picture. Now what have you learned?"

"For a start, the prison camps." Hines spread the maps on a marble-topped table. "Johnson's Island with the officers is the biggest prize, but with the prisoners at Camp Douglas at Chicago, at Rock Island in Illinois, and at Camp Chase near Columbus, we'd have twenty thousand men and over three thousand officers."

Thompson ran his fingers in a broad circle over Indiana, Illinois, Wisconsin, Michigan, and Ohio, the states known as the old northwest. His finger came to rest on Johnson's Island, near Sandusky, Ohio.

"The aborted plan from last year, how did they plan to get the prisoners away?"

Hines pointed to the small communities along the Lake Erie's north shore.

"The prisoners were to be taken to the Canadian shore and then on to Halifax. I don't know what they thought the British would do. We're safe in assuming there are about ten thousand British regulars. The rest is militia and not well trained, more like our social clubs before the war."

Thompson remembered the Southern training sessions and the evening parties that drew more men than the daytime exercise did.

"The element of surprise would have helped," Hines continued. "But I don't think the Brits would stand by if thousands of men moved through their territory. And it was late in the year. The late fall can bring massive storms, northern hurricanes. We must aim for a fair weather period, late summer or early fall at the latest."

Thompson absently tapped at Johnson's Island and western Lake Erie, and then moved his fingers west to Chicago. "What about Camp Douglas?"

"Eight thousand prisoners, give or take a few hundred," Hines replied. "But that's an estimate. I need to see for myself."

"Perhaps. But right now, I need you in Detroit. Well, actually in Windsor or Sandwich or whatever they call the Canadian side. I need you to meet a man who may be very important."

The explanation was interrupted as a clock struck the hour.

"We'll have to cut this short. I'll arrange a meeting for you and Clement Vallandigham."

He watched for a reaction but saw nothing from Hines.

"You do know who he is?"

"I met his supporters last year, part of my work with General Morgan."

A hint of a smile crossed Thompson's face. "I'm meeting the congressman in a couple of weeks. I'd like you to see him first."

Hines began to roll the maps but Thompson interrupted. "Leave those. I want a second look and there are others who should see them."

He hurriedly guided his guest to the door. "I think your idea of the farm nearby is a good one. Go ahead with those preparations."

Hines met the next guest on the stairway. He waited until he saw Charles Cole rap on Thompson's door.

* * *

RICHMOND, VIRGINIA: JUNE 1864

Mcgruder was apologetic. His concerns over Sarah's travel and safety appeared genuine but he had no one else to send.

The Army of the Potomac had dug in at Petersburg, and while Grant had lost thousands of men, the Yankees were still there, and Lee's losses were also staggering. Richmond was a giant hospital. Confederate wounded arrived daily by train, in long lines of horse-drawn ambulances, or in wagons and carts. A few wounded soldiers limped or staggered through the streets. Men with light wounds or no wounds were turned about and sent back to the army.

A stench hung in the early summer air, a hint of rotting flesh, mixed with whiffs of chloroform, dirty clothes, people, and animals. Several times, Sarah saw marching units and the inevitable discordant band move toward Petersburg. The faces were sad but stoic, in marked contrast to the gleeful mood in the early days of the war. Faces, Sarah decided, told the story. The South would fight on but for how long?

She stood with Mcgruder by the window at the Spotswood Hotel. The view was obscured by streaks and dust but there were more important things to do than clean windows. The outline of a carpet haunted the bare floor. Resourceful troops had cut holes for their heads and frayed carpets had become rough ponchos for protection from the wind and rain.

"It's not over," Mcgruder said, sensing her mood. "Don't let appearances fool you. The South has a few tricks to play and you are one of the prettier tricks."

She flashed a smile.

"Thank you, Colonel. A woman appreciates a compliment even if it's associated with those who turn tricks."

She watched for his reaction. First a blush, a sense of shock, and then a telling grin.

"Mrs. Slater, you continue to surprise. Perhaps someday I can learn more."

"Perhaps you shall, Colonel." She felt a draw to the man but she had been attracted before and felt sure there would be others in the future.

"Are there any special messages? I'll reach Thompson this time. Was I right to wait?"

"I think you were." The War Department was uncertain about the representatives in the British provinces. Too many people with too little experience were working alone. Thompson and Clay must seize control.

"This time," he told her, "confirm the message that Richmond is in the oil business and add that early—stress *early*—drilling results will come in late June."

"Excuse me, Colonel, but a child could create better code."

"Don't worry, we're not entertainers. Leave that for the stage. The message stands. We are sending you by a different route this time. Remember that your safety and the safety of others relies on secrecy."

"I understand."

A hard knock on the door from the adjoining room surprised them and was followed immediately by a loud question.

"Miss Sarah, that handsome Confederate officer still here?"

"Yes Sillery, he's just leaving."

"Oh goods, I gots something I needs him to carry."

Sillery stumbled into the room carrying a large, sloshing chamber pot.

"Me and Miss Sarah been saving material for the Niter Bureau. They needs this to make gunpowder, but the trashy hotel servants ain't coming to get it, so would yous carry it?"

She flashed Mcgruder a pleading look.

"Nice to see you, Miss Sillery, and may I say, your diction is definitely improving."

He took the chamber pot but recoiled from the smell. "Damn. When was the last time this was emptied?"

"Never you mind, it make good strong powder, me and Miss Sarah doing our part."

* * *

Two nights later, the women huddled in a rowboat. An elderly Negro strained on the oars while a white man in the bow peered through the Potomac mist. As the boat touched shore, the white man jumped onto the beach, glanced about cautiously and whistled softly three times. A moment later two figures emerged from the nearby brush.

"You are in for a long night, Mr. Jones. I have a passenger for your return trip." The man was young, barely in his twenties.

"Keep your voice down, for Christ's sake," the boatman snapped. "The whole Union army could hear you."

The young man stepped closer and whispered loudly. "There ain't a Union soldier within five miles."

"Let's get this done," the boatman growled.

As the women stepped ashore, a tall man dressed in a long black coat and carrying a small suitcase made his way across the beach. The younger man passed a large burlap bag to Jones.

"Go," the boatman ordered, pushing the craft back into the water and jumping on board.

"See you." The young man used a loud false whisper. "Stay dry."

The muffled splash of an oar answered as the boat moved toward the Virginia shore.

"Talkative, wasn't he?" The new guide now spoke in a normal voice. He pointed to the trunk. "The slave can help me carry the case. It's a half mile to the wagon."

"We'll manage," Sarah said, hefting one end of the trunk while Sillery grasped the other.

An hour later, the wagon rolled through rural Maryland. Sarah sat beside the young driver while Sillery perched on the trunk in the rear. The rising sun was warming the new day.

"It's usually quiet here," the guide announced, "and people are used to seeing me."

Sarah tried to study the countryside.

"You have a name?" he asked with rising irritation.

"I'm Mrs. Sarah Slater," she said, adopting a haughty air. "We were burned out by the Yankees and have nothing left." Sillery rolled her eyes at what had become a familiar story.

"And that trunk has all your worldly possessions," the young man burst out. "And family in Canada will keep you safe. Those people in Richmond should come up with something new. We're not rubes. We know as much as they do, and sometimes know it sooner."

He flicked the reins, asking the horse for more speed. "Richmond goes overboard with the cloak-and-dagger style, like a dimestore novel. Let's be honest. I'm John Surratt, postmaster, duly commissioned by the United States government. When you return, ask for me at Surrattsville or my mother's house on H street in Washington. Any business she gets will be welcome. She runs a nice clean boarding house but if she sees a hint of alcohol, there will be hell to pay."

"Haven't you already told me too much?" she asked. "Aren't you concerned about your mother's safety?"

"I haven't told you anything you couldn't learn in a couple of minutes out here. The ferryman, his name is Tom Jones. He didn't give you his name because you didn't ask."

She had felt no reason to ask. It was a matter of trust.

"Ask a few questions about Tom Jones and you'll find he has a nice little farm called Huckleberry, and people will tell you Tom was arrested and spent time in the Old Capital Prison. Tom makes a good living taking people back and forth across the river, and a few people might tell you he has connections to Mosby but they don't say anymore than that."

She thought he had finished, but a minute later, Surratt started again.

"And guess what was in that bag?"

Sarah wasn't sure she wanted to know.

"Newspapers," Surratt continued. "Ordinary papers from New York and Washington. The War Department reads them to learn which Northern regiments are being moved around or to study the casualty lists. And it's all thanks to a man in Washington who quite legally takes a subscription and passes the paper to me. Locals know all this but the big secrets are a different story. Only a few of us know about those."

CHAPTER 15

Quebec City, Canada East: June 22, 1864

"Crisis be damned! These bloody colonists can't make up their minds." Geoffrey Ralston hovered above Forsey's desk, the red of the army uniform giving him a majestic air, until one realized the uniform was worn by a junior officer.

For half an hour, he berated the colonies; the governor general, Lord Monck, whom he served; and the British army, which had sent him to the post. For the clerk, it was a welcome break in the day and a chance to hear the view from Spencerwood, Monck's Quebec City residence, even if the view was only a soldier's opinion.

"These men wouldn't know a crisis if it hit them in the head," Ralston went on. "And, so what if another government falls? Have an election, collect money from friends, buy the vote, and move on. And if guns were allowed in the legislature, John A. Macdonald and George Brown would be shooting. They hate each other, there's no chance of compromise."

"Mr. Forsey." Both men turned at the arrival of the chief clerk. "We're needed in the legislature." The usual calm demeanor of Hewitt Bernard was gone. "Bring a notepad. John A. and George Brown have an agreement on a new coalition."

He trotted off toward the chamber. "I never thought I'd see the day," he panted as the trio slipped into the gallery.

George Brown was on his feet, his voice choking with emotion. "If a crisis has ever arisen in the political affairs of any country that would justify a coalition, such a crisis has arrived in the history of the Canada."

"Well said, Mr. Brown," a Reformer cheered him on.

Bernard leaned to whisper to Forsey. "Brown has agreed to join the cabinet, and John A. will be sitting alongside him. The French, too, Cartier is in."

Brown cleared his throat. "We have two races, two languages, two systems of religious beliefs, two sets of laws, two sets of everything. It's been almost impossible for men of the two sections to come together. But Mr. Speaker, party alliances are one thing…the interests of my country are another."

The house exploded with applause while Forsey bent to Ralston's ear. "If the two of them work together, we might get something done."

On the floor, friends and political foes congratulated Brown.

"More talk," Ralston sniffed, unimpressed.

"They might agree on changes for the military," Forsey suggested.

"If you mean more militia and training, it won't work," Ralston told him. "Millions are needed to upgrade the forts and there's no sign of that. They expect Britain to carry the load, an Imperial obligation. Well, Britain is changing. England needs to spend at home, not pour money down a rat hole. Another war or revolution could erupt in Europe and the army will be needed at home, rather than to protect fractious little colonies."

* * *

WINDSOR, CANADA WEST: JUNE 9, 1864

The shrill blast of a whistle signaled another ship anxious to land. The twin-decked steamboat was one of a dozen or more that had touched the Detroit waterfront in the past day. Each weaved through a small fleet of sailboats and barges laden with lumber or livestock, crates or shipping barrels. Tom Hines watched as the ferry crossed the invisible border.

Windsor's Hiron House stood at the top of the embankment. A guest could look north across the river to the bustle of Michigan at war, or south onto the streets of a Canadian town where the war was a business opportunity, a place to seek refuge, or merely a distraction.

The hotel was being watched. The same scruffy men had been lounging at a tavern door when he passed yesterday. Simple tramps or binge drinkers would change position but this pair seldom moved as they watched the hotel entrance.

The men shifted as an expensive carriage rolled to a stop, the leather curtains drawn tight to shield the interior from prying eyes. One of two black coachmen jumped from the high seat to open the door, and, with elaborate care, dust the frames and the single step. A tiny boot surrounded by a sea of green muslin tested the step before a well-dressed woman appeared. She swayed and fought for balance before toppling onto the coachman, taking them both to the ground. Her scream spooked the horses. As the driver fought for control and a crowd gathered, Hines slipped into the hotel kitchen. A smile and a coin for a maid bought access to the service stairway and Clement Vallandigham.

* * *

The day was hot for early June. There was no breeze but Vallandigham waved for Hines to join him at the window. "Captain Hines, isn't it? Have a look at this, a little excitement in the street."

High-pitched curses echoed from below. The woman sat on a cane chair hastily moved from the hotel lobby. She rubbed an ankle and berated the hotel staff.

"Woman took a fall as she was stepping from the carriage," Vallandigham explained. "I thought a fine lady had taken a tumble but from the language, I'd guess she's little more than a trollop. Some gentleman must have lent her the carriage and servants. One hopes he's not shy. The story will be all over this town in an hour."

The two black coachmen lifted the chair to the door of the carriage and with a final rousing curse, the woman stepped behind the curtains. As the crowd broke, Hines saw the two scruffy detectives laughing and returning to their post.

"I hadn't arranged for entertainment, but do have some refreshments. Try a local specialty. This Walker fellow has a delicious recipe for whiskey." He poured an inch into a glass for Hines to sample.

"Now Captain, I agreed to this meeting with some reluctance. I know Jacob Thompson from my days in Washington, and I'll meet with him as an old friend, but I'm not sure why he asked me to see you."

Hines remained standing as the older man settled onto a velvet-covered lounge.

"I…we…have been impressed by your stand. Like you, we in the South want to end the war. We will do what we can to make that happen. As the supreme commander of the Sons of Liberty, you have expressed interest in a Northwest Confederacy. With a Southern ally, the Northwest would have access to the Mississippi and the markets in Europe. New England would no longer dictate the rules on trade, or transportation or policies like emancipation." Hines paused and took a sip from the glass.

"The original Sons of Liberty of 1776 didn't need permission from Washington. The Republicans snicker at the word "Copperhead," but they forget the revolutionary slogan, "Don't tread on me." The South remembers and knows what a Copperhead can do."

Vallandigham settled deeper into the lounge as Hines outlined the case. "We'd need to contact the men who come to seek your advice. We can find a common cause."

"What kind of help?" Vallandigham demanded. "The Confederacy can't supply campaign workers or elect a peace candidate. I suspect the South would offer guns and money!"

"We can do that," Hines assured him. "Mr. Thompson has funds available. I can help in other ways. Groups of well-trained men can operate independently, or a Southern army might move against the border states. Besides, what did the democratic process produce? They stole your seat by gerrymandering the district. They stole the governor's chair and here you sit in exile—for a year now—in a grimy little border town!"

Vallandigham rose and walked to the window before turning back to his guest. "What you propose has merit but it could bring more bloodshed, not less. There are men prepared for that. I'm not sure I am. I'll try to make the changes at the ballot box. We will have a peace candidate for president in the fall."

It was the answer Hines expected.

"Let us make the contacts. We have to be prepared!"

"Captain Hines, thousands of men are ready to step forward and create a revolution in Illinois, Indiana, and Ohio and probably in Michigan and Wisconsin. Lincoln trampled on their basic American rights. But I won't be publicly involved, at least not yet. As to the names, I'll give Jacob Thompson my answer. And Captain Hines, you seem to know about the men who came to see me. I can only assume that the Confederates have joined the Federals and British detectives in watching my every move."

Hines felt no remorse about a lie. "I wouldn't know about that."

* * *

Later, Hines summed up the meeting for Jacob Thompson.

"The contacts would help. There's a lot of ground to cover from Detroit to Chicago and south," Hines explained. "But what if his organization is not that strong? The Knights of the Golden Circle, the Organization of American Knights, the Sons of Liberty—none of them came out for General Morgan. I'd like to feel them out. Money is a different story. They'll take anything you provide."

"If there are any names, I'll get them to you," Thompson agreed. "And, is there anything else?"

"Will you use the front entrance at the hotel? It is being watched."

"Yes, let them think the Confederates are taking over the Sons of Liberty and for that matter, the Democratic Party. Keep them guessing. How did you avoid detection?"

This time Hines chuckled. "A friend of a friend who knew a lady that needs money and is an aspiring actress. It was, shall we say, an expensive but useful performance."

* * *

At the Hiron House, Clement Vallandigham paced the room.

Everything Hines said was on the mark. The congressional seat had been stolen. Anyone who knew politics could see that. The governor's race in Ohio had not been as close as expected but exile made him an absentee candidate. The upcoming presidential election was another matter. Lincoln could be beaten. The North was weary. Let Thompson and Hines act as the instigators. Let them supply the guns and money. He would remain above it all.

✓

CHAPTER 16

Chatham, Canada West: June 1864

Mary Ann Shadd Carey reread the letter. The goal was admirable and she needed the money, but it would mean more travel and time away. The newspaper was on a sporadic schedule. The *Provincial Freeman* had been her life, from selling subscriptions to typesetting and writing. She managed a few special editions but there was no money to resume regular publication.

Her mind often raced back to May of 1859, when John Brown had come to Chatham. Women were barred from the meetings but she quickly learned of a call for black revolt. The strategy had been plotted in the little church down the street. Had she been a man, she would have joined Brown's crusade. Instead, she helped Osbourne Anderson write *Voice from Harper's Ferry,* the book with a firsthand account of the raid.

The thought brought warm memories of the boy called "Oz," the happy times on her father's farm, teaching him the printing trade, and the sad thoughts of a man who should be considered an American hero but was living sick and destitute and with no one to care for him in the slums of the American capital. She knew the others involved. White men who secretly bankrolled Brown had suddenly sought refuge in Canada, fugitive financiers, as opposed to fugitive slaves. Unlike black fugitives, the white men soon returned to their homes.

Her neighbor, Gunsmith Jones, had warned Brown that the uprising would fail. She didn't believe it then, but she did now. The years in slavery had produced a breed that needed more encouragement than the words of a white man or the few black strangers who slipped onto the plantations.

And now, she was being asked to approach former slaves with the offer of a blue uniform, food and shelter, and monthly pay. The letter, in her hand, from her old friend Martin Delaney, offered a job as a recruiting agent for the Union.

She tapped her fingers on the desk and thought about what she would say to potential soldiers. It was better that the new recruits didn't know the hollow ring of words like equality, or that she'd had her own disputes with the missionary societies and the churches over what to do for the newly freed. Maybe it was better that they didn't know the black wasn't welcome in the North and perhaps would never be, or maybe that, too, could be changed.

From a desk drawer, she lifted a picture of Martin Delaney in uniform, a black officer, darker than three shades of midnight, and a black man proud of his color. What a contrast to her light skin, a legacy of white blood in her family.

The contrasts were more than skin deep. She had urged the blacks to migrate to Canada and to mix with whites. He wanted to take his people to Africa to create a separate black nation. But now, together, they might work to save the country they had been forced to leave, and recruit the men needed to replenish the depleted Union ranks. There would be no integration. The blacks would be in separate units. No one seemed to notice or care that both white and black men bled red.

She slipped a shawl across her shoulders and glanced around the office at the printing press and row of lanterns on the shelf. Selling lanterns had been her husband Tom's idea, a plan to keep the money coming until the press could support them. The dust covered lanterns showed the idea hadn't worked. And then Tom had died, leaving her to care for the children. She'd rely on her family to care for them if—no, she decided—when she went south. She glanced once more around the office and decided any work would wait for another day.

On the street, she adjusted the shawl. The weather was cooler than usual but the air was clear and refreshing. The crack of a whip caught her attention and she turned to see a driver urge his horses into a trot. She recognized Amos Baker, a free black man known for an independent streak and his ability to find business in both the white and black communities. The passenger was white. He caught her eye as the carriage rolled by and began to lift his hat before abruptly turning away. The polite greeting of white society faded on a closer inspection of her complexion.

Baker, too, had noticed the passenger's reaction.

"Those mulatto women keep their build more than the pure Negro," the young man remarked. "That woman must have been near forty but she's still slight."

"A matter of breeding," Amos Baker baited the passenger. "I find with the horses a little new blood brings out the vigor. Crossbreeding is acceptable for agriculture. Maybe it works with people."

The passenger turned to watch the woman as she made her way down the street.

"Perhaps in the slave trade," he said. "There's always a demand for smart house servants and stronger field hands."

"That particular woman has smarts. In fact, some folks think she's too smart for her own good," Baker told him.

"Her name is Mary Ann Shadd, or I guess it's Shadd Carey since she married. Husband died. His family are barbers in Toronto. Good solid work! But not good enough for her. Her family came here about ten years ago, when free blacks across America were being arrested under the Fugitive Slave Act. But the Shadds were different. Her father was elected to the township council." Baker saw the disgust flash across the passenger's face but continued anyway. "And she's always stirring things up, one way or another."

"So they're educated?" the young man guessed.

"You bet. She started as a teacher before writing for the newspapers, her own or any other that would take her work, and she wrote a pamphlet telling the world of the virtues of immigration to Canada West. But she upset a mess of people along the way."

"I have my own views," the passenger told him. "But an enlightened teacher must consider all opinions. Go on."

"A lot of different opinions on what to do with the slave," Baker continued. "Some people would send them back to Africa. Others say free the slave and let him fend for himself. One group says the freemen should stay among their own, but not her. She wants them to live alongside the white man; thinks the two races can get along."

Baker leaned back and pulled his vest tighter to fight the chill. "She doesn't hold with the begging, those folks who constantly ask for money. Her newspaper claimed men were raising money for causes that didn't exist and were taking advantage of white sympathy to line their pockets. You hear of Josiah Henson?"

"No, I don't think so."

"Ever hear of *Uncle Tom's Cabin*?"

"I didn't read it. It's trash."

"Josiah Henson wouldn't want to hear you say that because it's his life story and he gave the particulars to that Mrs. Stowe and she turned it into a book. And he still lives a few miles north at the Dawn settlement."

"It's a famous book now. He must be one rich darkie!" The passenger's tone was sharp.

"Funny you should say that," Baker responded. "Old Henson is pretty smart when it comes to money but Shadd Carey thought he was raising money for a project that ended years ago and when she printed that, there were a lot of unhappy people—black and white—especially the whites who thought they'd been taken."

"Sounds like the woman stirred up a hornet's nest."

"She means well, wants to raise her people up. It's just that some expect to be given a ladder and others are willing to claw their way up with their fingernails."

The passenger nodded. "Back home, we know the slaves can't take care of themselves. They wouldn't know what to do with freedom."

"A few of us know what to do," Baker corrected him. "Of course, in fairness, I've been dealing with this freedom thing all of my life. I was born free and been paying my way since the get-go. That's why I'm your guide today. I got a message that a Mr. Bennet Young wanted to see the Thames battlefield and would pay well. The message came through people who don't usually like to talk about what they're doing, so I didn't ask questions."

The passenger had a story ready. "I'm a college professor. I teach history in Kentucky and like to see what I'm talking about."

The driver was silent for only seconds. "Can't be much work for a professor when all the the students are in the army." Baker had already appraised his passenger: medium height with wide, muscular shoulders, and perhaps in his early twenties. The accent suggested the upper South.

"We had a fair number of travelers from Kentucky before the war, but I guess they have battlefields closer to home to study now."

The road ran along the banks of the river as it left the city and passed small farms.

"The steamboats only come as far as the city?" Young asked. "But the river seems broad enough for larger boats."

Baker allowed a trace of sarcasm in his reply. "Most history professors would know the British had a problem here. The river is too shallow for big ships. There are Youngs in Kent County—you any relation?"

"No, no family here," Young answered. "But I had a relative who passed through in 1813. We were raised on the story of the Battle of the Thames. Everyone knew of someone who fought Tecumseh."

Baker shrugged.

"All you will see is a stone on the side of the road."

Young did not want to miss the chance. Henry Harrison had used his role in the battle to win the presidency and another participant, Richard Johnson, became a vice president. Johnson was known as "Old Tecumseh." He fell from favor when he married a woman with Negro blood and fathered two daughters. But most men talked less about his relations and more about the battle: the cavalry charge, the British retreat, and who actually killed Tecumseh.

The field was as Baker described it.

Young walked the ground for an hour but time had moved on. The Battle of the Thames was more vivid in Kentucky than on the actual field.

Baker saw the disappointment. "What did you expect? A field full of tee-pees or a tribute to the gallant men of Kentucky?"

Young allowed himself another lingering look over the land. "I don't know what I expected," he said. "But maybe I'll come back to look another time."

Baker shook his head. "It doesn't do anything for me. Never has, so I don't know why people come, especially now."

For a moment, he considered speaking of the famous Tecumseh namesake, Gen. William Tecumseh Sherman, but decided he would rather be paid than argue.

Two hours later, Baker watched his passenger board an eastbound train at the local station. He had learned no more about the young man. Perhaps it was as he claimed. Still, he had been particularly interested in the river and neighboring roads.

V

CHAPTER 17

Washington: June 15, 1864

"**D**ress that line!"

George Grenfell studied a Federal patrol as the horses passed along Pennsylvania Avenue.

"Trooper! Don't be gawking," a commander yelled. "You are on parade."

Grenfell was tempted to join the line at the White House where Lincoln was available several days a week. But instead, he wandered the dusty streets of the capital, mentally preparing for his meeting.

"Right wheel." The cavalry troop swung onto the grounds of the White House and moved toward the small barn behind the presidential mansion. A few weeks of drill would turn them into a cohesive unit. He wished the Southern men had accepted the training and discipline in the same way.

Grenfell presented a pass at the entrance to the War Department offices. The signature of General John Dix, affixed in New York, would take him into the inner sanctum of the Federal war effort. The request for a pass had first been met with disdain, but Grenfell persisted and Dix passed the issue to Washington. Only the secretary of war could grant approval and as Grenfell climbed the stairs to the second floor office, he heard what must be the voice of Edwin Stanton thunder down the halls. It was gruff and no nonsense. He did not waste time.

"I must have a furlough. My wife is ill."

"Denied."

"My son is only fourteen," said a woman in tears. "He didn't have permission to join the army. Can you release him?"

"No."

And then Grenfell heard his name called.

Stanton stood on a small platform behind a high desk stacked with paper. The doors were open to adjoining rooms and Grenfell saw one man working alone. Through another door came the clatter of telegraph keys.

The secretary peered over the top of his glasses. The man in front of him could have been dressed for an English hunt with his tweedy jacket and pants, attire that must be uncomfortable for a late spring day in Washington. The Dix letter described Grenfell as about sixty and in robust health. He certainly was a mercenary, but surprisingly, he claimed to have given up the war. Dix was suspicious. In the past year, Grenfell had left the Confederate unit of John Hunt Morgan, apparently after taking the side of a black man in an argument. He next surfaced with the Virginia cavalry of J.E.B Stewart and later still, Union spies found him recruiting replacements for Morgan.

"Orderly!" Stanton called. "I want a stenographer!"

A young private armed with a large notepad arrived to stand beside the secretary.

"Now," Stanton said, pulling at his beard and looking over the top of the glasses that had settled down his nose. "To what do we owe this questionable pleasure?"

Grenfell stood at parade-ground attention. "Mr. Secretary, I have made a formal request for permission to travel the Northern states. I am a citizen of Great Britain but having served in the army of the Confederacy, I felt it appropriate to make a formal declaration of my presence. I have severed my ties with the South. My travel is purely recreational. I'm a great fan of the hunt and the Northern states have much to offer. I would prefer not to search out the provost marshal in each district to report my presence. With approval of this office, I could go on my way."

The private's pen raced across the paper. The scratching and the click of the telegraph were the only sounds in the room. Stanton continued to stare over his glasses, letting the silence linger, before he snarled another question. "And why should we believe you have forsaken the rebels?"

"Forsaken, is a strong word. I won't forsake my friends but my body tells me it's time for something less strenuous. We must be close to the same age and I'm sure you find times the body doesn't respond as it once did."

Stanton's stony composure was the only reply.

"I have the utmost respect for my former Confederate allies," Grenfell continued, "but I see no end in sight to this war. It will grind on and chew up men younger than I am. I want to see the Northern hills and the prairies and then return to England."

"Do you sense defeat?" Stanton asked. "With Grant threatening Richmond, the war will soon be over. The rebels are losing heart."

"Unfortunately, sir, I must beg to differ. I'm one man. Thousands are willing to fight on."

"Grant is about to overpower Lee. The Southern army is disintegrating."

"Again, I beg to differ. Lee has a hundred and twenty-five thousand men in the army of Northern Virginia. General Beauregard can provide another twenty-five thousand. And while Stewart is gone, his cavalry mounts eight thousand horses. No sir, the war will go on."

"So you don't think Grant can break through?"

"No, sir! Emphatically no!"

"You had differences with Morgan and with Stewart?" Stanton prodded.

"Speak well of the dead," Grenfell said slowly. "General Stewart's body is barely cold. I will say there is a different spirit in the East. When I arrived, Stewart's officers had been with him for two years or more. I was an outsider. I do know his men will fight on. Morgan and Forrest are another matter. Forrest runs hot and cold. Morgan has a new wife and I find that romance makes a man less lethal. He's more likely to contemplate a warm bed than a cold night in the saddle!"

Stanton considered the arguments. "You have been described as a mercenary, a man who sells his service to the highest bidder. I understand you fought in Africa, South America, and the Crimea. Would you consider the Federal army?"

"I'm honored. But as I said, I've grown weary. I'd rather follow a hunting dog than the dogs of war."

Again, Stanton was silent, lost in thought. "Will you take the oath of loyalty to the Union?"

"I couldn't do that, sir. I am a British citizen."

The private caught up with the conversation. The pen stopped.

"I may regret this but I will approve the pass." Stanton hesitated. "I warn you that at the first sign of any trouble, I will have you arrested. Is that clear?"

"Perfectly! And I thank you for your kind attention."

Stanton made no reply and went back to the papers on his desk as Grenfell marched from the room.

The private moved to follow but stopped abruptly at the secretary's hiss. "Not you!"

As the door closed behind Grenfell, the secretary turned to the nearby office. "Peter, did you hear all that?"

"Yes and those troop numbers are much higher than we believe." Peter Watson already had a pad in his hand to cross-reference the estimates. "He suggests twice what Lee has. Beauregard has only a third of what Grenfell claims and Stewart's Cavalry may be a menace but I doubt there are eight thousand. Morgan is preparing for another raid and Forrest is up to something. It's the opposite of what we believe."

Stanton cleared his throat and stretched his arms.

"Grenfell is either a liar or badly mistaken. But I know the feelings of growing old. Keep a watch. He may lead us to something. Private! Read back his last words."

The secretary and Watson listened again. Stanton hesitated only for a second when the reading was completed.

"Correct that record. Make a note that he took the oath of loyalty."

The private stared at the secretary before beginning to write. A moment later, he read it back.

"You are dismissed."

Stanton waited until the stenographer had left the room before turning to Watson. "There, Peter. If Grenfell is involved in anything, we'll have our records and we can put him away."

* * *

NEAR CHICAGO, ILLINOIS: JUNE 1864

"Nice quiet neighbourhood." Tom Hines almost shouted as he slipped into the seat beside Theo Schultz.

Even from a half mile away, the din was overpowering. Trainloads of cattle arrived at the Cottage Grove stockyards day and night. Some of the bellowing would end in the nearby slaughterhouses; the other animals would continue to bawl after sorting for shipment to the Eastern cities or the Union army.

"You get used to it," Schultz assured him, the German accent strong. Schultz was a large man with a barrel-shaped chest. A faded blue cap held shaggy brown hair in place.

Hines watched a group of men hover by a long wooden chute and roll a large wooden ball down an alley toward bottle-shaped targets.

"Ever bowled?" Schultz asked.

"Not if that's what they are doing," Hines answered.

"It takes skill," Schultz explained, "and it's a break from the slaughterhouse."

A shout went up as the ball knocked the bottles aside.

Schultz turned from the game. "And no doubt, money is at stake."

Before he could say more, a tall blonde woman approached the table to set glasses of foaming beer in front of them.

"*Danke*," Schultz said.

The women replied with a smile.

"Those workers are worried," he told Hines. "Survey crews are staking property lines for a new slaughter plant. The men will be out of work unless they get jobs at the new 'union' stockyards."

"I didn't come to talk about meat packing."

"No, I didn't think you did." Schultz leaned closer. "But see the men in the back corner? They're guards at what you came about but they only speak German."

"And you've had a few words?" Hines waited expectantly.

"A few conversations," Schultz smiled. "I'm learning about Camp Douglas."

"Go on."

"It's low ground, swampy—so wet the barracks are raised on four-foot stilts. It keeps the buildings drier and makes it easier to spot escape attempts. There's a wooden wall but it's not strong."

"How many prisoners?"

"Six thousand or more. The food is bad and there's sickness. The burial details take out dozens of coffins each day."

"Do you have a way to contact the men inside?" Hines asked.

"Dead men tell no tales," Schultz smiled. "Fellow that goes inside with the coffins likes cash."

"Keep him happy." Hines leaned forward. "When I leave, I'll forget my saddlebag. There are two envelopes inside. Take one and get the other to Breck Castleman."

"Breck's been to Bowling Green," Schultz said quietly. "He says the young lady is fine."

"Thank him for me. I'll be in touch."

CHAPTER 18

Toronto, Canada West: June 1864

Jacob Thompson, Hines decided, was learning. Their meeting was in
a private home. The owners had conveniently left for the day and
pulled the shades to block the summer sun.

Thompson stood with a large map of the Eastern United States
spread before him.

"I want to hear about your trip, Captain, but an urgent dispatch
just arrived." He ran a finger along the Virginia-Maryland border.
"Our losses are severe. Lee is digging in at Petersburg but needs to
relieve the pressure on his lines. He's sending Jubal Early to threaten
Washington."

Thompson became more excited as he talked. "And they want us to
create a diversion. What do you think?"

Hines had a simple answer. "We're not ready!"

"Not ready? We've spent weeks and thousands of dollars. It's time
to do something."

"If you want to create confusion, burn a few bridges or derail a few
trains, then we're ready," Hines explained. "But major raids need to be
organized and if we go off half-cocked, it would upset everything."

A flash of anger spread across Thompson's face. "So what would
you suggest, *Captain?*"

"The hotheads in the Copperhead movement might do the work
for us. Prey on their fears. Build on rumors. Spread word that the rich
Republicans are avoiding the draft. There's truth in that, anyway. Stir

up the black issues. Detroit's had one riot. The Federals moved whole regiments from Gettysburg to control New York after the riot last summer. Toledo is a powder keg just waiting for something to set it off."

Thompson still stared at the map but his face had lost the red flush.

"And work on the politicians. Invite old friends to this side of the border. Promise them guns, promise them money, buy newspaper editors, stroke egos."

Thompson was not ready for surrender. "We have to do something more."

Hines stepped forward but ignored the map. "I can send out a few men. They can loosen rails, set fires, and generally be a nuisance."

"The men are available?"

"A few."

"Send them and tell them to aim for anything to disrupt the Northern war effort." Thompson took a deep breath before moving to other issues. "Vallandigham has returned to Ohio. He may be allowed to campaign or he may be arrested. Either way, it stirs the pot. What have you learned?"

This time, Hines used the map. "Camp Douglas is like all Federal prisons, plenty of guards, not well trained, but lots of them. The camp is close to Lake Michigan, actually on the Stephen Douglas estate. I don't know what that says about Lincoln's respect for a former opponent."

Thompson shrugged. "I knew Douglas. A good Democrat but I never saw his property."

"You're not missing much," Hines assured him.

"The prisoners are from Kentucky, Missouri, and Tennessee and many are from Morgan's command, so they're fighters. If we had a ship, a couple of cannon shots would destroy the outer wall. We could carry enough guns to arm the men. Without a ship, it's more difficult."

Hines shifted around the table and pointed to Ohio. "Bennet Young is back from Columbus. There are six thousand prisoners at Camp Chase. But Johnson's Island has to be the main objective."

Thompson interrupted. "I have Cole on a survey of Lake Erie now."

"I'm not sure Cole is the best man for the job."

"Oh, come now, Captain. Cole may be loud but he knows the work. What is the problem?"

"He talks too much."

Thompson began to laugh. "No, no. He fits with the belligerent Yankee crowd, always willing to spout an opinion."

"And that's the problem."

"No. Let Cole continue his work." Thompson refused to reconsider. "Have you met Mrs. Cole? She's a big, brazen woman that also fits with that crowd. The Coles can handle the survey. Other men are better equipped to handle the ships but you can meet them later. You have other work to do."

* * *

OHIO: JULY 1864

The single horse and buggy was the best the livery shop had and Bennet Young was impressed. The horse showed no signs of tiring on the back roads of Ohio. He was less impressed with the man who slept beside him.

Someone somewhere vouched for Ike Pearson as a true Son of Liberty. He knew the password and the secret handshake but little else. Young hoped the other men sent off by Tom Hines found contacts that were more accommodating.

Pearson was to guide him to the rail lines crossing central Ohio, but motivating the man was like trying to push a large rock uphill.

"I'm the leader of the local castle," Pearson explained when they met. "I chair meetings but don't know about the work you propose."

"Do you have a crowbar?" Young asked.

Pearson was irked by the young man's tone. "Be a damn poor farmer if I didn't."

"Get it," Young ordered. "And a sledge hammer and a couple of small hammers. Oh, and a can of kerosene."

"Will I be reimbursed?" Pearson asked. "Tools and fuel are expensive."

Over the next few days, Pearson watched Young work on the railroad.

"The Sons of Liberty may need to know how to do this. Don't pull all the spikes. Pull a couple and loosen the rest. The wear of the trains going over will pop the spikes, the rail will come loose, and the next car will slam off the track."

Pearson preferred to stay with the buggy and act as a lookout, but with the flat Ohio country, a lookout wasn't needed. Young ordered Pearson to help on the track.

"Don't know as I like this," Pearson confessed.

"You need experience," Young suggested. "I learned a lot from General Morgan."

"I don't agree with Lincoln," Pearson expounded at another point. "A man should have the freedom to speak out. That's what I tell our men."

"But sometimes you have to act," Young urged. "It can't be all talk."

"And that's why I am recruiting members," Pearson countered.

"We need men who can follow my...well... *our* orders. A man alone can't do much but all of us together could accomplish great things."

Night was falling when Young picked a bridge over a small river for the final target. The railway line was silent but another freight train would pass soon. He pushed the brush into a pile beneath the trestle and ran his hand along the planks above. His fingers came away soaked from the kerosene. The match spread flame to the brush and began to rise.

Young sprinted back down the track, congratulating himself on what a single man could do. The flames had begun to light the sky when he reached the road where Pearson was to wait. But Pearson had whipped the horse to make good his escape.

Young would begin his return to Canada on foot.

* * *

WASHINGTON: JULY 1864

"I know they're tired but get those skirmishers forward." Gen. Jubal Early was fighting fatigue and morning heat.

"They're going, General," an orderly called as the first men went forward.

Early saw a sniper drop into a hollow and sight his weapon. The Confederate marksmen used any possible cover as they advanced on the Washington fortifications.

"Congratulations, General."

Early was startled. Intent on the movement of the skirmish line, he hadn't heard the other man approach.

"Oh, thank you, Mr. Breckinridge, but we aren't there yet."

"But so close. That's Fort Stevens ahead." A ragged round of rifle fire sprouted from the fort as he spoke.

"Not much of volley," Early observed. "The defenders of a capital city should be strong but the scouts say untrained men and convalescents are being forced to the barricades."

Breckinridge was more intent on happier times. "It hardly seems possible. I slept at Silver Springs last night and tonight I could see my old home. And look, they still haven't finished the capitol dome."

"Do you expect a parade to welcome the former vice president?" Early laughed. Breckinridge, now Early's second in command, had been one of the last Southern leaders to leave Washington. He had worked for compromise until the fear of arrest forced him to flee.

"Hah!" Breckinridge laughed. "You've done a magnificent job, General."

"Would have been a day earlier and a lot happier if we hadn't had that fight on the Monocacy River." Early stopped suddenly as he saw one of the snipers fall.

"God almighty, what I wouldn't give for more men!" He slammed a fist against a tree, "we can't hold Washington but we can raise hell for a few hours."

"General Breckinridge," the military title indicated Early had dispensed with small talk. "Give the boys an hour to rest and then order them forward. Sooner or later, the Yankees will send reinforcements and I want to be in the city before they are."

Breckinridge happily moved to spread the word.

Two soldiers left the line to weave back to the main Confederate position.

"Out of ammunition?" Early asked.

"Yes," one of them replied before he realized to whom he was speaking. "Yes, sir, General! I went through a lot of rounds. One fool was standing on the fortifications, a tall fellow with a big stovepipe hat. I put a few shots near him before they dragged him off. Just in the last few minutes, the Yankees are getting organized. I could see more men filing up to the fort. It's the outfit that wears the black hats."

"Yeah, I saw them, too," the other sniper added. "And out there you can hear the noise. All of Washington is sounding bugles."

"God almighty! Call General Breckinridge!" Early shouted to an orderly.

The puzzled snipers watched.

"Tell the rest of the unit to fall back."

"Fall back?" one of the snipers asked.

"God almighty! Don't you understand English?" Early snapped.

"Those new men are from Grant's army. If it's black hats, it's the Iron Brigade. They arrived in time to save Lincoln's capital and his sorry ass."

* * *

QUEBEC CITY, CANADA EAST: JULY 1864

"We're going to have more work than expected! Cancel any plans for the remainder of the summer."

Hewitt Bernard drummed on the arms of a chair. His expression showed that he expected no argument from a junior clerk.

"I understand, Mr. Bernard. These new reform proposals will need extra time and study." Forsey liked to demonstrate his grasp of the political climate. "The politicians think they know what they want but the written language confuses the issue. How many times did we redraft the provisions on Catholic schools?"

He stopped and waited. Bernard would sometimes accept his observations but on other days, he demanded silent obedience. The silent days usually followed a bad night with the minister. Bernard was the chief secretary to the attorney general of Canada West, and when John A. Macdonald entertained, Bernard picked up the slack.

"There's more, but I remind you of the pledge of secrecy," Bernard told him. "It's a union of all of the provinces, bringing the maritime colonies into the mix. If we can achieve a union in the East, the rest will fall in place. British Columbia will join if we win control of the Hudson's Bay Company lands. A new country would stretch from coast to coast, the entire northern sweep of North America."

"What will London say?" Forsey thought of the huge scope of the plan.

"I had the same question," Bernard told him. "Macdonald believes the British will welcome the idea. The timing is right. We'd still have the monarchy, the army and will still be British subjects."

"And the Americans?" Forsey asked. "American settlers are squatting on Hudson's Bay lands and Washington still dreams of annexation."

"But of course they are slightly distracted," Bernard reminded him. "So best to speed ahead."

CHAPTER 19

Johnson's Island, Ohio: July 1864

Reaching the island was easier than Annie Cole expected. The rules said only immediate family could visit the prisoners.

"There's no way a distant cousin can visit a prisoner," a corporal patiently explained as she began to dab at her eyes with the silk handkerchief.

"But Cousin Ben's mother is too sick to make the trip and I said I would come. Ben's a wild one. The rest of the family supports the Union and always has but Ben...well...I think he was lured into the rebel army. But Corporal, if you can't help, perhaps someone else could?"

And with the words, she dropped a ten-dollar gold piece on his desk.

She repeated the story to a sergeant the next day and after copious tears was ushered into the presence of a young lieutenant. His eyes immediately darted between the tears and her low-cut gown. She left the meeting with a pass and a promise to share dinner with the young officer.

*　*　*

A chorus of whoops greeted her as she entered the stockade.
"A woman and a looker!"

The guard who served as her escort stiffened but led her to the shade beside the barracks. Drops of perspiration rolled down her neck and she wasn't sure if it was from the heat or tension. This was the critical point. She had never met Ben Cooper.

A young man broke from the crowd and strode toward her.

"Cousin Annie. Is it really you?"

"Ben! Oh, thank God! We were all so worried."

The prisoner was tall, rugged, and definitely handsome. Cooper wore a dirty, white, cotton shirt and a faded pair of blue trousers. He swept her off the ground in a bear hug, squeezing her against his chest. His fingers pressed deep into the fabric of her dress.

"Cousin Annie," he almost sobbed and nestled his head in her blonde hair.

"Make it convincing," he whispered.

"Ben, it's really you! And you are safe!" She ran her hands through his brown hair, her mouth inches from his ear. "Don't make it too convincing, honey. No Southern gentleman would be groping a lady's derriere in public."

Cooper laughed and set her gently on her feet. He ran his hands across the back of her neck and she felt him guide a small piece of paper past the neckline.

The guard pointed to the chairs in the shade.

For the next five minutes, she held his hand and told him of the news from home. The guard listened as she described his mother's sickness and the problems around the plantation, but how Uncle Jack used his Union connections to get them black laborers—paid labor, of course, but anything helped. She was well into the description of Cousin Millie's new baby when the guard began to edge toward prisoners throwing dice against the wall.

"We have to make this quick," she spoke quietly. "We need to know what's happening inside, the number of guards, weak points, and who can be trusted. We're working to get you out but we're not ready yet."

He, too, spoke quietly. "Most of that is on the note in your dress."

Cooper glanced toward the guard and the game. "Is your name really Annie Cole?" Cooper asked.

"As good a name as any and I want the guards to remember me the next time I come. I will probably make several visits."

"Then it's delayed again?" Cooper asked. "We were told July 4."

She squeezed his hand gently. "We don't have a date but you haven't been forgotten."

"Tell them to hurry. Things are getting worse." Cooper spoke quickly. "The rations have been cut. The Yankees claim their men in Southern prisons are mistreated."

"We know!" She tried to sound reassuring. "And we need the leaders that are here, you see it's not just an escape this time—"

Loud shouts brought everyone's attention to the dice game. The guard grinned as two prisoners began to fight and roll in the dust. Still smiling, he pulled his revolver and fired a single shot in the air.

The players jumped back while the guard bent to stuff the money into his pocket.

Annie used the moment to pull a small envelope from her sleeve and press it into Cooper's hand. It quickly disappeared inside his shirt.

"This visit is over!"

Another guard moved to separate the man and woman.

"Just another minute," Copper pleaded.

"No! Trouble on the parade ground! Her time is up!"

"I'll go Ben! But I'll be back."

* * *

SANDUSKY, OHIO: JULY 1864

The lieutenant selected a table overlooking Sandusky Bay with Johnson's Island in the distance. His name was John Armstrong, and Annie Cole needed his cooperation. Their eyes met as she approached the table.

"My husband will join us momentarily; he's finishing…business affairs. So perhaps a sip of wine before he arrives?"

Armstrong raised his hand to summon the black steward.

"I must thank you again," Annie said, reaching across the table to touch his hand. "The family will be so relieved to hear Ben is well. And I feel better having seen the prison."

She delivered her words quietly. "We hear about the overcrowding, the filthy, vile conditions in the Southern system and think all prisons are the same. But seeing the conditions today, well, I feel much better."

"I am pleased to hear that, Mrs. Cole." Satisfied visitors were a rare commodity in Armstrong's work. "It isn't easy. Simple things take so much time. The ferry, for instance." He pointed through the window to the craft en route to the island. "It must be inspected both here and again on return. Trying to stay on top of supplies is a major headache. Costly, too, dealing with all the contactors. Hoffman, he's in charge of Federal prisons, runs a tight ship."

She watched as he spoke, noting freshly cut hair, a well-trimmed beard, and hands that lifted nothing heavier than a pen.

"Lieutenant, you are doing a fine job, and under very difficult conditions. Do you have to watch over the guards as well? Those poor veterans?"

"Oh, the Invalid Corps." Armstrong warmed with attention. "The Hoffman Brigade. A few need light duty while they recover from wounds but many are Ohio farm boys." His tone changed slightly with a note of condescension. "Some are here just to stay out of the war. And yes, I have to make arrangements to feed and house them. I have over a thousand men at times."

"And what about you? May I call you John?" She deliberately had worn a low-cut gown and made a point of leaning forward.

"I may join General Sherman's staff."

"You must be careful, John. I would hate to see you wounded, or worse yet, in a Southern death camp."

"Oh, I'll be careful, don't you worry."

Annie considered it the least of her concerns.

"It is obscene the way our men are treated," he continued. "Your cousin is in a palatial retreat compared to what the rebels provide. For a time we exchanged prisoners. Men like your cousin might be home by now if it wasn't for Jefferson Davis."

She leaned forward with a searching look.

"After the Emancipation Proclamation, Davis threatened to hang white officers caught leading Negro troops. Until then we had a steady stream of prisoners going north and south. Now the whole system is backed up."

"So there's no chance of exchange for Ben?"

"It's doubtful, Annie. He'll be a long time in prison."

A booming voice marked the arrival of the third party for dinner. "Charles Cole, Lieutenant. I do appreciate your help. Her news will be a blessing for the family. Even if young Ben was an upstart, and well— a traitor, I suppose—it's a relief to know he's well."

Cole quickly took command of the dinner arrangements including the demand for a second bottle of wine.

"And what do you do, Mr. Cole?"

The checked pants, the new jacket and shirt, indicated a man who preferred the good life.

"I'm in the oil business, Mount Hope Oil Company. If there's oil in Pennsylvania and in the Canadas, there should be oil in between and so I'm prospecting in this area. Annie and I will be circling Lake Erie this summer."

"Is your firm a large concern?" The lieutenant had passed through the oil fields and remembered only dirt and grime.

"Not yet," Cole confessed. "But people like Millard Fillmore are considering investment, so if a former president thinks it worth the risk, it must be."

"Yes, I suppose. Will you be doing the actual drilling?"

"Oh Lord, no! That's dirty work. We have Irish or Negroes for that. I'm in a supervisory role."

Cole leaned forward to capture Armstrong's attention. The lieutenant's eyes had drifted again to below Annie's neck. "A young man might want to give the industry some thought."

Armstrong reluctantly looked to Cole. "Perhaps I should. A man has to think of the future, although I was telling Mrs. Cole, I may be joining Sherman's staff."

"Really." Cole tried to sound impressed. "So you and the men will be moving on soon?"

"Oh, not the men, the Hoffman Brigade will stay and more may come. We had a couple of scares—rumors that the rebs were going to attack. Silly really, but Washington can send reinforcements in a hurry. I'm the one needed elsewhere but probably not before the fall."

"Excellent," Cole smiled. "My wife will want to see her cousin again. It would be comforting to know there was someone to watch over her."

As if to reinforce the idea, Annie shifted forward.

"And," Cole continued. "In the meantime, can you help me? Parts of this country are Copperhead and I won't do business with anyone who is disloyal. Can you identify any local people to avoid?"

The lieutenant shook his head. "I know my men and the army but I'm not familiar with local businessmen. I would, however, avoid Democrats. A deep pool of disloyalty in the party must be rooted out. I will not give them army contracts. But I will listen for any information that might be useful to you."

"Capital! Great news, isn't it, Pinkey?"

His wife's scowl broke his mood. "Er...dear...Annie," he stammered. "Pinkey is a pet name for Mrs. Cole from when we first met, when she was a humble working girl, but I did promise not to use it in public."

The lieutenant was a model of decorum. "Think nothing of it! It's forgotten."

"You are a gentleman, sir." Her voice was calm and low. "I wonder if I might impose for another small favor?"

"Why, anything at all."

"It's Cousin Ben. His clothes are disgraceful. If I buy some pants and shirts, could I bring them when I return next week?"

Armstrong considered the request and his tablemate. "It's against the rules but I can make arrangements."

CHAPTER 20

Niagara Falls, Canada West: July 1864

The man in English tweeds controlled a rough, yellow, snarling dog on a short leash, barely. He seemed oblivious to the stares of other travelers at Table Rock and their instant fear of the beast. The huge head and jaw were too big for the body and the dog appeared ready for the kill.

An attendant barred the entrance to the museum. "You know the rules. The dog can't come in. Tie him to the hitching post."

"Well then, I shan't come in!" George Grenfell made the English accent drip with venom.

He had entered his name in the museum guest book yesterday to alert associates of his arrival. Turning his back with a dismissive shrug, he walked toward the Clifton House Hotel. The dog's growl alerted him to the young boy.

"A message for you, sir." He waved an envelope but kept well clear of the dog.

"Down, Brutus!"

The dog refused the command until a strong tug on the leash reinforced the words. Reluctantly, he sank to the ground, his menacing eyes set on the boy.

"The man said to give you this."

"What man?"

The boy glanced over his shoulder with a bewildered expression.

"He was over there a minute ago."

"What did he look like?"

The boy was more concerned with the coin in his pocket than the man who gave it to him. "Don't know, sir."

He thrust the envelope forward only to jump back at a sharp bark.

"Enough, Brutus." Grenfell plucked the envelope from a shaky hand and ripped the cover. The brief note read, "85 Lundy's Lane. Hunter."

He smiled and stuffed the note in his pocket before he remembered the messenger. "You have been paid!"

It was not a question and the youngster abandoned hope of a second coin.

* * *

Tom Hines answered the door on Lundy's Lane, made an exaggerated bow and waved for Grenfell to enter.

The dog's growl was cut short by a jerk on the leash.

"Not to worry, Thomas. We are getting used to each other and he'll get used to you."

Grenfell marched inside to claim a plush chair. Brutus fought the leash but eventually settled beside him.

"I picked up the dog in New York State," Grenfell explained. "Had an excellent hunt. Been through the Adirondacks and the Finger Lakes and thought I'd try my hand here."

Hines sat outside of the dog's reach. "I'd have met you on the street but this area is crawling with detectives. Make yourself at home and perhaps the dog will settle in."

"Excellent hunting animal," Grenfell said, patting the dog's head.

"After only two weeks I've grown attached but I didn't think of the problems he'd cause. I couldn't get a hack and had to walk over the suspension bridge. Can we send someone for my bags at the International House across the river?"

"It can't be any of our men. The border patrol is checking papers, but one of the Canadian hires might slip over. How did you get across so easily?"

"I had Brutus and a letter signed by another centurion. I met their secretary of war, Mr. Stanton, in person. It's amazing what his signature will do. I carry what is called a protection paper, as all foreign travelers should. Stanton is a hard man, by the way, probably quite intelligent. Wanted to know about our forces in Virginia. I told him but the numbers may be higher than General Lee's records show."

Inflating troop counts was one of Morgan's tricks.

"Early used the same tactic," Hines explained. "He had ten thousand men but the papers tell of thousands more. Apparently, Washington is still in an uproar."

"And here?" Grenfell probed.

Hines rose too quickly for Brutus, who gave a sharp bark, a low growl, and tugged on the leash.

Grenfell smiled as Hines sat back down. "It's all right, Brutus. Thomas is our friend."

"Our first priority will be another home for your dog. As for the humans, we're waiting."

"In that case, I'll continue my tour," Grenfell announced. "I have never seen Montreal."

"Good. We may have a dispatch for Montreal. You could take it. Tonight, we'll have a reunion of sorts. Breck Castleman has arrived along with Theo Schultz."

"Ah, Breck. Good man! Does he have news of Morgan?"

"The usual. Not enough men but they hit Mount Sterling before he left. He brought money from the bank to cover expenses, another sixty thousand dollars for our coffers."

Grenfell scowled. "That's not good, Thomas. With plundering and stealing, the men are nothing more than thieves and there's a difference between thieves and soldiers. I warned Morgan, time and again."

"General Morgan will take care of himself. And if you can separate yourself from that beast, we'll have a good night."

* * *

By early evening, the dining room of the Clifton House was bedlam, upsetting the plans for a quiet dinner. "Greeley's here," a waiter blurted out as he approached the table. "Came over from the states this afternoon and tried to pass as a regular traveler but the desk clerk knew who he was. He was wearing that white linen duster, those long neck whiskers, and had a copy of the *Tribune* under his arm."

"Horace Greeley?" Grenfell was considering a memoir of his days in the South and the popular *New York Tribune* might be the place to publish.

"It's him, all right." The waiter glanced into the lobby before taking their orders and rushing to the kitchen. A moment later, he pushed through a crowd to the edge of the lobby.

"Sanders has Greeley involved in peace talks," Hines told his dinner companions. "He wants safe passage for a delegation to Washington for negotiations."

"Sanders...name sounds familiar. Who is he?" Grenfell wanted to know.

"He was some sort of American diplomat about ten years ago," Hines explained. "After that, he joined the European revolutions, and then joined us."

Theo Schultz spoke for the first time. "There are those who fought in the attempted revolutions. Many German immigrants are in that category. There's another group...the ones that only talked. Which is he?"

"I'm not sure," Hines confessed. "But Clay and Thompson are impressed."

"Tell us about the peace talks," Castleman demanded.

Hines spoke so only those at the table could hear. "A call for an end to hostilities and independence; the Yankees go their way and we go ours. But even Sanders isn't sure it will work. While he's upstairs talking peace, Thompson is just up the road in St. Catherines, trying to put more backbone in the northern opposition."

The waiter returned with their plates and more news. "The man with Greeley is John Hay, Lincoln's private secretary. The meeting with the Confederates is in J. P. Holcombe's room."

In his excitement, he tipped a bowl spilling gravy.

"Steady!" Grenfell scowled. "Worry about dinner before peace."

"Sorry, sir. I'll bring a fresh bowl and clean up the mess." He dashed toward the kitchen but stopped at the lobby door for the latest rumor.

"If it was up to that fellow, an armistice would have been signed." Grenfell began to eat but took only a mouthful before the noise from the lobby intensified.

Greeley and Hay descended the stairs to a barrage of shouted questions. Greeley wore a sour look. His younger companion showed no emotion.

"Is it peace?" A newspaperman demanded but any answer was lost in other questions.

"When will the armistice begin? Is emancipation scrapped? When will the men come home?"

Greeley and Hay ignored the mob and pushed through the lobby to a waiting carriage.

"They brought a letter from Lincoln," the waiter said, returning to mop the stain.

"The war may soon be over. My friend crossed the border for bounty money only a month ago. He looks smart—three hundred dollars and no war to fight."

"If there's peace, we'll be going home," Castleman suggested before he thought of the devastation in the South. "And there will be a lot of work. Rebuilding, for a start, and a few scores to settle…"

He had no time to finish as a heavyset man strode to their table. "Can't talk here," he said, addressing Hines. "Meet me at the falls lookout in half an hour."

"Gentlemen," Hines told his dinner guests as the man hurried off, "that was George Sanders."

* * *

The mist from the falls was a welcome relief from the summer heat. George Sanders was staring at the waterfall and turned at their approach.

Hines introduced his companions.

"Since Tom trusts you, I shall as well." Sanders fought a seething anger and the words came in a torrent. "Greeley wanted to stop the fighting. Hay brought a letter from Lincoln and not a shred of courtesy. It was addressed, 'To whom it may concern.' He had the gall to spell out conditions. As long as we accept the Union and abandon slavery, we can talk. And then he asks for proof that we have authority to negotiate."

"Surely you have that," Castleman interrupted.

Sanders stared at the young stranger for a moment. "Er, yes, though we do have to talk to Richmond. But what's the use? Without independence, there's no peace."

"So our other plans move forward?" Hines asked.

"Oh, we'll go through the process," Sanders assured him. "J. P. Holcombe has the letter, accepted with all the diplomatic niceties. We may publish the contents to show we were prepared to talk and Lincoln threw away the opportunity. If there's any upside, this will boost the peace Democrats."

The approach of a young woman had been drowned by the thunder from the falls. "Would you gentlemen like a souvenir? It's a dollar for a portrait at the Great Cataract." She pointed to where a photographer stood beside a camera.

"No, no picture for me." Schultz backed away.

"A dollar is a little high." Castleman was torn between a lack of funds and the smiling face that made the offer.

"My da...is trying to raise some extra cash. He might make a special offer," she said.

* * *

"Smile!" The photographer slipped under the hood on his camera only to reappear in seconds. "Sorry, I must have another. The little man moved."

"The little man doesn't want his picture taken," Hines muttered.

"Oh, another moment," Sanders urged. "One for the history books."

"Only a few seconds." The photographer slipped back under the hood. "Got it!"

The young lady wasn't at the gallery when Breck Castleman arrived the next day but the portrait was ready.

A second picture was already in a dispatch for the Secret Service office in Washington.

CHAPTER 21

Near Port Burwell, Canada West: July 1864

The summer was unusually hot and dry and crops planted with springtime hope began to wilt. A year earlier, Matilde's money eased the return to Canada West. Owen and Jimmy found harvest work and never spoke of the war. Jimmy's outbursts were rare but always connected with sharp noise. A gunshot from a far off hunter sent him cowering in a fencerow and the crack of a falling tree set his axe swinging in a mad frenzy.

Matilde and Jimmy settled in an abandoned cabin on the family homestead. No one asked for a marriage certificate and the swelling of her stomach discouraged speculation. A weak baby was born in a late March snowstorm and died in April. Jimmy didn't seem to notice and Matilde hid any emotion.

More trouble developed in early summer.

A local militia company was at drill when Owen went for supplies. An officer, resplendent in British red, shouted instructions while seated in his carriage. The men had no uniforms and instead of weapons carried hoes, forks, or sticks of wood. The exhibition offered free entertainment and Owen joined a small group to watch.

"Old Squire Barnes is having a hay day in his dress uniform. Must be bringing back memories of '37."

The squire was a fixture in the community. Barnes liked to tell of how he, and usually he alone, had put down the revolution. Twenty-five years had aged his body but in his mind, he was still a young gentleman. Friends from the old ruling families, known as the Family Compact, later provided financial backing to boost his career. The land-hungry Barnes had snapped up three farms abandoned when the revolt and the aftermath produced an exodus from the province. Another reward was the annual salary to lead the militia.

"Right turn," the squire ordered.

Most men complied.

"No, no, the other right!" he shouted.

"There's talk of more money for the militia," a spectator laughed. "The men will have to decide if they want smart uniforms or a rifle."

"Our government would have to make a decision for that to happen," another lamented, "And that doesn't happen much."

"Take a rifle," the first man suggested. "Use the gun around the farm. These boys won't be doing any fighting. That's the job of the British regulars."

The regulars were posted in major cities. Their numbers fell sharply during the Crimea War, and then rapidly increased during the *Trent* crisis, only to slowly decline in the last two years.

"Are those men Yankees?"

Owen felt a sharp pain in his stomach.

"What are they doing here?"

"Don't like it," the storekeeper said. "The two came in yesterday and said they were looking for deserters. I've heard of local men collecting a nice fat bounty, deserting, then going back and signing for another bounty. But one fellow got caught and the Americans hanged him."

Another man, a local farmer, joined the conversation. "So they squander men on the battlefield and off. Life's pretty cheap to the American army."

"Life's cheap in any army," the storekeeper said.

"Very good!" The drill over, the squire congratulated the men. "Now form two ranks, ten men each."

"Last night, those Yankees were talking up the American army, the good times, and all," the storekeeper continued. "Squire Barnes, of course, was right friendly and invited them to stay and watch this show. But they have no authority and shouldn't be here."

Another villager offered an explanation. "I'd bet our government is looking the other way to keep the Americans happy. Or maybe the government doesn't know they're here. Old Squire Barnes won't rattle any cages. Grant's whole army could come before he'd ask for instructions."

The militia finally managed to fill in the ragged ranks and the Americans began to inspect the troop. Owen took a step back as the crowd pushed forward.

One Federal walked with a slight limp. The other sauntered across the square as if he owned it. The body style, the walk, and the thinly veiled arrogance combined to shock Owen. The second man was Sergeant Hurley. Owen edged deeper into the crowd before slipping away to find Matilde and Jimmy.

* * *

Even the mention of Hurley's name changed Jimmy, as if a door opened in a dark corner of his mind. "The son of bitch." He began to shake. "He sent us onto the field at Gettysburg but he wasn't watching the enemy. He had his eyes on Jim Gready. You must remember, Owen. Gready was a gambler and kept cash in a money belt. The sergeant had been playing poker the night before and was a big loser."

Owen and Matilde waited in shocked silence.

"Hurley put Gready in front of him. In fact, everyone was in front of him. I glanced back when the order came to advance. Hurley waited for the first rebel volley and shot Gready in the head. A lot of the others went down, but from rebel fire. I went for Hurley but before I got ten feet, the rebels were on us. I don't remember much after that, except I did see Hurley pulling at Gready's belt."

Jimmy plunged a kitchen knife deep into the table. "If I see him, I'll kill him."

149

Matilde edged toward a thick hickory shaft that leaned against the wall. But as fast as the tantrum began, it ended. Jimmy sank into a chair and began to cry. Tears rolled down his face until he buried his head in his arms. Matilde's eyes were wet and she gently rubbed Jimmy's shoulder.

"Jimmy," Owen began quietly, "he doesn't know you are here and probably doesn't know what you saw."

"No! He knows and he's coming for me!" He sprang to where a rifle hung on the wall. "He's not going to get me. He won't take me alive."

He forced a window open and thrust the rifle through, sighting down the empty lane, and then as suddenly grew silent, back on picket duty, ready for a long night.

Matilde waited for a few moments and motioned to the door. "Owen, go home. Jimmy will stand the watch."

"It's happened before," she whispered. "He slips away. I hid the cartridges with the china. He'll fall asleep and tomorrow won't remember anything. Go quietly! Come back when we've had time to think."

"Maybe we should go to the sheriff or to Squire Barnes."

"Sleep on it," she urged, guiding him out. "Best you go quickly. There's rain coming."

The storm came with a rush of wind and stalled above the farms. Lightning was so close that Owen heard the snap and for hours, thunder rolled like heavy artillery.

Morning found him grappling with the dilemma. If he went to the sheriff, he would have to admit he deserted. But would anyone in Canada care? Would they care that Hurley, a murderer, was in their community? He had no answers.

Finally, he crossed the field to their cabin. The window where Jimmy had taken his post was firmly closed. There was no answer to his knock. No answer when he called out. No answer as he pushed the door open and entered the house.

In the front parlor, tables and chairs were overturned and Matilde's china, usually stored neatly, lay smashed on the floor.

Matilde was in the bedroom, sheets neatly arranged to her neck, and a single bullet hole in her forehead. Jimmy slumped at the kitchen table. The rifle was wedged between his legs and one hand had stiffened on the trigger. The top of his head was gone.

CHAPTER 22

St. Catherines, Canada West: July 1864

Jacob Thompson surveyed the meeting room. The Sons of Liberty sent a small delegation to St. Catherines and, in keeping with the zeal for secrecy, the delegates refused to use real names. With a few hours of work, he could determine the true identity of each man but he let them play the game.

Yes, they told him, the anti-war sentiment was growing. The lists of the dead and wounded were posted at newspaper offices, and each day produced more widows and orphans.

And yes, Lincoln's draft had a telling effect. Their region had already sent more than its share of men.

And yes, Washington was mounting attacks on democracy, or more precisely, on Democrats. Lincoln, Stanton, and Seward would stop at nothing to win the coming election. Loyal Leagues and other secret Federal societies received money and guns while the opposition was muzzled.

Thompson listened for half an hour before he rose.

"Mr. Smith," he addressed the obvious leader, "perhaps a private walk by the canal and some fresh air."

* * *

"One really must admire the British and their businessmen," Thompson said, indicating the bustle around the canal. A large sailboat drifted toward Lake Ontario and in the distance were the masts of other ships waiting to clear the locks.

"Built by a man named Merritt," Thompson continued. "Of course, nothing comes easily. His ideas were ridiculed. They called it Mr. Merritt's ditch and look what it's become, all from vision and hard work."

Smith tossed his jacket over his shoulder as they walked. "A lesson here for us, is there?"

"Perhaps," Thompson smiled, "We can provide the kind of assistance that Merritt eventually needed. We can offer encouragement and funds."

"Funds would be very welcome." It was Smith's turn to smile. "Elections are very expensive."

"We can help," Thompson assured him. "We're putting cash into the hands of newspaper editors. The editorials now have more bite. And there will be extra funds available if needed."

"It's all welcome, but..." Smith hesitated. "If we go beyond the ballot box we'll need other forms of support."

"That, too, can be arranged," Thompson said easily. "We can ship revolvers, rifles, and ammunition immediately."

"We'd only need them if other persuasion fails."

"Oh, I understand. The South wanted to negotiate in 1861 but it was up to people like me and Jefferson Davis to ensure we were ready if talks failed. I pledged my own money to buy arms. We didn't want the war but had to be ready. And you are dealing with the same deceitful rabble in Washington."

Smith grew silent and Thompson let the message sink in.

A sailor tossed a rope to snug a small schooner to the lock wall. As the rope tightened, two black men slung bags over their shoulders to carry to a wagon.

"Damn blacks are everywhere," Smith muttered as the pair returned for another load. "This was one of the stations on the abolitionist underground railroad. If I had my way, they would all be in the British colonies."

"You could make the rules. Indiana, Illinois, Ohio, Michigan, Wisconsin, all of the old Northwest could be a new Confederacy."

"It may come to that," Smith admitted. "And we're ready to fight if necessary but we need time. We can't be ready in a month."

"Speed up the process," Thomson warned. "The major Democratic rally set for Indianapolis will draw thousands. That could be the time for action."

"I'm not so sure," Smith countered. "It's hard to coordinate the action of all the castles. That's what we call our units. We need time, another month anyway…"

"And the other men feel the same way?"

"Oh yes, I'm sure. Give us a month. We can meet again and work out the details."

"Then we don't need to return to the others," Thompson told him. "You can pass on what we have discussed."

"I'll do that," Smith agreed. "That's what leaders are for."

Thompson offered the ritual secret handshake but as he watched Smith move off, he thought of what was missing. In 1861, Davis, Benjamin and himself, men with government or military experience, stepped forward. The Copperheads of the Northwest had only bit players.

Hines and Castleman lounged by the door as he returned.

Hines spotted a scrap of paper on the floor. After a quick glance, he showed it to Thompson. "August 16, the call to arms," it read.

"Damn. I warned them about this. They use phony names with us but leave hard evidence behind them."

"There was loose talk at the hotel last night, too," Castleman said as Thompson ripped the paper to shreds. "Thousands of men, Republicans burned in hell."

"I suspected as much. It's why I was deliberately vague on military support."

"Have you heard from Richmond?" Hines wanted to know.

"Morgan has moved into Kentucky," Thompson began, "to work north. Forrest could be ordered up the Mississippi. But the army won't commit until Sherman is dealt with. You will have at least a month."

Hines accepted the logic and added, "By then we'll have more men on the ground in Canada. There are only five, let's say, undercover at the farm, but more are coming."

* * *

LONDON, CANADA WEST: AUGUST 1864

Hines awoke to the distant peal of church bells. The summer sun warmed the hotel room and a light breeze brushed the curtains by the open window. He poured what was left of the water into the basin, bent, and immersed his face, shaking his head slightly to stir the tepid water, before reaching for the towels.

The journey from Chicago was interrupted by a series of breakdowns and delays. More soldiers than usual watched the American ferry from Port Huron but the customs shed on the Canadian side was closed and no one checked papers. It was well past midnight when he reached London's Tecumseh House.

He shaded his eyes from the bright sun and gazed from the third-floor room. The station below was quiet but in the rail yard, men worked on the engines. Several blocks away, he saw colored faces en route to a small frame church. That was the black section, he recalled, close to the tracks and to any work the Great Western Railway might offer. He remembered one street name and smiled. It seemed to demonstrate the Canadian way: not white, not black, but Grey Street.

A single bell began to toll from the black church. The bells that awakened him had come from the larger cathedral up the street. Jacob Thompson would be in the sea of white faces at the Cathedral of St. Paul. A few black faces would be sprinkled in the congregation but not enough to raise concern.

The Americans had completed a study of the escaped slaves in Canada West. The Freedmen's Inquiry Commission was the work of abolitionists and would boost the emancipation process. The Buxton experiment was praised and while the authors found

grudging acceptance of Negroes in the large cities, they found prej-
udice in smaller centers. The first Africans were welcomed but now
many as sixty thousand might be competing for jobs and money.
Hines heard the same complaints in Canada West that he heard in
Illinois. There were too many colored people and more might be
coming.

* * *

Jacob Thompson would not recall the words of the sermon, but
instead would remember the British regiment and the pews filled with
scarlet. Pockmarked faces and scars offered mute evidence of brushes
with disease or combat. Their barracks, a block away, showed obvious signs of wear. No amount of fatigue duty and paint would conceal
the evidence of a government reluctant to earmark cash for colonial
defense.

He glanced across the church to where a visiting officer sat. He had
a casual introduction and suspected Lt. Col. William Jervois might
inadvertently help the Southern cause.

The director of fortifications for the British army had completed an intensive study of the colonies. His first report to the
British and Colonial governments was shelved, but in a sign of
growing unease he had been dispatched a second time. He was to
review again the garrisons and posts that faced the American border. Thompson had learned of the growing debate and the Confederates had planted questions about the Northern intentions.
Would Lincoln, Seward, and Stanton be content to disburse the
army when the war ended or would they send the forces against
the British colonies?

As the service ended, the troops marched off while Jervois mingled
with the congregation. He would hear of how about important the
local garrison was to the fate of the empire. Let unsaid would be how
important the garrison was to local business.

* * *

LONDON, CANADA WEST: AUGUST 7, 1864

"Hurrah, hurrah for the First Hussars," a child's voice and applause rose from the street. The commotion brought the men to the windows of the Tecumseh House to peer below. A glance told Tom Hines that the twenty riders were part of a new Canadian volunteer cavalry on drill.

"They have smart uniforms," Breck Castleman smiled.

"Yes, they look impressive," the man who called himself Jones added to a few murmurs of agreement.

A dozen members of the Sons of Liberty had arrived for the meeting, men from across the American Northwest with their hands out. They sought more money, more guns, and the one thing the Confederates could not promise: more time.

Ten rebels had already started for Chicago, travelling by boat from Goderich in Canada West. With stops along the way, the voyage might take a week. A second week would be spent surveying the city and making the necessary contacts.

Another fifty men would slowly make their way by land, arriving in time for the Democratic convention. Thompson, Hines, and Castleman assured the meeting that the Confederates were ready. All that was lacking was the assurance that the Sons of Liberty would join when the signal came.

Thompson rapped on the table. "We can't be definite, for obvious reasons, but General Morgan is prepared to move north. The Federals will commit troops to stop him and that will make things easier for us. Colonel Jessop from Morgan's command will mount diversionary raids along the Ohio River. Captain Hines is in contact with the prisoners at Camp Douglas. That's six thousand men. Add them to your force and the whole Northwest belongs to you."

Thompson was threading a fine line. He needed to inspire the Sons of Liberty without raising fears of what might happen to homes and families. It was no time to conjure images of a city in flames or unruly gangs. "Now you must move quickly to establish authority. New leaders will have to step forward and those leaders will come from the men in this room."

157

Jones, Smith, and the others all nodded their agreement.

"The South has no designs on territory," Thompson reminded them. "But when we regain control of the Mississippi, we will want to re-establish the old commercial ties."

"All sounds fine," Jones said, glancing at the faces around the table. "But I'm just not sure we have the time to get men in place."

"Yeah, in my county, the revolvers arrived but there was no ammunition and a lot of the farm boys need training," another man voiced his concern.

"A few more weeks would make a big difference," another added.

"Gentlemen," Thompson said, rising from his chair. "Perhaps a rest will do us good. Let's meet again tomorrow morning."

"Yes," Jones sighed. "Dinner and a good night's rest will make our decision easier."

"But we can't wait long," Hines said, ignoring Thompson's warning glance. "Time is running out."

* * *

"There can be no delay," Hines told them the next morning. "My men are on their way. If we can't act when the Democrats open their convention, we'll lose a golden opportunity."

Thompson absently opened an envelope.

"There will be no better time. Confederate forces are on the move—"

"A moment please," Thompson interrupted. "This letter may change things." He waved a sheet in the air.

"Judge Bullett has been arrested in Kentucky."

"No, it can't be." Jones voiced the shock that showed in other faces.

"Oh, it's true." Thompson grew angry. "Joshua was here last week and returned with money for the organization. I warned him to carry gold or greenbacks but he disregarded my advice. The Federals have my check. The connection will be used to discredit the Democratic Party and the Sons of Liberty. And someone from your organization must have turned him in. You've a traitor in the ranks."

"That seems a little strong," Jones began but stopped as Hines rose.

"You have to act now," he warned. "You can control your own destiny...wait long enough and a squad of men in blue, perhaps black men in blue, will take you away."

Jones looked up and down the table before he spoke. "We can try." He hesitated. "But I think we will need more time."

CHAPTER 23

Meadville, Pennsylvania: August 1864

The travelling wore on Annie Cole. The journey took them into hamlets called towns, or towns called ports with little more than a rough beach, a dock, or a small river draining into Lake Erie.

Charles Cole met local business leaders, but not before carrying art supplies to the shore. While he discussed oil speculation, his wife sketched harbor facilities and landmarks. No one seemed to notice as she painted fortifications or the position of a gun battery. Charles Cole had grown more belligerent as the summer progressed. Part of it stemmed from her demand for separate rooms. Only once had she given in to his desire and then only to win an appeal for cash. Cole had needed another handful of greenbacks to convince her to follow him on a visit to an oil-boom town.

One glance and Pit Head repulsed her. The settlement was a collection of shanties arranged in haphazard fashion across a small valley. The few substantial buildings were framed with rough, fresh-cut wood. The structures lacked permanence; each was built to be dismantled when the owner moved on.

Rains left the main street a sea of mud. Horses and mules struggled to haul wagons filled with equipment for the wells or returned with smeared wooden barrels of crude.

Drill sites sent black grease sliding down a river bank to mix with the crude sloshing from overfilled barges. The water was coated with petroleum. On the bank, she saw three young children skimming oil into small containers.

Cole left her in the lobby of what passed for a hotel. A long sink running the length of the wall allowed each arrival to wash away the grime but offered nothing to clean the residue that clung to clothes.

The lobby was reminiscent of a busy New York depot with every passenger late for a train. In the corner, a harried telegraph operator bent over his key to send a constant stream of messages to the outside world. By his side, a cue of anxious men waited their turn to advise of a deal completed or to wire for more cash.

She made her way toward on empty chair but a man pushed past and sat. As she considered the next move, she heard a soft male voice. "You are welcome to a seat."

He rose from a small couch and motioned to an empty space. She noted blue eyes, a small well-trimmed moustache, and clothing that suggested a man who cared about appearance. A hint of male cologne drifted over her.

"Why, thank you. It is a pleasure to see that gentlemen exist."

"The pleasure is mine." His eyes sparkled as they settled together.

"I'm J.W. Booth."

"I'm Annie, Annie Cole. My husband," she said, slipping into her charade, "is looking for investment properties, but promises to return soon. I hope he does!"

"Pit Head is not a place one expects to find a lady," Booth told her. "So this is a delightful surprise. A few hours ago, I looked and smelled like a driller but this so-called hotel does have a private bathhouse."

"So you are in the oil business?"

"Like your husband, I suspect. Perhaps we should compare notes."

"I'm sure Charles would be delighted," she told him, knowing that Cole would welcome any information. And it would give her time to learn more about this man. "You are so young, Mr. Booth. I imagined investors to be older. You must have a magic touch?"

"I have been lucky. I am taking a break from a career which rewarded me well but I want to consider other possibilities." His eyes indicated possibilities beyond material gain.

"What did you do?"

"I am a thespian, an actor, who comes from a long line of actors."

"The Booth family. Of course. You played Cleveland last fall. I saw the posters but I was—well—er—I was committed elsewhere. I hope to see a performance in the future."

"I have booked two shows in Meadville. It's not that far away."

"What a surprise. Charles and I will be there this weekend." She didn't know or care what plans Charles might have.

Booth produced a card with his name and picture. "Show this to the theater manager. Two seats will be reserved on Saturday."

He rose with a lithe motion. "I will look forward to seeing you and," a polite afterthought, "your husband and perhaps dinner after the performance?"

"That will be grand."

He gave a slight bow and moved away but the scent of cologne lingered.

* * *

MEADVILLE, PENNSYLVANIA: AUGUST 13, 1864

Annie Cole was no judge of drama but Johnny Booth on stage was as captivating as he was in person. Booth performed scenes from his Shakespearean repertoire. She could feel his eyes on her in her front-row seat.

Charles was on his best behavior. He led the audience in a long round of applause and chatted with those around him. "Remarkable. I saw Edwin Booth in New York and was impressed, but this younger brother puts him to shame. This young man ranks with his late father." Annie doubted if Charles had seen the other Booths but when it came to acting, Charles could turn in a masterful performance. It continued at a late diner as the Coles joined Booth in the hotel dining room. First, the talk was of acting, then of the oil business, and finally as the night wore on and the wine bottles emptied, of the war.

"I was there when it started," Booth told them. "I was in Richmond and joined the militia when it was ordered to Charles Town, so I was in the ranks when old John Brown dropped into eternity. We saw him as a crazy old fool but the North has made him a saint, and how many good men have gone to their graves for his silly cause?"

"I couldn't agree more," Cole said.

Cole was holding his liquor better than usual. Perhaps it was the meal and the food but she could detect only a slight slur.

Charles glanced around the almost deserted dining room but still lowered his voice and leaned toward Booth. "I fought for the cause. I took the oath of allegiance to avoid the hell holes of Yankee prison camps but I haven't given up."

The two non-combatants locked eyes across the table. One, she knew, was a coward and had probably thrown down his weapon at the first sign of danger. She waited to hear the other man's story.

"I've travelled the South since the war began," Booth continued. "I can do more outside of the army than in the ranks. I pass what I see to the right people. And the medical supplies, the quinine, I've smuggled south has aided many a soldier."

Cole motioned for wine. "I may be more effective in—shall we say—the special service."

"What sort of special service?" Booth asked.

"Special operations, action behind the lines, can't say more than that."

Annie bit her tongue. Charles had never come this close to talking about their work in public.

"Oh, Charles, you are no spy. Pay him no mind. He's rambling."

But Cole was beyond advice. He had found a like-minded soul. "Perhaps, you should meet my friends—in Canada."

"Charles!" She tried to change the subject. "The friends in Canada are interested in oil, not war."

"Loss of work needs to be done!" Cole went on, the slur more pronounced. "Bring the war north, make them suffer, cause all kinds of hell…more than one way to skin a cat." He made less sense with every sentence. "Or take the head off a snake; that would do it. Cause bloody hell in Washington!"

She glanced at Booth and saw a half smile.

"That's an interesting idea, Mr Cole. What would you do? Blow up the capital? Shoot General Grant? Perhaps kidnap Lincoln?"

"Piss on kidnap! Kill him, a gunshot. Or something from the theater—a poisoned cup. That would do it." He motioned for Booth to draw closer. "You are one of us. I can see it. Go to Toronto or Montreal and meet Thompson. No. No, Thompson doesn't have the guts. Talk to Sanders…to George. He's the one with ideas and guts."

Cole sank in his chair, the energy spent.

Annie called to the waiter. "Excuse me, my husband is indisposed. Can you help us get him to the room?"

* * *

Cole awoke in an alcoholic haze and lurched from the bed to the adjoining room.

"Annie," he whispered loudly, "Annie? Pinkie? Are you here?"

A shawl was tossed carelessly across a chair, the only sign of recent habitation. Cole stumbled across the room and pulled a chamber pot from beneath the bed. As he emptied his bladder, fragments of the evening returned. Annie smiling at Booth across the table, Booth telling of travels in the South, and welcoming Cole's idea to do away with Lincoln.

He buttoned his pants and swayed before spotting a half-filled bottle. He sniffed and lifted the bottle for a deep gulp. Refreshed, he tottered to a chair by the window, planting the bottle on the sill while he absently pulled a pocketknife from his jacket. It took him the rest of the bottle to finish his handy work.

Scratched on the glass was, "Abe Lincoln departed this life by effects of poison, August, 13, 1864."

He untied the curtain, letting it fall across the window to hide his masterpiece. He'd show her in the morning.

Two rooms away, Annie Cole stirred. Booth—Johnny—lay beside her. His arm and hand lay across her stomach, and in the moonlight, she read the tattoo, J. W. B.

She would have to ask why he had ruined those perfect hands with a meaningless tattoo. But it was just one of the many mysteries that surrounded her sleeping companion. Johnny had his secrets!

CHAPTER 24

Washington: August 1864

"They're turning on women and children!"

Lafayette Baker thought it sounded just right, a mixture of shock and indignation. To add to the performance, he stormed around the War Department office.

"Jubal Early should be hanged for burning Chambersburg. Oh, I know it was one of his officers but a commander takes the blame. Asking for ransom and firing a town is beyond the rules of war."

"Save your indignation for another audience! We're no angels. The rebels consider it tit for tat," Peter Watson said, rejecting the theatrics. "I didn't ask you here to talk about Chambersburg. What's the latest from Canada?"

"Everything's connected," Baker told him. "Chambersburg, Early, and the Confederates in Canada. Early wanted to free the rebel prisoners at Point Lookout but we were moving them north before the rebels could get there."

"The connection, I suppose, is the prisoners?"

Baker needed no prodding. "Think of Camp Douglas, Rock Island, Camp Chase, Johnson's Island, and a handful of smaller prisons. The rebels want to free the prisoners and they're counting on the Sons of Liberty to join them."

"And will they?"

"A year ago, the men in the Northwest might have tried, but the war machine is now cranking out jobs and money. The Sons of Liberty are little more than hot air."

"And the Confederates don't know that?"

"A few suspect it. We could arrest the agitators anytime but then the rebels might try something on their own. That's when it could get dangerous."

"You have a watch on them?"

"Oh, Mr. Watson, a near perfect watch. The rebels disappear but we track their associates and sooner or later, a head pops up. And we watch Democrats. A few arrests would make people see what the Democrats are up to. It might win more votes for Mr. Lincoln."

The administration was growing desperate and even the president was losing hope. The desire for peace was growing but there was no end in sight to the war. After the debacle of the peace talks at Niagara, Lincoln allowed a secret mission to Richmond suspecting correctly that it, too, would end in failure.

A miracle was needed before the fall elections but Watson knew that miracles didn't just happen. They could be made.

* * *

AMHERSTBURG, CANADA WEST: AUGUST 1864

The bag tossed carelessly from the top of the stagecoach landed with a thud at the feet of John Yates Beall.

"Careful, David," the black driver cautioned his assistant. "Don't damage the luggage."

At home in Virginia, Beall would have delivered a tongue-lashing but this was no time to attract attention. News travelled fast through the black communities and there were more black faces than he expected.

From the coach he had glimpsed what once was the fortified stone complex of Fort Malden. With proper artillery, the location controlled the entrance to the Detroit River and passage to the Upper Lakes, but other passengers told him it was now an asylum for the insane. The stone walls built to keep invaders out kept the deranged contained.

He reached for the bag only to see it disappear into the hand of young black boy.

"I'll carry it for you, sir. Will you be going to the Frazer House?" The youngster moved off without waiting for an answer. "That's where most gentlemen stay, where the steamer stops, and only steps from the government dock. I'm Cletus Washington."

Beall guessed the boy was about twelve, tall for his age but thin and none too strong. The bag scraped the surface of the dust-covered street.

"Been mighty hot lately!" Cletus switched the bag to the other hand. "Get quick storms though, cool it down right quick."

Beall remembered the process in Virginia. A young black would serve in silence. Here, the attitude was different.

"First time in Amherstburg?" the boy asked. "Lot of Americans come, even old Abe Lincoln."

Beall maintained a strict silence but the boy was undeterred.

"Yup, Abe walked right down this street. Just imagine that stove-pipe hat moving through the crowd. I didn't seem him myself but I heard about it. Mrs. Lincoln has family across the Detroit River and they came over to look around."

A whistle sounded in the distance.

"That will be the steamer from Sandusky," Cletus told him, suddenly picking up the pace. "She'll arrive in about ten minutes but don't worry, we'll get you to the Frazer before she docks."

The boat emerged from behind the line of buildings to fight a strong current as it edged toward the landing. Painted on the paddle-wheel were the words "*Philo Parsons.*"

"How often does she run?" Beall watched the ship approach.

"Oh, you can catch that one or another boat any day but we better hurry. Those passengers will be looking for rooms, too, and first come, first served is the rule. Best you hurry, sir!"

Cletus broke into a jog, tapped a reserve of energy and leaped the steps onto the lower veranda. "There you are!"

In the South, he would stand patiently. Instead, he extended a brazen black hand. "Folks have paid me as much as a dollar to hall their bags."

"Where I come from, young black men should never appear saucy."

Cletus flinched and the coin the man produced was much less than he expected.

"In the future, mind your manners."

The man turned his back to enter the hotel. Cletus went in the opposite direction. He ran to the dock, arriving in time to help a pretty white women collect her bags.

* * *

THE FARM, CANADA WEST: MID AUGUST 1864

George Ellsworth was the last to arrive. The man, nicknamed "Lightning," was awkward on a horse, an unlikely choice for the cavalry. But John Hunt Morgan hadn't cared about his riding ability and neither did Tom Hines.

Ellsworth had trained under Samuel Morse. He refused to say if his name came from his speed on the telegraph key or a shock from a summer storm. But he was the "damn Canadian" who helped outfox Union forces, tapping the lines to read Federal orders or send messages to confound the enemy.

"Captain Hines?" The surprise showed as he pulled the horse to a stop and swung down to the ground. "No one told me you were here."

"The world is full of surprises." Hines took the extended hand. "And it's Tom—no more mention of captain."

"That's fine, never did care for the military mumble jumble."

Both men froze as a howling mass of canine energy charged toward them.

"Brutus, heel." The British voice carried across the yard.

Ellsworth stepped behind Hines. "Oh Christ, that bugger will kill me."

Grenfell had never forgiven Ellsworth for an incident earlier in the war. The telegrapher had taken Grenfell's mount during a skirmish but came out on the wrong side of the fight and lost the horse. Later he learned Grenfell had hidden a small bag of gold coins in the saddle. The pair adopted an uneasy truce but the animosity remained. The dog took an instant dislike to Ellsworth.

"Come inside," Hines laughed. "The other men will step in if it comes to blows. Besides, it's time to talk of what's ahead."

The farm operation had changed since Hines arrived in April. In addition to daily chores, Linslow and Fletcher began to box rifles, revolvers, and Bowie knifes. A steady stream of shipments marked "Sunday school supplies" went to sites in Indiana, Illinois, and Ohio.

With the hint of fall in the air, Homer Linslow lit a fire and then glanced at Hines.

"Go prepare the demonstration, Homer. We'll join you later."

Linslow plucked a jacket from a hook, picked up a small satchel, and limped into the dusk.

As the door closed, the other men turned to Hines.

"First, Homer is being sent away for his own protection. A stranger has been asking questions in the neighbourhood. Since Homer isn't coming, the less he knows the better. The rest of us will be in Chicago when the Democratic convention begins."

Hines rubbed his hands before the stove and began to explain. "I'll start with a quick lesson in presidential politics. Lincoln and Andrew Johnson have been nominated on what's called the Union ticket. The Republicans know they can't win under their own party name and the president is so unpopular he may even be replaced. General Freemont heads a third party bid for the White House but he's not likely to get far. That leaves the Democrats as the only hope for the people who want to end the war."

He waited a moment, glancing at the ten men in the room—the ten he had selected to lead the operation.

"As the Democrats open their convention, the telegraph lines will be cut. Only one wire will be intact, and it will carry a report that Union troops are breaking up the convention. George, word it for maximum confusion; 'Federal attack on the Democrats, Lincoln bids for dictatorship,' that sort of thing."

Ellsworth began to think of the new assignment. The other men waited for Hines to continue.

"We won't be alone. Fifty men are on the way from Canada and Confederate units will be slipping in from Missouri. Our biggest asset will be the Sons of Liberty, a group with thousands of supporters. With their help, we're also going to storm Camp Douglas and free our prisoners."

The room was silent as the extent of the plan began to sink in. Hines waited a full minute before he resumed.

"The Sons of Liberty will be taking over the city hall, the armories and other key locations. The Federal troops in the city are not well-trained, so most will give up and we'll be able to handle any that don't. It won't matter what the convention does because the Sons of Liberty will create a new Northwest Confederacy.

"It's an ambitious plan, Thomas." The British voice pronounced judgement. "As you gentlemen may be aware, I am officially a non-combatant having given my pledge not to engage in hostilities, but I will come as an observer. But here's an important question: Will the right people lead this new Northwest Confederacy? They must be men with spunk, not disorganized rabble."

The room was silent again.

"We have to hope so."

A knock on the door interrupted any further questions.

"The demonstration is ready," Linslow called.

"We'll be right there, Homer."

Hines scanned the room, briefly searching each face. "This must sound very ambitious. I'll go over the individual assignments tomorrow, so save any questions. And while I can't give details, I can tell you our plans coincide with another major rebel raid .The Confederate leadership believes these co-ordinated actions will change the course of the war."

* * *

Linslow was waiting outside by a large pile of branches and discarded wooden timbers. A burning torch offered the only light. He held a small glass bottle.

"Each man will be given a small valise with three bottles inside. The bottles will be wrapped and well protected, but avoid hard vibrations. Now watch."

He hurled the bottle onto timber. The glass shattered and a strong stench like rotten eggs drifted over the men. Brutus sniffed the air and growled as a sheet of flames erupted and spread across the wood.

"Greek fire," Linslow laughed as the flames rose. "It's your new secret weapon."

CHAPTER 25

Amherstburg, Canada West: August 1864

Beall was tired after the afternoon walk, a lingering effect of the bullet that ended his career with Stonewall Jackson's Foot Cavalry. Months of recuperation with family in Iowa and Canada West had helped rebuild his strength, but physical exercise left him drained. He drew relief from the warmth of the last rays of the sun as he waited on the upper veranda of the Frazer House.

The day had been a disappointment. Only half of the men had arrived to take lodging around the town. Another ten, the key players, had been delayed.

The other problem lay with the Sons of Liberty. He suspected the local leadership was adept only in sharing secret handshakes.

Beall spent a single night at the Windsor "castle" before moving downriver. In Amherstburg, sailors waiting for lake work would be a familiar sight.

The woman walked in the path of the setting sun and only when she drew near could he see her face.

"Oscar?" she asked.

Beall had tried to memorize the names used by the Confederate Secret Service. The cipher worked for written messages when there was time to think. Remembering the oral codes and the constant changes were another matter. The women solved his dilemma.

"Carson sent me. I'm Belinda."

It all flooded back. Belinda was the agent from Sandusky. Carson was the code name for Jacob Thompson.

"It's a pleasure to meet you, Belinda." He guided her to the end of the veranda, casually leaned over the railing, and finding no one in listening distance, motioned to a pair of high-backed chairs. "I believe we are to discuss investments in the oil business."

"My husband has been investigating several properties," she told him, completing the passwords and countersigns and then sighed with relief. "My name is Annie but I guess it doesn't really matter. Charles, er, Captain Cole has gone to Erie to make final arrangements."

She felt uncomfortable calling Cole, a captain. She doubted he had earned any rank but Thompson accepted his story and his refusal to use an alias.

"Why Erie?"

"It's the homeport for the *Michigan*. Captain Cole has been wining and dining the officers."

"He's working alone?" Beall was shocked.

"No, no. There are local members of the Sons of Liberty, at least a dozen."

"Even a dozen can't take on the crew of *Michigan*. Those are professional sailors."

She had the same misgivings but answered with what Charles had told her. "He plans a special chemical ingredient for their dinner."

"Does he have anyone on board he can trust?"

"That's why he's in Erie. He thinks a few can be bought."

"*Thinks?*" Beall didn't like what he heard. "What about the island?"

"They're ready." She knew the prisoners would move at the first sign of rescue. "They have only a few revolvers and pieces of lumber. But they're ready and want to know when."

"As soon as the rest of my men arrive, but that could be the middle of September. There's a delay."

Her heart sank. The best hope for success was a coordinated push timed to the uprising in Chicago.

"Tell them not to worry," Beall assured her. "When the Northwest blows, the confusion and uncertainty will last for weeks and with the ship we can range across the lakes. But tell Cole he needs more men in the town and on the *Michigan*. A delay will give him more time."

He rose to leave but her hand on his arm stopped him. Ben Cooper had raised a question.

"The prisoners want to know where they are going."

"Tell them they're going back to war."

* * *

HALIFAX, NOVA SCOTIA: AUGUST 20, 1864

Hundreds gathered along the Halifax waterfront as the rebel warship docked. The *Tallahassee* was only ten days out of Wilmington but the voyage shocked the American coast. Thirty-three ships had been captured and all but a handful burned. From New York to Maine, ships fearfully scurried to port and insurance rates soared.

Officially, the need for coal brought her to Halifax. Unofficially, she had passengers to disembark. Only the officers on the *Tallahassee* had uniforms. The crew wore civilian garb and matched the appearance of the locals who clambered along the docks.

Commander, John Taylor Wood, hand picked the ten men leaving the ship. The special crew included mechanics, engineers, and artillery officers, and with their experience, a captured ship could quickly be turned against the enemy. Wood had honed their skills in successful raids on the Chesapeake to the delight of his uncle, Confederate President Jefferson Davis.

The men who slipped ashore in Halifax exchanged places with ragged workers sent through Weir and Company, a Halifax shipping agent engaged by the South. In the confusion on the docks, no one paid attention to the two large crates offloaded from the ship or the exchange of men. Escapees from Northern prison camps would keep the *Tallahassee* at strength as she returned to the South.

* * *

CHICAGO, ILLINOIS: AUGUST 27, 1864.

Tom Hines was uneasy from the time he stepped on the station platform in Toronto. He scanned the crowd, watching for any small mistake that would give a detective away, but saw nothing. If someone was on his trail, the fellow knew his job. Grenfell created a scene demanding his dog ride alongside him and while he argued with the conductor, Hines slipped aboard. Grenfell would be remembered; the other raiders would escape scrutiny.

The first hours were quiet but the train grew crowded as it crossed Illinois. Rowdy Democrats en route to the convention packed the cars and a hundred miles from Chicago it was standing room only. Grenfell wasn't bothered. A growling Brutus ensured extra space.

At the Richmond House, raucous delegates paid no heed to the small group claiming to be part of the Missouri delegation. The impromptu speeches, the music, and offers of liquid refreshment turned the hotel corridors to a circus but in a quick meeting with leaders from the Sons of Liberty, Hines heard assurances that all was in order. His Confederates were in place, those who had sailed from Canada West, those who took the trains, and a few who arrived on horseback.

Clement Vallandigham made a triumphant entrance with the Ohio delegation but deliberately moved to the opposite side of the lobby when Hines caught his eye. He offered no recognition.

* * *

At the beer garden on Cottage Grove, Theo Schultz struck up a conversation with a guard from Camp Douglas.

"I work more hours." The man struggled with English but was determined to learn the language. "The commander says all guards must work. No break for many days. Maybe when the new troops come."

"New troops, more troops?" Schultz asked.

"Ya, lots more soldiers to come. The big-bang guns, too."

"Big bang," Schultz was puzzled for a moment. "Big guns—cannon?"

"Ya, and they aim in…not out…aim at the prisoners. But no big balls, the shells spread out like the shootsguns."

"Cannister?" Schultz asked.

"Ya! That's the word." The guard sloshed down the last of his lager and slapped the glass on the table.

"Another?" Schultz asked.

"Ya!"

* * *

Two miles away, Billy Parker, a late addition to the raid, strolled through the city. He explored communities of ragged shacks, packed three-story tenements, and finally a neighborhood of fine houses where a dozen cows fought for space on the street.

"Get out of the way!" a boy driving the little herd yelled. "These cows have to be milked and be back on the common pasture by dark. The rich folks are waiting for fresh milk."

"Do you drive them to their houses?" Parker was intrigued. "And back to the pasture?"

"Of course," the boy scowled. "Democrats must all be country rubes. How else would you get the milk? I'll be glad when this convention is over. Rubes like you and horse soldiers are scaring the cows."

Parker was amused. "You should be used to cavalry and crowds in this city."

"Well, yeah, rube," the boy said, slapping a cane across a cow's rear. "But the last couple of days there are lot more soldiers on foot and on horseback. A few blocks over, they are so thick I couldn't drive the cows through."

* * *

George Ellsworth silently moved his lips sounding out each word on the poster before edging his way to the counter in the Western Union telegraph office.

"I can read and that's about recruiting," he proudly told the agent and pointed to the poster. "But I want to know how to send a message."

"Simple. Compose a message, pay me, and I send it."

"You can send it from back there where those army folk are?" Ellsworth asked and peered at soldiers huddled over instruments at the back of the office.

"It might be delayed," the agent confessed.

"The army telegraphers get priority. New orders are being processed for fresh troops."

"Maybe I'll just wait," Ellsworth decided. He motioned the agent to bend closer. "I hear the army is going to bust up the convention so Lincoln won't face another competitor. You be careful. Those soldiers are as likely to bust a fellow's head as look at him."

And then he slipped away to tell Tom Hines what he had learned.

* * *

Hines slammed the door to a large meeting room, leaving Parker and Shultz to lounge in the hall and ensure there was no interruption. He walked quietly to the table where Breck Castleman was seated. A day ago there had been thirty members of the Sons of Liberty, tonight only a dozen.

"We're ready," he told them. "How many men can we count on?"

From the street, he could hear chants from exuberant delegates but the men in the room were quiet.

He repeated the question and finally Hiram Smith, one of the leaders from southern Illinois spoke.

"Only about half of my men have shown up, although there may be more scattered about that we can't locate. The crowds are bigger than we expected and it makes it hard to find our men."

"Shouldn't your people be finding you?" Castleman asked with contempt.

Smith shrugged. "We gave them money but only about sixty men are where they were supposed to be and some are so far gone in cider they won't be any good. Besides, they may not be needed. With Vallandigham running the convention, we'll have a peace platform."

"I agree, Mr. Smith," Vanecker, a delegate from Iowa, chimed in. "There may be no need for violence. Besides, my men are local politicians, all charged full of piss and vinegar but I wouldn't count on them in a fight."

"We had an arrangement, gentlemen!" The words from Hines were now icy and menacing. "We gave you money and we gave you guns. Confederate troops are at the Ohio border. If you want to control your destiny, this is the time. Think what five thousand men could do. The city can be yours."

Vanecker spoke for the others. "We'll be hard pressed to find five thousand men, especially when they see the extra Federals parading around."

"Those troops are here to break up the convention and to intimidate you." Hines fired the words across the room but the response was only shuffling feet.

Smith summoned the courage to speak. "Now Mr. Hines, we appreciate what you have tried to do. But we've been talking and we don't see how it can done."

"What about the prisoners, the men at Camp Douglas? Bring me five hundred men and we'll have them away."

"Seems to me, that's a problem, too," Vanecker said. "There are extra guards and cannon. Any attack would be suicide." He faced Hines square on. "And any commander who would order one would be guilty of nothing short of murder."

"If you are afraid, others have courage." Hines let the words hang. "With only a few men, we can take the prison camp at Rock Island. That will draw off the Federals. When the troops leave Chicago, you take control."

"That might indeed help the rebels." This time, Smith was back in the argument. "But we've been talking and thinking and decided to stay quiet. Remember Morgan's raid last year. Hell, you were part of it. The stealing and the marauding worked people up. The same thing could happen again and frighten them back to the Union. No,

Mr. Hines, it won't work. We'll beat Lincoln in November without bloodshed."

"It's a mistake. You are losing a great opportunity! Perhaps the last chance!" But Hines's words had no effect.

"Good luck, Mr. Hines," Vanecker said, leading his group from the room. "No hard feelings. Perhaps with an armistice or the end of the war, we'll meet again."

"I am sick of liars and thieves," Hines told his dwindling group of associates as the door closed behind the delegation.

"And what will we do?" Billy Parker asked.

Hines stared to the street below. In the gathering dusk, the delegates marched with torches and burning brooms en route to the convention.

"Billy, we need you to collect the cases of Greek fire. Bring them to me at Walsh's house. He'll still be reliable and can help us find more men in the future. You know where that is?"

Parker nodded. "I'll find it."

"Time is something we have in abundant supply," Hines reminded him. "So be careful and don't hurry. We'll leave a few cases with Walsh and Breck will take the rest. He can find targets for those bottles. There are twenty steamers at a time tied up in Louisville."

"We could use the Greek fire now," Parker urged. "We have our own men—we could burn Chicago."

Hines thought for a moment. "No Billy. We haven't sunk that low."

"What will you do?" Parker asked.

Hines took one last look at the crowded street.

"Billy, we need you in Toronto. Go with Bennet Young. I want to be here should the *Michigan* suddenly appear off Chicago."

CHAPTER 26

St. Lawrence River: August 28, 1864

There was no question about economy. The leaders from the Canadian provinces needed to make an impression and chartering the *Queen Victoria* was a first step. Her black hull and funnel was a familiar sight along the St. Lawrence, but those watching from shore would be surprised at how few passengers were aboard.

Paul Forsey closed the cabin door and reflected on his good luck. Junior clerks seldom had their own accommodation and he would have the room until Charlottetown. After that no one knew what would happen.

Through the summer, proposals were drafted and redrafted while the leaders of the Canada East and West bickered. Finally, a plan emerged to unite all of the British colonies. The next few days would show if Nova Scotia, New Brunswick, Prince Edward Island, and Newfoundland would accept the proposals.

Forsey made his way aft to where John A. Macdonald offered an afternoon "cordial." Macdonald had been on his best behavior, confining his prodigious appetite for liquor to moderate consumption. On only a few days had Hewitt Bernard sheepishly announced, "Mr. Macdonald is indisposed," but there would be abundant temptation ahead.

On the rear deck, the men stood with glasses of wine and large cigars; D'arcy McGee and Macdonald, Alexander Galt, the Finance minister, William MacDougall, another cabinet member and the two Frenchmen, George Etienne Cartier and Hector Langevin, political

181

leaders in Canada East. Forsey and Bernard would be the only staff to support the contingent.

"Our junior clerk has come to join us," Macdonald said, gesturing to the steward for another glass. "No work today. Review the papers tomorrow. Captain Pouliott expects with the storm past, the ship will make a fast run to Charlottetown."

"Have you crossed the water, Mr. Forsey?" McGee sauntered to his side.

"Just once, sir."

"Try it again! John A. and I find the trip soothes the mind. We have work in the next few days but on an ocean crossing, there's time to relax."

"I'll keep that in mind." But Forsey suspected the only way he could afford travel was on the government account.

"A fine day," Cartier observed in English, stepping from under an awning and into the sunshine. A burst of smoke and cinder from the funnel swirled in the wind and Cartier retreated for shelter.

"And now we know why the owner installed the awning," Galt brushed ash from his coat.

"And we wouldn't want him to sue us for damage," Cartier said, kicking a glowing ember across the varnished deck and into the river. "The ship owner will try for every cent. He should be thrilled that government largesse is filling his coffers and let's hope he remembers us at the next election."

Cartier and Langevin stepped to the rail and began to speak rapidly, an animated conversation that Forsey, with his growing knowledge of French, realized dealt with riverfront property. The English speakers drifted into conversation a few feet away.

"This is my first major trip in almost a year," William MacDougall told them, "And I'm hoping this one is happier."

MacDougall was a longtime intimate of the power brokers of Canada West, but he changed his opinion so often he was known as "Wandering Willie." His public career had begun with a newspaper and culminated in the leadership of the Reformers and "Clear Grits."

George Brown had taken control but MacDougall maintained influence.

"Sandfield Macdonald sent me to Washington last fall. I didn't accomplish much on the trade issues but I did see Lincoln in action."

"He can be hard to read, a mix of intellectual and bumpkin," Alexander Galt interjected, "I met him in '61, during the *Trent* crisis. Secretary of State Seward was making all those threatening noises, and some of the Yankees wanted to end their Civil War, and take on the British. The British were ready for a fight and I suppose we were too. Anyway, it was Lincoln who helped defuse the tension."

"A huge relief," Macdonald said, signaling for another glass. "Lincoln did have an ulterior motive. Much of the American gunpowder was imported from England. He wouldn't have been able to fight for long."

"Lincoln was trying to gain control," Galt told them. "In the first few months of his administration, everyone thought the cabinet was running the show. Seward and Chase believed it was their administration."

"Seward still thinks he's running the show," MacDougall told them, "He and Stanton try to run the government but every now and then Lincoln yanks on the chain."

"How long were you in Washington?" Forsey blurted the question and received a harsh glare from Bernard.

"Just a few days in Washington and then to Gettysburg." MacDougall didn't notice the exchange between the clerks.

"Lincoln went for the dedication of the national cemetery. It was macabre. I was delighted that the president kept his speech short. The air stank! Dead horses and mules still lay in the fields. And while the Union dead were reburied, the rebels were still in shallow, sometimes very shallow, graves."

He took a long drag from the cigar and expelled a cloud of smoke.

"You won't be able to see for the cigar smoke in Chicago this week," McGee said, turning the subject from the battlefield. "Gen. George McClellan will have the nomination unless Clement Vallandigham nominates himself. My friends in the states think the Democrats can win the election."

"McGee, your friends are Irish! And most of them can't vote!" Macdonald's words set off a round of laughter.

"True! But they have a grand old time talking about it!"

As the laughter died, McGee grew serious. "Agitators in the Irish community believe the training in the American war is necessary to prepare for the next one, the fight to force the English from Ireland. One group suggests seizing Canada. It sounds silly, but with access to money and guns, well…"

"What does your brother in the American army hear?" MacDougall asked.

"Much less from the rank and file since he's been promoted, but he says the Irish questions are very much alive. The Americans have been quietly recruiting in Ireland and thousands of immigrants join the army as soon as they step off the boat. I worry what will happen when the war ends. Those immigrants know only what they learn in the army, and that's fighting by day or carousing at night."

"The Americans may have to face up to the future sooner than they expect," MacDougall told them. "If McClellan wins, there's a chance of a truce, an armistice."

"But consider the dead," McGee argued. "Anyone who suggests a ceasefire will be admitting the war was a failure, nothing but a tragic waste of men and money."

"Something will have to give. On a purely financial basis, the crisis is growing." Galt took special interest in government budgets and spending. "The war costs millions each day. Both North and South will soon be bankrupt."

Macdonald passed an empty glass to the steward and waved away a refill.

"In a few minutes, perhaps," he told the waiter and waited as the man moved to serve the French contingent.

"I've had a private letter from Washington," he told them. "The story making the rounds says Lincoln knows he can't win." He glanced to where Cartier and Langevin stood.

"Cartier heard the same thing through the French consul although he won't admit that's where his information comes from, just as I can't say where I get my information. Unless there is a great military victory, very soon, Lincoln's goose is cooked! And then what happens? It likely means more uncertainty along our border."

"Have you given more thought to a force of special detectives?" McDougall asked abruptly. "The Confederates are travelling the provinces and are up to no good. The local police have their hands full. I've thought of someone for the job. Gilbert McMicken was in the freight-forwarding business and a customs collector. From what I hear, he's desperate for cash and is taking Southern money to move escaped Confederates to the East Coast."

Macdonald responded quickly. "I do remember him from the legislature. I wish it was my idea." A smile worked across his face. "McMicken was a Tory, as if that would matter to me. And since the suggestion comes from a Reformer, they can't accuse me of hiring only Tories."

He raised his hand to gesture for more wine. "Now perhaps we should join Cartier and Langevin and consider our current challenge. George, Hector," he called across the deck. "Time for food to wash away the wine." He led the small parade to the tables in the stateroom.

Forsey brought up the rear, mentally prepared to add the conversations to the pages of his journal. He glanced across the deck to commit the scene to memory, but jumped at a blast of the *Queen Victoria's* whistle. The captain warned another ship to give way, a battered little steamer churning in the opposite direction.

* * *

THE ST. LAWRENCE RIVER NEAR MONTREAL: AUGUST 29, 1864

Storms and strong winds on the Gulf of St. Lawrence had delayed the passage but the engineers kept the paddle wheels turning. Rough seas might take a toll on novice sailors but not the former crew members of the *Tallahassee*.

185

The weather calmed as the ship passed into the St. Lawrence River and under the British guns at Quebec. Only hours from Montreal, the men were called to the ship's salon. The once elegant room had been stripped and now offered only a long table bolted to the floor.

The *Maria Victoria* was owner Patrick Martin's pride and joy. She was part of a small fleet that successfully carried cargo from Montreal to the American seaboard. Martin, an early Southern sympathizer, had given up a successful liquor business in Baltimore to move his wife and children to the safety of Montreal, after he ran afoul of American officials.

A portly man sat by his side. He had taken special interest when the men moved the heavy crates into an empty cabin and when a young sailor used a special key to open the locks. In the crates were five explosive devices to mine the entrance to harbors or shipping channels. A second box was lighter and contained what appeared to lumps of coal, but each was packed with explosive. A single lump could destroy a boiler on a ship or a railway locomotive.

Martin rapped the table sharply and in the ensuing silence, the quiet was broken only by the dull thump of the paddle wheels pressing through the water.

"I wanted to talk to you before we reach port. You all know me. This charming fellow," he gestured to the other man, "is my partner, Alexander Keith. Mr. Keith's uncle is a very prosperous brewer in Halifax. The uncle, however, does not share our Southern sympathies, so we call our Mr. Keith, 'Keith the younger.' If you return through Halifax, ask for Keith the younger. The elder will slam the door in your face or call the sheriff."

Keith barely budged and gave no sign he was paying attention as Martin continued. "When we reach Montreal, move quickly to the Railway Depot, and take the train to Windsor in Canada West. There, Master Beall suggests the Heron House, a hotel on the river. Ask for 'Defiance' and someone will come for you. After that, it's Beall's show."

"How much do you know about the plan?" asked one of the men.

"The target is Johnson's Island. But I don't know the details."

"What about you, Mr. Keith? How did you get involved?"

Keith blinked to clear his eyes and mind. His voice was high-pitched and had the hint of New England. "Me, I hate to see a tyrant boot upon a noble people!" He squirmed slightly, not used to the attention, but willing to accept any that came his way. "I work the supply side ensuring material is ready when the ships come in. And recently, I've been arranging for the shipment of a locomotive."

"A railway locomotive?" The question came from the back of the room.

"What other kind of locomotive would there be, you ninny!" Keith snapped. "Of course a railway locomotive! We bought it in Philadelphia. In Halifax, we load it on a ship and run the blockade. All it takes is balls and a good strong ship!"

Keith saw a quick flash of anger on Martin's face and knew he was saying too much. "But mostly, Patrick and I line up cargo for the South. Don't think this business is easy or safe. We've lost two ships and if it weren't for the insurance," he glared at Martin, "that I demand we carry, we'd be out of business."

"We'll count on all of you to forget what we've talked about," Martin added. "We'll be in Montreal in two hours. Don't miss the train."

* * *

CHARLOTTETOWN, PRINCE EDWARD ISLAND: SEPTEMBER 4, 1864

"Would you like a hammer?" D'Arcy McGee laughed and bit into the lobster meat as Paul Forsey worked valiantly to extract a small piece from the shell.

"Practice, practice. That's what it takes," McGee laughed again. "My visits to the Eastern provinces allowed me to perfect the art."

The shell slipped from Forsey's hand and flew across the buffet table.

"Ah, never mind. There's more and more of this," McGee said, reaching for another glass of champagne, only to bump against the outstretched arm of John A. Macdonald.

"Mr. McGee," Macdonald laughed. "Great minds think alike."

Forsey suspected both men would end the evening floating on a sea of alcohol but a celebration was in order. The members of the Coalition had whet the appetite of the maritime colonies and a new country might soon stretch from the Great Lakes to the Atlantic.

He reached to sample the crab and followed the politicians as they ate their way down the table. Rich banquets followed each day of the conference in Charlottetown.

"It's going well," Macdonald told McGee. "The ground was well prepared. The work of the clerks in drawing up the proper language and considering all the possibilities put us where we are. Bernard deserves congratulations."

Forsey waited for praise for junior clerks but Macdonald reached for the roast beef.

"Have you canvassed all of the delegations?" Macdonald asked.

"It looks good," McGee told him. "Nova Scotia and New Brunswick are with us but I'm not sure about our hosts here in Charlottetown."

"I'm surprised." Macdonald edged closer to McGee, making it harder for Forsey to hear. The clerk leaned in to pick at another plate of lobster.

"An agriculture minister should know his work," McGee explained. "I had a tour of the countryside. This island is close to revolt. There's real anger about the rents charged by absentee English landlords. The best solution may be to buy the landlords out."

"Oh that," Macdonald scoffed. "I've hinted a new federation might find the funds to do the job. Let it rest until everyone gathers in Quebec City. Ah, move down just a bit so I can reach the potatoes."

"A new nation and an ample table are the dream of every Irishman." McGee smiled before correcting himself, "Or perhaps that's for the old country. This is the new one!"

CHAPTER 27

Chicago, Illinois: September 5, 1864

"It's trouble, Thomas. It could be the end." George Grenfell's words were weighted with grudging resignation. "Lightning has seen the messages and not just one but several. The whole North will celebrate."

The winds off Lake Michigan brought a hint of fall. The fireplace was burning brightly to throw heat and light across the two men. The dog was quiet, accepting Hines as a regular visitor, but maintained a constant surveillance. The head came up as Hines replied.

"It's only one city, and perhaps it a strategic withdrawal to bait Sherman. Gen. John Bell Hood may be setting a trap."

"Oh, come now, Thomas. We both met the gallant Hood. The man is aggressive and brave, even after losing a leg and the use of an arm, but he is not gifted with great intelligence. Granted, he has a gift for winning important friends. Jefferson Davis took a shine to him. But now he faces Sherman and a Yankee army, not a sympathetic politician."

For Hines, the disappointments were compounding, the failure of the Sons of Liberty and now the fall of Atlanta.

Grenfell continued to speak. "It's said Hood deals with great pain. You know the sort, bravery in equal dose to the pain medication. As to the value of Atlanta, think of the factories, war supplies, and railroads. Lincoln has a victory and a new lease on electoral life. The people will support the war if the Union is winning. Grant couldn't give him the breakthrough in Virginia but Sherman gave him Atlanta."

"Lincoln still has to win that re-election," Hines reminded him, "And there are two choices—more war or peace."

"Oh, Thomas, I wish you had a better grounding in the fine art of the politician! See here, all credit to Clement Vallandigham for taking control of the Democratic convention and getting his peace plank. On the surface, we should be expecting an armistice at any moment but look at the candidate. His critics may be right. General McClellan's best attribute is that he looks good, or as they say, he sits a horse well. He might reject the so-called peace plank. What was Vallandigham's advice in that letter he sent McClellan?"

He thumbed through the newspaper to find the article. "Here. *"If anything implying war is presented, two hundred thousand men in the west will withhold their support and may go further still."*

Grenfell flipped the paper aside. "But where were the thousands of people promised you? All talk! The party is split, with Democrats who want to fight on and Democrats who want peace. That's not the recipe for an election victory, especially if Lincoln has wind in his sails."

Hines stared silently into the flames of the fireplace.

Grenfell groaned as he pulled himself from the chair and walked painfully to the tumbler on the nearby table. "I'm getting old, Thomas! The arthritis from too many cold nights is settling in. I planned to return to Canada for hunting and fishing. But damn, it was growing cold there three weeks ago. I think Brutus and I will move south into Illinois and hunt prairie chicken."

The younger man stared through his glass toward the flames. "I've had a message from Thompson, who thinks there's life in the Sons of liberty."

"Then the man is an asshole!" Grenfell snorted.

"He's keeping the pressure on," Hines told him. "Jeremiah Black came to see him. Judge Black was in President Buchannan's cabinet before the war. He served with Thompson and Stanton and says Stanton sent him to Toronto."

Grenfell paid closer attention.

"According to Thompson, more than blood scares the Yankees. The Northern economy is on the verge of collapse, the costs are mounting daily, and the debt is climbing. In fact, Stanton is so worried he wants a guarantee of personal protection."

"The Secretary of War is ready to piss his pants!" Grenfell was enjoying the image. "Ha! Stanton making overtures to save his own skin? What a delightful thought!"

"So you can see why Thompson wants to press on."

Grenfell grew solemn again. "And I'm sure you will, Thomas, a soldier to the end."

He lifted a blanket and draped it across his legs. "I'll be content to leave the thrill of battle to someone else."

* * *

CHICAGO, ILLINOIS: SEPTEMBER 7, 1864

The dog growled and stared at the door. The knock came a few seconds later.

"Easy, Brutus, we know that signal." Grenfell opened the door a few inches and then all the way.

"Thomas, I hadn't expected you so soon."

In the hallway, Hines stood with a newspaper clasped in his hand. He moved slowly into the room and handed the newspaper to Grenfell.

"What is it?" Grenfell looked at a page of the latest dispatches. "I told you it would be in the papers. The Yankees are going to use the fall of Atlanta for all of its worth. They haven't had much to cheer about these last months."

"Not that. Read on." The voice was choking.

Grenfell scanned past the headlines on Sherman and Atlanta. Then he saw, *"Late dispatch from Tennessee. Rebel General John Hunt Morgan killed by Federal forces."*

He stood frozen as the memories flooded back, Morgan and the 2nd Kentucky, mounted Cavaliers, the dash and the spirit at the beginning, the column of fours in the bright spring sunshine of the Blue

Grass. John Morgan was always up for a challenge, but here finally was the challenge that was too much.

Brutus groaned and settled on his haunches. Grenfell forced his eyes to focus. *"Loyal woman brings Union force to Greenville. 100 Confederates killed."* He crunched the paper into a ball and threw it across the room.

"He wouldn't listen! I warned him a year ago. The discipline was falling apart. And the women…And in the end, one does him in."

He saw Hines brush his eyes.

"Were you at the wedding, Thomas?"

Hines managed to answer with a muffled, "No."

"That was the beginning of the end," Grenfell decided.

"Mattie was a child. He brought her shoes, and pins, and cloth when he should have been thinking about the men. General Polk, in his bishop's robes, read the service and Jefferson Davis was there. Yet after that, Morgan was distracted. And in the end, perhaps Mattie wasn't enough. Read between the lines and you see another woman or perhaps a woman scorned."

Grenfell stared off into space. "The last of the cavaliers! Jeb Stewart is gone, and now Morgan."

"It was the general's style," Hines was finding his voice. "I remember when he crossed the Ohio on the Great Raid. The Yankees were close but he took the time to greet me as he would at his home."

"He was what the South wanted, what they all wanted to be." Grenfell leaned forward rubbing his hands across his knees. The dog rubbed against him. "And another hundred men are gone with him. Guns and uniforms can be replaced but the Confederacy is running out of men."

"There's still fight left," Hines reminded him. "Basil Duke will soon be back in action."

"General Duke is a fine man and Morgan's brother-in-law, as is A. P. Hill, generals all, and all part of the family connections of the Southern aristocracy. I wonder if that's why we British like you. The upper classes do stick together. I suspect Duke will have Morgan's command, or what's left of it."

CHAPTER 28

Amherstburg, Canada West: September 10, 1864

The farms along the Detroit River appeared solid and prosperous. Brick houses replaced log cabins, but Beall noticed a cluster of shacks, the homes of former black passengers from the underground railway. He considered knocking sharply on the door to witness the shock of the men and women inside. He might find a familiar face, one that had disappeared in the night from Walnut Grove, the family home near Harper's Ferry. The armies had left a trail of destruction in their wake. His once-prosperous farm was devastated and the slaves were gone.

He slowed the horse to a walk as he inspected the countryside. Colonel Steele, a Southern sympathizer from Kentucky, moved to Essex County when the war began and had been conspicuous in support of the Confederate cause, offering shelter to escaping prisoners or Southern refugees, and today there were very special guests. He turned from the main road and down a rough track. Most trees were still green but the first of the autumn leaves were showing. In the distance, Lake Erie threw waves against the sandy beach.

The horse spooked as a man stepped suddenly onto the track and a second man, revolver in hand emerged. The horse reared and snorted and Beall fought to regain control.

"Looks like you've done some riding." The man with the revolver leaned against a tree. The gun was pointed at the rider.

"Done my share," Beall patted the neck to quiet the animal. "Used to do more but I'm in the oil business now."

"Ain't that a coincidence. We're in the same business and looking for new property. Head to the house and meet the men. The two of us will stay in case there are uninvited guests."

Beall rode on toward a two-story, brick house. A group of men were clustered around two wooden boxes at the door to a barn and a tall man broke from the group.

"I'm Beall," he announced, "Acting Master John Yates Beall."

"I'm Carmen Giles, late of the CSS *Tallahassee* and the Confederate Torpedo Bureau," the tall man said.

"Pleasure to finally meet you, Mr. Giles."

Beall swung from the horse and passed the reins to another sailor. "Now, Giles, perhaps you would introduce me to the crew." Beall liked what he saw. The men were young but each one had service in the Confederate Navy on blockade-runners, or under Wood on his raids along the Potomac and the Chesapeake. More men were coming but they were soldiers. He had met only one, Billy Parker, who brought orders from Thompson.

The rebel master plan was in shambles. Chicago had failed. One small Confederate unit had seized and burned a steamboat on the Ohio but that was the extent of the revolution. Still, the message was emphatic. The raid on Johnson's Island and the capture of the *Michigan* must proceed.

Giles, he noticed, seemed uneasy. The introductions completed, he asked for a moment alone. "What is it?" Beall asked.

Giles lead him to the two crates. "Someone has tampered with the explosives and a few charges are missing."

"Missing, what's missing?"

"The large torpedoes are here but we had sacks with the fake coal and several lumps are missing from one bag." Giles showed his anger and frustration. "Only one person was really interested in them, the Canadian, Martin's partner—Keith. Alexander Keith."

Beall recognized the name. "I was warned off by the people at Weir's. They said not to trust him."

"No one told us anything!"

"God damn!" Beall kicked the lid, slamming the crate shut. "Mr. Giles, it was your responsibility. You could be removed from duty! But that won't happen because we need every man! Are you certain none of the crew is involved?"

"I'm the only one that knows how to handle torpedoes. I've made such a big deal of the danger, the other men are afraid of them."

"Very well. We'll let Thompson know what we suspect. Get the men together."

Inside the house, Beall rolled out the charts. "We have a week to prepare and then we are going to give the Yankees a surprise."

"Excuse me, sir!" Giles spoke from a seat at the window. "Riders coming."

Beall moved to the window to study the two horsemen trotting up the laneway.

"One of them is Colonel Steele," Giles said and waved a sailor with a rifle away from the window.

"And the other is Jacob Thompson," Beall told them. "He's come for a final inspection."

* * *

SANDUSKY, OHIO: SEPTEMBER 15, 1864

The other attacks might fail but Charles Cole knew his work was about to pay off.

Annie had returned from Canada and the latest meeting with her contact and brought his orders. Cole intended to take the matter up with "Oscar" when they met, and Oscar would learn who was really in charge.

The attack would come soon. The cannon fire would be the signal for the prisoners to attack the guards. Cole knew the guards would have the upper hand but what were a few gunshot wounds compared to the brilliance of his planning?

Had "Mrs. Cole" been more receptive, she could have joined his private, pre-raid party, but through the summer, Annie had grown remote. Something had happened between her and the actor, Booth, but he pushed Annie from his mind and returned to the woman stretched on the sofa. Large breasts were peeking around two buttons that held a thin blouse in place. And she was a bargain. Business was slow, she admitted, and would be until the next Federal pay parade.

"Would you care for some wine, Delia?"

Cole kept the expensive whiskey for himself. The local wine would do for his guest. He poured a full tumbler of whiskey and half filled a wine glass.

She rose and walked toward to him but he held the glass out of reach. "Take those stockings off and do it slowly."

The demand became a performance as she bent and slowly removed the stocking. He allowed her to sample the wine and refilled his own glass before the second stocking came undone.

"I'll need help," she told him, pointing to the blouse and then turning to indicate the ties on the corset. She heard the lurching step and felt him fumble with the strings before tearing the undergarment away. His breathing grew heavier. She let him pluck at the buttons on the blouse before guiding him to the couch. In a few short minutes, she earned her pay.

"I may want you again, Delia," his breathing was ragged. "I expect to come into money very soon. Cost will not be an object."

She rose and walked naked across the room. "Rich uncle dead?" the voice was low and taunting as she topped off the glass.

"Nothing that pedestrian, my dear." His words had a slight slur. "It's the war. I am about to be well paid for a very dangerous assignment."

"Oh my!" she cooed.

Other customers during the past three years had offered similar stories and failed to impress her. But Cole took her response as an invitation. He ran his hand along her thigh and up across her stomach.

"Let me draw you a map," he told her. "Very soon, we'll cross the mountains," the hands floated across her breasts and drifted lower.

She gently pushed him aside. He accepted the rejection and poured another glass.

"I'm going to capture the *Michigan* and free the prisoners on the island."

"You are what?" She was used to surprises, but this was different.

"This weekend," he told her. "I've made friends on the ship. Men like Murray, the gunner, and the chief engineer, and the second mate. We're going to have a party on board. I'll provide the booze and add a secret chemical concoction and when they pass out, I will seize the ship."

He wagged a finger as a warning but his whole hand moved. "Go away this weekend. The streets won't be safe."

"And you are going to do this all alone?" she laughed.

"No, no." Cole grew angry. "The Sons of Liberty take my orders. I have them coming by train to take the town."

Cole made an extra effort to stand erect but the whiskey was taking its toll. "I command a Confederate force that will swoop down from the sea."

"And where do they come from?"

"Canada. Let me shows you on the map." He reached toward her but lost his balance and collapsed to the floor and his eyes began to close.

Delia waited to be sure he was asleep before pouring a full glass of whiskey and retrieving her clothes. She had heard wilder stories but the Federal sheriffs would sometimes pay for information. They might even reward her as loyal Union woman.

* * *

CANADA WEST: SEPTEMBER 15, 1864

The cars on the Great Western were crowded and passengers from Chatham had to search for a place to sit. A slim, dark-complexioned woman stood for a moment in the aisle, looking at the bag on the seat. Bennet Burleigh grudgingly shifted his case to the floor.

"Thank you, sir." The diction reflected culture and education. She was well dressed and carried a simple carpetbag but on closer inspection, her complexion gave her away. Light-skinned black, he decided; a servant trained to carry herself well.

"Bennet Burleigh, ma'am." With hours left on the trip, he welcomed any distraction. "Travelling far?" he asked.

Obviously a Scot, she decided. Burleigh was a young man, well muscled and average in height. His eyes were bright and intelligent, his clothes were neat and clean, but the hands were calloused and under the fingernails was an oily stain.

"Detroit, then Chicago, and southern Illinois."

"And won't that be a difficult journey for a woman of color, on her own, or will you meet the mistress en route?" A smug look crossed his face.

"I am a free woman," she snapped. "Quite capable of taking care of myself."

What business was it to him, she wondered? Did he feel coloreds should ride in a separate car?

He turned to watch the passing countryside, deciding she was what friends in Richmond called "an uppity bitch."

"And you, sir. Are you going far?"

He would have thought nothing of conversation if approached by a black man in Glasgow. In Richmond, he might simply ignore her but he wasn't sure on the proper tact in Canada West. "To Windsor," he answered.

"Quite a few of your people are there." She emphasized "people" to drive home the fact that he, too, was different. "Probably a few bagpipers and lots of whiskey."

"We don't all overindulge."

"And we aren't all ignorant slaves. And with that settled, we can converse as intelligent adults. My name is Mary Ann Shadd-Carey."

He fumbled for a reply. "Is that Miss or Mrs.?"

"Mrs. I am a widow. My husband died two years ago."

"It must be difficult. Do you have family to support you?"

"Oh, I have family but I look after myself."

"A trade, then?" Burleigh tried to imagine her as a seamstress or a house servant, and settled on seamstress. The tongue was too quick for a respectable household.

"Yes, I publish a newspaper." She opened the bag and withdrew a broadsheet. "It's a special edition. We don't publish every month."

The front page of the *Provincial Freeman* was filled with announcements of hotels for coloreds, colored doctors accepting patients, and stables where colored business was welcome. The typeset was as professional as anything he had seen in Britain, in the South, or in Toronto.

"All news about colored people?" He was mildly intrigued.

"The information is useful to black and white," she told him. "Since our circulation extends into the United States, we carry articles of interest to all."

A headline told of recruitment for a black regiment. He had seen enough similar ads to know the bounty offered was lower than for white men.

He pointed to the address in the ad. "Does this Delaney really expect to collect men?"

"Mr. Martin Delaney has been very successful. He's already filled regiments in Massachusetts and Rhode Island."

She wouldn't speak of Delaney's problems. He had been forced to escort new recruits to ensure the full bounty was paid.

"But why is he recruiting in the West for Eastern regiments?"

"The black population in the Northeast is small, and men who can go have already signed up. He's hoping to recruit escaped slaves."

Burleigh knew of Southern officers who considered black soldiers an insult and ordered extra fire on their ranks. Others, however were surprised by the courage and the fighting ability of what had been considered a docile, unintelligent people.

"Why aren't white men joining up?" he asked.

"Because they don't have to," she sighed. "Each black recruit means a white man doesn't have to fight. It's not right but what is in this world? Our men are proving themselves. We must ensure the rebels are beaten. Imagine the life of even a free black person, anywhere in the United States, if Jeff Davis has his way."

Burleigh could have told her that the fate of the blacks was an afterthought in the Confederacy. Richmond concentrated on independence. He might have said slaves were only useful for digging entrenchments. But he kept silent.

"And we're proving our value," she continued. "The whites can't turn against us if we help win the war. They need us. That's why Lincoln issued the Emancipation Proclamation."

"How does freeing slaves where he has no influence help anyone? Slaves in the border states are still slaves."

"Read the document," she advised him. "It's a war measure allowing the Union to accept black recruits."

"The Union is taking any recruit," Burleigh countered. "Britain, Ireland, and Germany are scoured for warm bodies. They take the poor devils that can't even speak the language, give them a uniform, press a gun in their hand, and send them off to die. But I guess a black man can die as well as a white man. That's what they call equality."

"Those poor devils you describe are white. Mine are black, and as to equality, that will come."

She spoke with a mix of determination and resignation. "After we are truly free we can work for equality."

"Do you write as well, Mrs. Shadd?"

"Shadd-Carey," she corrected him, "And yes, I write for the *Freeman* and for other papers."

"Other black papers?"

"Yes, only the black papers," she admitted. "It's sad. A writer's color should not matter. But it does."

Mary Ann settled back and in a few minutes appeared to doze off.

The train was arriving in Windsor when she stirred. Burleigh was silent until the train lurched to a stop. "Can I carry your bag?" he asked.

"No need for that. I'll fend for myself."

The conductor made no offer to take her luggage but did reach for Burleigh's case.

A loud voice startled her as a rich Southern accent carried across the platform.

"There you are, you old dog! Welcome to Windsor."

"Oscar, by God," Burleigh laughed and charged across the platform to grasp the man's hand. "It's time to start the party."

ν

200

CHAPTER 29

Lake Erie: September 18, 1864

The waves were running to four feet as the northwest wind freshened to gale force. The door to the pilothouse opened but was caught by a gust and swung until it slapped hard against wooden sheeting. A wet and windblown Bennet Burleigh pulled the door shut, grimaced, and shook his body like a wet dog.

"Foul night, Master Beall." A single oil lamp washed the cabin with a wavering light. A young Confederate sailor on the wheel fought to keep the ship on course.

"It is that, Mr. Burleigh." Beall stood at the rear of the cabin. His attention was torn between the chart and a speck of light from another ship a half mile away. "Giles is keeping that other pig on station." He grasped the chart table as another large wave rolled under them. "We were greedy and kept two ships, but if we get through the night we'll be ahead of the game."

Over the course of the war, the *Philo Parsons* carried everything from soldiers, to fugitive blacks, furtive businessmen, draft dodgers, and ladies of questionable repute. Beall had literally jumped on board at the British dock in Sandwich as the ship began the run to Sandusky. The rest of his crew and two large crates were loaded at Amherstburg.

Sunday morning was quiet but a few hours later, a line of thunderstorms swept the lake. Beall waited nervously for the storms to pass and for the ship to make the first scheduled stop at Main Bass Island.

A few passengers left, along with the captain. His departure indicated there was no fear of any rebel attack.

An hour later, the Confederates struck.

"This ship is now the property of the Confederate States of America." The words reinforced by rebel guns brought instant surrender. Passengers and crew were herded to the main cabin while the Southerners fanned through the ship. Within minutes, an engineer was back. The boiler was in good condition but there was only enough wood for a day and not the two days as expected.

The ship reversed course, returning for more fuel at Main Bass Island and to leave the passengers and original crew. But as the *Philo Parsons* prepared to leave a second time, another steamer reached the dock. The *Island Queen* was jammed with dozens of Union soldiers. Beall waited for signs of guns or cannon but the soldiers were unarmed. A quick volley brought surrender. And a second set of prisoners was confined to the island.

Any soldier worth his weight would try to alert the authorities. But only rowboats remained on Main Bass, and no rowboat could cross the lake as the weather worsened.

Beall glanced across the water, reassured by the light on the *Island Queen*. The chart showed the ships a few miles off Pelee Island and in position for a rendezvous.

"We've had a few surprises but it's gone remarkably well and we're a few hours early."

"Yes, everything seems under control," Burleigh agreed. "The men not on duty have managed to get some sleep and we'll relieve the crew on the *Queen* when the weather clears. I managed to get some rest, so if you want relief, now's the time."

Nervous energy made Beall reluctant to leave the bridge. Instead, he wrapped a blanket around his shoulders.

"Wake me at first light," he ordered. Both men knew the sleep would not be deep.

* * *

WEST HOUSE, SANDUSKY, OHIO: SEPTEMBER 19, 1864

Annie Cole's sleep was full of nightmares. She was standing at the prison waving frantically, but each time the prisoners moved, the Union cannon opened fire and cut young men to shreds.

"Ben!" She willed him to rise. The lower torso responded. The upper torso remained on the ground, the head rising with an expression of sheer terror.

She woke, sat up straight, and tried to shake the image. She had seen Ben only yesterday for the final message. He had been smiling, confident, and hugged her fiercely.

On the signal, the prisoners would attack the guards with wooden clubs and their few revolvers. The youngest and fittest would be ferried to the mainline and commandeer trains for a fighting trip south. The men too weak for action would be ferried to the Canadian shore. The prison complex would be destroyed.

Last night, Cole had been fortified with wine but able to sketch the plan. Gunner John Wilson Murray had reaffirmed the invitation for dinner on the *Michigan*. When the officers passed out, Cole would lock the hatches to confine the crew below deck and by then, Oscar and his men would be at the harbor entrance.

"A damn fine job, Annie," Cole had tipped another glass. "You've been a fine distraction for those nosy Yankees, allowing me to do my work."

He had turned his back, bent to pull a loose board from the floor, and removed a small case. "Here." He thrust an envelope toward her. "A thousand dollars, just in case we are separated. We lived well this summer but there's money left."

She wondered how much would be returned to the Confederate treasury but a tap at the door interrupted her thoughts.

"That will be my special guest." Cole shoved the case back in the hiding place.

"You should go—unless you'd care to stay? The three of us could have a good time." He opened the door and waved the woman into the room.

"Delia, this is another friend of mine…this is Annie." He saw the scowl on her face. "But she's leaving."

* * *

OFF PELEE ISLAND, LAKE ERIE: SEPTEMBER 1864

The lookouts spotted the approaching sails at first light. Waves still crashed against the ship but the broken sunshine hinted at fair weather. Beall was awake and on his feet at the first shout.

"Two ships, due north. Wait—make it three. There's another one, more like a fishing smack, low in the water."

"Have the cook serve breakfast, Mr. Burleigh. We may not have time later."

"Already done. The crew was fed while you were having a beauty sleep and the cook brought a plate for you."

The charts had been rolled aside and a steaming mass of eggs and bacon waited.

"Those ships should be on us in half an hour."

"Any sign of recognition?" Beall scooped the food with his bare hands.

"Signal, sir," the lookout called, training spy glasses on the approaching ships. "From the small boat."

Beall spat the food on the deck to clear his mouth.

"Someone with a semaphore flag on the deck. In code…sir…our code…It reads, "We've struck oil.""

The two sailing ships were the type that carried the bulk of the cargo on the Great Lakes. The fishing boat was handled by an expert. Ropes were loosened and the sails furled as the craft approached the *Philo Parsons*. The crew members appeared to be little more than children. One, he guessed, was barely a teenager. The other, perhaps a bit older, was dressed in knee breeches and was barefoot despite the cool breeze. Beall's shock grew as the sailor lifted a cap and let the wind blow through a long mass of red hair.

"My God, Burleigh! The Canadians are using women."

Within minutes, the fishing boat captain swung onto the deck of the *Philo Parsons* to meet a half dozen armed sailors. He raised empty hands.

"Which of you friendly spirits would be Oscar?"

"That would be me." A man stepped from the pilothouse with an outstretched hand. "And since we're past the planning stage, I'm Acting Master John Yates Beall, Confederate States Navy."

"Eramosa Willis, captain of the fishing smack tied alongside. Pleased to meet you, finally!"

"The next few hours will tell the tale. You have done as promised with the two ships but the fishing boat, that's more than expected."

"I thought a Lake Erie fishing boat would attract less attention for any last-minute scouting. Carson—well, since we're using real names now—Mr. Thompson suggested I bring her along."

Beall scowled. Thompson should have left the details to him but a short visit to Sandusky might be in order. Willis could make the trip.

"The sailboat captains. How much do they know?"

"Nothing except they've been chartered and paid in advance. In fact, very well paid," Willis said.

"We'll keep the destinations quiet for a few more hours. Have them take up station with us. Later this afternoon, we'll move down the lake. Meet us on your way back."

"I'm not sure of the plans," Willis ventured. "A friend came by in the spring to pick up charts and I figured you were going to hit Johnson's Island. No one's told me how. And these ships and men," he gestured to the sailboats, "don't have arms or crews with fighting experience, unless you count a tavern brawl."

Beall found he was warming to the fisherman. "Don't worry. Their job will be to move the less mobile prisoners from the island to the smaller ports and even creek mouths in Canada. I'll give you full instructions later. Any fighting will be finished before we bring them to the harbor. Now, how many men can those ships carry at a time? One hundred?"

Willis considered for a moment. "We can pack them tight. The weather should improve soon so the trip won't be rough. So maybe one hundred and fifty."

"Good, that will make our work easier." Beall was relieved.

"And the *Michigan*?" Willis asked.

"Will be in our hands by tonight," Beall replied. "I'll take command and stay until the prisoners are safely away. The *Michigan* will be flying Confederate colors and we'll carry the war up the lakes to Chicago."

"You won't be hitting Canadian ships or ports. We are officially neutral, you know?"

"Ah, Mr. Willis, I am well aware of the Neutrality Act. I jumped onto this ship yesterday so the leader of the expedition didn't violate the precious neutrality by asking the captain to tie up on British soil. Mr. Thompson demands we respect your neutrality. Why, Jefferson Davis demands it! And we could have tried to land the bulk of the men in Canada but decided not to. We'll only drop a few on that British naval reserve land on Point Pelee and at Rondeau. The most seriously ill will be taken where our people can meet and care for them. Is that enough, Mr. Willis?"

He didn't wait for a reply. "Can you make Sandusky and back by dark?"

Willis glanced at the racing clouds. "Easily!"

"Good. Now check on the cannon across the channel from the island. The *Michigan* should be at mid channel. Take a look around the harbor and tell us what you see."

Willis moved to return to his boat.

"Uh, Mr. Willis, one other thing." He pointed to the crew on the fishing boat. "Do all Canadian fishermen employ females?"

"Oh that," Willis laughed. "That's just Erin. She thinks she can do anything a man can do and usually can. I know women are supposed to be bad luck, but Mr. Beall, there are cold nights on this lake and a man like me, well, he likes to stay warm."

* * *

THE WEST HOUSE, SANDUSKY, OHIO: SEPTEMBER 19, 1864

Annie Cole could see nothing unusual at the prison. The supply boat had come and gone with no sign of increased surveillance.

A few minutes before noon, Cole pounded on her door. "Annie, I need to see you."

He pushed past as she opened the door and glanced around the room. "Alone are you?"

She nodded, angered by the suggestion.

"Just checking, my dear."

"Everything looks normal."

"That's it, then. I'm going to send the telegram to Chicago. They failed badly a couple of weeks ago but will have the chance to redeem themselves in a few days. Murray is coming for me and by late this afternoon our work will be done. Stay off the street. The Sons of Liberty are a rough crowd and hard to control. I'll send someone for you later, maybe that young Confederate messenger Hemmings—the one you said was sweet." He watched her face. "I love when you blush!"

She slammed the door behind him and threw herself on the bed. Perhaps if she could sleep the time would pass faster.

* * *

A noise from the hall woke her, footsteps from heavy boots. She cracked the door to peer down the hall.

The man Charles called Gunner Murray stood at Cole's door. He knocked loudly and called, "Charles, time to go."

Someone stirred in the dark hallway behind him.

A man with a stick? she thought. Immediately, she saw her error. A rifle was pointed at the door.

"Soldier," Murray turned to one of what she saw was a troop of soldiers. "When I tell you, kick the door down."

"Cole!" Murray shouted. "Charles Cole, you are under arrest. Open the door or we'll come in and get you!"

Dazed, she watched as they smashed the door. The commotion brought other hotel guests from their rooms and she was able to join the crowd in the hallway. Cole was dragged away in handcuffs.

"A damn rebel," an excited guest announced. "He was plotting to take the *Michigan* and free the rebel prisoners."

* * *

LAKE ERIE: EVENING OF SEPTEMBER 19, 1864

Beall's fleet sailed to within a few miles of Sandusky. As Willis predicted, the weather improved. Erie's waves dropped to a gentle swell and the wind eased. The sun was dropping when the lookout spotted the fishing boat. Willis had crowded on extra sail and the little boat flew across the water. Willis didn't wait to tie up but jumped to the deck of the *Philo Parsons*.

"Where's Beall?"

"Right here, Mr. Willis." Both Beall and Burleigh stepped from a cabin.

"It's blown!" Willis blurted out.

"They know something. The waterfront is an armed camp."

"Hold on!" Beall ordered. He pulled the Canadian into a cabin. Burleigh followed, slamming the door.

Willis began again.

"The battery was reinforced while we were there. The Yankees have moved more cannon into place, along with extra powder and supplies. And, the *Michigan*. Gun ports are open, the guns run out. The crews are standing by every one of them."

The two Confederates stood stunned.

"Maybe a drill," Burleigh said, grasping at straws. "A new commander trying to work his people into shape?"

"We wondered, too," Willis told him. "And since everyone was on edge, we figured it best to tie up and not just sail in and then disappear mysterious like. While we were there, a squad marched a man in handcuffs to a boat and rowed him to the *Michigan*. People on the dock said he was a Confederate spy."

"We're screwed! After all this and so close!" Burleigh slammed the wall in frustration.

Beall remained silent, and then said, "It may be a mistake, a false alarm."

"Not from what I saw, Mr. Beall. I'll bring Erin and Rufus up. She can tell you what they saw."

"That's a good idea. Lash your boat to the side and bring them up."

As Willis hurried off, Beall turned to Burleigh.

"Lock them in this cabin. Willis, too. I need time to think and I don't want the crew to know."

* * *

SANDUSKY, OHIO: EVENING OF SEPTEMBER 19, 1864

The hotel staff knew them as Mr. and Mrs. Cole despite the separate rooms. With Cole in custody, the Yankees would come for her.

She froze at a light knock on the door. The tap was repeated. She put her head against the door, listening for boots but there was only another tap and a soft whisper, "Mrs. Cole. Are you there?"

She swung the door open and almost leaped into the arms of the young Confederate. Charles Hemmings was frightened, too. He pushed her into the room and locked the door.

"They have Mr. Cole. I've been watching from across the street."

"Yes, I don't know what happened. Charles had paid off Murray but that's who grabbed him. I don't know where they took him."

"To the brig on the *Michigan*. And that woman he's been seeing— what did he call her? Delia—she's involved somehow."

She felt sick. Surely, Charles had been smart enough to keep his latest tryst confined to the hotel room.

"How do you know about her?"

Hemmings stammered a reply. "Charles, uh Mr. Cole, took her to dinner the other night. I was in the same dining room. He introduced us."

"Charles has a taste for the good life and his good life includes many women."

"He picked a bad one," Hemmings told her. "She went to the sheriff's office and a few minutes later she and a couple of deputies came out, friendly as all get out. When they put her on the train to Cleveland, she looked like the cat that swallowed the canary."

"Oh, Charles! You are such a fool," she spoke aloud, forgetting the young man.

"We don't have much time." Hemmings would not be ignored. "The Sons of Liberty are supposed to be all over town but won't move if there is no signal. What are you going to do?"

The half-packed suitcase lay open on the bed. "Someone has to get the word to Toronto. Maybe they can help or arrange for a lawyer."

"Good idea. Get to Thompson." Hemmings agreed. "But as to the lawyer, I wouldn't count on much. If solid Union men can be thrown in jail without trial, imagine what will happen to a Confederate."

She slammed the suitcase before dragging Hemmings to the hall. There was no guard on Cole's room. "Come quickly."

The wood around the lock was splintered. The door swung open with a light push and she dashed to the loose board by the bed. The case was still there.

She tossed her own bag to Hemmings.

"Take this."

Cole's bag was heavy but manageable.

"Mr. Hemmings, I hope we meet again. But now go!"

He nodded, stunned by the events of the last few hours.

"Go while you can," she urged. "And we will both survive."

* * *

LAKE ERIE, ABOARD THE *PHILO PARSONS*: SEPTEMBER 20

"I'm sorry I had to do this." Beall spoke to the trio confined to the cabin.

Willis was upset. The woman appeared to enjoy an adventure, the youngster didn't seem to understand.

"The crew had to hear it from me," Beall told them. "I thought there was still a chance to take the *Michigan*. It would have been a nasty fight but could have been done. Half the crew was ready but the other half, the ones that Thompson sent, had cold feet. We'll deal with them later. Unfortunately, I have bad news for you, Mr. Willis. Your boat is at the bottom of Lake Erie. We couldn't tow it and it's probably best if you are never associated with this raid."

Willis clenched his fists but relaxed at Erin's touch.

"A small consolation but you are not alone," Beall continued. "The owners of the *Island Queen* will be looking for compensation. She's sinking as we speak. As to your boat, I'll verify any value you think reasonable."

Willis stammered a question, "The other ships?"

"We thanked them, told them to keep the money, and wished them god speed."

Willis fired a series of questions. "Now what? Do we remain as prisoners? For how long?"

Beall responded after a tired smile. "We're just off the Detroit River. I'm going to stop at Amherstburg. Most of the crew can scatter from there and you shouldn't be seen with them. Burleigh and I will take the *Parsons* up the river and sink her. You shouldn't be seen with us, either so…according to those charts, there's a landing place on what's called Fighting Island. We'll drop the three of you there."

He saw the grudging acceptance from Willis.

"Now if I may suggest, the air in this cabin is rather stale. I have ordered the crew not to use this side of the deck to protect…well, let's say to protect your privacy."

With that, Beall returned to the pilothouse.

"So Eramosa is getting a new boat." Erin's Irish lilt broke the silence as they emerged on deck. "A week ago you said the boat was finished, and Rufus spent most of our trip bailing. You got the best of the deal."

The conversation was interrupted by cheers as a flag began to rise above the *Philo Parsons*. It snapped in the breeze only to snag as the wind whipped the rope.

The Confederate battle flag had been carried deep into the North but refused to rise above half-mast.

211

CHAPTER 30

Chicago, Illinois: September 22, 1864

Two light taps, a pause, and a heavy knock. Hines sprang from the bed and pulled the gun from the holster on the bedpost. He placed his back against the wall and swung the door open. The drawn curtains left the room in darkness.

"Tom," George Ellsworth whispered from the hall.

"Come in, George, and close the door."

He waited until he was certain that Ellsworth was alone. "Sorry, George, we can't be too careful." Hines lit an oil lamp and turned up the wick.

Ellsworth clutched a newspaper but offered a flimsy telegraph form. "It was sent three days ago but just arrived. Tom Wallace, that's the name, you are using, right? The message doesn't make sense so I figured it was in code."

Hines grabbed the telegram and read, "Close out all shares of the Mount Hope Oil Company at 3 p.m. today."

He felt a rush of adrenaline. The *Michigan* was in Confederate hands and loose on the lakes. There would be a second chance to free the Chicago prisoners. If the telegram was sent three days ago he had only hours to get word to Camp Douglas. The *Michigan's* guns would soon arrive to smash the walls. He began to think of all that needed to be done.

"More news from the East," Ellsworth said, raising the newspaper. "And a real hornet's nest. Thompson's men sank two ships on Lake Erie and tried to capture the *Michigan*."

Hines seized the paper. The editors had rushed to print. First, it said two ships had been destroyed, but a later dispatch suggested the vessels had only been damaged and the *Michigan* was still in Federal hands. A spy, perhaps the ringleader, had been arrested.

Hines had to wonder if the delay in receiving the message was deliberate. His elation vanished. Cole knew too much.

Ellsworth watched, mystified by the mood change.

"We've got to go, George."

The telegram was pushed into the chimney of the oil lamp to erupt in flame and curl into black soot.

"Let's go." He shoved the telegrapher's lean frame into the hall. "Go out the front. Get what you need and tell the others to make for Toronto."

Hines ran for the rear stairwell to the kitchen and livery stables.

It took Ellsworth a minute to reach the lobby and the safety of the crowded street. A bearded man watched him go before speaking to his companion.

"Ellsworth is small potatoes. We can get him anytime, but we bag Hines and we have the major player." He glanced at the clock above the hotel desk. "Wait another five minutes to be sure the building is surrounded and we'll take him."

* * *

QUEBEC CITY, CANADA EAST: SEPTEMBER 22, 1864

"Mr. Macdonald."

He turned to see the junior clerk racing toward him.

"Another dispatch from Windsor," Forsey panted. "It must be more on the Lake Erie raid."

"I'm sure all is in hand," Macdonald said, stepping away from the waiting carriage. He had only begun to read when the stiff breeze pulled the page from his hands. The paper swirled to fall at Forsey's feet.

Forsey bent to retrieve it, saw the note began with, "My Dear Attorney General," before he felt Macdonald's hand on his shoulder.

213

"Confidential," Macdonald announced coldly. He turned his back and began to read. A minute later he folded the note and placed it in his coat.

"No need to file this. Just more on that botched rebel raid." Macdonald turned to step into the carriage but stopped and turned back to Forsey. "You open the daily mail?" he asked.

"Just one of my duties."

"Watch for any letters from McMicken in Windsor or elsewhere in the Western District. No need to send them through the ministry channels. Bring them to me. I'll do what needs to be done. No need to involve anyone else."

"But I'm to file all correspondence..." Forsey began. He stopped when he felt the icy glare. "Yes, sir. Whatever you think is proper."

* * *

CHICAGO, ILLINOIS: SEPTEMBER 24, 1864

Martin Delaney enjoyed the shock he produced. Black men in blue were becoming a familiar sight but he was different, a black officer, a black major. His uniform was pressed, the buttons gleamed, and the boots were polished until they shone.

"Congratulations, Martin!" Mary Ann Shadd-Carey admired the appearance of an old friend, "Or, should I call you Major?"

"When we're alone, call me Martin. Beyond this office, it should be Major. The white officers expect nothing less and I have to measure up."

Delaney had been a doctor and struggling writer and she, an impetuous but struggling editor when they met in Chatham.

"The first effort was successful?" he asked.

"We put ten men on the cars for Rhode Island last night," she smiled, "Mostly freemen from Chicago. Next week, I'm going to the contraband camps around Cairo and Mound City."

"It may be dangerous," Delaney warned. "But more former slaves are arriving daily. Even after Fort Pillow, men are coming forward. Forrest did allow his men to murder black soldiers but the affair been blown out proportion."

"But Washington?" she asked, "Has Lincoln demanded retaliation?"

"No. Army commanders don't want to roil the waters. Only the white officers leading black regiments paid much attention. The rebels have threatened to kill any officer who leads black troops."

Delaney began to beat his fist against his hand. "White men are treated as prisoners of war. For a black, capture means a return to slavery and brutal whipping."

"How are black men treated in our army?" She wanted reassurance.

"An army is slow to change," Delaney replied. "Most white officers expect manual labor, give them shovels instead of guns, but yes, our people have been used as cannon fodder."

She waited, certain Delaney would offer more.

"At the Battle of the Crater, those mine explosions at Petersburg, our men were to have the element of surprise but their commander was drunk and sent them to a slaughter." The fist began to hammer against his hand. "We need black men led by black officers. But even the suggestion strikes fear into the white community, conjures an image of servile insurrection and Southern belles fighting off the bucks from the slave quarters."

"It was a different story when the masters came to the quarters," she reminded him.

"The whites don't understand, or don't want to, but a change is coming, a move to total unrestricted war. Sherman wants to make the South howl. An African Corps would make rebels howl, scream, and run for cover. I've heard of black men putting the bayonet to captured rebels. That will make them think."

She felt a sense of revulsion. Where would it end? Would it be possible to overcome the hatred? "What will you do when it's over, Martin? Will you still want to move our people to Africa or stay here and work for change?"

"Our own land and our own country is the best solution. The races don't mix. So yes, I believe emigration is the answer. Post-war America will welcome the idea."

He opened a desk drawer to count out one hundred dollars.

"I'll pay you before the accounts are lost in some supply officer's file…ten dollars a head."

"Do you ever think that we are now making money off black bodies?" she asked. "I've been compared to a slave dealer and told my ranks are no different than a coffle of slaves."

"And how do you respond?"

"I don't bother to answer. There is no sense wasting words on that sort."

He chuckled. "Be mindful of the danger, Mary Ann."

"There's danger everywhere. The raiders on Lake Erie were awfully close to home in Canada and last night, soldiers stormed a hotel just down the street."

"Yes, I heard. The ring leader got away but at least another rebel is on the run."

* * *

WASHINGTON: SEPTEMBER 1864

Sherman's telegram announcing the fall of Atlanta changed the mood in Washington. Edwin Stanton, usually so reserved, grinned with delight when Peter Watson brought the news. And, the secretary of war smiled broadly, when told of the deepening split in the Democratic Party.

Stanton motioned for Peter Watson to close the office door. This would be a private meeting with no notes or no witnesses, the way both men liked it.

"Freemont will withdraw from the presidential race before the end of the month," Stanton predicted confidently. "And McClellan with his ego will beat himself. He won't accept the peace plank and that divides the Democrats. But we can't stop."

Watson pulled a sheet of paper from his suit.

"I've some suggestions. First, regiments we know will vote for Lincoln can be furloughed home. That helped beat Vallandigham in Ohio last year. For the men left in the field, hurry along promotions and on Election Day, ballots for the notorious Democrats might be lost.

"And extra rations, a bit of alcohol," Stanton added quickly. "Keep the army happy. What next?"

"The Copperheads can be used to our advantage. The idea of a revolution is actually driving nervous Democrats to us."

Stanton understood. "Fewer people will support the Democrats if they are identified as Copperheads or cutthroat traitors. We can exaggerate the threat of terror. We might have to send troops to supervise the vote in the big cities and if soldiers scare away Democratic votes on Election Day, that would be too bad."

Watson glanced again at the list.

"The last thing may be beyond our control. Perhaps a hint the British are too close to the Confederates, perhaps a strongly worded diplomatic note with threatening language. At the very least it would make the British more eager to police the border."

Stanton lifted his hand. "We can't go far."

"The British won't do anything," Watson scoffed. "Talk tough. They'll fall in line."

CHAPTER 31

Johnson's Island, Ohio: September 25, 1864

For an instant Robert Kennedy felt a surge of hope but the sound was distant thunder and not cannon fire.

Like the other prisoners, he had waited for the signal for the uprising but instead extra guards had appeared on the wall and searches began. The guards could have been following a map, one that marked the location of hidden revolvers or the wooden staves stashed under a barracks.

Only one inmate was seized. Ben Cooper was hauled to the cells and took his secrets with him. The prison authorities ordered a ban on visits and cut rations but only Cooper was marked for special treatment.

Kennedy watched the line of dark clouds approach. A native of Louisiana was no stranger to summer storms or hurricane winds.

A bolt of lightning struck near the shore where work parties had been cutting winter firewood. Another flash illuminated a line of stumps, a small dock, and a rowboat straining on a rope.

The first heavy drops of rain began to pound the barracks from a sky turned an ominous green. The wind blasted the prison and littered the parade ground with debris. A section of roof flew from the next building to slam the prison wall and open a twenty-foot breach.

"It's a tornado!" Another prisoner was shouting over the howling wind. "Hug the ground! This whole building could go." But the wind died and was followed by sheets of torrential rain.

Kennedy left the shelter on the dead run, slowing only to pick his way through the damaged wall, and in minutes reached the boat. He thanked the laziness of the Yankee officers who had left a set of oars. The Lake Erie Islands and the Canadian shore were only a few hours away.

* * *

CANADA WEST: SEPTEMBER 1864

Beall arrived in a driving rain, pounding on the door to wake Willis. The conversation was strained but Erin offered shelter for the night. By morning, the tension eased and Beall began to tell of the final stage of the Lake Erie raid.

"Burleigh and I flooded the *Philo Parsons* when we got to Windsor," he told them, "but we knew she could be raised. Everyone slipped away but Burleigh. I warned him about taking the pianoforte. He couldn't move fast with the weight and the constables charged him with illegally importing goods, and then let him go, so they obviously didn't know what to do."

Erin moved quietly about the kitchen and set breakfast plates.

"The urchins have been fed," she said in answer to Willis's unspoken question. "I thought it was best, with company and all."

Willis turned to Beall. "And what are you doing now?"

Beall began to answer but was swept by a spasm of coughing. He thumped his hand against his chest. "Sorry. It's grown worse these past few weeks."

He saw the compassion on Erin's face.

She's pretty, he thought. And she looks much better in a dress than disguised as a sailor.

Willis impatiently toyed with his meal.

"We've been busy," Beall finally began. "We planted the torpedoes near the mouth of the Detroit River. Keep a sharp watch in that area. The torpedo expert thinks they were damaged and may not pack a full charge but there's enough powder to cause a major explosion. You remember Giles?"

"We didn't meet many people locked in a cabin," Willis snapped.

"Oh, I forgot that." Beall shrugged before he continued. "Later we sort of borrowed a long boat and would have given a scare to Erie, Pennsylvania, but a storm drove us back to shore. So, I sent the crew to Toronto and I came here."

"Why?" Willis wanted to know. Erin's eyes jumped from her plate to send him a reassuring glance.

"We have a line on another ship, one we will own and control. She'll be a privateer and if the *Michigan* should come for us, so be it."

Willis thought of the effect that a well-armed raider could have on the lakes. The shipping channels were among the busiest in North America.

"I want her on Lake Huron before winter," Beall explained. "We'll need a quiet spot to arm her. Do you have a chart of Georgian Bay?"

Erin had almost finished breakfast. The fine hands that held the fork would soon hold a pen. She began to clear the table but had a question.

"British or Canadian ships? Will you attack them, too?"

The answer was soft but emphatic. "We don't want to!"

He turned to Willis. "Tell the local sailors to carry a British flag. At the start, we won't attack the Union Jack. Of course, if the Yankees begin to hide under British colors we'll have no choice."

Erin began to wash the dishes.

"And we could use a man who knows the lakes."

A plate slipped from usually steady hands to smash on the floor.

"Take it easy, Erin!" Willis rose to calm her before turning to their guest. "I'll need time to think."

That night Willis was almost asleep when Erin turned to him in bed. "John Yates Beall is a Confederate. He's at war and has the protection of his government. You will have no protection. They would consider you a pirate."

He felt a slim leg cross his body as she nestled against him.

"I haven't decided yet. Let me think."

CHAPTER 32

Southern Illinois: Fall 1864

The sentry didn't answer her question, concentrating instead on a passing riverboat. Mary Ann Shadd Carey waited before asking again for directions.

"The contraband camp." He finally pointed up river. "But don't go there. Ain't no place for a white woman." He studied her for a moment. "Or, on second thought, you might fit right in."

He chuckled before adding, "Although the bucks prefer younger women."

The camp resembled a crowded Oriental harbor, a makeshift village on barges connected by planks. The smell was overpowering. Rotting garbage sloshed on the water. On one barge, a few people watched a card game while on another a man plucked a banjo. It was the best the army would provide for colored refugees.

A stout black man wearing only trousers and a beaten straw hat looked down from a deck.

"I'm looking for Frank Lucas."

"What's a white lady want with the likes of him?" The man scratched his stomach. "Are you his old mistress? If so, he don't want to see you."

The itch satisfied, he moved to the edge of the boat.

"I'm not his mistress but show respect. Get your clothes and help find him."

"Come this way," he said, reaching for a shirt drying on the railing.

The minister at the black church had suggested Lucas. He was recognized as a leader, able to read and write, and perhaps was officer potential. Lucas had promised to assemble a group of refugees.

Her message would be different from that of a plantation preacher. It would not be a call to suffer or endure subjugation to win a life of ease in the next world. Instead, she would urge them to seize a new opportunity and do it now.

"Mr. Lincoln wants you for his army," she began as she had a dozen times in recent weeks. "He wants to end slavery and is willing to pay and provide clothes, food, and a gun."

She avoided comparisons with white soldiers who drew more pay and lived in better conditions.

"There's a new bounty, a payment for each man who volunteers. Two hundred and fifty dollars cash money. The money will keep your women and children until you come back."

"And what if they don't come back?" The question came from a tall, gaunt woman. "What happens then?"

"Martin Delaney is a black man in charge of this recruiting drive." She delivered her well-rehearsed answer. "He wants special help for the families of anyone seriously injured or—God forbid— killed."

"And how do they determine family, missus?" The speaker was an older man, the body strong but hair already white. "I was married on the plantation but the white minister says I'm living in sin and never had a proper church blessing. Will a white government take the word of a black woman if her man is dead and buried?"

She silently thanked the foresight of Delaney in preparing for the question. "As each of you signs up, we'll take a record of a wife or family. It should satisfy the requirements."

"Whole thing, don't really sound different than what we've seen," the older man spoke up again. "Two years ago the master sent me and a couple of others to dig ditches at a rebel fort. White man told us where to dig and when the work was done, old master gave us a reward."

"You won't be digging ditches," she answered. "We have men working with the artillery, firing those big guns, and we have whole regiments of foot soldiers. They fight as well as any white man!"

"But we'll be fighting our own people." The old man was persistent.

"We were raised in the South and feel close to the master and the family. Why, some of our men went with the young masters, got a gray suit and fought right alongside of them. And two boys from the next plantation have been playing in a rebel band since this war started. A lot more black folk in those rebel armies than the Yankees realize."

"You are too old to fight anyway, Uncle." Lucas moved beside her. "The rest of us will do more than beat a drum. The young men need a better life, with their own land and making their own decisions. That's what freedom is about."

"You don't know freedom," the older man shot back. "Freedom is a word conjured up by folks like this lady. We been living in freedom since we came north and what has it got us? A bed full of bugs on a barge that was used to haul cattle or coal or both. Back home, the white folks knew us, understood us. Up here, they don't know us. And they don't like us!"

Lucas spoke before she could muster any argument. "And that's what we have to change! We're going to carve out a place for ourselves and we're going to start by becoming soldiers."

"Be sure the secesh don't catch you." The older man was not finished. "The rebels don't like it when their people turn. Old General Forrest was a slave trader, so he knew the value of a black person, but he let his men kill blacks when they tried to surrender. The Southern folk are fine gentlemen but they do insist the African know his place. You don't cross them."

"I'm not afraid." Lucas dismissed the older man and turned to the others. "You can stay with him or go back south and crawl on your knees for forgiveness, but I'm going back with a gun in my hands and demand what's mine. Anyone interested, come see me and Mrs. Shadd Carey. We'll be leaving for the East in a couple of days. Ride the railcars all the way, just like the white folk."

By day's end, Lucas had added seventy-five names to the list of recruits. "Others will come," he told her. "I'll take the first group. I'll look out for them. You should be pleased."

"Oh, I am, although that older man upset me. What if more of our people think that way?"

"Face it, a lot of them do. There were plantations where the slaves were part of the family, and well treated, as long they behaved. Since the war began, the Yankees have been demonized. Word went around that the Yankees wanted to kill people, burn the cabins, and eat the babies. If you hear that enough, you come to believe it. And the old man was right. Blacks are with the rebels, cooking, cleaning, or nursing, and sometimes fighting. But they don't know any better. Nobody tried to reach them."

TORONTO, CANADA WEST: SEPTEMBER 1864

The last thing Clement Clay wanted was an argument with a temperamental young man but it was the next item on the agenda. The man—the boy—waiting outside could wait a few minutes more. The letter for Judah Benjamin was important and must be worded precisely.

"Lincoln and his Union Party have been buoyed by the fall of Atlanta, and while I personally think it doubtful that the Democrats can win, we must do all in our power to encourage the hope for an armistice. A great military victory and a Southern army pushing toward the Ohio River would add to the pressure for a negotiated settlement."

His thoughts would be in Benjamin's hands by mid October. He signed his name and glanced out the window waiting for the ink to dry.

Bright clear weather brought the oarsmen to Lake Ontario for what might be last race of the season. The young Floridian was in the heat. After the debacle in Sandusky, Charles Hemmings had earned a chance to relax. Clay watched as his racing skull edged into the lead as the boats crossed the finish line.

Clay placed the letter in the Richmond pouch before admitting another intense young Confederate.

"It's not fair, Mr. Clay! I was ordered to return from Chicago." Bennet Young didn't wait for the door to close before he began to speak. "Captain Hines will confirm it. But Mr. Thompson thinks I'm a shirker and that's not the case! I was under orders."

"All a misunderstanding." Clay's tired smile was meant to reassure. "We'll set the record straight. Try to understand that Mr. Thompson is under a great strain."

Young seemed to relax but quickly added, "I'm not a coward."

"Thompson has worries of a personal nature," Clay confided. "The Yankees are taking personal retribution. His home at Oxford in Mississippi was deliberately torched and his wife given only moments to get out. She's coming here but he's worried and will be until she is safe. I'm taking over a few of his duties."

The hard look in Young's eyes began to soften.

"I'm interested in your opinion," Clay told him. "Our raids have been less than a success but because of us, thousands of Union soldiers are compelled to remain in the North. Hines will stir the pot in the Northwest but I'm wondering if we can add pressure elsewhere. Take a look at Vermont. It's not far from Montreal. See if there's anything a small group could do. A scare just before their elections would help."

"I can leave tonight. Two weeks will be enough. I've been on my own before."

"Be cautious," Clay warned. "And, let's keep this to ourselves. We won't bother Thompson."

Young saluted. "Thank you, Mr. Clay. You won't be disappointed."

***

CENTRAL KENTUCKY: SEPTEMBER 1864

A midnight crossing of the Mississippi cost more than Mary Ann Shadd-Carey expected but the guides were adamant. The costs rose with the danger. They spent the next day hidden in dense Kentucky bush until the guide kindled a small fire at dusk and a few men straggled in.

"So we'll be free but in the army?" The questions began immediately. "The white man will be telling us what to do?" A tall man edged closest to the fire.

"And we will have food and clothing? But we have that. Things haven't been bad these last few years. The men are gone, most overseers are gone, and all we have to do is please the lady of the house."

"And what happens when the master comes home?"

"Reckon there will be more work!" The man told her before asking, "What will happen when the army has used us up?"

"With the bounty money, you can buy land and make decisions on your own."

"But we're doing that now. Each one of us has a little money hidden and long as we stay close, we do what we want. The work isn't bad and we're used to it. Buying land takes a heap of money. The poor white folk can't afford it."

She heard grunts of agreement.

"This may be your last chance. If the rebels win, there's no chance. You will spend the rest of your lives here."

"We've been here a long time now. Don't see much reason to move."

"You can be sold!" she warned.

"I'll take my chances. I can be shot and killed or be like some of the ex-soldiers come home with only one arm or one leg. Least ways I have all my parts."

The other men begin to snicker.

"Look missus. I thank you for coming all this way but we'll be staying."

"And when you are old and can't work?" She tried one final argument. "Maybe the master won't take care of you. You'll be shipped south, sold for a dollar a pound, and worked to a death in a field in Mississippi or Alabama."

It didn't work. She left empty-handed.

V

CHAPTER 33

Southern Illinois: October 1864

The scent of blood hung over the prairie where Grenfell's gun dropped the birds. Brutus tore two apart but Grenfell salvaged a third before it, too, became bloody pulp. He was distracted by the dog's fury and didn't notice the riders until they were near his camp. The glare of the sun made them hard to distinguish but he saw that neither man wore a uniform. The dog crouched, forgetting his bloody work, and bared his teeth with a threatening growl.

"Looks like you've had a good day." Tom Hines pointed to scattered feathers.

"Middling day, Thomas," Grenfell relaxed on seeing an old friend. "Brutus took most of my share."

The dog settled, his tongue licking at the blood and meat lodged in his teeth.

Hines considered the animal before he swung from the saddle. The other rider was Theo Schultz.

"What's up?" Grenfell asked. "Have you given up the war for the life of the sportsman?"

"I wish it were that simple," Hines replied. "We've had another setback."

Grenfell brought them to a small fire where a battered kettle steamed. A blanket was spread on the earth and he reached to retrieve tin mugs. Shultz rejected the offer, instead pulling a flask from his jacket.

"Snn-chapps?" Grenfell asked, drawing out the word, trying, but failing to break the German's mood. "A foul mood? What's happened?"

"Breck's been captured," Hines began. "He was out of uniform. He could be hanged."

Grenfell absorbed the news quietly.

"I have no doubt Castleman was out of uniform or spying. I'm surprised he wasn't hanged immediately as another example of military justice. And let me guess: You'll help him escape. Let's see, it would be you, Schultz, and the legions of the Sons of Liberty. Wake up, Thomas! You'll be behind bars and the Northern friends will do nothing."

"No, we've made contact," Hines explained. "We sent a message with his mother and he says not to try but we did send hacksaw blades."

Grenfell growled in disgust. "Sent, no doubt, with his sainted mother. What if she had been caught and thrown in prison?"

"We had to try!" Schultz said angrily. "We couldn't give up and go hunting."

"But what good did you do?"

The dog settled to watch the two visitors. Hines kicked absently at the fire before he spoke.

"We did have to try. Breck would have done it for us. But it's out of our hands. His family has connections on the Union side, good strong connections at the highest levels—even to Lincoln. And we'll keep working for on other solutions."

"Do you believe that?" Grenfell was testing him.

"There will be surprises on Election Day," Hines told him. "Thompson wants a series of attacks to disrupt the vote in New York, Boston, and Cincinnati, and of course, Chicago."

Grenfell shook his head in disgust. "And for assistance, the Sons of Liberty, those brave, well-organized souls."

"Them, too." Hines smiled.

"What do you mean, too?" Grenfell asked.

"The army. General Hood will bait Sherman from Atlanta with a move to the north and west. If Sherman follows, Hood turns and fights. If Sherman stays put, Hood will move into Tennessee and Kentucky and up to the Ohio."

"Thomas," Grenfell interjected. "We've talked of Hood. The man's brains rest on his saddle. I think you've been listening too much to those schemers in Toronto."

"But if it works?" Hines asked.

Grenfell considered the possibilities. With a Southern army in the North, Grant would be forced to shift the army of the Potomac. Lee would be able to break free of the entrenchments at Petersburg. Sherman would be isolated. And, the Northern cities would be torn by revolution.

"The South will be in control. But only if it works!"

"I'll need help," Hines told him. "Someone I can count on. Schultz is on his way to Kentucky. He'll take what he learns to Hood. I need you in Chicago."

Grenfell stared at the young Confederate. "I'm tired, Thomas. I though this hunt would make me feel more alive, but I'm tired. Or maybe old is a better way to put it."

"Come to Chicago," Hines pleaded. "I need someone with experience."

"It's true you'll need someone but I'm not sure I'm the man."

"There's no one else. Come to Chicago."

––*

DETROIT, MICHIGAN: OCTOBER 1864

It would be another late night but for Col. Bennett Hill, long hours came with the job. As the Union officer commanding in Detroit, he could be called day or night, and frequently was, but late at night was quiet and the best time to think.

Hill tapped tobacco into his pipe and looked across the river. Lights were glowing in Windsor where he suspected bands of rebels were gathered. He didn't trust the Canadians. The concern with neutrality was one thing but harboring criminals was another.

He lit the pipe and studied a long message from Justice Joseph Holt, the report from a summer-long inquiry into the Sons of Liberty. Holt warned of the growing threat from the secret societies, the thousands of men who joined the shadowy groups, of the guns and weapons seized, and of the leaders, primarily Democrats who were under arrest.

Hill would do as ordered and distribute Holt's work but he suspected the conclusions were overblown. Still, the judge must have reasons for timing the release for the final weeks of an election campaign.

Beneath the report was another on the Lake Erie raid. He had saved copies of anxious telegrams sent from Edwin Stanton's office on the day of the raid, the warnings flashed around the Great Lakes.

"*War Department, Washington, September 20.*

This department has just received information that rebels from Canada have captured two steamers on Lake Erie. You will proceed immediately to take such measures as you find proper."

A near thing, but Washington knew the initial warnings came from Hill's office. The sheriff in Sandusky said he learned of the plot from a local prostitute, while John Brown Jr., who had forsaken his father's war to tend a vineyard on a Lake Erie Island, said he rowed his boat to Sandusky to sound the alarm.

But Hill had his own account. A shabby rebel had come to his office, the same man who had brought the unlikely story of a Confederate attack on Chicago late in the summer. This time, however, the information had proved correct.

Hill closed the file. For now, his district was quiet and if the rebels across the river were making plans, he expected to hear the details well in advance of any action. There was even the Canadian detective McMicken. The two men met quietly to share information and their superiors were not aware of the contact.

CHAPTER 34

The Farm, Canada West: October 1864

Homer Linslow stirred the ashes before dropping another log into the cabin stove. The fire would ward off the autumn chill.

Horses, sold to the American buyers in the spring, would provide the only income from the farm. The crops planted with high hopes had withered in the summer heat. In any other year, he would have worried, but the Confederates paid well for his hospitality.

John Yates Beall had stopped in, resting for a day before continuing north. Beall, Linslow learned, had been raised on what was once a model farm in Virginia and showed a polite interest in Linslow's small acreage.

Beall had written an open letter to a newspaper defending the action on Lake Erie. He repeated the story for Linslow, hinting the dream of Confederate action on the Great Lakes was not dead.

He had been the most generous of the visitors, leaving twenty American dollars. Glancing around the room, Linslow doubted the latest guests would be able to scrape up twenty dollars between them.

Charlie Hemmings was the youngest but served as their guide. Linslow guessed John Headley to be about twenty. He wore a goatee and spoke with the air of one raised in Southern society. Robert Martin appeared to be the same age. His blond hair hung to the neck and, like Headley, he sported a goatee. The fourth man, Robert Kennedy was clean-shaven but his hands, red and blistered, caught Linslow's eye.

"I got some salve," he said as Kennedy rubbed his palms.

"I'll try anything. They burn something fierce. Two days pulling on oars and look at the result."

"Rob escaped from Johnson's Island," Hemmings blurted out. "And he's not used to oars the way I am."

"Try this." Linslow took a tin from a cupboard. "We use it on the cows when their teats are tender. Works real well."

Kennedy began to rub the ointment between his palms.

"Any trouble after you reached Canada?" Headley asked Kennedy.

"I just followed the directions. There was one Canadian who had a lot of questions. McMicken. You run across him?"

No one had.

"He wanted to know where I landed, who I saw, and so on. I wouldn't tell him and so he got huffy but eventually paid for my ticket to Toronto."

"The border was in a panic when we came across," Headley volunteered.

"We kept our mouths shut and kept moving."

"I must have been just in front of you," Hemmings said proudly. "I was in Sandusky and had to warn the local people. Then I followed Miss Annie back to Toronto."

"I believe it's Mrs. Annie," Martin joined the conversation. "And she's too much woman for a boy. She and Cole had a business arrangement. Does Thompson know she was a hooker?"

Hemming looked on in shock. Headley and Kennedy watched in silent amusement.

"You didn't know?" Martin asked. "Hell, you could read the signs a mile away. Well, most of us could. You and Thompson must be the only ones in Toronto who think she's a lady."

Martin cut off Hemmings' stammered reply.

"And don't take on so. Maybe she'll do you for free. Although a boy your size might want to start with something smaller."

Headley was laughing. "Just like the old days with Colonel Martin stirring up mischief in the camp. You may as well laugh, Charlie. You'll

232

hear worse things in life. Homer! Any of that Canadian whiskey hid away?"

Linslow shuffled to a cupboard and removed a large jug. Two hours later, he shuffled happily for another, pleased that he at least could hold his liquor.

Hemmings was snoring loudly on the bed. Kennedy had been silent for half an hour. His head rested on the table. Headley and Martin, like Linslow, seemed unaffected.

"Here's to the next chapter and life at sea." Headley raised his glass but abruptly lowered it.

"It's all right," Linslow reassured them. "I don't talk. Besides, Mr. Beall and I were comparing notes just the other day."

"When was he here?"

"About a week ago. Said he was going hunting at Balsam Lake. That's about a day's travel."

"How did he look?"

"A bit tired. He said his lungs were acting up and he wanted fresh air."

"I know the feeling," Martin interjected. "I took a minie ball in the lungs and there are days it's hard to move."

"Is Beall coming back?" Headley asked. "We are supposed to join him at a place called Port Colbourne later in the month but we could wait here."

"Wouldn't mind the company," Linslow told them. "But he was going to Trenton, where the Trent Canal empties into Lake Ontario. From there, he can take a train or boat to Toronto. He's got his eyes on another ship, doesn't he?"

Headley and Martin exchanged a glance before Headley answered. "We don't know. We're ordered to report to him but weren't told why."

Linslow's mind was racing. "Port Colbourne. I'll wager it's another attack on Johnson's Island."

"One hell of a place," said a slurred voice from the tabletop. Kennedy slowly raised his head. "Hell of a place. Glad to be gone. Shudder to think of the winter."

And with that, his head sank to bounce on the table.

CHAPTER 35

Quebec City, Canada East: October 1864

Paul Forsey planned to work on his private journal until he heard the tread of military boots. The journal was in the drawer before Geoffrey Ralston entered the room. The short Quebec City summer was ending and a chill had returned to government offices. Both men pulled chairs to the fire and like old conspirators began to share their stories.

"So, Lord Lyons has gone and I'm glad."

The British consul in Washington had arrived in mid September for an unofficial vacation and complained of a headache. It grew much worse with word of the Lake Erie raid. Ralston served as his aide.

"With the fuss on the lakes, the first days were exciting but then it became a social whirl. Dinners with the cabinet, lunches with the governor general, and countless carriage rides with Monck's family. I felt rather silly riding along as an escort but he promised the right people would hear of me."

"The battlefronts seem quiet," Forsey observed, "but the war appears to turning against the South. And Lincoln may be re-elected."

"The North fears a major defeat. Heavy casualties could affect the vote," Ralston explained. "But if Lincoln wins, the gloves come off. Grant and Sherman can destroy what's left of the Confederacy."

"And then what do the military minds expect?"

"Two options, really. The Yankees might occupy and tame the South. The other, more dangerous for us, is that the armies remain intact and move against us—or Mexico—or both. There's no love lost in Washington for the British or for the French. It may be time to kiss up to Billy Yank."

"The government here will do nothing to anger them."

"And what of the Canadian Confederation?" Ralston asked.

"The devil is in the details but representatives from all the colonies will meet in a few days."

Ralston rolled his eyes. "What has to be settled?"

"Well, almost everything," Forsey admitted.

"And assuming they agree, a big assumption, how quickly will this union happen?"

"As soon as possible. Macdonald wants it done fast before the Americans do any meddling."

"I also hear Macdonald is looking for bomb factories?"

"What are you talking about?" Forsey feigned ignorance.

"Macdonald is asking for military expertise in Canada West."

The formal request had crossed Forsey's desk only a day earlier. "Again, confidentially?"

He waited for Ralston's agreement.

"One of the Lake Erie raiders has a relative with a foundry in Guelph and is trying to mold cannons. Also there is a report of a house in Toronto with bombs, grenades, and other infernal devices stored in the basement. If it's true the rebels are planning new action."

Ralston rose to leave. "Best be off and clean my kit. An officer never knows when he might see active service."

***

TORONTO, CANADA WEST: OCTOBER 1864

"She didn't feel right coming down the lake," Beall said, completing inspection of his new command. The *Georgian* was safely moored to a Toronto dock.

"It's the damn propeller," an older man answered. "When Thompson or Clay provide the money, have it repaired."

Dr. James Bates was a former Mississippi River captain who used his money and knowledge for the Confederate cause.

"We'll get steam up tomorrow," Beall decided. "Most of the crew are in Toronto; the rest will join at the Welland Canal."

As he unrolled the map, he remembered the Irish girl who had copied the chart. She would be worried, knowing her companion was to join the crew, but Eramosa Willis and his knowledge of the lakes would be a welcome addition.

"I'd like to have installed the ram," Beall told Bates, "but any structural work attracts attention. We can fix it when we load the cannon. Until then, we'll look like any other ship."

Bates pulled a small flask from his pocket, took a healthy pull, and passed it to Beall. "This flask kept me company many a night," Bates said. "Have to be alert for currents and shifting sand bars."

"When did you come north?"

"When the Mississippi grew too dangerous and we had to stack bales of cotton around the deck to stop the bullets. The damn guerrillas didn't care which side you were on. I could have stayed on the river, but I got out. I'm doing all right now, as long as someone doesn't wreck my ship before she's paid for."

"I know, Doctor. The money should arrive with the crew."

"Don't understand that either," Bates replied. "You don't seem to have any trouble getting money or men. Down South, the Confederates are running low on warm bodies."

He took another pull on the flask, washing the liquid around in his mouth, and swallowing before offering the flask to his companion. He showed obvious relief when the offer was refused.

"I hear things are so bad for manpower that the South is ready to arm the Negro," Bates said.

Beall continued to study the chart before the long silence forced a reply. "Blacks have been with army all along," he reminded Bates. "Did the laboring jobs so white men could fight."

"No, no. This time the idea is to give them guns and send them into battle."

"I can't see that happening," Beall told him.

"Neither did I but I have a nephew at the headquarters of Gen. Pat Cleburne. Cleburne is British, or Irish, so doesn't understand our ways. He suggested arming the slaves and giving them freedom if they perform well. He wrote a proposal, bounced the idea off army friends, and sent it to Richmond. Jeff Davis stopped it cold. But that was a year ago and the army ranks have been decimated so the Confederate Congress is taking it up."

"Couldn't work," Beall told him. "Blacks will fight. But if they were freed, fortunes would be lost. A prime slave might fetch over a thousand dollars. Planters would need compensation. The big planters wouldn't stand for it and besides, who would work the plantations?"

"I'm telling you what I've heard," Bates told him. "Don't get all fired up at me."

"Nonsense," Beall continued. "I don't buy the argument that arming a slave leads to insurrection—the majority are as loyal as we are. But freeing them won't work."

"But there are lots of them," Bates reminded him. "And when we stopped importing from Africa, the owners bred more. There are millions of those warm black bodies, four million, I hear, and more being made."

He took another pull from the flask.

"Have you seen a breeding farm?"

"No."

"Well, I've heard about them. They work them blacks until Christmas and then light a great big, old, Yule log, one that will burn for two or three days, and pretty quick the quarters are filled again with pregnant woman. Just like cattle when you turn the bull loose. Scientific agriculture. Use the principles of breeding like with sheep, or cattle, or horses."

"You've been listening to abolitionist bullshit. The breeding stories are bullshit! You do have to provide shelter, food, and supervision; and teach them where the boundaries are; and it costs money. The Northern factory owners can turn an employee out but we provide for an old or unproductive hand."

237

"I'm telling you what I heard," Bates said defensively. "Millions of slaves and the army wants men. Hell, they'll breed enough to replace anything lost in battle. Besides, maybe the black population needs a culling."

"Nonsense. Don't repeat it!"

* * *

SOUTHERN ILLINOIS: OCTOBER 1864

"I got the first shipment in August," Matthew Evans explained. "The fellows at the depot helped me load the buckboard. The boxes of 'Sunday school books' were really heavy but they know I come from a God-fearing family and that I'm a good Christian, and active in the church."

Evans was a storekeeper, a prosperous merchant, a good Democrat, and, as Hines knew, a Southern sympathizer. The two men sat in the kitchen of the house attached to the general store.

The shipment was destined for the Sons of Liberty but a series of arrests disrupted the process. The man who was to collect the shipment was in prison.

"The boxes are in the shed," Evans explained. "I pried the lid on one and got a Colt revolver, but no one has told me what to do with the rest. The gun is in the store. A man has to protect his family."

Hines could hear the rest of the family in the next room. Two boys and a girl were screaming happily.

"I let them make noise in the afternoon," Evans's wife offered justification. "If they play hard all day, they sleep at night. And I don't have the help I need. Back home, there were servants, but here all I have is Aunt Jean. She's getting old and doesn't hear so well, so the noise doesn't affect her."

An aging black woman worked silently at the kitchen counter.

"Aunt Jean!" There was no response, so she raised her voice. "Aunt Jean, leave us now! Clean the bedrooms."

The black woman slowly covered two tins and lifted them to a cupboard. "Yes, Miss Emily. Will we be having company for supper?"

She stared hard at the young visitor. The dust on his clothes told the story of recent travels and he seemed wary, on constant guard.

"No, our guest will leave soon. Look in on the children on your way."

"Whatever you say, Miss." Her tone was a mix of insolence and resignation.

"She grows more impertinent every day," the white woman complained. "She thinks she should be free and keeps asking for her papers, but we tell her Lincoln hasn't freed her. His proclamation doesn't apply in northern states."

"Emily, Mr. Beecham, didn't come to hear about domestic affairs."

"Never mind," Hines reassured the couple. "Everyone has the same problems. That's why we're working so hard on the election."

He rose to retrieve the saddlebag. "There's a hundred dollars in gold." He set a small bag in front of them.

Evans hefted the sack, loosening the drawstring to peer at the coins.

"Convert the gold to greenbacks," Hines instructed. "Gold is rising against the dollar so you should have plenty of cash to spread around."

Hines suspected part of the conversion rate would go to Evans. "I've also brought pamphlets to pass out. They show the true Unionist aims for our society."

He flipped the paper open. "Many people are upset over this amalgamation of the races."

He waited for the shock to appear.

"Amalgamation? You mean mixing the races? White women and black men?

"Oh Lord, Matthew!" Emily Evans sagged in her chair. "They can't expect us to stand for that. It's against the laws of God."

"Just proof of what we're up against," her husband told her. "The Black Republicans will create a world of mongrels. Freeing the Negro, and making him an equal, or allowing the Negro to vote is bad enough. Many poor white men can't vote and shouldn't be allowed to, either, but this. The Negro will see it as sanction for rape."

"It's why we have to work harder to elect Democrats," Hines reminded them. He had doubted the value of the pamphlet, but each time he displayed the paper, the reaction was the same.

"No white man will vote for them after they see this," Evans declared. "This will decide the election."

Hines began to rise but Evans had another question. "What of the Southern army?"

"President Davis has ordered General Hood into Tennessee," Hines told them. "In a few weeks, Confederates will water their horses in the Ohio."

"And the Sunday school books." Evans suddenly remembered the shipments.

"We'll make arrangements soon," Hines told him. "But be careful who you speak with. We're too close for mistakes!"

"I agree completely," Evans assured him.

In the room above, Aunt Jean raised her head from the floorboard knothole, her hearing no longer a problem. Friends at the black church would know whom to tell about the stranger and the shipment. As to amalgamation, she'd keep that to herself. No self-respecting black man would lay with Emily Evans and the thought of Matthew Evans and a black woman was enough to make her laugh. An old lady would be more than he could handle.

CHAPTER 36

Quebec City, Canada East: October 10, 1864

"Gentlemen, can we begin?"

Sir Etienne Taché's voice and gavel could barely be heard over the buzz of conversation but slowly the men from across the British colonies took their seats.

Taché, the nominal premier of the Canadas, had been elected as the chairman. Macdonald, considered the power behind Taché, took a seat nearby. Brown chose the opposite side of the table.

"A few more formalities before the real work begins," Hewitt Bernard whispered to Paul Forsey. "We'll only take a few notes. There will be no formal record of the proceedings."

Newspapermen who sought admittance were turned away. The Quebec conference would be conducted in private and any opposition kept inside the room.

"Very well." Taché rapped the gavel again.

"To review, Mr. Macdonald's motion to affirm the desirability of union is approved. Mr. Brown's motion for a new agreement to embrace Federal principles is approved."

Both men had used dry parliamentary language and only hours into the conference, Forsey wished for McGee's passion.

"Mr. Macdonald has the floor," Taché announced.

Macdonald rose. "We can save time," he smiled. "The less time in this room, the more we can enjoy what Quebec City has to offer. No one goes home hungry...or dry."

The words brought a few chuckles.

"You all know," MacDonald said, growing serious, "a sectional rivalry has gripped this province and we believe the solution lies in new arrangements that still guarantee the rights established in the past. Why reconsider the right to the French language, the French civil law, the role of the Catholic Church or related institutions in this province? They exist and there is no need to change them. But we do need a strong central regime with national powers. The folly of strong provinces or states shows in the turmoil of our southern neighbor. We must learn from their mistakes."

"I stand to agree," George Etienne Cartier rose. "My people have the most distinct culture. We are different, partly by history, by culture, and by language. And we can protect our culture without outside interference."

He turned to face Brown. "The idea we would submit to the commercial interests of Upper Canada has and will be rejected. But we can see the future. We can better protect our interests inside a new confederation."

"Now, don't think you are special," a Nova Scotia delegate warned. "We too have a distinct culture and local traditions to protect."

"Gentlemen," McGee sprang to his feet. "We're going in the wrong direction. Instead, think of a new nation with equal protection for all. I dream of the time when we speak not as Frenchmen or Englishmen, or Scots, or God love us, Irish. I dream of the time when we all take pride in being Canadian."

* * *

QUEBEC CITY, CANADA EAST: OCTOBER 15, 1864

"Miss MacDougall doesn't like her rooms," the young Miss Cole explained. "But I think the Hotel St. Louis is fine. The dinner was superb and soon the ballroom will be aglow."

"Oh, do you think so?" Frances Monck, the niece of the governor general, suspected the country girl would be impressed by any hint of city. The women she knew only as Mercy Cole and Miss McDougall, the daughters of two colonial delegates, could hardly be expected to know of the better things in life.

"And the decorations add so much," Mercy bubbled. "The Union Jacks draped from the ceiling add a regal touch."

"I do like the posters advocating union," Frances said. "The staff tried hard, but the days of rain make Quebec City so dreary. Have you been able to leave the hotel?"

The answer from Mercy Cole was lost as the band began to play. She raised her voice and began again. "No, Miss McDougall has been feeling poorly. She's staying in tonight. Hopefully, when she feels better we can see the sights."

The women moved to seats at the edge of the ballroom.

"Does your father feel they are making progress?" Frances Monck asked. The conversations at the governor general's residence indicated the meetings had degenerated to bickering.

"Oh, he hasn't said." Mercy watched the first couples take the dance floor. "Father doesn't feel a woman needs to know of such things."

"And what is a woman to know of?" Frances sniffed. "Eventually, we'll take our place beside the men. Wouldn't you like to know the plans for the Kingdom of Canada?"

"Is that the name for the new country? Oh look!" She pointed. "Mr. Cartier is on the floor. He dances well into the night. I wonder how the men do it. They dance and party all night and the next day are back at work."

"Oh, they all enjoy the evenings," Frances observed. "Except, perhaps, Mr. Brown. I suspect he retires to his room at night and writes to his wife."

"Isn't that sweet," Mercy sighed.

"I'm sure those young officers would like to write to you." Frances nodded toward the array of red coats across the ballroom.

"One of them spoke to me at the ball last night." Mercy smoothed her dress before she confided, "His name was Ralston."

"Forget him," Frances warned. "He's an aide for my uncle and is not well connected. You can do better."

"He seemed nice," Mercy said. "But men are hard to understand. Mr. McGee was so drunk he made a complete fool of himself last night. And Miss McDougall said Mr. Tupper was very aggressive when he danced with her."

A tall, slim officer crossed the room and bowed in front of the women. He extended his hand to Frances but she politely declined.

"We must be so careful," Frances whispered to her young friend. "A woman has to find the right sort of man."

* * *

QUEBEC CITY, CANADA EAST: OCTOBER 16, 1864

"Like Great Britain," John A. Macdonald explained again, "one central parliament."

"We've already agreed on federal union," Brown insisted. "A central parliament and smaller parliaments for each province."

"The provincial parliaments are very important," Cartier interjected. "They must protect the local interests."

"Any progress?" Bernard whispered, slipping into a seat beside Paul Forsey.

"Not really." Forsey slid a private page of observations beneath other papers.

"Let's leave it for now," Taché suggested. "Could we consider the Senate?"

"An elected Senate," William McDougall proposed.

"Nonsense," Macdonald countered. "Don't use the American model. Next, you will want to elect judges and dogcatchers. The Senate will be appointed. The government of the day can select the members."

"You'd make it a house of ill repute," McDougall shot back. "You would pack the chamber with old cronies. The Senate should not be the preserve of the rich."

"The rich are a minority," Macdonald smiled. "And must be protected."

"Enough!" Brown shook his head. "I agree with Macdonald. The Senate should be appointed. An elected senator would feel he had some power. He won't."

"Yes, but the Senate will provide a reliable income for friends of the governing party," Macdonald said. His comment brought laughter around the table.

"Let's leave that. Where are we on the division of powers?" Taché asked. "Do we need to identify them?"

"Oh yes," Macdonald proclaimed. "Mr. Brown and I are in full agreement, a long list of federal powers and a short list for the provinces."

"Yes." Brown offered a rare smile. "The provinces should deal with strictly municipal issues. Let them build roads and bridges."

"It makes you wish the British has solved these problems years ago," Forsey said quietly to Bernard.

The chief clerk smiled. "The British are masters of change. The first union added English-speaking areas in a bid to control the French. Then after the strong American colonies staged the revolution they decided to keep our colonies weak. Now Britain will agree to what we propose because it needs a stronger union to face those same Americans."

"But without two east coast colonies," Forsey suggested.

Bernard nodded. "Canada West already carries substantial debt. Macdonald doesn't believe we can afford to buy out the landlords on Prince Edward Island. Without that promise, P.E.I. is out. And, Newfoundland is depressed. The colony will need ongoing support from Great Britain."

The gavel struck again.

"The franchise?" Etienne Taché struggled to move the agenda forward.

"Full suffrage," William MacDougall suggested. "Every man should have a vote."

"No, no." Macdonald was exasperated. "The winds have blown the American disease into MacDougall's head. We have to maintain the property qualifications. Next, MacDougall will say that women should vote."

Brown interjected before MacDougall could reply. "Ownership and property brings out the best in people. Retain the property rules."

"We are favoring the upper class," MacDougall charged. "And look who is making policy. A room full of lawyers. Where are the tradesmen and farmers?"

"I'm the minister of agriculture," McGee laughed. "That should count for something."

"And I'm a cabinet maker," Macdonald added, "and a damn fine one, too!"

* * *

ST. ALBANS, VERMONT: OCTOBER 19, 1864

Bennet Young looped the horse's reins around the hitching post and saw a hat wave in the distance: the signal that all was ready. He slowly removed his top coat to reveal the gray tunic, pulled his revolver, and entered the bank.

"Raise your hands and don't move," he shouted. A companion armed with a rifle followed him through the door.

"We are Partisan Rangers of the Confederate States of America. No one needs to be hurt. Where is the bank manager?"

Young swung his revolver slowly around the room, passing over customers, until he saw a short fat man in shirtsleeves and wearing an eye visor. "That's me." His raised hands shook and his voice quavered.

"Open the vault and empty the money drawers." Young waited as the man scurried behind the counter.

"The vault is on the other side of the room," Young spoke quietly and poked the nose of the revolver across the counter.

The manager quivered and the gun he had snatched clattered to the floor. Seconds later, he was nervously cranking the wheel to open the vault.

The lessons Young had learned under Morgan were paying off. His men had carefully observed the town and the bank operations for the past week. Other raiders were making withdrawals at two nearby banks and twenty other rebels were about to make their appearance. He glanced at the clock and yelled, "Hurry it up!"

The manager soon had two bags to deposit at Young's feet.

"Everyone to the village green." The customers gasped as he continued. "The bank and other major buildings in this town will be burned. Federal forces have destroyed towns and villages in the South. The North is no longer safe from Confederate retribution."

The customers and staff streamed from the building to join a parade of townsfolk herded by the sudden appearance of mounted men.

"All as planned," Young called. "Start the fires."

A rider slapped a horse to mount the wooden sidewalk and threw a small bottle against the building. A burst of flame erupted where the bottle smashed.

Gunfire drew him in the opposite direction. The riders were firing into the air while other partisans smashed the vials against walls and through windows.

"Let's go!" Young draped the bags of cash on either side of his saddle. A rebel yell mixed with random gunshots as the men galloped toward Canadian border.

* * *

QUEBEC CITY, CANADA EAST: OCTOBER 20, 1864

"Defense is the chief item for today's discussion," Taché announced as the Quebec conference resumed for the morning session.

"Governor General Monck has joined us along with Maj. William Jervois of the Royal Engineers, the Deputy Inspector General of Fortifications. Major Jervois will begin. He's spent a good deal of time in the provinces in the last two years."

"And touched off a firestorm," Macdonald interjected.

"I must apologize," Jervois said. "My report was meant for the British army and not the *London Times*."

"Was the *Times* correct?" George Brown demanded. "Is Canada West indefensible?"

"Let the major deliver the details as he chooses," Taché suggested.

Jervois moved to a large map of British North America. "I won't spend a great deal of time on the Maritimes. Obviously, Halifax plays an important role in imperial defense, with the Atlantic fleet and the

West Indian squadron. The Admiralty will ensure the safety of Nova Scotia and New Brunswick. The work to improve those fortifications has been underway for two years."

The eastern delegates were relieved. The British would continue to spend on supplies for ships and men.

"Our concerns are here." Jervois moved to a second map.

"The facilities in Canada West have been allowed to deteriorate and there is only a token force in towns like Amherstburg, Port Lambton, London, and along the Niagara Frontier. Repairs or improvements have been repeatedly postponed. The works at Toronto are virtually nonexistent, so the largest fortifications in Canada West are at Kingston."

Macdonald leaned forward at the mention of his home but slumped back, stunned by what he heard next. "The fortifications at Kingston, the Martello towers, and Fort Henry are obsolete. The improvements in armaments, in both range and destructive power, as we have seen in the American war, would bring destruction in a matter of hours. The entrance to the St. Lawrence and the Rideau Canal route to Ottawa will fall easily to a determined enemy."

Jervois waited for his words to sink in before he continued. "My recommendation has been to first improve the armaments at Montreal and here in Quebec City. In the event of war, our small forces in the western districts would conduct a fighting retreat to Canada East. It would be several weeks or depending on the season, months, before the Navy could begin to land reinforcements and our battalions reclaim lost territory."

"Lost? More like abandoned territory," Brown growled.

"There's no choice." Jervois was blunt. "The cost of modernizing the facilities will reach into the millions. Moreover consider the time for construction. If the Americans were to advance in the next two years, Canada West would be lost and a large portion of Canada East."

"What about the lakes?" a New Brunswick shipbuilder asked. "A strong armed fleet could be constructed quickly."

"And could give the Americans an excuse to attack," Jervois said. "It would be a direct violation of the Rush-Bagot agreement that limits naval vessels."

"Urgent for the governor," a red-coated messenger called as he scanned the room for Lord Monck.

"Might we take a break?" Taché suggested.

* * *

"We have a new issue, gentlemen," Macdonald announced as the session resumed. "The governor general has been called away. Mr. Cartier and I, as the ministers responsible for the militia, will join him shortly." The words brought silence to the room.

"Yesterday, a small force identified as Confederate partisans attacked the town of St. Albans, Vermont. Banks were robbed, fires started, several people shot and at least one person killed."

"Just another incident in their unfortunate war," a delegate suggested.

"Unfortunate for us," Macdonald continued. "Twenty-five raiders escaped across the border, pursued by American forces. The Americans caught the leader but the attempt to return him to St. Albans was thwarted by a British military officer and our local law officers. The Confederate, several of his companions, and the cash from the bank robberies have been taken for safekeeping to the jail in Montreal."

Macdonald paused and ran a hand through his hair before beginning again. "Two issues emerge. The Confederate leader claims he was acting on the authority of his government and so will seek the protection of our territory. And second, the Americans are warning that their forces will cross the border in force if there are further incidents. Gentlemen, if there was ever a time to display British North American unity, it is now."

CHAPTER 37

Montreal, Canada East: October 29, 1864

A light rain and mist washed over the long line of carriages. Paul Forsey stood by the doorway watching the guests arrive. The always-immaculate St. Lawrence Hall had been given an extra cleaning for the dinner and ball.

The confederation package had been completed after two long weeks in Quebec City. The politicians chose a glittering social event to unveil the details.

It had all been very businesslike, Forsey decided. The resolutions were simple, straight forward, and dealt with the technicalities of government. Little in the dry principles of the Quebec City resolutions would equal the stirring calls for life and liberty and the pursuit of happiness outlined in the American constitution. Canada's leaders opted for peace, order, and good government.

Each delegate had signed the final agreement but Forsey smiled as he thought of the missing signatures that would never be acknowledged: Bennet Young and John Yates Beall's. The rebels had inadvertently turned the tide. Beall's raid on Lake Erie had started the process and Young's sally into St. Albans finally had convinced the colonies to stand together. Defense had become the decisive issue. But he doubted anyone would admit it and in a few years, few would remember.

The first strain from the military band called the swirling mass in the corridor to the main ballroom. Men and woman, dressed in their finest, were eager to partake of the food and beverage at government expense.

Geoffrey Ralston sauntered through the door and bowed to a society matron before joining the clerk. "Aren't you going in?" Ralston asked.

"No need. I brought notes for Macdonald and now I am excused until the festivities move to Ottawa."

"I haven't been there yet," Ralston casually noted. "I expect to have my fill of the place when we move next year."

"The move could be delayed. The construction on the new Parliament buildings is well behind schedule, and surprise, surprise, over budget. It may be an omen. The contractors of Ottawa are learning to play the government game."

Ralston shrugged. Anyone connected with the military knew the problems with contractors.

"Ghastly decision, never did like the idea of moving the capital into the wilderness. We won't see—"

Ralston froze and offered a stiff salute as a line of British officers made their way to the ballroom.

"Sir Fenwick," he muttered when the officers had passed. "All of the high and mighty."

"He had to be here. It would have been an insult if Sir Fenwick Williams, the commander of the British forces, failed to make an appearance."

"Yes, well," Ralston agreed reluctantly. "Since he lives in the St. Lawrence Hall he can slip away if needed."

"Why would he have to?" Forsey asked.

"Rumblings of more trouble from the Confederates. General Dix in New York issued an order allowing the Yankees to pursue rebels into Canadian territory. Lord Lyons was having dinner with Dix when the word of St. Albans arrived. He agreed with the Americans at first, thinking it was a case of plain robbery, but then had second thoughts. He convinced Washington to rescind the order. However, we think the extra troops are being sent to the border."

Forsey decided instantly to add the latest threat to his private journal. Only a few insiders would have access to the information. His journal might become a major book.

"The Americans are doing more than rattling sabers," he told Ralston. "Their Congress is threatening to cancel the reciprocity agreement. An end to free trade would be bad news for the people who sell in the United States, a lucrative business these last few years."

"Rebuilding forts and building the army in a time of economic distress will be even tougher on politicians," Ralston surmised. "What would they do?"

"Turn to Great Britain," Forsey suggested. "These side issues will surface as the Colonial Office mulls the accord. Maybe Sir Fenwick will intervene. He has connections at the highest levels."

"Ah, but on the wrong side of the blanket," Ralston laughed. The British commander was rumored to be illegitimate and a half brother of Queen Victoria.

"But don't raise that in the wrong circles," Ralston sobered. "Sir Fenwick can be ruthless to those who offend him."

"Wouldn't dream of it," Forsey replied, and thought of his book.

"My God, the nerve," Ralston whispered and pointed to a couple crossing the foyer. "The key man in the Confederate Cabinet boldly appears. He must have rooms in the hotel."

A blonde and strikingly beautiful woman was on Jacob Thompson's arm as the couple climbed the stairway to the upper floors.

"Ironic, isn't it?" Ralston suggested. "The Canadians are celebrating a plan for a new country on the first floor while the Confederates upstairs are no doubt plotting to destroy another."

* * *

Sarah Slater gasped as the music from the ballroom rose in volume. "My heavens, that's Dixie!"

"A very popular piece of music," Thompson said, waiting as she searched for the door key. "Music doesn't stop at the border."

Slater gave up and knocked lightly. The door opened immediately.

"Sillery, Mr. Thompson will be joining me. Would bring us some brandy?"

Moments later Thompson watched as the servant set the tray on the table.

"To your health," Sarah took a delicate sip. "I believe you have a message for Richmond?"

"The letters will be delivered later tonight. The documents are innocent enough, requests for confirmation of orders, that sort of thing."

"Would they apply to Mr. Young and his men?" she asked.

"Yes and that will surprise no one within a hundred miles of Montreal. If we can prove he was acting under orders, the Canadians have no reason to hold him. However, I am more concerned about your safety."

"Don't worry. I've made the trip several times."

"I don't like it and I'm especially concerned after the events with Mrs. Greenhow."

"What's happened?" Slater asked. "I never met the woman but certainly admire her."

Rose Greenhow had become a Southern legend, gathering military information. Her arrest led to several months in prison and she was banished from Federal territory. But the 'Rebel Rose' managed to further embarrass the Union with a book and a successful lecture tour in Britain.

"Use the past tense—admired," Thompson said sadly. "She's dead. She demanded to be put ashore when her blockade-runner was attacked. The sea was too rough."

He saw no need to tell Slater the grisly details. The body had washed ashore. The gold and the dispatches Greenhow carried were stolen and the body was shoved back into the ocean. The currents carried the body to shore a second time a few hours later. The man who had admitted to stealing the gold claimed to know nothing of the papers.

"Holcombe was with her, in the same boat, and got our report to Richmond. But it underlines the danger of your work."

He had a sudden vision of Sarah Slater, lying inert on the ground as soldiers groped her clothing. "So you really must be careful."

"I'm not afraid," she reassured him. "Is there a verbal message?"

"Tell Secretary Benjamin that Clay made a mistake. He gave Young permission to strike at Vermont, denied it, and only confessed when our men were captured. As a result, Young and his people aren't sure whom to trust."

Thompson was more nervous than she had noticed in the past.

"Also advise Mr. Benjamin we have major plans for election day," he continued. "An attempt will be made to fire the major cities."

He read the confusion on her face. "Fires will be set," he explained. "The more, the better. And the Sons of Liberty will seize major arsenals. It will be a day the Yankees won't soon forget."

As she repeated the message, she grasped the significance. The war would be carried to the great industrial cities of the North.

* * *

PORT COLBOURNE, CANADA WEST: NOVEMBER 2, 1864

Only one of the ships waiting at the Welland Canal held Erin Brady's attention. Beall's *Georgian* was moored offshore and Eramosa Willis had climbed aboard an hour earlier. In Erin's bag was a hundred and fifty dollars in gold, his payment in advance.

The shops that lined West Street bustled with the last-minute rush of the dying shipping season and British troops who had assumed guard positions in the last few days added to the confusion. A day earlier, Beall slipped ashore evading both soldiers and detectives.

"The fuss from St. Albans," he told them when they met at a local inn. "The Yankees are on edge. Buffalo is a mass of blue and the tugboats are carrying cannon. But don't worry, Miss Erin. We'll be on the British side of the lake and if our propeller isn't fixed, we may have nothing but a leisurely sail."

"It's not fixed?" Willis thought immediately of the luxury of steam-driven power in the fall gales.

"The chart shows a harbor at Port Stanley. If I order parts, they can be sent by rail and we'll fix it there. Perhaps the little woman could send a telegram for me."

"I don't want her involved," Willis interrupted.

"It's just a telegram. I can do that." Erin placed her hand on his arm. "I'm going to take care of things for the next few weeks anyway. Now what about that message?"

Beall found her more attractive each time he saw her. "Actually, two telegrams. One goes to the York Boat Works for the propeller, the other to Mr. Godfrey Hyams. I need a couple of barrels of potatoes."

"We can get potatoes anywhere along the lake," Willis told him.

"But Hyams needs the business. He's sending supplies to reach us at Port Lambton and can add the potatoes."

"The crew is aboard?" Willis asked.

"All we need," Beall told him. "Two men were ordered back to Toronto for another mission. Both were officers under the late General Morgan, but they weren't sailors, and that's what we need."

Willis wrapped his arm around the woman. "There's nothing to worry about, and the money will carry us through the winter."

"No attacks? No Johnson's Island?"

"Not on this trip, Miss Erin," Beall smiled. "Not on this trip."

CHAPTER 38

Chicago, Illinois: November 3, 1864

At the Richmond House, he was Henry Wallace, an implement dealer from Louisville, in Chicago to meet potential customers. Some clients might actually register at the hotel, Hines told the clerk as he scanned the names of newly arrived guests.

Had the clerk been more attentive, he might have noticed the flash of a smile. The writing was bold. The name of George St. Leger Grenfell of Great Britain stood out and minutes later, a growl told him he had found the right room.

"Thomas! I was expecting you." Grenfell's voice was strong but he moved painfully toward his place near the fire.

"Pull up a chair. Take the chill off. I feel bad forcing the chamber maids to carry wood for a daytime fire but the warmth helps and climbing a few flights of stairs won't hurt them."

Brutus watched Hines take his seat before dropping between them.

"My hunt was successful but with the cold coming on I decided to make one last stop before I return to England."

"You didn't come to join us?" Hines asked.

"I'm not sure what help I could be. I can't move fast, although I hope with the warmth the bones and muscles will loosen up."

Hines felt a surge of sympathy. "Even guidance would help."

"I'm not sure, Thomas, but tell me the latest."

"It promises to be an exciting election." Hines began to detail the latest plans, but Grenfell stopped him.

"Thomas! The Sons of Liberty cannot be trusted. The newspapers are full of stories about a big and powerful secret organization but something is suspicious. The Republican papers carry the most threatening reports. Is the Lincoln Administration trying to scare the people with talk of revolution? If so, it is working. The states that had elections in October supported Lincoln."

"This time, our plans will work." Hines was emphatic.

"Why this time?" Grenfell retorted. "The money spent to elect peace movement candidates is wasted. McClellan's message is falling short. The Democrats are going to lose the election."

"We're prepared for that," Hines told him.

"How? Through the Sons of Liberty, or the Knights of the Golden Circles, or the Order of American Knights?" Grenfell scoffed. "Read the papers. Judge Holt investigated all those groups. If Holt can determine how many there are, you can be damn sure the Federals know who they are and where they are."

"But it won't be just us." Hines tried to remain calm. "Men are ready in other cities. Headley and Martin are in New York. Others are in Cincinnati and Boston. The major cities will be in flames on election night."

Grenfell slumped back in his chair. "And how would the deaths of thousands of innocent people aid the Confederate war effort?"

"They are all Yankees!" Hines exploded. "The Union army has burned houses and towns. The Northern cities can blame their own armies for what's to come."

"And then what happens? Lincoln will still be in the White House. The Federal armies are still in the field. Will they retaliate?"

"Perhaps they'll sue for peace," Hines shot back. "Perhaps they'll recognize the South and let us go."

"Remember the nursery rhyme, Thomas. 'If wishes were horses then beggars would ride.' Perhaps, perhaps, perhaps…"

Brutus interrupted the argument by growling and lunging at the door. A timid knock came a second later. Hines sprang to his feet, reaching for his gun.

"Relax, Thomas." Grenfell stiffly made his way to the door. "I sent for food and a newspaper."

A porter took one look at the dog, set the tray on the table, and quickly retreated to the hall.

"Help yourself," Grenfell told Hines. "You may not have regular meals in the next few days."

Hines picked at the tray as Grenfell scanned the newspaper and then snorted. "They've done it again! There's a warning from Seward, the secretary of state, based on information from the British provinces. It seems there's a plot to burn the major Northern cities."

Hines choked and spit his food into the fireplace.

* * *

LAKE HURON: NOVEMBER 1864

The *Georgian* was under full sail to conserve the coal supply but as Eromosa Willis scanned the northern horizon, he saw dark clouds building, a first hint of a November storm. To the south was a smudge of smoke. The *Michigan* remained in striking distance.

The propeller had given out on the second day of the voyage. The new parts had been waiting in Port Stanley and the repairs made, but the ship was barely underway before the *Michigan* appeared. She came toward them on a collision course and only turned at the last minute, steaming past with guns run out, and then like a cat watching a mouse hole, the warship took up position a few miles astern.

Canadian customs agents added to the tension at Port Lambton, the last port before entering Lake Huron. For three hours, the British scoured the *Georgian*, looking for war material but finding none. Two wagons loaded with supplies were waiting and the customs agents demanded a check on each box and barrel. The loading was nearly complete when Beall lost patience. "Where is the coal?" he bellowed. "I ordered coal and there's no sign of it."

"Don't know about coal," a dockworker called back. "We won't see another shipment till spring."

"What kind of god-forsaken port is this?" Beall pounded the rail. "All we see are petty bureaucrats, sticking their noses in places where they don't belong, and no damn coal!"

He began to pace the deck, fuming over the slow pace. The agents used steel bars to pry the lid from each container.

"Ah hell!" he finally shouted pointing to the remaining barrels. "Leave the potatoes. We've enough food and we could lose the wind."

"And who will pay?" an angry teamster shouted from the dock. "A half day's work has been lost in carting from the depot and it will be another half day to take them back."

"Giles," Beall signalled to the crewman. "Pay that man to shut him up."

Giles swung easily onto the dock and began peeling off bills for the teamster. "Ship the rest back to Toronto."

"I've got papers, sir, but I can't read." The teamster pulled a sheet from under a wooden block on the wagon seat. "Perhaps you'd have a look."

Giles glanced at the documents. Godfrey Hyams had been careful. His name was missing. The address was a warehouse in Toronto and an E. Brady had shipped the goods.

"Yes, it's fine," Giles told him. "Send it back."

"An awful fuss over potatoes," the teamster told him.

"Don't worry. You've been well paid."

Giles, too, was losing patience and Beall had begun to draw in the ropes holding the *Georgian* to the dock.

"Here." He pushed several coins into the teamster's hand. "This should cover any inconvenience."

"Well, thank you, sir. You're a gentleman."

Giles didn't hear. He was back over the rail and onto the *Georgian* as the ship got underway.

The teamster watched until the ship was a speck on Lake Huron. There was no hurry now; he had been paid. He snapped the whip to turn the horses when a customs agent called out. "We'll have a look at those barrels before you go."

"Look all you want! I have all the time in the world."

Moments later, an agent lifted a lid and called to a superior. "Better look at this. The potatoes are seasoned with revolvers!"

The supervisor cursed. Minutes earlier and he would have seized the *Georgian*. He ordered a message sent to the *Michigan*. He didn't like sharing his information with the Americans but his orders suggested this was a special case.

* * *

Aboard the *Georgian*, Willis scanned the sky. The wispy clouds had given way to an ominous black line.

"A moment please, Mr. Willis." Beall motioned to the chart room and turned the wheel over to a young sailor.

"Keep her on this tack," he ordered, "and watch the horizon for our shadow."

"We're going to make a detour," he told Willis, pointing to an isolated dot on the map. "I scouted this area and found a perfect spot, a deserted lumber camp. In two days, a wagon will arrive with the first of our cannon."

"Where are you finding cannon in the wilds of Northern Canada?" Willis asked.

"Remember Burleigh?" Beall asked.

Burleigh was the Scotsman and second in command of the Lake Erie raid.

"He has family in Guelph," Beall explained. "The family has a foundry. Two guns are ready. Two more will be ready soon. In the meantime we'll test the cannon and reinforce the bow. I want her ready to ram."

Willis glanced at the chart. The lumber camp was miles from the nearest town.

"Have you forgotten the *Michigan*?" he asked.

"No chance of that. We have to lose her. We'll hold this course till dark and light the boilers."

"Get steam up now," Willis urged. "There's a squall line out there and this time of year it could be the forerunner of a major storm."

"Then wait for the storm," Beall ordered. "We'll move to full steam when the squalls hit and lose the *Michigan*. We'll give her a surprise next spring."

CHAPTER 39

Nashville, Tennessee: November 1864

Theo Schultz watched as another squad of Union soldiers made their way toward the fortifications. He estimated over a hundred men, blue suits fresh and clean, the ranks dressed with each man in step, and each carried a new Spencer repeating rifle. Any Confederate attack would face a large, well-armed force.

Forts and gun entrenchments stretching three miles into the countryside defended Nashville, and another Federal army was on the way. Thirty thousand men would bolster the force occupying the Tennessee capital—unless, of course, John Bell Hood could stop them, and having just left the Confederate camp, Schultz knew that the rebel general intended to try.

Schultz urged his mount forward but stopped as another squad moved from a side street. In place of weapons, the black men carried shovels and tools. He had seen their work in Kentucky and Tennessee. The railway bridges, the easy targets for Morgan and Forrest early in the war, had been rebuilt as forts and bristled with gun platforms. The raiders who once burned the bridges resorted to tearing up a few rails.

The well-to-do inhabitants fled to the perceived safety of Nashville, leaving elegant homes and plantations deserted. Once-well-groomed lawns sprouted rifle pits or makeshift barricades. Productive farmland grew only weeds. In the city, streets seethed with people, horses, wagons, and carriages, and he blended into the crowd, working toward the roughest part of the town, the district known as "Smokey Row."

The paint had faded on the sign that identified Blocker's Tavern but someone had retraced the hand that pointed to the stable in the rear. His horse turned skittish as he turned into an alley with the decaying carcass of a mule and piles of manure.

"Boy!" He caught sight of a figure in the shadows of the barn. "Boy, get out here and take this animal."

"Don't know as we have any room but if there is, you have to pay in advance." The youngster moved into the light.

"Don't get lippy with me, boy!" Schultz told him.

"I don't have to do anything I don't want to! And I especially don't have to listen to a damn Dutch man."

"Don't get saucy, Jethro. Uppity Negroes get whipped."

"But you have to catch 'em first, Mr. Schultz." The youth offered a smile. "I didn't expect you. Only a week since you left."

Schultz began to empty his saddlebag.

"Figured I would make sure you were behaving, you being a country boy and all."

"Doing fine, thanks to you. Got a warm place to sleep and all the food I need. It's better than grubbing in the hills."

Schultz discovered the teenager in an abandoned barn near the Kentucky line, the only survivor of a guerrilla raid. The bodies of a white man and black woman lay beside a burned wagon nearby. The teen had told of four men who showed no interest in anything but the man's wallet and when he was slow to deliver, the gunfire began. Jethro had escaped to the shelter of the woods. He asked for help to bury the victims, his master and a house slave, and told how twenty other slaves, the master's family, and their most valuable possessions had been moved to Texas. Schultz had no need for a slave but Blocker's Tavern gratefully accepted another hand.

Jethro moved to loosen the saddle cinch. "Still dangerous outside of the city?"

"Worse every day." Schultz slung a saddlebag over his shoulder. "You are safer here, even if you have to work for a living."

Schultz pointed to the horse. "He'll need feed."

"Figured as much. You'll want to see Miss Abigail. This time of day, she's usually in the upstairs parlor."

Schultz made his way through the crowded barroom. A few blue uniforms stood out among the rough apparel of other customers. He caught the bartender's eye before climbing a narrow stairway to the second floor.

"Gonna cost you extra this time of a day," a woman called. "Girls had a busy night; aren't many up yet."

"There will be a bonus in it." Schultz leaned into a room at the top of the stairway. The woman sat before a mirror, running a brush through long brown hair. She wore a heavy housecoat and little else.

"Oh, it's you!" The woman was in her late twenties, full bodied and fleshy. She pulled him into the room and pushed the door shut.

"Your timing is excellent." She guided him to the bench by the mirror, and then perched on the edge of an unmade bed. The housecoat slipped from her legs as she bent to pull an envelope from under the mattress.

"The latest on the garrison," she told him.

"It's the best we have on what's here and the supplies ordered for men on the way, requisitions for food, ammunition, medical supplies, and a pay shipment. If the pay comes through, there will be prosperous times at Blocker's Tavern."

She spoke with a nervous energy, in sharp contrast to other woman in her trade, who he often found slow and lethargic, at least until his time began. With Abigail, it was the opposite. She made him forget that another man was waiting.

Abigail Blocker knew her business. She chose the edge of Smokey Row, sensing potential clients would stop at Blocker's to avoid the crime and violence deeper in the district. Her girls used separate bedrooms and not the cribs, the tiny makeshift cubicles frequented by the lower army ranks. When the authorities decided to register the prostitutes of Nashville and inspect for venereal disease, she marched her workforce to the inspection station and won a clean bill of health for each employee.

Expensive brothels catered to the upper class, but Abigail's clients were clerks, merchants and junior officers who knew as much or more than their superiors did.

"They know the rebel army is closing in," she told him. "A week ago, there was talk of impressing men and cleaning up the city, hauling off the garbage, and not letting dead mules decay on the street. Instead the men work on the barricades. A few months ago, that was black work and not fit for any white man."

"Is that more of Johnson's doing?" he asked.

"He prefers Mr. Johnson," she corrected him. "The Emperor of Nashville. He's white trash but struts around in fine clothes. To think a man like that, a tailor, could be vice president."

"Only if Lincoln wins the election," Schultz reminded her.

"He'll win here. Johnson demands a loyalty oath from every man who votes. The only ones that accept are Union men or turncoats who live on government contracts. And that's another thing. Anyone with an army contract had to 'donate' to the campaign. Lincoln will win here."

She shook her head in disgust but then rose to run her hand across his face.

"Shave and bath might be in order, comfort you don't find in any country tavern. Jethro can bring water."

"I don't have much time. It's easier if I'm past the pickets by sunset." He struggled for something to say, something to dampen the desire. "How's the boy doing?"

"He's a good worker, but do I pay him or you? Negro work gets paid now, by Yankee order. If it's a slave of a loyal Union man, the master gets the money. If it's a slave of someone with suspected loyalty, the money goes to the Negro."

With each movement there was a flash of skin. Schultz found it harder to concentrate. "Pay him. He's doing the work and he's not my slave."

"Are you a closet abolitionist? Many Germans oppose slavery. Why, there are whole units in the Federal army under that German officer...what's his name?"

"Sigel. Franz Sigel," he told her.

"Oh yes, I remember now. I fights with Sigel," she mimicked a German accent. "That's the only English they know."

She grew more serious. "How did you end up as a courier? You could have been an officer. You speak perfect English and use the German tongue."

"I had close friends in Kentucky and tagged along. Some had slaves but I never did. And I never felt the need to live with Germans. I wanted to go my own way."

The brief explanation ended as he rubbed a hand along her neck and began to fumble with the buttons on the housecoat.

"You are in a hurry," she laughed and slipped the garment from her shoulders.

* * *

"There's no charge." She smiled and retrieved the housecoat. "We seem to be similar creatures."

His visits to Blocker's had increased in the last few weeks and more than dispatches made him look forward to her company.

"Abigail." His eyes locked with hers. "Be careful. The Yankees would delight in carrying you to prison."

"And you?" she answered. "The Yankees would like to see you swinging from a tree."

"Maybe in a few months—" he began, only to be silenced by her fingers on his lips.

"Maybe things will change. I'm giving up my role in this business. Oh, I'll still run the girls but I have no desire to work, myself. I may sell Blocker's and use the cash to disappear and start fresh somewhere else. Maybe California."

"We should talk," he told her. "Not just yet but soon."

He pushed the papers into a slit at the bottom of the saddlebag.

"About Jethro?" she said quietly. "The Yankees seize young black men. Manumission papers might prevent that. He could claim to be free. If you don't object, I could draw up the papers."

"Do that," he replied instantly. "But don't tell him. The boy isn't capable of making his own decisions but have the papers ready."

"And when will you be back?" she asked.

"I expect to be close to Nashville for the next few weeks, and north after that, but I promise I will be back."

"You always have a room at Blocker's."

CHAPTER 40

Chicago, Illinois: November 3, 1864

"Mr. Beecham?" The woman's voice was loud and shrill and it took a moment to connect the Beecham name. He used it in the southern counties but not in Chicago.

"Is it you, Mr. Beecham?"

Hines turned to see a distraught woman hurrying down the wooden walkway.

He concentrated. Matthew Evans, the storekeeper in Southern Illinois. The woman was his wife, and she was forcing other people off the walk as she hurried toward him.

"Mrs. Evans! What a surprise."

"Oh, thank God. It is you! Matthew's been arrested!"

"Good heavens, Mrs. Evans. There must be a mistake."

He scanned the street looking for a quiet spot, a restaurant, a hotel, somewhere they could speak in private. He guided her to the entrance of an alley. The pedestrians hurrying home in the gathering dusk would pass them by.

"Now, tell me what happened."

The woman's cloak was covered in dust and her hat was askew.

"What happened?" he repeated.

"We came to Chicago to visit relatives," she said, her voice tinged with panic. "Mathew wanted to bring a box of Sunday school books. He had an address, so we went there. But before he could unload, soldiers stormed the house. This is a Christian country but they ripped the books and said they found what they wanted. Matthew started to speak but they hit him so hard I thought he might be dead but he came around…and then they took him. They told me to keep quiet or I'd be going to prison, too!"

"When was this?" Hines asked.

"Oh, I don't know. What am I to do? I can't visit relatives if my husband brings scandal on the family. I don't know what to do!"

"Think!" Hines demanded. "When did this happen?"

"Oh, it can't have been more than an hour ago. What am I going to do? I need a place to stay! What hotel will accept the wife of a criminal? My reputation is ruined."

"Mrs. Evans!" He grasped her by the shoulders. "I'm sure this is a horrible mistake. Now, we're going to get you a cab. Do you know the address for your relatives?"

"Yes…it's—"

"Good. Tell the driver."

He dashed to flag an empty hack before he returned to her.

"One more thing. Did Matthew tell anyone else about the books?"

"No! Who would he tell? No one knew except Aunt Jean, our black servant. She helped load the wagon. Why would the army care about Sunday school supplies? We're good Christian folk!"

Hines held the carriage door. "Try not to worry. I have friends in the police force. I'll ask if they can help."

He nodded to the driver and Emily Evans waved from the window with tears coursing down her face. "Oh, thank you, Mr. Beecham! I feel so much better!"

I wish I did, Hines thought. If Evans had been arrested the Federal forces were closing in. There would be precious little time to warn the others.

* * *

The brandy was half gone but the muscle pain persisted. The ache reinforced Grenfell's decision. The game was for young men, men who were physically strong, and not for an old man all but crippled.

Brutus growled, aroused by the voices in the next room.

Another Confederate in the adjoining room had a visitor, a man named Shanks, and his appearance was the last straw. Shanks claimed to have escaped from Camp Douglas by hiding in a supply wagon. Grenfell was suspicious. The escape was too easy and the Shanks he remembered from Morgan's cavalry was a liar.

So when Hines arrived, Grenfell would do his last service for the Confederacy and expose Shanks for what he was, a horse thief and a con artist. He would warn Hines to choose better company, shake the hand of the young scout, wish him well, and tell him to visit England when the war was over.

Brutus rose and growled but Grenfell didn't budge. Instead, he stared into the fire, thinking of family he hadn't seen in ten years.

An axe smashing the door broke the spell. Blue uniforms flooded the room.

"George St. Leger Grenfell, you are under arrest for treason."

The dog moved to the attack position.

"Down, Brutus," Grenfell ordered and turned to the soldiers. "Put the bayonets aside. The dog won't hurt you. I'll put a collar on him."

But a circle of sharp steel prevented any movement.

"Aren't you brave! I'm an old man, sick, and unarmed."

"Get up! And keep your mouth shut!"

A colonel levelled a revolver at Grenfell's head. "Up, and up slowly."

"Slowly is the only way an old man can move." Grenfell rose. "But this is wrong. I'm a non-combatant. I have a pass from the secretary of war."

The colonel ignored him and turned to a young soldier. "Don't stand there. Cuff him."

Brutus rose as the handcuffs snapped in place.

"Down, Brutus," and the dog reluctantly obeyed. He waited patiently for another command but Grenfell was hustled away.

"What about the brute?" a soldier asked.

"I don't care," the colonel answered. "We've got we came for."

"Excuse me, sir," a young lieutenant interrupted.

"The Sanitary Fair, where they raise money to help the wounded, needs exhibits. We can't show Grenfell in a cage but we could show the animal and we were told to get as much publicity on this raid as possible."

The colonel considered for only a moment. "Do it, lieutenant. Make the proper arrangements and when the fair is over, shoot the dog."

CHAPTER 41

Richmond, Virginia: November 3, 1864

The Confederate offices in Richmond were abuzz, a feeling of official optimism unlike anything Sarah Slater had seen. The journey from Montreal had gone without incident despite the most recent change in itinerary. The two women spent a night at the Surratt boarding house in Washington and with morning, John Surratt arrived to guide them to Confederate lines.

"Damn soldiers are everywhere," Surratt muttered, "And Lincoln wants more. If I'm drafted, I'm going to buy a substitute. I can get a black one, cheap. White men cost more. Ah, damn!" He pulled the horse to a stop and set the brake.

A freight train blocked their path as it crawled across the Long Bridge to Virginia. The flat cars were packed with row after row of cannon.

Sarah's gaze moved from the bridge to tents that spread for miles along the river. Thousands of tents meant thousands of men.

"I'll take you to Surratt's Tavern," John explained. "Ma's rented it out but we still use it. A fellow from Mosby's command will take you the rest of the way. I thought of signing up with Mosby. Just a few irregulars keep the whole Union army on edge."

"Why didn't you join?" she asked.

"Boy, you're got a lot to learn. My job is too important. The Confederacy needs me where I am."

* * *

A battered cart carried her the final few miles to Richmond, the contrasts growing with each mile. Once white tents were a dirty brown and the rebel lines appeared as thin as the soldiers who manned them.

Judah Benjamin was gleeful when Sarah delivered the message from Montreal and he demanded that she wait. The president was in his office and should hear the news firsthand.

Jefferson Davis was gaunt, the curtains drawn to ease the strain on his eyes, and he rubbed his forehead to fight a constant headache. He stood as she entered and brightened when told of Thompson's message.

"Mrs. Slater, the women of the South have been our strongest supporters," he told her. "And when this war is over I'll see you recognized for the work. I know it is dangerous. Do you travel alone?"

"I have a servant," she answered.

"Watch her," Davis suddenly warned. "The servants aren't as faithful as we once thought."

* * *

The Indian summer chill settled as soon as their bodies parted. She reached for the blanket and nestled back against him. For the first time, she realized how much she had missed him. Their relationship had blossomed through the summer and built to a new climax with each return to Richmond.

"Can you stay?" she asked. "I've given Sillery the night to herself."

"Only for an hour, I have duty tonight."

Mcgruder's duty would take him to the seamy side of Richmond, into the taverns and gambling dens in search of federal spies, turncoat rebels, or simple deserters.

"The president seemed tired," she told him, "And he warned me about Sillery."

"It's not Sillery," Mcgruder scoffed. "It's everything tied to the Negro. He's agreed to consider enlisting blacks but his supporters are planters who would lose valuable assets. Since property is the jurisdiction of the local government, any decision would have to be approved, state by state, and so it's a bureaucratic mess."

"Why warn me to watch Sillery?" she asked. "Surely, the president doesn't get involved in such small matters."

"Davis likes a hand in everything," Mcgruder explained, "But he had a scare with a small fire at the executive mansion and the next morning, a slave was gone, along with silverware. Almost certainly, the Yankees played a part. We know there's a spy ring or rings in Richmond."

"But there's no problem with Sillery!"

"None. Her daughter is in good hands in Georgia. She knows that."

Relieved, she faced him, balancing her head on her hand. The long blonde hair hung to her shoulders.

"And what about us?"

"We've had this conversation," he reminded her. "We'll be together, I just don't know where. Tell me how the war ends."

"It could end quickly." She thought of the uprising planned for Election Day.

"If Lincoln loses, the North will agree to talk. And even if his Union Party wins, the fires and riots will tear the North apart."

"I wish I believed."

She watched as he began to dress. "How can you continue if you feel that way?"

"What else can I do? Perhaps we know too much in Richmond. We know reinforcements aren't coming. There's no one left to send, maybe not even black men."

She reached to take him in her arms. "So what do we do?"

"Our duty, as trite and silly as sounds. But we also have to think of ourselves. I have money set aside. Take your cash to Montreal on the next trip. It would be safer there."

He pushed her back gently to admire the face and body. "Have you been to Europe?"

* * *

TORONTO, CANADA WEST: NOVEMBER 5, 1864

"Brown! Brown! Brown!" The chant intensified as George Brown stepped onto the balcony at the Queens Hotel.

Toronto Mayor Francis Henry Medcalf joined him to wave to the crowd in the street below.

"I wasn't sure anyone would stay," Medcalf shouted to be heard. "Ordinary folk don't seem to care about this confederation and our Orange brothers were told to assemble at seven and it is after nine."

Brown smiled and waved but carried on a conversation. "We were delayed by an accident at Port Hope; a railway worker was killed while coupling cars. We would have been delayed further if Brydges hadn't ordered the body removed. The local officials jump when the president of the Grand Trunk tells them to clear the track."

"I hope the accident wasn't an omen," Medcalf replied.

"Don't go superstitious." Brown continued to wave. "If we hear anything, it will come from labor agitators. They'll claim the hours for the railway crews are too long. Ignore them. Other men want work."

"Speech! Speech!" the crowd shouted. Brown stepped forward.

"My friends," Brown raised his hands. "We have an accord to form a British North American Union!"

The crowd roared approval with more chants of "Brown! Brown!"

"They like it," Medcalf laughed.

"Ha, yes," Brown told him. "They can see we put the French papists in their place."

He stepped forward again. "Canada West can move forward. All of the lands to the west, the Hudson's Bay Company lands, wait for the plow. Our nation can stretch from sea to sea."

It was Brown's night and his alone. John A. Macdonald had slipped away from the victory tour before it reached Toronto.

* * *

"Toronto is showing its best to the folks from the East," the mayor proudly told Brown after meeting with the delegates from the Maritimes. "I doubt they can match this grandeur in Halifax."

"It gives them something to aim for," Brown agreed.

The glow of the gas lamps illuminated the famous "red room" of the Queens Hotel. Chairs, couches, and wallpaper were in shades of crimson. Even the marble in the fireplace was tinged with red.

"Mr. Medcalf," Brown drew the mayor aside, "I have disconcerting news that I didn't want to share with the mob. Your foundry does ship to the United States?"

"Oh, yes," Medcalf explained. "Products from the machine shops, agricultural material, steam boilers. The Americans take a goodly share."

"You may want to explore other markets. The Americans have given notice. They will end the free trade agreement. They claim it's in response to the Confederate raids but of course, a high tariff protects their domestic business. Our union will make easier to supply the other colonies but our markets are smaller. The American action is a year away but I thought you should know."

"Thank you, Mr. Brown." Medcalf began thinking of the steps to shelter his business.

"I have better news, however, for your political hopes," Brown continued. "You won't have to face George Allen in the next contest for mayor. Allen's name is on the list for the new Senate. He'll have other fish to fry and a healthy stipend, to boot. So you see, the Senate is already serving a purpose."

* * *

NEW YORK CITY, NEW YORK: ELECTION DAY 1864

The small hotel room was covered in newsprint—a newspaper was spread on the table; another, on the bed; and parts of a third crumpled on the floor.

"Chicago was a failure but there's nothing of Boston or Cincinnati," Robert Martin told them. "Maybe like us, they're delayed. The troops were moved in after Seward's warning on incendiary attacks."

"I wish I trusted the newspapers." John Headley tossed another broadsheet onto the floor. "The Chicago story says Grenfell was captured but he's the only name I recognize and there's no mention of Tom Hines. From all I can read, they faced the same problems. The local supporters had cold feet and big mouths."

Robert Kennedy ran his fingers across another edition. "Grenfell's dog is on display at the Sanitary Fair. People are going to pay good money to get a look at the animal."

"We've got more to think about than the dog," Martin told them. "Ben Butler will keep his extra troops in New York until he's sure the city is safe. Let's meet here next week. In the meantime, John can make contact with the chemist. The New Yorker's let us down there, too. The Greek fire should have been ready today."

* * *

WASHINGTON: NOVEMBER 9, 1864

"I hope you slept well, Mr. Watson!" Edwin Stanton's voice boomed across the War Department office. "You'll need the rest. The assistant secretary of war is going to be a busy man."

Peter Watson rose to pump Stanton's hand.

"Congratulations! It's doubtful anyone will know the full extent of your work, but I believe you saved Mr. Lincoln, and the country. History will show a huge Electoral College victory for the president, and 55 percent of the popular vote, but few will realize how close it was. We won Connecticut by only two thousand votes and just seven thousand in New York. The voting furloughs for the troops turned the tide in Pennsylvania, Illinois, and Indiana. A rough calculation shows we took 80 percent of the soldier vote."

"I was worried and so was Mr. Lincoln," Stanton admitted. "The big cities, New York, Detroit, and Chicago went better than three to one for the Democrats. The foreign element, the so-called working class, are easily led or bought."

He began to polish his glasses. "And no post-vote trouble. Busting the rebel ring in Chicago on election eve helped. It thwarted their plans and it shows that fear works. More voters went to the devil they know. You'll hear complaints of people kept from the polls by soldiers or of strange mistakes in the counts, but ignore them. We won!"

"And now, to win the war." Watson moved to the large map of Virginia on the wall. The markings showed the line of forts and trenches stretching to within a few miles of Richmond.

"Grant can rebuild his forces and take the gloves off in a spring campaign."

He turned from the map to face the secretary. "Sherman wants to march through Georgia and link up with the naval forces at Savannah. Hood is the fly in the ointment. Grant says if he was Hood, he'd bypass Nashville and drive deep into the North."

"I know Grant's concern," Stanton hissed. "Yes, it's a worry. But we've sent reinforcements to General Thomas."

"Old slow trot." Watson laughed at Thomas's nickname. "Thomas is methodical and doesn't like risks. Hood is the opposite, with a reputation for being impetuous."

"Hood must be destroyed," Stanton repeated. "His army stopped. A breakthrough in the Northwest would destroy our work. We'll have to light a fire under General Thomas or we'll replace him."

"And on the political front?" Watson asked as he moved from the map.

"Emancipation," Stanton barked. "The original proclamation may not stand a court test. It would be dreadfully embarrassing if the courts ruled against the president. Congress can now pass a permanent measure to eradicate slavery. It was best not to raise the idea during the campaign. Why work people up. But now we can act."

"A constitutional amendment," Watson mused, "The thirteenth amendment...lucky thirteen."

CHAPTER 42

Richmond, Virginia: November 10, 1864

Dan Mcgruder imagined the scene; a restless horse stomping, a rider waiting anxiously, but there were no messages from the North and no word on the election result. The delay might stem from a broken axle or a disabled horse but at the Confederate War Department, the silence fueled hope. If Lincoln was beaten, Washington could be in chaos, or fires and riots might have disrupted the railways and made travel impossible.

He thought of other times when Richmond waited in suspense. The news from Gettysburg was slow to arrive and Lee was said to have won a major victory. The first of the wounded painted the true picture a week later.

Mcgruder decided the worst of the rumors came from inside the Confederate government where wishful thinking ran out of control. A year ago, he would have rejected the premise of a tottering Confederacy as preposterous but each night brought more evidence of decay.

He thought again of Sarah. Her money would be safer in Canada and so would she, but she refused to end the trips to Montreal. He had tried to convince her she wasn't needed, that someone else could do the job, hinting that other couriers worked the same route.

The sound of a galloping horse brought him back to reality, a courier with the latest news. A glance at the rider's face told all he needed to know. The first newspaper confirmed it.

"Lincoln re-elected, supporters celebrate in the street. Joyous reaction to huge victory."

He walked slowly to where Judah Benjamin waited. Benjamin could tell the president.

***

TORONTO, CANADA WEST: NOVEMBER 15, 1864

Jacob Thompson settled back as the Negro driver climbed to a seat high on the carriage.

"Have you seen much of Toronto, Dr. Blackburn?" Thompson asked.

Blackburn was in his mid forties and wore a long black coat. He squirmed trying to find support in the sagging leather. "I hadn't planned on a sightseeing tour."

Thompson leaned out the window, snapping his fingers for the driver. "Take us around Queens Park," he called and then turned to his guest. "The British have high praise for your efforts in Bermuda. One of them whispered of special recognition from the Queen."

"I've worked with the Black Jack most of my life." Dr. Luke Blackburn explained. "I developed immunity so the disease doesn't affect me and I learn more with each outbreak. A few people take the yellow fever and recover but when the symptoms progress to bleeding it's often fatal."

"And you do know how the yellow fever is spread?" Thompson noted a drop of sweat had formed on the doctor's balding forehead.

"You weren't told?" the doctor asked.

"I've been distracted by other events. Why don't you explain?"

"There's not much to tell. I believe the sickness can spread through contaminated clothes. I sent clothing to Northern suppliers but there was no outbreak."

"You may be too modest," Thompson told him. "An outbreak at New Bern in the Carolinas has decimated the local garrison."

"I didn't know. And I wasn't sure how our leaders would feel about my work."

"We are past the ethical stage, especially with the Lincoln re-election." Thompson tapped his fingers against the window frame. "Besides, the same tactic was used before, British and Americans gave blankets from small pox victims to Indians."

"And you would authorize future action?" Blackburn asked.

A cold smile flashed across Thompson's face. "You have more?"

"I had the crates shipped from Bermuda. The disease won't spread in the cold weather but when spring comes, I can try again."

"Then do it!" Thompson was emphatic. "If it's discovered, deny any involvement as I will."

"I understand," Blackburn told him. "There are things done in war that should not be discussed now or in the future."

Thompson glanced to the street. If the driver took the expected route, they would have a few more minutes.

"There's another matter. You spent time in Halifax? What do you know of Alexander Keith—Keith the younger? We believe he stole explosives."

"Explosives?" Blackburn was shocked. "What sort?"

"It's not my speciality," Thompson admitted, "but the devices came from the Confederate Torpedo Bureau. Quite ingenious, with gun-powder packed like a lump of coal."

"Keith was a partner of Patrick Martin, a blockade runner. The last time I saw him was with that actor, Booth."

"I know Booth and yes, I remember Martin," Thompson recalled. "We charted his ship."

"You won't do it again," Blackburn explained. "Last month, the *Maria Victoria* wrecked on the St. Lawrence. It was very strange. The weather was clear, the sea was calm, but the witnesses saw her erupt in a fireball. The boiler could have blown but from what you say it was probably something more."

"So it might have been one of our devices?"

"Quite possible. Keith was his partner and the boat was insured to the limit. Keith convinced the insurers to pay and disappeared with the money. Martin's wife and children are left with nothing."

"And no one knows where Keith went?" Thompson asked.

"Not a clue! Had a woman in Halifax but she hasn't seen him. His family will have nothing to do with him. But you might quiz Godfrey Hyams. He did work for Keith."

The two rode in silence for a few minutes, watching the street. The day was mild for mid November.

Blackburn eyed a group of young men in matching green shirts. "What are they? Local militia?"

"Oh, don't the Canadians wish that was the case," Thompson laughed. "They're Fenians. Four hundred of them marched around with pikes at Queens Park a couple of weeks ago. They're Irish, and want to seize Canada and exchange it for Ireland."

"Now, that's a proposition," Blackburn scoffed.

"The Canadians are nervous. The provinces are torn with Protestant and Catholic rivalry and those men make it worse."

"It sounds silly," Blackburn told him.

"It does," Thompson agreed. "But many Fenians are Yankee veterans. If sober, they know how to fight. And, if the British are watching the Fenians they pay less attention to us."

CHAPTER 43

Northern Georgia: November 12, 1864

The Union semaphore flags waved from the hilltops and suggested new orders would arrive by morning. The wounded and semi invalids had been sent to safer territory further west. The trains bound for Atlanta carried only fit men and war essentials.

On the valley floor, the soldier known as Owen Wilson wrenched a plank from a veranda to build a campfire. The house, probably offering little more than basic shelter a year ago, was a now a shell, picked clean by scavengers from both sides. Only enough wood remained for a small fire.

The papers identified him as a private, enlisted at Detroit, September 1864, another soldier who collected a three hundred dollar bounty. He couldn't remember where the money went or when he changed his name from Owen Burwell. Liquor dulled but never completely erased the flashes from the past.

It had been five months since Jimmy had killed Matilde and turned the gun on himself. Owen had placed Jimmy's body beside her, doused the sheets with kerosene, struck a match, and watched the flames take hold. He waited outside until he saw men galloping toward the smoke. The local sheriff led the way, the squire whipping his carriage horse to keep up, and the two men in blue uniforms. He remembered crawling into a haystack and listening to the conversation through the crackle of the fire.

"Anyone inside has had it," the sheriff called as the men and horses milled in the yard. "Search the barn and then we'll go to the other house."

Sgt. Levitus Hurley, a man Owen had hoped never to see again, had spurred his horse, forcing the animal into a tight side step to where the squire sat. "You will send someone to check for bodies," he ordered before realizing he had no jurisdiction. He added, "Won't you please?"

"We will, Sergeant! We want to know what happened here, too."

"I appreciate the help," Hurley told him again. "I saw that one who called himself Owen Burwell slinking away yesterday. I know he, his friend, and that woman stole an army payroll."

"Rest assured, Sergeant, we'll keep looking. But there's no one named Burwell around here. There's a little Port on Lake Erie by that name but—"

"And I remind you," Hurley interrupted, his anger rising, "a lot of these boys are using phony names and enlisting in our army. A lot are bad apples, rotten to the core. We waste time in rooting them out. America will remember who helped us and who didn't when the war is over."

In months following the fire, Owen worked his way across the province. When the demand for farm labor fell with completion of the harvest, he boarded a ferry for the United States and the nearest recruiting office.

A shout from the dusk brought him back to Georgia.

"Wilson, is that you?"

"Who else would it be," another voice giggled, "He's the only one that doesn't like to see the sights."

"Look what we brought." The first man held a jug as he approached the fire.

"Mulroney and Flaherty will take care of what ails you with a little nip of Oh Be Joyful."

Owen reached for the jug.

"Took it off a colored man we met up the road," Mulroney told him.

"Should have seen him run," Flaherty giggled.

The two soldiers made a striking contrast against the fire. Pat Mulroney was tall, a shade over six feet, his frame packed with muscle. He towered over Mike Flaherty by eight inches and where Mulroney was solid, Flaherty was slight, his face pockmarked from small pox.

"Ah, the fire feels good. Takes the damp off the night," Mulroney sniffed the air. "There's no sign of winter quarters. We'll be moving out."

Mulroney could read the signs of army activity. He and Flaherty had served in a British regiment but a pompous commander, strict discipline, and poor pay had soured their experience. Both men deserted from a border garrison, leaving behind red tunics, to fit out hours later in Union blue.

"What else have you heard?" Owen asked.

"We aren't going west," Mulroney told him. "A railwayman says after Sheffield's army leaves for Nashville, Sherman will rip up the rail link, so we'll live off the land."

"Betting is, we're going east, maybe to the ocean," Flaherty added. "There's nothing to oppose us except old men and boys. Their General Hood took his army west, expecting Sherman to follow, but Uncle Billy let him go."

"When will we move?" Owen asked.

"Next few days, I suspect," Mulroney surmised. "A couple of outfits have been ordered out at daylight but they're going to Atlanta and carrying matches. There won't be much left of the city, or its factories or railways. There won't be anything for the rebels to come back to."

CHAPTER 44

Toronto, Canada West: November 16, 1864

"A word, please, Mr. Thompson?" William Cleary slipped into the office and closed the door quietly.

As clerk for the Confederate Commission, Cleary handled the official letters and was well aware of unofficial communications. "There may be another...issue...developing," he said quietly. "A friend of Burleigh's brought disturbing news. Canadian detectives arrested him yesterday."

"Damn!" Thompson slammed his fist on the arm of his chair. "The cannons?"

"They seized two and wrapped them under a cover so no one would know what they took—except Burleigh, of course. Everyone saw him led off in shackles."

"The Yankees have been stepping up the pressure since the St. Albans raid. The British may have decided the less the Americans know, the better. It would be very embarrassing if Confederates were found molding cannon in the heart of Canada West."

"The other guns have been shipped," Cleary assured him. "We had them freighted to Beall."

"Inform him," Thompson ordered. "If they have the second in command from Lake Erie they'll want the leader. As to Burleigh, let's wait—or maybe that lawyer friend of yours could make discreet inquiries."

He waited a moment but Cleary stayed by the desk. "Something else?" he asked.

"The visitor, sir," Cleary told him. "He won't speak with me—says his business is with you and you alone."

The stranger had arrived earlier in the morning, demanding an immediate meeting with Thompson.

"I thought if I waited, he might give up," Thompson smiled. "But no such luck! Bring him in."

Thompson rose to stretch his legs. He had no appointments but it was not unusual for mysterious visitors to arrive.

The man Cleary ushered into the office was in his late fifties, tall and rigid with a bald head seemingly held in place by a clerical collar. He waited until the clerk had left the office.

"It is a pleasure to finally meet you, Mr. Thompson. I am the Reverend Kensey Johns Stewart and I am here to ease your burden! You were told to expect me?"

"I'm afraid not, pastor," Thompson replied. "But anyone who can ease my burden is welcome."

"Shall we pray?" The pastor raised his eyes to the ceiling. "Lord, accept the pleas of your servants as they toil in a foreign land. Protect our President Jefferson Davis, our gallant General Lee, General Longstreet, General Hood, and all Southern men who fight to defend our homes and our Christian constitution. Hear, oh Lord, as we beseech you to smite our enemies. May they see the error of their ways and repent and if they fail, smite them with plagues and hellfire and brimstone. Amen."

Thompson was poised to guide him from the office at the "Amen," but the pastor gave him no opportunity.

"Now Mr. Thompson, I come with the blessing of God and Jefferson Davis. I have met with the officials at the highest level in our brave Confederacy, and I have taken our esteemed General Lee into my confidence. He is, after all, a relative by marriage."

"Well, that's very interesting—" Thompson began, but was cut off as the pastor continued.

"I am short of funds and will need to access the money forwarded from Richmond. The twenty thousand dollars in gold; I'd like it this afternoon."

"I don't know what you're talking about," Thompson told him, "and I'm not about to provide cash for every damn fool that comes to my office."

"I won't accept profanity," the reverend interrupted. "Perhaps that profanity has turned the Lord against you. How else can we explain your failure?"

"My failure?" Thompson sputtered.

"Well, you can't call it a success. The money was sent. I want it now."

"I don't know anything about money."

"It was sent by special courier. The president felt it unsafe for me to carry such a large amount across enemy territory. If it's not here, it's been stolen. Thou shalt not steal!" he thundered, waving his hand at Thompson.

"Oh, Christ!" Thompson barked. "Cleary?"

"Blasphemy, too! Repent or be consigned to hell."

The door opened as Cleary arrived but the tirade continued. "You and your associates are on the road to ruin!" spouted the reverend.

"Cleary, what do we know of a special delivery for Rev. Kensey Johns Stewart, funds from Richmond?"

"Nothing. A courier is due but there's been no communication about any Rev. Stewart."

"Thieves! Money changers!" Stewart was in full cry. "The good Lord threw them out of the temple but they have returned!"

"Mr. Cleary," Thompson growled. "Give the reverend one hundred dollars from our emergency account. Be sure to get a receipt! And then see him out of this office. You will learn where the good pastor is staying, and if there is a need for further communication, talk to him there. He is not—I repeat, not—to return here!"

* * *

CHICAGO, ILLINOIS: NOVEMBER 20, 1864

Relief washed across Mary Ann Shadd Carey's face when she finally found the office of Martin Delaney.

He smiled broadly when he saw her. "I'm about to transfer to Washington and was afraid I might miss you."

Despite the roaring fire, Delaney's office was cold. The papers on the window ledge rustled as wind whistled through the cracks around the poorly built frame. The entrance to the building was down an alley and five blocks from the Union headquarters.

"We have shelter but the white army considers us second rate," Delaney saw her glance at the window. "I am supposed to be glad I have an office. Still, I suspect it's better than how you have been living for the past few weeks."

"I manage," She slipped into a chair. "The weather isn't the worst of it. It's the attitudes—on both sides. We've signed all we're likely to get from the contraband camps. Going into Kentucky and Tennessee proved a waste of time. The freed slaves not taken for labor are used as servants and staff for army officers. They get food and clothing and little else but they seem to have no desire for anything more. The wives and daughters find piece work as washerwomen or domestic servants."

"Our people should not work as domestics," Delaney interrupted. "It's beneath them! That sort of work should be done by the Orientals. The Southern planters know the value of a black man —they didn't want to risk slaves on railways or in building canals or levees. They found it was much less expensive if they lost an Irishman."

"Our people worked side by side with the Irish when they built the railroad across Canada West, and they got along quite well," she told him briskly. "Of course, our people were freemen."

"I suppose the men must support themselves," Delaney relented. "When the war is over, they'll need jobs. The poor whites will have more competition, and won't like it. However, our cousins prefer the South. There are upwards of four million slaves across the cotton belt. There have been ample opportunities for them to get away, but in the grand scheme of things, very few have. We've really seen only a trickle reach the North."

"But how many black men are in the army?" she asked.

"About a hundred and fifty thousand," Delaney told her. "But that will grow."

"Do we know how many are in the Confederate army?" she asked suddenly.

He was silent, surprised by the question.

"I don't know actual numbers, but not more than a handful," he answered. "There may be some misguided freemen, and God knows the Confederates are using plenty of slaves around their camps. I take it you ask because of the rumors of Southern emancipation?"

"I met slaves in Kentucky who were as rebel as their masters. And yes, I've heard the talk. The rebels would train slaves to fight and consider emancipation when the war is over."

"That should be seen as a final, desperate act!" Delaney told her, "showing the South is out of men and out of ideas."

"Have they lost that many?" she asked. "One hardly knows what to believe."

"There are thousands of graves," he told her. "The glory is gone from the rebel cause. And don't forget those who deserted or refused to fight."

"But that's not new," she told him. "Early in the war, the railway added extra cars to the trains from Windsor to accommodate the people fleeing into Canada. So really, what's changed?"

"We have!" he told her. "If not for us and the foreign elements, the North would be out of men too. Instead, Federal armies are close to full strength but there will be a call for more men. Lincoln is not about to let up."

"I was worried about the election," she told him. "The voters had been worked into such a state I feared they would vote against the Union."

"*White* voters," he reminded her. "Only a few black men have the right to vote. That has to change. Think back to Canada. Your father and the men of Kent proved they could elect a black man to the township council. Think of how millions of black men could affect an election.

"And black women," she reminded him. "We should vote, too."

"Oh, Mary Ann! Fight for women when the war is over."

"We should be working for it now!" She was angry but Delaney would have no part of the argument.

"We'll take care of men first. I want a black army, led by black officers. The slaves would come to us in droves. That's the way to run the war!"

"Well, haven't you become militant, very militaristic, and more uppity than usual?" she chided him.

He allowed a smile before he continued. "It's the only way. We won't have another chance. We have to win total freedom, and the army is the only way to do it. The white man's civil war must become a black man's revolution."

"And a black woman's?" she asked again.

"Later! That will come later! We've come too far to be distracted. It's why I'm going to Washington. I need to be close to the decision makers—maybe the president."

"I'm going home!" she told him, and immediately regretted her tone. "I need to see the children and get away from guns and uniforms. And I'm disgusted by North and South. Federal soldiers burned Camp Nelson in Kentucky to deprive black women and children of shelter. And the husbands are in the Union army."

"It's war," was the only defense he could offer. "And if you feel that way, this may be a good time to go."

"Why?"

"There is a rebel army in Tennessee. Should they get by the Union forces around Nashville, there's nothing to stop them before they reach Ohio. And remember—at Gettysburg, the rebels rounded up colored people, the free and the slaves, and sent them south. They would do the same in the Northwest."

"I worry about the counties along the Ohio River," she said. "I heard so many stories about disloyalty and guerrilla units and hidden guns, and all that talk about the Sons of Liberty."

"That was a game. A man's game. The talk was engineered by Washington to frighten voters into casting a ballot for Lincoln."

"I'm not so sure. There were dangerous men on the loose through the summer. Look at what they tried to do here. Free the prisoners, burn the cities. It was barbaric!"

"Well, you don't have to worry about it anymore," he assured her. "Go back to Chatham. I'll send word if I need you."

* * *

NEAR ATLANTA, GEORGIA: NOVEMBER 17, 1864

"Wilson, I need to talk to you!" The lieutenant on horseback called the foot soldier to his side.

"We have orders to move for another two miles before we camp, and if we have more light we'll make better time. Take a dozen men and set these rail fences alight. They're dry, they'll burn well, and they're far enough from the road to allow the men and wagons to move down the middle."

"We'll make a perfect target," Owen cautioned. Unlike many officers, Lieutenant Carswell would accept advice from the ranks.

"Don't worry. Kilpatrick's cavalry is sweeping through the fields on both sides. They'll scare out any rebs. Light her up!"

Atlanta was thirty miles behind, and like the houses and plantations along the march, had been picked clean by Sherman's forces. The men had been told to forage liberally, and took the orders to heart. Anything of value was taken, and much of what could not be carried, was destroyed.

The dry grass made perfect kindling. The flames spread to the wooden rails and leaped to fight the gathering dusk. With the extra light, the blue regiments picked up speed. The marching men mixed among wagons loaded with food and ammunition and sagging with the weight of confiscated goods. On one, a grandfather clock was wedged against the seat, surrounded by chairs, a bed frame, and stacks of clothing.

Wilson set the torch and watched the flames take hold. He thought momentarily of the work to build the fence—of the rails split and assembled to keep the livestock in the fields—but there was no livestock left to hold. Horses had been confiscated by the Federal force, cattle driven into the herd at the rear of the column, and the few pigs gutted. Useable meat was tossed into army wagons to be cooked in camp and any remains left to rot.

In the distance, a regiment began to sing. *"John Brown's body lies a-moldering in the grave,"* the voices sang, rising in volume. *"His soul goes marching on,"* they continued. Other units joined the chorus:

> *Glory, glory Hallelujah!*
> *Glory, glory Hallelujah!*
> *Glory, glory Hallelujah!*
> *His truth is marching on.*

The fires raced along the fencerow to writhe like giant red and yellow snakes on either side of the Federal force.

Owen watched shadows in dark blue, flames reflected from buttons and bayonets, and dust mixing with smoke. No rebel snipers disrupted the column. The very sight of the passing army would frighten any sane man.

* * *

That night he met the Frenchmen.

The soft strains of music caught his attention, a contrast with the bustle of the army settling for the night.

"You like the music?" an accented voice asked.

"Yes, it's different," Owen answered.

"Well, *vive la difference!*" the soldier stepped out of the shadows. Like Owen, he wore the rumpled blue jacket and pants. Another soldier leaned over his instrument.

"His grandfather teach him to play the violin, not the fiddle that the others play—the violin," the man continued. "Some nights he play the happy song, but tonight he is sad. I am Gaetan Malo," the man said, and offered his hand.

"Owen...uh...Wilson," he replied but focused on the violin.

292

"That is Jerome Tessier," Malo said. "And we are part of the Quebec contingent in General Sherman's army."

A baffled Owen turned to Malo, "Quebec contingent? I know there are people from the British colonies, but I didn't know of a regiment from Quebec."

"Ah no, mister, just me and Jerome. We collect our bounty in New Hampshire with many others of our people. But the army, she works in strange ways. We end up with an Illinois regiment and they don't understand us. Jerome does not speak the English so I speak for both."

Something in Malo's tone and face made Owen relax. "Actually, I'm from Canada West, but I don't talk about it much."

"Hah! These Americans don't know about other places—or care," Malo smiled. "And hey, with their armies, maybe they don't need to."

The music continued.

"Jerome—he is very sad tonight, maybe he thinks of his girl back in Lévis. She is a pretty one and he miss her a lot."

"Do you miss a pretty one, too?" Owen smiled.

"Ah! Gaetan miss all the womens not just one," Malo chuckled. "Come, we have wine that has been—how you say, 'liberated'. Share it with us."

Wilson later decided it was the wine, but as the evening progressed he told Malo of his home, of the army life, of Jimmy and Mathilde and all of his experience in the past two years.

"Sometimes it helps just to talk," Gaetan told him. The soft strains of the violin matched a gentle Southern night.

"Jerome. He has no one to talk to but me," Gaetan explained. "He says he don't want to learn English. When this is over he will go home and speak only with his own people."

Malo shook the last bottle and offered it to Owen. "We finish it! We find more tomorrow."

Owen happily agreed, stretching out and watching Jerome.

"He is also sad because of what he sees," Malo spoke quietly. "He does not like the destruction. He says his grandfather tells him of the other war, what we call the Conquest, when General Wolfe defeats Monsieur Montcalm. Wolfe burned the little farms around Quebec

City. He turns the woman and children out as General Sherman does. I tell him, look: we survived, our people survived. We always remember but we survive."

"I knew of the Plains of Abraham," Owen replied, "but I never heard of the farms and houses that were burned."

"Hey, Gaetan can teach you a lot, mister," Malo laughed. "Maybe before we get where General Sherman wants to go, I can teach you more."

* * *

The rank and file weren't told their destination. A soldier with a friend in Sherman's small headquarters unit said the armies were aiming for Savannah on the Atlantic coast, but others felt the destination was farther north and Richmond. The men gauged progress by the clouds of smoke that showed buildings destroyed and, with their destruction, the war-making capacity of the South.

Flaherty and Mulroney linked with a unit of men scouring for food, weapons, or anything of value.

Owen had been left to fight a team of badly trained horses, recruited from a Georgia homestead, when he heard the first explosion. The team reared and tried to run, but a nearby squad grabbed the bridles and harness.

"Wonder what that was?" Owen asked. The horses were stomping and fighting their bits. "Wasn't loud enough for artillery."

As he spoke, another blast came from up the road.

By the time he had regained control of the team, the first soldiers had come running back.

"Torpedoes. Land mines," one panted and leaned on the wagon to catch his breath.

"The friggin' rebels have planted explosives in the road."

"Anyone hurt?" Owen asked. He began to swing down but stopped to study the ground where his feet would land.

"Yeah, two men blown to hell," the soldier was trying to catch his breath. "The Frenchies. The one that did the talking stepped on one of those infernal devices and gets blown up. We yelled and told the other one to stay put, but he don't understand nothing. He runs ahead and gets blowed up, himself."

Owen slumped onto the wagon seat.

"Wait here until the road is cleared," a lieutenant ordered.

The words were barely out of his mouth when another wagon rolled up. Two ashen Confederate prisoners were tied together and surrounded by Union soldiers.

Behind the wagon were several Union officers on horseback.

"Holy shit, Uncle Billy," a soldier observed.

Owen raised his head in time to see a red beard flash by. A large slouch hat covered the rest of the face, the uniform covered in dust. The horse was short, and the rider's feet appeared to drag the ground.

"William Tecumseh Sherman," another soldier whispered, and then shouted, "Three cheers for Uncle Billy!"

If Sherman heard, he gave no sign.

"Them torpedo things will surely anger the general," a soldier announced as he stared after the departing figure.

"He don't like to see lives thrown away. That's why he had us marching all around Atlanta during the summer. He doesn't like to see men cut down for sport."

"Guess you weren't at Kennesaw Mountain," another soldier spoke up. "He threw the whole damn army against rebel works. I lost good friends that day."

"Yeah, well, that's one of the few times he didn't look for another way," the first soldier defended his general.

"He does what he can to save a Union life."

"Yes, you're right." The lieutenant joined the conversation. "He doesn't like to waste people. Those Confederate prisoners, on the other hand, are a different story. The rebs have to crawl around looking for the mines. If they find one, they remove it. If they don't see one, and get blown away—well, the road is clear and none of us get hurt. Sherman sent a message through the lines and told the rebels what he was going to do. Figures that may make them stop planting the damn things."

* * *

A half hour later, there had been no more explosions, and the column prepared to move forward.

The lieutenant looked about before ordering the advance.

"Any of you close to the fellows who were killed?" he called. "They have to be buried."

"Nah, they was foreigners," a soldier answered. "They kept pretty much to themselves."

"I'll do it," Owen volunteered. "We had things in common."

"Well, it won't take long," the lieutenant predicted. "There won't be much left to put under."

CHAPTER 45

New York City, New York: November 24, 1864

John Headley awoke with a start and groped for his watch. In the soft glow of the lamp, he read 7:30 p.m. Earlier in the day, he had checked in, dropped a single suitcase, and left to repeat the process at another hotel a few blocks away. The rest of the men followed the same pattern.

Tonight the action would begin. Headley's case lay empty on the hotel room floor. He spread papers and clothing at the foot of the bed, lifted the drawers from the night table, and placed them on the mattress along with anything else that was combustible.

The bed sagged under the weight as the nightstand and an upholstered chair were heaped on top.

It was time.

He tossed the bottle gently it in his hand, watching the fluid begin to froth, and then hurled the bottle to shatter on the heap of wood and cloth. In an instant, the overpowering smell filled the room, and a second later, the flames erupted.

He moved quickly into the hall, pulling the door closed behind him. A glance showed no one in the corridor, so he took precious seconds to insert the key and lock the door. Those who would respond to the alarm would face another obstacle. Already he could feel the heat building through the door.

Within two minutes, Headley was down the stairs and into the street en route to his next target.

The first of the fire bells rang as he left the second hotel. The alarm came from several blocks away, proof that the other Confederates were busy. The fire attack on New York had begun. The streets were soon filled with panicked New Yorkers.

"Don't know what's happening," a man shouted to his companion. "Fires are breaking out all over."

"We've got to get out," a second man panted. "People are spooked. We could be trampled by the mob."

Headley could smell smoke, but there was no telltale glow on any horizon. The fires would take time to reach the roofs and streets.

For an instant, he felt compassion for those that might be trapped, but he forced the thought from his mind. It was war, and retribution for the thousands of Yankee torches used in the South.

For over an hour, he fought the crowds, slowly making his way toward the river, where dozens of boats were moored for easy access to the warehouses. Their crews were peering anxiously in the direction he had come, and a squad of Federal sailors began to take up position to limit access to the Navy ships. The easy targets were hard to find, and he had one last bottle of the Greek fire.

A barge stacked high with hay caught his eye. He glanced about to be sure that no one was watching. He put all his strength into hurling the final bottle near the metal casing that held the anchor chains. He saw it smash and ignite, and watched the first of the flames begin to eat at the forage. At worst, he reasoned, there would be hungry Yankee horses. At best the flames would spread along the waterfront.

* * *

Kennedy was the last one to return, clutching a liquor bottle as he swayed into the room.

"It was hot and thirsty work. A man needs refreshment," he laughed, and took a pull from the bottle. "My kind of Greek fire, soothing and lacking the burn of cheap rotgut."

"You are late," Robert Martin told him. "We expected you two hours ago."

"I was delayed at the theater." Kennedy delivered an elaborate bow. "A little bonfire at Barnum's. It was like a free night at the circus. So I stayed to watch the show."

"And you've been drinking all night?" Martin asked.

"No! Only since breakfast," Kennedy grinned.

"You are done for the day." Martin told him. "The last thing we need is a drunk. We'll stick together until we leave for the depot and Toronto. The Yankees will be watching everything."

"Do you have any idea what went wrong?" Headley asked. "The fires were started in my two hotels, but must have burned out. The only place where the flames took hold was on a hay barge on the river."

"The newspapers tell of fires across the city," Martin told him, and pointed to the stack of papers spread across the table. "But little damage. The flames were discovered or simply burned out."

Martin continued. "There was panic, especially at Barnum's"—he looked at Kennedy—"which wasn't on our list. The crowd at the Winter Garden Theater smelled smoke and started to leave but one of the Booth brothers stopped their special show and told them not to worry."

"There was a bunch of people that charged out into the street," Kennedy told him. "Maybe not everyone, but enough to fill the street. I thought the whole block would go up."

"Same with me," another man added. "The fire was going when I closed the door. But I went by this morning there was soot on the window but that was it."

"Could it be the chemist?" Headley wondered aloud. "Maybe the mixture wasn't strong enough, or perhaps was deliberately sabotaged?"

"Or maybe the Greek fire formula," Martin suggested. "Maybe that's why there were no fires at Boston and Cincinnati on Election Day. We'll find out in Toronto."

"We could find out now," Headley told him. "I'll swing by the chemist's shop for a little chat."

"No, that's dangerous," warned Martin. "The police have descriptions. The descriptions don't match us, but stay off the streets. One paper even says Tom Hines led the raid. Our best plan is to get the men away. They'll be needed for other work."

CHAPTER 46

Near Franklin, Tennessee: November 30, 1864

Theo Schultz stepped ahead to lead the horse. With the congestion along the hillside road, he could save the strength of the tiring animal.

"Guns," a rebel lieutenant bellowed as he galloped from the front. "We need the guns at Franklin! General Hood wants them now!"

An artillery officer inspecting a gun carriage with a broken wheel rose from his knees. The spokes had given way and blocked the track. "Push it to the side," he ordered the crew. "Take the barrel off and we'll find a wagon. We don't have enough cannon to leave one behind."

"Hood wants the artillery now," the lieutenant said, forcing his horse into the man's face.

"We're moving as fast as we damn well can," the artillery officer shouted. "The equipment is wearing out."

"Damn your equipment. Move it along. We've got one hell of a fight brewing."

The lieutenant spun the horse, turning the way he had come.

Schultz stepped into a ditch to pass the obstacle.

Ahead, he saw gray troops rise from a brief rest to double time forward.

The growl of massed rifle fire ahead underlined the urgency.

What had been a perfect Indian summer day was fading to twilight as Schultz approached the main rebel line.

Packs, overcoats, and blankets littered the road. The Army of Tennessee had lightened the load before attacking the Northern army.

A cluster of black servants remained to protect abandoned property. The gunfire had grown louder and Schultz was forced to shout.

"How far ahead?"

"Just to the top of that hill," one black shouted back. "And on the other side of the hill it's open ground to the Yankee line."

"And the army has gone forward?" Schultz called.

"Oh, yes, sir. A great sight—bands playing, the line must have been three miles across. My master said it was like Pickett's charge at Gettysburg, but General Hood had been at Gettysburg and he wouldn't allow that kind of result."

"But, it's open ground?" Schultz asked.

"Yes and the Yankees are entrenched with a river behind them. A bunch of veterans pinned papers on their backs. I can read. It was their names and hometowns. They don't do that unless they might not come back."

"Out of the way!" a series of shouts came as more lines of gray and butternut jogged forward.

"What's happening?" Schultz yelled to the closest men.

"Reserves going in," came the answer. "Hood must have them on the run if we're going in at nightfall."

"I'll be praying for you," a chaplain called. "Remember any man that falls for the cause, will dine with the Lord in Heaven tonight."

"Will you be joining us for supper?" A grizzled veteran asked. But the chaplain had moved to the rear.

Another voice spoke. "You can leave the horse and join us."

In the uproar, Schultz hadn't heard the man approach. He saw insignia of a rebel major.

"No, I'm a courier with a message for Hood," said Schultz.

"Bullshit!" the major spat.

Schultz pulled the envelope from his pocket. The major scowled and squinted in the fading light.

"His headquarters is to the right—a plantation house back of Franklin."

The chastised major stalked off before waving his hat in the air. "Hurry it forward, boys. We've got the Yankees where we want them!"

In the confusion at the headquarters, it was twenty minutes before Schultz found an orderly to accept his message.

"Doubtful if there will be a reply tonight," the young officer told him. "General Hood believes the Yankee line is weak and it will take just a nudge to break it. We're hitting them head on. Find somewhere close to rest. Hood will need you in the morning."

CHAPTER 47

Franklin, Tennessee: December 1, 1864

The noise and a shudder in the earth woke Schultz. He shook his head to clear his mind and felt the ground shake again. The deep-throated roar came from the rear, meaning the Confederate artillery had arrived.

The small fire that offered warmth last night had burned out. The other men who had gathered by the flames, like him, were too tired to search for wood. A layer of frost covered sleeping bodies.

Schultz rose and stamped his feet. Despite the gloom of the coming dawn, he could see shapes, men hurrying in and out of Confederate headquarters a scant hundred yards away, but he turned the other way and climbed slowly toward the top of the rise.

The concussion from another round of cannon fire shook the last of the fall leaves from the trees. The artillery that was delayed yesterday was making up for the absence this morning.

Schultz topped the ridge to look toward the Yankee position. Confederate shells threw up clouds of debris, and there was no return fire. The Federal line appeared empty. At first he felt elation, until the light grew to allow him to see the shapes on the battlefield.

Soldiers and stretcher-bearers were moving cautiously, choosing each step carefully as they wove through a vast carpet of dead and wounded.

"Theo?" He turned to recognize another scout.

"General Hood wants you! He'll be moving to the Carter house," the scout said, pointing to a building closer to the abandoned Union trenches. "But I don't think you need to hurry."

"Is it as bad as it looks?" Schultz fought a weakness that swept over his body. "Thousands must be lying out there."

"No one has the official casualty numbers but it's bad." The scout toyed with his riding gloves. "We may have lost six thousand men. General Hood sees it as victory, since the Yankees pulled out during the night and left their dead and wounded behind. He's moving on to Nashville."

"What with?" Schultz asked as shock gave way to anger. "The best fighting men in the Army of Tennessee are lying out there."

"And some of the best leaders," the scout agreed, glancing back toward the headquarters. "I counted five generals laid out on the veranda of the Carter house this morning."

Schultz was silent and surveyed the field as the scout continued.

"Pat Cleburne was missing. He had two horses shot out from under him and was pressing ahead on foot and waving his cap to rally the men. The general's Irish brogue came back in a battle and they heard it strong. He said if they were going to die, they'd die like men."

"But he's missing, you said?" Schultz asked. "Maybe he'll turn up among the wounded."

"Well, I said he *was* missing," the scout clarified. "But they found his body propped up among his men. Cleburne may have had an Irish premonition. He stopped at a church yard a few days ago and said it would be good place to be buried."

Schultz listened as the scout ran through the long list of officers who were missing or dead.

He watched a lone figure moving gingerly and making odd movements among the fallen. The man bent to lift a head and struck it hard with the hammer he carried.

Schultz gagged. With the hospitals filled there was no hope for the grievously wounded.

"What's left?" He tried to steady himself. "If you're right, Hood has lost a third of his army."

"Take that up with the general," the scout suggested. "I'm sure he'll be interested in your opinion. He'll be waiting for you at the Carter house."

* * *

The Carter family home had been transformed into a makeshift hospital and was already overflowing. Frantic surgeons worked over men on the lawns and in the nearby sheds.

"Ah, the Dutchman," Hood exclaimed. Army staff had lifted the general to his horse and secured ropes to hold him in the saddle.

Schultz did his best to imitate a salute. He looked closely and saw Hood's eyes were glazed. Perhaps the rumors were true, and the pain-killers had clouded the commander's judgment.

"I'll make this quick," Hood told him, although his speech was slow. "I'm moving to Nashville immediately. After we take the city I will reorganize, and re-equip, so the drive north will face a temporary delay. In a few weeks, we'll come. We can move either north of the Ohio River, or swing east and catch Grant in the rear. I want recruiters sent into Kentucky."

"I'll tell them, General." Schultz touched his hat and swung his horse to the north.

As he trotted down the roadway, he saw the burial squads at work, hundreds of bodies ready for the long trenches.

The general may be optimistic, Schultz thought, but he's out of luck with volunteers. Hood had expected new recruits in Tennessee but only a hundred men came forward. It would be the same in Kentucky. Despite the general's swagger, he feared Hood had wrecked the Army of Tennessee. It would be hard, if not impossible, to find man-power to rebuild it.

CHAPTER 48

Collingwood, Canada West: December 1864

A heavy, wet snow added to the gloom. The *Georgian* rocked and pulled on the ropes that held the ship to the dock. The deck was stacked with lengths of sawn lumber, the lumber that could fetch thousands of dollars in the big American markets.

Eramosa Willis slid sideways into the narrow space between the stacks, making one last check that the ropes and chains were tight.

The cannons were stored in two heavy crates to protect them from the winter snow and lumber piled to shield them from prying eyes. The ship was being watched, but the weather drove the detectives to the shelter of a nearby tavern.

One rope had worked loose, but it took only a quick pull to wrench it tight.

The deck was slippery as he made his way back to the main cabin.

Through the slanting snow, a lone sailboat made its way to harbor. In a matter of days, the cold and ice would end the shipping season. The harbor was rapidly filling with ships tied up for the winter.

Willis swung the cabin door open. A small stove was bolted to the floor and a makeshift chimney carried the smoke through a porthole. On this day, it warmed the main cabin, but in a few weeks—in the depths of winter—only a small radius around the fire would offer comfort from the cold.

Erin was peeling potatoes for their last meal on board. Beall had left for Toronto and the rest of the crew had been paid off a week earlier.

Willis removed his wet coat and hat and hung them by the stove.

"Everything seems fine," he told her. "The local man takes charge tomorrow and we can be away."

"I won't be disappointed," Erin said, pulling a sweater tighter. "It's too cold and the storekeeper expects the winter will bring several feet of snow. We get a few inches at home and call it a blizzard." She watched as he rubbed his hands. "But it's not the cold. Someone is always watching."

"That's what they get paid for," Willis reminded her. "The lawsuits over this boat will keep the lawyers going all winter. Major Denison thinks he'll win control but I've never seen a lawyer move fast. Those detectives are there to make sure no one pulls a fast one. And what they don't know is they're guarding the supplies for next spring."

"The cannons, you mean?" she asked.

"Yes and a few boxes of explosives, plus a crate of revolvers."

"And will you come back in the spring?"

"It's good money, Erin, and Beall knows what he's doing," said Willis. "I made more on one trip than I usually make all year."

"But it's dangerous!" she scolded. "Beall may be all right, but the others frighten me. I wouldn't trust that Hyams in Toronto." She paused. "I haven't told you about that."

"About what?" He took a seat across from her. She appeared thinner than usual and lost inside the bulky sweater.

"The shipment to Port Lambton," she told him. "Hyams put my name on the shipping documents, so the police came to see me at the boarding house. I played the part of a poor, dumb, Irish girl and told them I didn't know what they were asking about, but I'm not sure they believed me. They kept asking questions about the *Georgian* and about my family, and was I a Catholic and did I support the Fenians?"

"The Fenians?" Willis asked. "What do you have to do with them?"

"Nothing—except I'm Irish and that seems to be a crime in this province." The lines across her forehead were becoming more pronounced and that, he knew, was a sign of growing anger.

"They had the name E. Brady, and I told them it might be my brother, Ed."

"I didn't know you had a brother," Willis said.

"I don't," she scoffed. "But it made them go away. What was in those barrels? I was told to order potatoes."

"Ammunition and revolvers," he told her. "Beall confessed after we left Port Lambton."

"So he knew, and he knew what it might mean if I was caught!" Her anger was growing.

"No. I mean, he thought Hyams would be bright enough to use a phony name. Beall wouldn't have done that to you," he assured her. "Take it up with him in person. We're going to meet in a few days. He wants to talk about the spring."

"He wants you to sign on," she corrected him. "What will it be in April? The *Michigan*? An attack on Chicago? I have nightmares," she said, and began to sob. "I see you on the gallows and I see your body swinging back and forth."

"Erin, the money!" He put his hands on her face and wiped away a tear. "Their war can't go forever."

She tried to smile, "And what will you do with all of the money?"

"I'll probably hire a respectable housekeeper," he laughed, lifting her off the chair and carrying her to the nearby bunk.

CHAPTER 49

Georgia: December 1864

The embers from the burning barn carried to the sheds and slave quarters, and soon there would be nothing but smoking ash.

The house was empty, stripped to bare floor and walls by the former occupants. The ruts across the lawn showed where heavily loaded wagons had been hours before.

"The livestock has all been killed and it's starting to spoil," a soldier told Lieutenant Carswell.

"Very well, I will consider this an act of provocation on the part of the owner and under General Sherman's orders, I will retaliate. Wilson! Fire the house!"

He spurred his horse to return to wagons already filled from the foraging in the Georgia countryside.

Wilson flipped turpentine-coated torches to Mulroney and Flaherty, and pulled a match from his pocket. "Usual drill," he told them. "We'll start on the second floor and move down."

All three reeked of smoke. Soot stained their coats and boots.

"Should be able to do this fast since there isn't much left."

"Just as well," Mike Flaherty confessed, his pockets bulging as he made for the stairwell. "The watches, the rings, the jewelry from that last place are weighing me down. Let's get this done and look for fresh pickings tomorrow."

"They sure picked this one clean," Pat Mulroney observed as he looked for flammable kindling. "There's nothing but bare walls."

"I'll fix that." Owen used a bayonet to hack at the walls. A pile of plaster and dry wood began to rise at his feet.

"Do that in the other rooms and smash the windows. Make sure there's lots of air. We don't want it to burn out."

"You think the rebs are getting smart?" Flaherty asked, his voice echoing down the empty halls.

"More like they had time to get stuff away. If we can see the flames in the distance, they can, too. This owner must have had plans. He even got his slaves off."

Mulroney smashed into a bedroom door. It splintered and broke into pieces. "Stronger than it looked," he rubbed his shoulder before kicking the pieces on top of the other debris.

"Light her up," Owen called. "The lieutenant is anxious to get away and I don't want to be left behind. The rebel cavalry likes to jump on stragglers."

The upper floor began to fill with smoke.

Owen stood at the top of the stairway to be sure the fires spread, before retreating to the lower level and repeating the process. He found the entrance to the cellar, wrenched the door open, and was about to fling his torch down the stairs when he heard a muffled cough.

He shouted to the other two men, drew his revolver, and edged down the steps. A cough came from the left, where flickering torch light revealed a door on the back wall.

He could hear the footsteps of Mulroney and Flaherty on the stairs.

"Best to get out of there," Flaherty urged. "The house was dryer than shit. It's burning fast."

"Cover me," Owen ordered, throwing the torch on the floor and hefting his revolver. With one kick, he broke down the door.

"Don't shoot!" a woman called, "We coming out." There was another muffled cough.

"I's sorry, auntie." This time it was a child's voice. "I got choked up and had to cough."

"Both of you, out!" Owen reached to grab the arm of the child, pulling her into the basement. She was black, as was the woman who followed her.

"Up the stairs." He pushed them across the room to where Flaherty, with a torch in one hand, used the other to shove them. The small party reached the kitchen, gulping in air tinged with smoke.

Flaherty suddenly grabbed the woman, shoved her hard against the wall, and lifted her dress to waist level.

"We don't have time for that," Owen began, and then as quickly stopped.

Flaherty had ripped a cloth belt from under the dress and shook it. The sound of coins carried above the crackle of fire.

"Knew I felt something that wasn't right," he explained, and casually tossed the belt over his shoulder. "Best we check it later. It's time to go."

From the lawn, they watched the flames devour the house. The woman was silent. The child appeared confused.

"Just what we need," the lieutenant snarled. "We got more than enough blacks in camp. This whole day has been a waste of time. Now—"

His words were cut short as a bullet whistled by. A second shot from the other side sent a young private to his knees.

"Reb cavalry!" a trooper shouted.

"Close up, close up!" the lieutenant yelled, jumping from his horse to seek protection.

Owen shoved the woman and child to the shelter of a wagon.

The gunfire grew louder and closer.

Owen sighted his revolver, searching for a figure or a horse amid the smoke, but could see nothing.

The gunfire pinned the Union troop to the ground. The only movement came from the wounded private who writhed in pain. But as suddenly as it began, the gunfire slowed, and in the distance the men could hear the sound of a bugle.

They saw a flash of rebel gray as the horsemen raced off across the field. At the same moment, a Union cavalry troop charged into the plantation yard.

"Need help, sir?" a sergeant asked, addressing the lieutenant. Carswell rose to brush the dirt from his clothes and looked to the mounted man.

"Sergeant Abbott, Kilpatrick's Cavalry, at your service."

"Yes, thank you, Sergeant," he replied meekly. "Damn rebs got the drop on us."

"Yes, sir, we saw that." With a wave of his arm, the sergeant sent half of the unit in pursuit.

"Strange," he told Carswell. "We've been over this land again and again and there's been no sign of them. The closest of Wheeler's reb force is twenty miles away. And that was a fair-sized party—must have been at least thirty. They don't gather that way unless there's something special."

"Well, a foraging party is an easy target," Carswell began but was interrupted as another trooper galloped to the yard.

"They were watching this place, Sergeant," he called. "We found a pair of spy glasses."

"Lucky you came by, Sergeant." Lieutenant Carswell began to relax. "Perhaps we can ride together to the main camp. I'd feel better with the extra protection."

* * *

Night found them safe in the heart of Sherman's army. William Tecumseh Sherman had sixty thousand men, and though he had divided his army into three, there were enough troops to fend off anything—the cavalry or the few bands of Georgia militia—that the Confederates could muster.

Owen lounged by the campfire and considered a visit to the contraband camp. The escaped slaves had attached themselves to the rear of each of Sherman's units, feeling safer and freer under the protection of Union guns.

He knew the camp would be full of soldiers looking for women.

"Wilson?" Flaherty called softly as he approached the fire. "If you're going to the colored camp, I've got something for you."

Flaherty had disappeared when they returned to the main camp. Now, he sank to his knees by the fire and smiled at Owen.

"That woman we found this afternoon is something else." He spoke quietly as if to protect an important secret.

"She was a mite uppity until I offered her my jug and told her she had better enjoy herself. The jug helped. She's a wild one—and a talker! And I don't mean just grunts and groans, although she uses those, too. The woman knows her way around."

Owen considered for a moment before asking, "Where was the kid?"

Flaherty chuckled. "That one is a little too young, but she's there, sleeping in the next tent. And you know what? The girl is what the Confederates were after."

"What are you talking about?" Owen asked, confused.

"The Negro wench has been watching that child for months. When the owners left, she was told to stay, because some rebel officers would come for her and the girl. We arrived before they did."

"Why would the rebels be interested in a child?" Owen asked.

"She don't know," Flaherty told him. "But they're willing to spend big money to protect her. She says the child was brought to the plantation earlier this year with instructions to take good care of her."

"You're not making sense!" Owen told him.

"I have one hundred American dollars for you, too," Flaherty smiled, "And another hundred for Mulroney. There was four hundred dollars in that belt I took off her rear this afternoon. She won't complain, because no one would believe her anyway. The money was to cover expenses while she took care of the kid. Now she'll be living off the Union army."

"I don't believe you," Owen said bluntly.

"Well, get off your ass and come with me. You can hear it from the horse's mouth." Flaherty extended his hand to lift Owen to his feet and led the way to the colored camp.

"Right in there!" he said, and pointed to a tent, one of the dozens used as shelter after being cast off by the army.

"They sure is popular females," an elderly black man told them from a few feet away. "First you, the Union soldier, demand the bump and grind, and now back for more with a friend. But I'm afraid youse is out of luck. They gone."

"What do you mean, gone?" Flaherty pulled back the flap on the tent. "Hi honey," a large black woman said, smiling. He let the flap fall back.

"Like I tole you, she's gone. The child, too," the old man continued. "Couple of white men came up, had a word with her, and she grabbed the child and went. Wasn't like you," he said, looking at Flaherty. "They didn't do the bump and grind."

"Were these Union men?" Owen asked.

"Don't think so, sir. They weren't wearing the army blue. Dressed like some of your bummers. But they weren't no white trash—no, sir. Acted like Southern gentlemen."

CHAPTER 50

Toronto, Canada West: Mid December 1864

"I'll be glad to get home." Clement Clay coughed and cleared his throat. "This climate is too damp and too cold."

Clay would leave for Halifax in the morning. The meeting would be his last task in Toronto.

"Take this." The Reverend Stewart offered a half-filled glass. "Natural water is as good a tonic as you'll find. The temperance people are correct. The evil of the distillery and the brewery must be stopped. People become besotted fools. And with that comes the fornication. Our men should be chaste."

For Clay, the spasm was past. The sermon was not.

"I thought Jacob Thompson was a Christian gentleman, but he can't control the men. The man has a foul temper. Has he stolen my money? Twenty thousand in gold was sent and all I've seen is a few hundred dollars from Thompson's poor box. I am not a pauper, and a man of my station must have the funds to support his family."

"Go easy on Thompson," Clay warned. "I've had my differences, too, but the man is doing his best. He's fighting a war on many fronts."

"The Lord has not rewarded his efforts," Stewart thundered. "The entire mission is a litany of failure and when I came to help, how did he reward me? He turned me, The Reverend Kensey Johns Stewart, a true Confederate and man of God, out of his office and left me with a simple clerk."

"That clerk knows as much of what's happening as Thompson and I," Clay assured him. "As to the money, well that's why I'm here. We did have a message from Richmond and so we can advance some cash but our funds are stretched tight."

"A product of Thompson's insatiable demand for luxury," Parson Stewart suggested. "He might as well have bought the Queens Hotel. This whole place is filled with people living on his account."

"There are other expenses." Clay raised his voice in a bid to silence the parson. "Like lawyers. The men held in Montreal are waiting for freedom and we have others behind bars on trumped-up charges, and what about the men in the Northern states? Would you deny what they need for dangerous missions?"

"I wouldn't deny sustenance to our brave Christian fighting men but, Mr. Clay, you and Jacob Thompson had access to thousands and thousands—perhaps millions—of dollars. Where has it gone?"

The parson opened a note pad and picked up a pen as if ready to take an accounting.

"Rev. Stewart!" Clay snatched the pen away. "We'll account for those funds in Richmond. I won't play a game of sums but I will tell you, in confidence, of two of our major expenses. But the information cannot go beyond this room."

"My word or my oath on the Bible? The choice is yours."

"Your word will suffice," Clay told him. "Perhaps you remember John Porterfield. He is watching our financial resources. Last summer he almost cornered the gold market in New York. You may recall the American greenback took a heavy fall against the price of gold during their election campaign."

"How would I know? I do not associate with money changers," the parson sniffed.

"If he had more time he would have undermined the financial system. The economic blow would have been worse than the damage a Confederate army could produce and with no bloodshed."

"But he failed."

"Yes. Their treasury officials got wind of the scheme. But it gave them a scare."

"An expensive scare, no doubt." The parson was unimpressed. "Did his scheme turn a profit. No? I suspected as much. Yet another case where Thompson and associates mismanaged accounts."

"Have you had dinner?" Clay appeared to change the subject.

"Yes, of course." The parson relaxed and rubbed his stomach. "One of the joys of Toronto is the food, all kinds and ample portions. I had an excellent leg of lamb and—"

"And what do you think soldiers were eating tonight?" Clay asked. "Was leg of lamb served in the trenches at Petersburg?"

"No, of course not, but there's plenty of food in the South. I admit there is a problem getting it to the men. The military supplies should take the priority in shipping."

"And did you see any bacon?" Clay asked.

"Very little pork is left in Virginia," the parson replied. "My hogs were slaughtered and left to rot. My entire property was destroyed. I tell you, when I saw what the Yankees had done, my heart hardened and I pledged before God to do all in my power to defeat the enemy."

"And that's why I raised bacon." Clay struggled to keep the conversation on track. "Nassau bacon?"

"Oh, it's putrid. Often spoiled. Awful stuff." The parson appeared sickened. "Soldiers eat it when there's nothing else. Fresh meat is much more beneficial."

"But there's little fresh meat reaching Richmond, so those shipments of bacon that come through the blockade are keeping our men alive."

"I suppose," the parson agreed. "But surely the buyers could force the people of the Bahamas to produce a better product."

"Nassau bacon doesn't originate in the Indies," Clay announced. "It comes from the American Midwest." He relished Stewart's shock.

"Bev Tucker—you must remember Judge Tucker's family—well, he's been working on this for months. The meat is packed in Cincinnati, shipped to New York, then Nassau, and through the blockade to our ports. It's not the best system and some of the pork is spoiled. But it's better than starvation."

"Ha!" the parson smiled. "So our men are surviving on stolen Yankee bacon."

"No, not stolen," Clay told him. "It's bought and paid for with cotton. Tucker got the trading permits to make it to happen."

"Then it's a deal with the devil," the parson exploded. "How can you allow it?"

"The cotton is getting to the Connecticut mills anyway. This way, it's not all lost to the crooks making a fortune off the war. Thompson, Tucker, Cleary, Porterfield, and I have done things we are not proud of but they had to be done. Perhaps, you should consult with your conscience and your God before you condemn us."

The parson fell silent and a full minute passed before he spoke. "I won't give you my blessing, Mr. Clay. I think there are other ways to win our freedom."

"I'm not asking for your blessing," Clay told him. "I'm going home. I'll make the run through the blockade and go to Richmond to lay it all before Jefferson Davis."

"It's for the best!" Rev. Stewart decided. "I can take over the operations when you and Thompson are gone."

"I'm sorry to disappoint you but that is not going to happen. The message from Richmond told us to provide funds, but there's no directive for you to take command. Sorry, Rev. Stewart. You are another foot soldier."

* * *

QUEBEC CITY, CANADA EAST: DECEMBER 1864

The weather was mild and the sunshine drew Paul Forsey to the streets, a short walk to escape the office. At first he didn't recognize Geoffrey Ralston. The British officer was dressed in army fatigues and loading trunks into a wagon.

"You could help," Ralston called to the driver, who remained on the seat, leisurely rubbing the reins. "I said you could help," Ralston repeated.

"*Pardon, monsieur?*" The driver looked down. "*Parlez-vous francais?*"

"You understood English well enough when we engaged your services," Ralston snarled and mimicked a French accent, "Oui! Oui! Two dollaars."

The driver shrugged but made no move to help.

"Need a hand?" Forsey asked politely from behind.

"You bloody well know I do, you—" Ralston's tone changed as he recognized the clerk.

"Oh, it's you. I was expecting my brother officers. Grab the handle and lift."

As the trunk slid into place, Ralston spoke. "I guess you know the fat's in the fire."

"Not sure what you mean," Forsey replied. "Where are you going?"

"Ordered to Niagara." Ralston dropped his voice and moved closer. "Five of us to supervise the militia."

"A training exercise in December?" Forsey asked. In order to hear over the din on the street, the pair moved closer together.

"The official orders go out tomorrow. The militia is to guard the border, every crossing between here and Windsor. The Confederates may be planning another raid but actually, I think the deployment is to reassure the Americans."

"The official orders come tomorrow?" Forsey tried to make sense of it all.

"We need officers in place before the troops arrive," Ralston told him. "A thousand militia men will need supervision. The regulars stay here but can move quickly."

Ralston glanced toward the driver but the man continued to stare into the distance.

"I'm glad to be away. It beats dealing with the French or those little Irish bastards. We found some Fenians in the ranks, had to drum them out, and one was in my unit. If it were my choice, he'd have been flogged. But some bright spark turned him loose."

"It's a well-kept secret, then." Forsey steered away from regimental scandal and back to the borders. "But why Niagara? Why not a Quebec border point?"

"Yes, Montreal, or the Eastern Townships," Ralston agreed. "But someone has decided to move the men around. Maybe it's to ensure the militia get extra pay for being away from home, or a hidden subsidy to the Grand Trunk. But my orders say Niagara."

"*Monsieur, allez,*" the driver interrupted.

"Oui, Oui." Ralston turned to Forsey. "You've picked up French. Tell Johnny Baptiste to go to the Grand Trunk depot and wait for me there. I have to get my personal bag."

Forsey relayed the instructions as Ralston dashed back inside. The driver listened patiently and smiled.

"These red coat buggers think they own us! Piss on them, I say. But I take their cash."

CHAPTER 51

Nashville, Tennessee: December 16, 1864

Jethro Schultz pulled the blue overcoat tighter, pressed hard against the trench, and wished again for Blocker's Tavern. Beside him, a white private picked his teeth and ignored the bullets and shrapnel buzzing above.

"Keep your head down, young fella. A few more hours and them Johnnies will be licked. They're kicking up a fuss right now but there's a lot more on our side than theirs."

They both winced as a shell exploded a few feet away and delivered a shower of mud.

"Damn, I hate being wet." The private knocked a fresh clump of dirt from his uniform. "First rain, then snow and freezing rain and sleet, and this ungodly Nashville muck."

Another shell sent more mud and debris into the air.

"Guess, we ain't going nowhere," he told the shivering coat beside him. "At least not until the cavalry can root out those guns."

He plucked a clean piece of wood shaving from a coat pocket and began again to work on his teeth.

Jethro hugged the trench but touched the uniform jacket. The small bulge reassured him. The paper was there and if he survived, the few lines of script would mean a new life. "Where are you from, boy?" The white man asked as if they were meeting for a street-corner conversation.

Jethro wanted to answer, but no words came. Instead, in his mind he saw the squad of Union troops streaming into Blocker's. Miss Abigail told them they wouldn't find anything and they didn't, except for the Negro stable boy. It was the last straw for Miss Abigail. She called the Union troopers every foul name she knew but to no avail.

"He's a child, big for his age," she screamed. "He doesn't have the sense to look out for himself."

Finally, she dashed into the tavern, returning to shove a paper in the officer's face. "The boy is free!"

He glanced at the page and shrugged. "Slave or free, he's got to work."

It was the only time he saw her cry. She clutched him as he had seen her squeeze customers and pushed the paper into his hand. "Take this, Jethro. The manumission paper says you are free. Your name is Jethro Schultz. Theo left it for you."

There was no time for questions. A corporal had used a bayonet to prod him away, leaving Miss Abigail and her girls wringing their hands, crying, and shouting at the departing soldiers.

The paper impressed the white men at the army camp. He had a choice, they told him: dig or join the army, wear a new blue uniform, get paid, and dig. So he was in Union blue, willing his body tighter against the muddy trench wall.

"Been in the colored corps long?" The white private's voice remained calm despite the bedlam.

"No, suh!" Jethro found his voice only to lose it as another shell burst close by.

"Not many of us been in the army long," the white man said. He picked up a discarded rifle and brushed the mud from the gun site. "Must have belonged to a sharpshooter," he observed. "Damn fine gun and I guess it's mine now."

"Yes, suh." Jethro repeated the words that always impressed a white man.

"I saw a bunch of the sharpshooters in action at Franklin," the private explained. "That's where I learned to keep my head down."

Another shower of mud and stones underlined the danger. "You from around here?"

"Yes, suh."

"I'm from Canada West."

"Yes, suh!" the "suh" all but drowned in rifle fire.

"Fair number of coloreds in Chatham." The private continued a one-sided conversation and hefted his new rifle. "But where I'm from at Glencoe, they are a pretty rare sight."

"What you doing here?" Jethro forced the words but hugged the wall as another shell exploded.

"Same as you," the white man answered. "Waiting for General Thomas to kick the ass of John Bell Hood. Hood only has one leg. Thomas could catch him pretty fast and we could get out of here. Hell, after Franklin, Hood didn't have much left, but Thomas lets him set up a siege and look where we are."

"Yes, suh." Jethro was gradually finding comfort in company.

"When this fight is over I'm going to get smart," the man continued. "Yes sir, Private John Eddie is going to apply to the quarter master corps. I'd rather drive wagons and lift supplies than spend my life in a ditch. Couple of fellows from home are already doing that. What you say, boy? You want to come?"

"Yes, suh!" Jethro responded as a shell slammed into the rim of the trench. Neither man felt the explosion or the tons of earth that buried them.

* * *

RICHMOND, VIRGINIA: DECEMBER 17, 1864

Richmond Society welcomed a 'starvation party' but the men and women attending would do all in their power to forget shortages and rising prices. The bandleader tapped his foot and brought his baton down to lead the ensemble into the haunting strains of "Lorena."

"Colonel Mcgruder!" The woman's voice was sharp and insistent. "Please order them to play something happy. It's a beautiful song, but we need something upbeat."

"Yes, ma'am. I'll speak to them directly."

"Now! I won't have the night off to a bad start with sorrow and tears. Ask for something bouncy, even an old Virginia reel. The general told me I could count on you."

In seconds, he was leaning by the bandleader's ear. The hostess saw the baton strike the music stand at mid verse and in another moment the quartet burst into the first bars of "Listen to the Mockingbird." She nodded in approval.

Mcgruder cast an admiring glance over the women as the room began to fill. The young belles might not have the latest styles, but wore what they had with panache.

A glimpse of long blonde hair falling in ringlets to a shoulder brought thoughts of Sarah. She would be in Montreal, if all was well. Once past the American capital, the threat of discovery dropped.

Sarah wore a threadbare dress as she departed to blend easily with other Southern refugees. She would be wearing the latest styles from London and Paris when she returned. The updated wardrobe, purchased in Montreal, allowed her to mix with the wives and daughters of the prosperous Yankee merchants on the return trip. In Richmond, she would sell the new clothes and start again.

Despite the efforts of the hostess, the conversations turned to the battlefield.

"Sherman is finished," a one armed officer told a Confederate senator. "He'll run out of supplies or Hood may return and finish him off."

"I wouldn't count on that," the senator confided. "Hood's orders are to drive north. The communication lines are down but the last message from Tennessee said the Yankees were in retreat."

Mcgruder turned his attention to the table weighed down with delicacies.

"You are Colonel Mcgruder, are you not?" The question came from a young officer who was also sampling rare sights and smells. "I'm Capt. Sam Davis. General Winder says you need a courier."

Mcgruder stuffed a large tart into his mouth and began to chew. Winder had mentioned Davis, praising his work in the prison camp at Andersonville. But Davis could wait. The tarts were in short supply.

"I'm eager to go," Davis told him. "Montreal is exotic and as close to Paris as I'll get for awhile."

Mcgruder moved his tongue inside his month to get the last of the sweet. "Are you a relative of the president?" he finally asked.

"Oh no, or at least not that my family knows of."

"The accent?" Mcgruder asked. "Not deep South. Perhaps Northern Virginia?"

"Close. I'm from Delaware," Davis told him.

"That could be advantageous." Mcgruder eyed a steaming mince pie.

"You could sound Yankee. Some men open their mouths in the North and are suspected immediately."

He caught a servant's eye and motioned to the pie. "A good-sized piece and the same for my friend."

"Thank you, I will." Davis watched as the knife sliced the portions.

"Do they eat like this in Montreal? I might regain lost weight."

Mcgruder saw that Davis was thin but no thinner than the men in the Lee's army, men in the trenches instead of at a Richmond soiree.

"And I have a smattering of French," Davis went on.

"Let's move to the other parlor," Mcgruder suggested. The black servant had been hovering nearby as the two men talked.

"And thank you for your service," he said, politely dismissed the servant. "You are to be commended for your professional manner and appearance."

"Thank you, sir. I'll tell Miss Van Lew. She'll be right proud to know that folks appreciate what she taught me. She told me to help out tonight. She says they need high-class servants."

"Perhaps bring us wine," Mcgruder ordered and led Davis to the quiet of the nearby room.

"I'll need to review your record. But there should be no problem. We need a courier for a mission immediately."

"I'll pack tonight," Davis smiled.

"That won't be necessary," Mcgruder told him. "We'll put together what you need. You do realize if captured, the Yankees will treat you as a spy."

"Not worried, sir. I've had experience dealing with the Yankees, what with the prison and all. I'll be able to get through and I do look forward to seeing the French colony."

"The British colonies," Mcgruder corrected him. "The British conquered Quebec a hundred years ago and from what I hear, neither the British nor the French have forgotten. But Montreal is not the destination. It's Toronto."

"Toronto." Davis failed to hide his disappointment. "I'm not sure how to get there."

"We'll take care of that and—"

"The wine." The servant had approached silently.

Mcgruder lifted a glass from a gleaming silver tray to toast a new protégé. "To your health."

The servant, he noticed, hovered near each group before offering a refreshment. Elizabeth Van Lew had done a good job. The woman was a well-known eccentric in dress, appearance, and attitude, even visiting the enemy prisoners at the various Richmond jails. People called her Van Lew, Van Loon, or sometimes Crazy Bett. It didn't matter; she had a way with Africans.

* * *

SAVANNAH, GEORGIA: DECEMBER 26, 1864

"I tell you I'm poisoned," Pat Mulroney said, rocking back and forth in pain. "Those damn Negros slipped something in my dinner. I need a surgeon to relieve me ailment."

"Ah, the surgeons don't want to see you," Mike Flaherty told him. "Buck up. Be a man."

Mulroney couldn't answer. He was doubled in pain.

"Maybe we should find him a doctor." Owen Wilson stood in the opening of the tent. "A night in the sick ward might do him good."

"No sick ward," Flaherty declared. "They keep records like in the British army, where you been, what you ate, and who you been seeing, and later they can bring you up on charges. Mulroney goes and tells them he forced those Negras to give up their plates and we'll face a court martial sure as you live."

He bent to stick his face close to Mulroney. "So live with the pain or face the punishment."

"There's a Southern hospital tent up the street," Owen told him. "Maybe someone can look at him. They won't keep notes for the Union army."

"Yes," Mulroney quaked. "Anything. Get me there."

* * *

"We don't treat Union soldiers," a young orderly said, barring their way. "Go to your own people."

"I'm dying." Tears streamed down Mulroney's face. "I can't handle the pain."

Mulroney screamed and sank to the ground.

"What is it?" An older man appeared.

"He's Union, Doctor. I don't think we should treat him."

The doctor shot a withering glare at the orderly and pointed to an empty cot. "Bring him here."

The bed covering had a large reddish-brown stain but Mulroney didn't notice.

"Hold the light." The doctor gave a lantern to Owen.

"I think it were oysters," Mulroney said, rubbing his stomach. "It hurts something fearful. And my body is shutting down. I can't pass water."

Rough hands opened Mulroney's tunic and pants, producing another scream of pain. The tent was ringed with cots. The men who could watched the latest procedure.

At length, the doctor straightened and Owen saw his face. The moustache and the eyes were familiar.

"Oysters," the doctor announced, "are not the problem. You've been sticking your pecker where it don't belong. You are poxed. The Spanish lady or whatever you want to call it. But it's treatable. I'll mix a potion."

Owen followed him to a chest filled with bottles, vials, bandages, and what looked like a hand saw.

"Dr. Secord? Do you remember me? I'm from Canada West. We met in Gettysburg."

"I can't remember everyone." The voice was gruff as he rummaged through the supplies. "There it is." He scooped up a small jar.

"But you are from Canada and that's my home, too."

Secord gave Owen a second look.

"My friend, Jimmy, had nostalgia. You told us to take him home."

"Sorry son, I don't remember. You see a lot of faces and many things you'd rather forget."

He poured the contents from the jar into vial. "I hope your friend recovered."

"He was better for awhile but then he killed himself and his woman."

The hands shook so violently Secord stopped the preparation.

"I'm sorry! I wish we could save them all. Sometimes I think the ones that die on the battlefield are the lucky ones. The wounded get what scant treatment we provide."

He tried again to mix the medicine.

"Your friend has to be more careful around women. And you, you went home and like a bloody fool came back."

"Guilty," Owen agreed. "There was nothing left there to hold me."

"We're all damn fools," Secord decided. "I had a chance, too. I slipped away and got to New York. What a cesspool, the high and the mighty with fancy homes and carriages while the poor live in filthy tenements and work like slaves. I bought medicine and smuggled it south. The advance of General Sherman leaves me behind American lines for the second time. There won't be a third. I'm going out on the first ship."

"And going back to Canada?" Owen asked.

"Yes, I think so. What about you?"

"I'm not much for thinking about the future."

* * *

329

TORONTO, CANADA WEST: DECEMBER 27, 1864

Eramosa Willis raised his hand for another glass. He looked to Erin and saw her nod as the waiter approached. "More whiskey and a glass of the wine for the lady."

Erin saw the waiter smirk at the mention of "lady." Conventional ladies weren't often seen in his establishment.

"He's not often late!" she said.

He scanned the faces men entering the room.

"Wait, there's one I know. Robert Martin. He came up in the fall."

"Willis, isn't it?" Martin asked. A Canadian, he remembered, a man whom Beall trusted completely.

"That's right! And this is my...friend, Erin Brady.

"Friend?" Martin appraised the woman, eyes drawn to missing buttons that exposed her throat and the top of her chest.

"Friend," Willis replied. "Trusted friend."

"My apology," Martin lifted his hat. "When a man is always around other men he forgets his manners."

"We're expecting John Yates Beall," Willis announced.

"Then you haven't heard?" The response was awkward. "He's missing. The Yankees may have him."

"Nonsense. He's too smart for that."

Martin saw the fear flash across the woman's face.

"Let's hope so," he resumed. "The Yankees were moving several of our generals from Johnson's Island to another prison in New York State. We tried to stop the train and get the generals away but we failed. Most of the men got back to Toronto. Hemmings is hiding in New York State, but there's been nothing from Beall."

"We were supposed to meet tonight," Willis began. "To talk about the *Georgian* and next spring."

"A lot of things can happen between now and spring. I'm going home in the New Year. John Headley and I will see what mischief we can cause and get away from these amateurs."

"Amateurs?"

"Not all of them," Martin corrected himself. Tom Hines knows what he's doing. Kennedy was all right, but we think he's been arrested in Detroit. Some one must have talked, again. Most of the others think war is a game. Parson Stewart is a good example."

"Oh, we've met," Erin chimed in. "First, we were sinners because we aren't married, until he discovered a larger sin. I was raised a Catholic and he could lead the Orange Lodge. Surely, you don't need leaders like that."

A high-pitched English voice interrupted the conversation as a man tried to lead the patrons in song.

"And there's another loose cannon," Martin told them as the man swayed and lost his balance. "Godfrey Hyams. Stay clear of him."

"Oh, we're aware," Erin hissed but fell silent at a glance from Willis.

Another man had climbed on Hyam's chair and called for a toast to the South.

"Look, Tom Hines!" Erin jumped to her feet but was pulled back.

"No, he looks like Hines," Willis told her.

"Other people have made that mistake," Martin laughed. "He's an actor, John Wilkes Booth. He claims a plan to ensure Southern independence. He wanted me to join but I don't think so. He does have a way with the women. Mrs. Cole," he said, stressing the Mrs., "Is quite taken and she has free time, with her husband in prison."

Willis bit his tongue. Beall had warned them to let no one know of their knowledge of the Lake Erie raid.

"Do you find Booth attractive, Miss Brady?" Martin asked.

Stunned by the question, she looked across the room. Booth had begun to recite what sounded like Shakespeare.

"It doesn't matter," Martin said before she could answer. "Stay clear. There are men I'd follow, but not Booth. Now Tom Hines, I'd follow to hell and back."

"And what have you heard of him?" Willis wanted to know.

Martin considered his answer, reassured by the faith that Beall had placed in the couple. "He got away from Chicago and I heard he was ordered to Richmond. But I'll let you in on secret. There's a woman in his life."

"A woman," Willis whistled. "I had no idea!"

"He's serious about her. I wouldn't be surprised to see them married. But he won't talk about her because he's afraid people will hurt her to spite him."

"Tom Hines married?" Willis was shocked.

"It happens," Erin told him.

* * *

NIAGARA ON THE LAKE, CANADA WEST: DECEMBER 31, 1864

A trio of bagpipers led the first of the militia, the advance guard of the men to take up positions along the Niagara River.

"Eyes right," the command lifted over the unit and Geoffrey Ralston returned the salute. The men were from a university military club but in the torchlight of a winter night, they could be mistaken for veteran regiment. With luck, their presence would deter any further Confederate raids and the American forces gathered across the river.

An Irish voice drifted from a group nearby.

"I haven't heard the pipes in three years, but of course they were playing Irish tunes. Bugles and bagpipes led the Irish Brigade onto the field at Fredericksburg. That's where I damaged my arm and I was a lucky sod."

"You always was a lucky sod," a companion agreed. "You are so lucky, I'll buy a round! Let's get out of the cold."

"I was discharged after that." The man was rooted on the field where the Irish Brigade had fallen. "But I can still fight."

"Let's go back inside," his companion urged.

"I'd go back to the wars," the veteran continued. "But not against the rebels. I'd have a go at the bloody British and get the red-coated bastards out of Ireland."

"Ah, shut your trap!" another man warned. "They'll lock you away."

"I'll have my chance. Wait and see. My chance is coming!"

CHAPTER 52

Journal of Paul Forsey,
government clerk, January 1865

*W*hat a difference a year makes! Twelve months ago, a stalemate threat-ened our faith in government but now we have an agreement to cre-ate a new nation. The details must be ratified but the confederation proc-ess appears on track. The creation of two levels of government is certain to brighten my prospects for promotion.

Macdonald has a full plate. The rebels continue to threaten cross-border raids, the Americans stand ready to retaliate, and the Irish here in the colo-nies are a growing irritant. Gilbert McMicken has been ordered to create a Frontier Constabulary to police the border.

The Americans appear ready to crush the Confederacy. Grant is poised outside of Richmond and Sherman has cut a swath through Georgia. But there is more evidence of the brutality of their war. Hundreds of Federal prisoners have starved at a prison camp called Andersonville. The Southern armies are beaten, but the rebels refuse to quit.

* * *

TORONTO, CANADA WEST: JANUARY 1865

Annie Cole clicked his glass, hoping the champagne would revive his spirits.

"And what did you see in the Canadian oil fields?" she asked. "Are they as advanced as the fields in Pennsylvania?" Conversation was a way to keep John Wilkes Booth from drifting into a morose silence or sleep.

"Dirty and smelly and filled with the wrong class of people," was the weary reply. "Canadian riffraff, Yankee businessmen, and British who have fallen on hard times. And they don't like the Negro taking the white man's work. They lynched an African last fall."

He took a sip from the glass before he spoke again. "The first blush is off the rose. Canadian fields that went into production before the discoveries in Pennsylvania are playing out."

"So the oil boom is over?"

"Sooner or later, someone will strike it rich again."

"Will we be part of it?" she asked.

"I've been pulling out," he confessed. "I sold most of my own holdings but there's a small interest in your name in Pennsylvania."

"And the rest of it?" she asked, thinking of the money she had advanced.

"We do have expenses, Annie. A private suite costs money and with the travel, the oil fields, Washington, Boston, Montreal..." He reached for the champagne. "You do have to pay for the best."

She nodded in agreement. The suite was her private domain when Johnny was on the road, and she lived well. She thought of Charles Cole confined to a cold prison cell but pushed the image from her mind. Cole had given her a thousand-dollar bank draft but the case retrieved from his room had contained another fifty thousand.

Thompson had not asked for an accounting and instead provided extra cash for her return to Sandusky. Legal fees for Cole's defense were a waste of money, she had decided. With the feelings in the North, Cole would never be acquitted, so more Confederate funds had gone into her private holdings.

"How long can you stay?" The champagne finally brought a spark to Booth's eyes.

"Only a day, and then to Washington."

"Have you told Thompson?"

"No, Sanders is better at this kind of thing. He heard me recite 'The Charge of the Light Brigade' in Montreal and was moved to tears. We hit it off and when I told him of my plan, he saw the wisdom of my thinking."

"Will he join you?" she asked.

"I want his connections in Richmond. They have to know when the American president is coming."

Booth began to pace the room. "Sanders will make the arrangements. We need a train after we cross the Potomac and I need soldiers to protect us. Our route will be through John Mosby's territory so his guerrilla's will slow any pursuit."

"And protect you. If anyone can carry this off, it's you; but I wish you had more help."

"I have all I need, the more men in the game, the greater the danger of discovery."

She felt a surge of pride. He trusted her with what could be a matter of life or death. "Do you still plan to seize him at the theater?"

The idea of taking Lincoln in a crowded theater seemed preposterous until Booth made her understand. As a well-known actor, he would attract no suspicion and he knew his way around the rabbit warrens of the backstage. When the gaslights went out, Lincoln would be lowered to the stage and carried away.

"The theater, or the street," he told her, his eyes burning with that special intensity that drew her to him. "The important thing is take their president. We can demand anything. Free our prisoners! Recognize an independent nation! Anything is possible!"

She watched in awe, as captivated as his theater audiences, and she gloried in each private performance.

"I could help, Johnny!" She imagined sharing his life on stage and off. "I can come to Washington. No one would suspect a woman."

"No, Annie. I want you safe. You will be my refuge, my shelter from the storm."

CHAPTER 53

Quebec City, Canada East: January 1865

"What a magnificent scene. Makes one proud to be part of the British Empire."

Paul Forsey tried to conceal his surprise. Capt. Dennis Godley, late of her majesty's Seventy-eighth Highlanders, and the principle secretary to the governor general, was actually speaking to him.

"It does that," Forsey answered, but he wondered which sight inspired the captain. Was it the improvised ballroom inside Spencerwood where the regimental band provided music for dancing? The official residence was being restored after a fire and the low lamplight hid the remaining blemishes. Or, it might be the roofed skating rink where the young people of Quebec City demonstrated their ability on ice and threw swirling shadows along the walls of the torch-lit arena?

"I've seen indoor riding arenas," Godley told him. "But a covered ice surface. The British people always adapt to new conditions."

Forsey would have described the rink as a French innovation borrowed by the English.

"Forsey, isn't it? Clerk with the ministry?" Godley intoned, "Lieutenant Ralston implies you know the local politicians."

"He's overstated my importance," Forsey said, feigning modesty.

"I'm well aware of that. You are a humble clerk and never forget it." Godley reverted to his true character, arrogant and officious to the point where, behind his back, he was called, "The Almighty."

"But be that as it may. Lieutenant Ralston believes you have an ear to the ground. So what do you hear of Cartier?"

Forsey stammered, "He's back from Washington."

"Good God, man!" Godley exclaimed. "The news boys at the depot know he's back. What did he accomplish with the hurried trip? What is it the French call him? "Petite Georges?" What did little George accomplish?"

"I'm not completely sure, Captain," Forsey tried to explain. "He hasn't briefed the cabinet."

"Hasn't briefed them, eh? He was probably in a hurry to get to the warm bed of his paramour. Ha! He thinks we don't know about her or the fallout with his wife's family."

For an instant, Forsey wondered if the captain had been sampling the alcohol in the regimental medical supplies.

"So what's the unofficial story?" The red coat, the tartan kilt, the dress sword all leaned to demand an answer.

"Apparently, he convinced the Americans that we are doing our best. He met with Secretary of State Seward as well as President Lincoln."

"At least he saw the right people," Godley agreed. "But how did he cover up the mess in the courts? Here are the Confederate raiders from St. Albans, the American demands for extradition, and George Etienne Cartier appoints an old French friend to hear the case. And this fabulous judge decides the case is not in his jurisdiction, sets the rebels free, and returns the money they stole. How did he explain that?"

"I don't know, Captain." Forsey stated the obvious. "But the main culprits have been arrested again and are back in jail and I suspect he explained the legal complexities and the varied interpretations of the Webster Ashburton Treaty on extradition."

"Come come, Mr. Forsey!" the captain interrupted. "I'm not asking for a lecture on law. I'm asking what he accomplished!"

"He thinks they were satisfied. He thinks they understand."

The captain made his customary snap judgement. "What bloody nonsense! Only a colonial politician—only a *French* colonial politician—would jump to that conclusion. The Americans are up to something."

"The border has been quiet for two months," Forsey reminded him. "The crisis may be past."

"Not bloody likely with rumors of new raids every day. The Confederates aren't about to give up if they can string the Yankee rear."

"Macdonald has begun to worry about the Fenians as well as the Confederates," Forsey told him.

"That's a laugh," Godley fumed. "No sir. Worry about the rebels. Tell that to the nation builders. And that's a joke, too. The sooner these colonies are united, the sooner British forces can be withdrawn. Bloody colonies are a waste of time and energy."

"That unification may take longer than first thought."

"What? I thought Macdonald had it all in hand."

"In Canada West," Forsey told him. "But there's a problem in Quebec. Cartier's opponents call him a *Vendu*—a sell out. The French fear they would lose influence. Cartier argues that more local control would come through the separate Quebec parliament. There hasn't been a National Assembly since the revolution in 1837."

"There they go again!" Godley said. "National Assembly. What nonsense. The sooner the French are put in their place, the better."

"It's just language, just semantics," Forsey tried to explain.

"Obviously, that won't wash in Canada West," Godley interjected. "There are more English than French. It's time the French changed their way."

"That's what George Brown has been saying. Of course, he's just saying it in English in Canada West. No one in Quebec wants to hear him."

"Not surprising," Godley announced. "Anything else of note?"

Forsey hesitated before he continued. "To make the Americans feel better, our government will offer a cash payment to the town of St. Albans."

"Dangerous!" Godley fumed. "It's admitting fault."

"And dangerous if we don't," Forsey told him. "We couldn't fight off the Americans but maybe we can appease them. Buy time. That's Macdonald's strategy. They don't call him old tomorrow for nothing."

* * *

TORONTO, CANADA WEST: JANUARY 1865

"Stand by the fire, Captain Davis, this won't take long." The woman threaded the needle and began to stitch the lining into the heavy winter coat. "I usually leave this for the servants, but Major Denison explained this could be sensitive and asked me to do it."

"And I appreciate it," Sam Davis turned from the fireplace. "Your husband has been very kind."

"I should have used a larger needle." She rose to change position and two pieces of linen slid from beneath the lining.

"I'll get them." Davis bent and glanced again at the written words. A reader would need access to the Confederate codes to make sense of the gibberish.

He stuffed the linen inside and held the coat as she resumed stitching.

"I used to do my own needlework but since I married, the servants do household chores." She tugged to be sure the lining stayed in place. "Perhaps not the work of a seamstress but it will keep you warm."

Davis slipped on the coat and walked about twisting and turning.

"It holds well, and there's no sound. Paper can bunch and rustle and draw attention."

"When will you leave, Captain Davis?"

He removed the overcoat and hung it by the door, "Later tonight, unless there's a last-minute change."

"Do you worry about the danger?"

"No sense worrying."

"I always worry when my husband is away—and he doesn't have to cross enemy territory."

"But he always makes it safe and sound, Mrs. Denison," a voice boomed, "and so will Captain Davis."

George Denison entered the room brushing snow from his militia uniform. "Sorry I'm late. The drill was ragged and I ordered an extra hour. It's the only way to make soldiers."

Davis suppressed a smile. The true test came in battle.

"A good stout horse and sleigh will speed you to the depot." Denison explained. "He'll be here in half an hour so we must hurry along. Mrs. Denison, I will need the sewing basket for a minor alteration."

Denison pulled a penknife from his pocket, sliced two buttons from the coat, and produced an identical set. "Have a look," he urged the courier. "A clever Confederate used photography to shrink the messages to a size of a button."

He rummaged for a needle. "Sanders sent them. It must be important."

He tugged on the first button before moving to secure the second. "Also, tell them the Parliament plans legislation to control aliens in the provinces, but I wouldn't be concerned. Look at the American demand for border passports. Bogus passports are for sale on the street. The one you will carry, by the way, was created especially for you."

Denison gave a satisfied sigh as he tugged on the second button.

He passed the coat to Davis. "Tell the men in Richmond to pay attention to this drive to unite the British colonies, to form our own Confederacy. The ties to Great Britain will remain. We won't become a third-rate republic run by a mob."

"I'll pass it along," Davis told him, turning at the sound of a tap on the door.

"That will be the driver. I wish you a safe journey."

Davis pulled on the coat and fastened the new buttons. "I hope to meet again."

"Perhaps on the next visit," Denison suggested. "God speed, Captain!"

CHAPTER 54

Savannah, Georgia: January 1865

"I tell you, it was her!" Mike Flaherty slammed his fist against the table. "It was her and the kid was with her."

The three soldiers had drifted from their unit as Savannah was secured. Other soldiers might be content in wet tents, but after bumming the trio wanted freedom and found it in a house abandoned when the owners fled.

"Mike, me boyo, we believe you," Mulroney told him. "But why we do care? Blacks, mulattos and Southern white woman are all looking for the protection of the Union." He rubbed his crotch. "Believe me, I know. Why on God's green earth should we traipse around the city looking for a mysterious black woman?"

"I'd like to hear the answer." Owen emerged from a bedroom at the sound of the raised voices.

"You don't have to traipse around the city," Flaherty told them. "She's only a couple of streets over."

"Mike, Mike, Mike." Mulroney shook his head in disbelief. "Don't be a lovesick youngster. The woman is black, coal black. She won't fit with society friends in Dublin."

"I don't intend to marry. I want to see her again. Maybe spend a few minutes alone."

"Have you been drinking, Mike? Have you been holding out on Pat?" Mulroney stretched to full height, "What ails you?"

"Oh, come on," Flaherty whined. "Besides, she was going into a fine house. Who knows what we might find?"

Owen pulled a chair close to Flaherty. "Are you bored? Uncle Billy is going to have work soon. We're off to the Carolinas. Save your strength to keep up with the army."

"All's the more reason. Nobody knows what's in the future, so I'm going today." Flaherty jumped to his feet. "Come with me or stay here. It's your choice but I want my money back."

"Wait a minute!" Owen thought back to the contraband camp. "What money? You paid her for services rendered."

"Oh, there was some service," Flaherty admitted. "But the money was like a loan and she up and disappears that very night."

"This makes a difference," Mulroney declared. "I'll not have my friend cheated. I'm with you and unless I miss my guess, Private Wilson will join the party."

The house was only two blocks away but night was falling when they reached the door.

"Look your best, boys," Flaherty urged them. "Square the shoulders like you was being inspected by Uncle Billy." He slammed the knocker hard against the brass setting and then twice more before a tall black man appeared.

"Yes, sirs."

"Came to see Lucy," Flaherty declared and shoved past the servant.

"Lucy? She has a name?" Owen followed Mulroney into the house.

"Can I help you, gentlemen?"

A white man, whose dress and bearing indicated Southern gentry, stood in the archway of the main hall.

"Looking for the black wench, Lucy," Flaherty announced and swiftly added, "on orders of General Sherman."

A wide smirk crossed the man's face. "Really, I had dinner with the general last night."

Flaherty shifted nervously. His eyes sent a silent appeal to his companions but neither man reacted. "Maybe we have the wrong place," was the best that Flaherty could offer. "Please excuse us, sir."

"No, Private. I will not excuse you." The voice was strong and sharp. "What are you are doing in my house and why you are looking for my servant, Lucinda?"

"Don't really matter, sir, wasn't important," Flaherty stammered.

"On come now, private! Why do you want to see her?"

"Doesn't matter. We'll be on our way." Flaherty saw his two companions edge toward the door.

"Not so fast! General Sherman says we will not be harassed but three vagabonds charge into my home. Again, Private, why do you want to see Lucinda?"

"Owes me money." Flaherty decided to brazen it out. "I gave her money in a contraband camp and I'd like it back."

"That's a lie," the homeowner snarled. "Lucinda has never been in contraband camp."

"Was too. She and the black kid. I gave her money, because, well, she was kind to me, and she up and disappeared. But I saw her and the child today, coming into this house."

"More nonsense. Lucinda and her daughter have been in Savannah since August. I take care of my people. I wouldn't let them run around the countryside to be polluted by who knows what! Accept my explanation or we'll see General Sherman tonight."

"Won't be necessary," Flaherty bowed and again edged toward the door. "Mistakes happen. Black women look alike."

He started down the steps and did not pause until he heard the door close behind him.

"Keep moving," he muttered. "She ain't worth the bother. Shit! The last thing I need is a session with Uncle Billy."

The servant watched as the three soldiers faded into the darkness. "They're gone!"

"Then no time to waste. Prepare the carriage. We'll leave for Richmond tonight. I want that brat off my hands. If she's so important to Mcgruder, he can look after her."

* * *

RICHMOND, VIRGINIA: JANUARY 1865

The sound of the slamming door echoed down the hall of the Spotswood. Sillery Fraser was tired from the latest journey from Montreal and after the meeting with Dan Mcgruder, she was angry.

"Sillery, the child is safe," Sarah spoke sharply. "They lost track of her when Sherman marched out of Atlanta, but she's safe in Savannah. Dan wouldn't lie."

"My daughter was supposed to be safe in Atlanta." She spat out the reply. "They should have known that Sherman would move that way. Besides, you don't understand. My child is black. She's not like me. She's a darker shade. And for all their high-blown talk, Yankees don't like blacks of any shade. Grown men can't protect themselves. She's a child."

"Maybe you should have stayed to protect her," Sarah snapped, instantly regretting the words.

"I was hired to protect you," Sillery retorted. "I had the French language and I can handle a gun or a knife." Tears welled in her eyes.

"Sillery, I am sorry. All of this is wearing on me, too. The last trip frightened me. That Yankee squad came so close to where we were hiding. We'll all be glad when this is over."

"Sarah, you don't understand." Sillery wiped a sleeve across her face. "The war may end for the whites but not for my people. Don't you see? There is no difference for an African, North or South. Where does that leave me? Where does it leave my daughter?"

"But Dan is bringing her to Virginia," Sarah reminded her. "She'll be safe near Richmond, and you can see her. Surely, that means something!"

"Oh, it does. It truly does," Sillery again dabbed at her eyes. "But what's safe? The whole Yankee army is a few miles away."

"But they can't break through, and what if there's an armistice? You heard Dan. Old man Blair, from Lincoln's cabinet, is in this very hotel tonight. He's meeting Jeff Davis," Sarah explained, "and that could lead to peace, or at least to negotiations."

"Won't do any good," Sillery made up her mind. "Northerners aren't going to give Jeff Davis time to rebuild the army."

She saw the surprise on Sarah's face.

"The Yankees are making money, good money, off the war. Think of the fancy stores and the carriages and the fancy people in the North. Where's the money coming from? It's from their factories and war contracts. No missy, the North won't agree to any armistice. Your Southern friends will have to fight to the end or give it up. So you tell Colonel Dan to get my daughter close and to keep her safe because someday soon I'm going to collect her and be gone."

"I'll tell him," Sarah shot back. "And I'll remember this conversation when General Lee smashes the Union army and we are victorious!"

"Yes, ma'am." Sillery dropped back into the slave vernacular. "Yes, ma'am, I suspects you will." She bowed and strode from room, slamming the door behind her.

* * *

OHIO: JANUARY 1865

The whistle of the steam engine woke him as the train slowed for another tiny depot. Sam Davis wiped the frost from a windowpane to see cold travelers waiting for the dubious heat of the railway cars.

Two of the new passengers, obviously old friends, greeted each other loudly before a tired conductor guided them to empty seats.

"So how are the missus and the kids?" one asked.

"Missus is fine," was the answer, "but the kids are rowdy."

Davis shut out the conversation and drifted to sleep. He awoke to a light tap on the shoulder.

"Have I seen you somewhere before?"

It took an instant to remember the train and the men. "I don't think so," Davis replied. He reached for his watch and saw he had been asleep for three hours.

"Don't often forget a face. I'm Robert Gerry and this here is my old friend, Pat Sumnall. Were you in the army?"

Davis thought fast. "Well yes, what regiment were you with?"

"Ohio Volunteers, hundred-day men. We signed up to guard bridges and railways but we didn't count on Jubal Early, and to make a long story short, we spent time in a rebel prison."

Davis rose and pulled on his overcoat. "Well, we didn't meet in the army. I joined the Third Minnesota and that's a long way from Ohio."

"Face is so familiar," the man persisted. "Did you serve in Virginia?"

Davis racked his brain for a quick way to end the conversation. "No. When the war began, I joined in a hurry but I had an accident two weeks later and was released. That's why I'm a civilian today."

"Sure look familiar."

"You don't look familiar to me."

Sumnall joined the interrogation. "When you talk like that—all snooty like—the voice sounds familiar, too."

Davis gave him careful study and noted the bright red scar that ran from ear to throat. "I don't mean to be impolite, but I don't know either of you."

The train slowed for another depot. The station sign read Newark and a squad of Union soldiers lined the track.

"The troops must be wrapping up a furlough," Davis announced, hoping again to distract the two men. As the train stopped, troopers moved to block each door of the car.

"Yes. Lucky ones are on furlough. Unlucky ones are in other places," Gerry sneered. "Or in a pest hole like Andersonville."

As the first soldier stuck his head cautiously into the coach, Gerry waved and shouted. "Get on down here!"

Sumnall jumped to his feet to aim a revolver at Davis. "It's him all right! This is the bastard that ran the camp at Andersonville! We wired for the army. Had time to watch sleeping beauty and remember all those days in hell."

Other passengers stood to stare.

"Let's hang him right now. String him up to a telegraph poll and let him dangle!" Gerry shouted.

"Or, one bullet right between the eyes."

"My name is Willoughby Cummins!" Davis shouted above the commotion. "I'm a travelling salesman. I have papers to show it."

"Bullshit. He's no Willie—whatever," Gerry sneered. "His name is Sam Davis; the louse killed our men in Georgia. Hell, shooting or hanging is too good for him. Chain him and leave him to starve."

"Let me show my papers," Davis appealed to a trooper with stripes and reached toward his travelling case. "They're in my carpet bag..."

The butt of a revolver sent him into temporary oblivion.

* * *

Davis awoke with a pounding headache. He blinked repeatedly to clear his vision. The memory returned; the two ex-prisoners, the Union soldiers. He ran his hand across the back of his head and held it in front of his eyes to study the blood.

A few feet away, flames leaped behind a grate on a pot-bellied stove. On the other side of the room was a barred door.

His coat was filthy but the lining was intact. He tore at the lining as he staggered to his feet. He grasped the bits of linen and he pushed them through the small grate on the stove. In seconds, the messages erupted in flame.

"Search him again!" The iron door swung open and three rough jailors sauntered into the cell.

"The coat," one ordered.

Davis slipped the overcoat off. A knife appeared and slashed the lining to strips of rag.

"Nothing," the searcher announced. "Except the watch, which he won't need. Nice little timepiece, should fetch a few dollars!"

"Check the seams. The damn rebels are hiding material there, too."

"Nothing! Maybe he ain't a rebel. The papers say he's British."

"He's a reb with friends in Canada. They're tight with the Confederates. He's the one from Andersonville and he'll swing. Check his clothes. Tear them off him if you have to."

The rough hands pulled at his clothes until he sat naked on the floor. The clotted blood on his head became a small stream.

"Didn't find anything. What now?"

"Leave him! The sheriff from Cincinnati is on his way. He can take over."

The trio snickered as Davis pulled on the torn clothes, including the sleeveless overcoat.

"Latrine?" he asked. "I need a latrine"

"You bet you do, Johnny. I'm not going to clean up your shit and piss."

The rough hands pushed him into what he guessed was an exercise yard and he staggered to where a plank rested above an open trench. With his back to the jailors, he tugged at the buttons on the overcoat.

"Shake her well, Johnny," a jailer laughed.

He damned Denison for his needlework, until both buttons popped into his hand. He let them slip into the trench to send a small ripple across turgid water below.

With a deep breath, he turned, dropped his drawers, and perched on the plank.

"Hope the bugger ain't constipated," the jailer called. "We ain't got all night."

* * *

CHAPTER 55

Washington: January 1865

"We're making progress, Private Edwards, I can feel it!" Major Martin Delaney was in rare form. The tent on the grounds of the Arlington estate was damp from winter rains but any complaint about accommodation was forgotten. "I have my meeting with Mr. Lincoln."

"With the president." the private wanted to be sure.

"Yes, yes, who else? On February 8th, I'll walk up the driveway at the White House, shake his hand, and have his full attention."

"Sounds real fine." The private guessed this would be a good day. The major could be as cool and remote as white officers were.

"Please take notes?" Delaney spoke with a friendly, informal tone. "Scratch out the main thoughts. I'll review them later."

"Yes sir." The private searched for pen and paper.

"Are you a free man, Cyrus?" Delaney asked as the private slipped into the chair.

"Yes. Was born free and had me some education, not that it did much good. I worked as what you'd call a laborer in Boston, but then signed up for the army. Army brings out strange things in people. A man may find he can shoot and do brave things and others, like me, can make sense of forms and orders."

"And you like the work?" Delaney asked.

"Yes, sir, I do!" He felt no need to speak of the perks—a semi-dry tent roof, regular meals, steady pay, and no drill.

"Have you been south?" The major took a cigar from his pocket and rolled it between his fingers.

"No, Washington is as far as I've been. A colored man—especially a free colored man—ain't safe in the South."

"But what if you went as a free colored man in uniform?" Delaney asked.

"Not sure I'd want to go."

Delaney lifted the cover from the oil lamp to light the cigar. "What if you had a full army with thousands of soldiers?"

"Probably feel safer," Cyrus Edwards answered.

"And what if it was a black man's army," Delaney asked, "An army of colored men, led by black officers? Would that make you feel better?"

The private considered. "I guess, but I'm not much for the drills. I'm better taking notes and writing."

"Then start, Private," Delaney ordered and Edwards bent to the paper.

"Let's start with thirty thousand men, colored infantry, colored cavalry, colored men for the heavy artillery, and especially colored officers. The freed slaves will rush to join us and we'll welcome them. And a special note. I'll want teachers and doctors with my army."

The pen was flying across the paper.

"Discipline, note that. No raping, no murder, but we'll forage at will."

Delaney drew on the cigar and blew the smoke across the tent. Through the entrance, he could see the white columns of the Arlington estate and the black men and women who called it home.

"Location. Note location," Delaney turned back to Edwards. "Sherman cut a swath through Georgia and moved on. Our army can take over counties or states and hold them. Eventually, we could carve out a black homeland."

"Got it, sir." Cyrus Edwards drew a thick black line.

"Manpower! Four million slaves and less than two hundred thousand under arms. If we recruit more of our people, Lincoln can terminate the draft, a big political plus. But a question private, mark it down: where does Lincoln stand?"

The pen stopped and the private cleared his throat.

"What is it? Spit it out."

"I thought everyone knew where Mr. Lincoln stood. He's for freedom for the black man."

"Ah, but he may want to colonize the Negro. How would you like that? How about going to South America or some bug-infested Caribbean Island, or Africa?"

"I don't want to go to Africa," the private muttered.

"Africa is not as bad as it sounds. Colonization might work," Delaney said.

"Are you serious? They'd send us away?"

"Virtually every American president has given lip service to the idea," Delaney explained, "and I have to find out if Lincoln is an exception. Maybe he has a plan for a black homeland in America, in the South or perhaps in the West."

"So we'd have to fight Indians to make a home?" the private asked.

"Perhaps. Make a note of that, the Indian Territory."

The pen began to scratch again.

"Money, support, training." Delaney gathered speed. "The compensated emancipation in Washington was a sop for the politicians who owned slaves but if there is aid for the slave owner, there must be money to help the slave adjust. I'll try that one on the president, too."

The tent was filling with tobacco smoke.

"Sure makes me glad I'm free," the private said.

"Yes, good," Delaney said absently, and then, "Mark that down too…Freedmen—more work for the Freedmen's Bureau."

He pulled again on the cigar and the private waited patiently.

"That will do for now. Mr Lincoln and I should have quite a conversation,"

CHAPTER 56

Quebec City, Canada East: February 3, 1865

"Our gallant knight and prime minister struck the first blow." John A. Macdonald smiled as he read the first summary of the Confederation debate.

"With grace and good taste," George Cartier agreed.

"I liked his tone." Macdonald studied the words of Sir Etienne Taché.

"He made the right points—confederation or we may be forced into an American union, either by violence or a steady slide. I'm not sure I like the reference to a war of the races...ah, wait...He said the English-French war actually *ended* with responsible government. Still, I don't like to see the language and race issues raised."

"It's there, admit it," Cartier was blunt. "Unity of the races is a Utopian concept, simply impossible."

"Be that as it may, but let our opponents raise it."

Applause erupted as Taché re-entered the House, his presence a courtesy to the other speakers. He walked slowly and appeared unsteady as he reached the seat.

"Politics takes a toll," Macdonald observed. "He's an old man. Imagine what he's seen, the War of 1812, revolution in '37, all the years of watching the provinces change, and finally a title. He could be happy and retired but craves the cut and thrust of the House."

"And what of the power behind the throne?" Cartier smiled. "Is Macdonald's speech ready?"

"I'll concentrate on procedure. I'll stress there can be no amendments, the Quebec resolutions must be accepted as they stand. Even a hint of change will derail the process."

"The Honorable member for Kingston," the words produced another series of cheers and Macdonald rose.

"We are here to embrace the happy opportunity of founding a new nation…"

* * *

JOHNSON'S ISLAND, OHIO: FEBRUARY 5, 1865

The conversation in the cell block died, replaced by the sound of boots stamping the wooden floor as guards snapped to attention. Sam Davis could hear hammers and saws. The gallows must be near completion.

The door to the inner cells opened for a Union officer. Col. Bennet Hill was the only contact with the outside world. Guards brought food and water and emptied the slop pail but were under orders not to speak.

There were only two men in the cells on Johnson's Island. Ben Cooper had been confined since the aborted raid in September. Cooper was morose and painfully silent. Davis had seen the look, hundreds of times, at Andersonville.

"No news." The Colonel waited as a guard opened the cell door and thrust a chair inside. He carried a notebook and pen; his gun remained with the guards in the outer room.

"Don't expect a reprieve, Davis. We have no mercy for spies."

"I am not a spy! I told you that. And, I told the military court."

"If you say so." Hill repeated the facts in the case. "Rebel officer, out of uniform, in disguise, captured deep in Federal territory, no papers aside from a dubious passport issued under a phoney name in Canada. That's the evidence, Sam."

"Has there been anything from Thompson?" Davis asked.

"Nothing more than I told you. He considers you a prisoner of war. We see it a different way. The war has gone on too long for any chivalrous compassion."

Hill bounced the notebook on his knee and studied the young prisoner. "Tell us about the messages and we might be able to do something."

"I told you, I destroyed the messages. I don't know what they said."

Hill opened the notebook. Davis had repeated the same story since his arrest.

"And you won't tell us where you came from in Toronto or who you were to meet next?"

The question went unanswered. Hill flipped a page. Washington was showing a growing interest in the Southern prison camps.

"Still about five thousand men left at Andersonville. The other prisoners were moved. Know anything about that?"

"I'm not surprised," Davis answered. "We tried to move them last summer. But cavalry raids disrupted the plans. Of course," Davis said, trying to turn the tables, "we thought it strange the Federals didn't try to free them. The Union army was close. We offered to release them, forget an exchange, just provide transportation to your lines, but no one cared."

"I've have noted your feelings." Hill tapped the notebook, "But that didn't give you the right to starve them."

"They got as much to eat as we did," Davis told him. "Conditions were bad but there were twenty-five and sometimes thirty thousand prisoners. And they weren't officer class. Some of the enlisted men were the scum of the earth."

"And that gave you the right to murder them?"

"We never murdered anyone!"

"And what of the prisoners shot for approaching the deadline?"

"Get off it, Hill! What about deadlines at the Northern prisons. And, don't take on airs over the food. Southerners ate dogs and rats at Camp Douglas. Chicago was up the road with lots of food. Starvation in Northern camps was deliberate."

Hill set the pen down. Why discuss the claims of abuse in Northern camps? Instead, he prodded Davis about the Confederate system. "Shelter, the men had no shelter."

"We tried! We built hospital wards but didn't have the manpower or medicines." Davis clenched his fist and slammed the wall. The wood from a knothole popped and cold air blew in. "This is shelter? One stove to heat the whole building? No one froze to death at Andersonville. You are no better than we are!"

"What about women at Andersonville?" Hill asked.

"Two women and they claimed to be with their husbands," an angry Davis snapped back. "If they were abused, it was by Yankee soldiers. At least we knew about them. You didn't know about the woman at Johnson's Island until she gave birth."

It was not a great moment in the history of the Lake Erie prison but Hill had hoped that aside from the local paper, the birth had gone unnoticed. The mother and child had been sent south.

"And if you love the Negro, why do you allow servants to stay in this camp? Maybe you should fix the problems here."

"Guard, open this cell."

Hill faced the prisoner as the guard hurried down the corridor. "Our scouts have seen the burying ground at Andersonville, more graves than they can count. We can hang the camp commander. And when he's gone, we'll come for the subordinates, and for a time you ran that camp. But then, you don't have to worry. You'll have swung."

* * *

THE CAROLINAS: FEBRUARY 1865

Sherman's army moved at a crawl after two weeks of steady rain. The pioneer corps felled trees for corduroy roads but the weight of the wagons pushed the logs deep into the muck.

"Wilson, move your wagon up." The order came from what was once the clean, immaculate Lieutenant Carswell. The mud had turned man and horse into a sodden mess. The yellow stripes on the sleeve were covered with the residue of the South Carolina soil.

"Once started, don't stop!" the lieutenant ordered. "About a hundred yards ahead, around that bend, the road gets better."

The wagon in front bogged to the axles and only with eight black men pushing and lifting did it break free.

"Where are Flaherty and Mulroney?" The Lieutenant moved his horse closer.

"Bumming," Private Owen Wilson said. "I drew the short straw and the wagon."

"Warn them to stay close," Carswell spoke quietly. "Rebs are causing headaches. Stay within a mile of the main column."

"Things are picked over close in, better chance of finding supplies where the army hasn't been."

"Warn them! I'm not going back for men in trouble. Now move it along."

The reply was a sharp snap of the whip. "Git up, mules!"

Savannah was a distant memory. Sherman's army returned to a familiar pattern, scouring plantations and farms for anything of value.

The wagon ahead lurched over a log dropped sharply into a pit and came to an abrupt stop. A shouted order sent two Negros to each of the wheels to lift and push. As he cracked the whip over the mules, he heard the snap of a second whip and saw a white sergeant send rawhide to within inches of the black men.

"Pull!" The sergeant snapped the whip to underscore the order.

The wagon broke free and lurched forward, throwing a young black off balance. The man slipped and could not recover before the wheel rolled across his ankle. The other blacks responded to the wail of pain and began to lift him to the roadside.

"Leave him." The sergeant snapped the whip. "We've got more. Leave him for the surgeons or the rebs. Keep the wagons moving."

The mules found temporary footing and pushed slowly forward. Owen glanced to see the man on the edge of the track, his foot twisted at a bizarre angle. He cursed his luck that this was his day on the wagon.

The Federal army was bringing a special hell to South Carolina, the birthplace of the secession. But the opposing rebels were better equipped and better trained than the ragtag militia units of Georgia had been. Small, determined Confederate units delivered death with professional detachment.

The convoy ground to another halt. The Lieutenant galloped forward shouting orders to keep the train moving. The shouts and curses from other drivers faded. The mules balked when they turned the corner to enter a path hacked through tall pine trees. Owen raised his whip but froze at the scene ahead.

Two blue clad bodies dangled from a branch about ten feet above the ground. Nailed to the bottom of the tree was a rough sign reading, "These were thieves."

He heard the low voice of the lieutenant.

"Sorry Wilson. I know they were your friends."

Mulroney and Flaherty had made their last forage.

* * *

LOUISVILLE, KENTUCKY: FEBRUARY 1865

The clatter of dishes and the buzz of conversation carried from the dining room but there was no sound from the hotel hallway and no sign of guards. John Headley rechecked the ammunition and hefted the gun. "Time to Go?" he asked Robert Martin.

"A few more minutes. Give the dining room time to fill."

Martin walked quietly to the window. A carriage waited in the alley below.

Andrew Johnson was two rooms away. The next American vice president had stopped in Louisville while en route to Washington for the inauguration. A single clerk was with him; he had no other protection. The former tailor was the best-dressed man in Louisville. In a few minutes, he would be in the hands of the rebels.

"It's now or never."

A few steps took them to Johnson's room, where Martin knocked and called, "Message for the vice president-elect."

There was no reply. Headley moved closer and cocked the revolver.

Martin banged harder. "I have a message for Mr. Johnson."

"A minute, please," a voice finally answered.

The door opened to reveal Johnson's assistant, hair tousled and clothes askew.

"Must have dropped off to sleep." He peered at Martin. "A message?"

Martin forced the clerk into the room. Headley waved the gun in his face. "Be quiet!"

Martin crossed the suite to the bedroom door and glanced to Headley before aiming a powerful kick. The door swung open to reveal only a rumpled bed.

"Johnson! Where's the vice president?" Headley poked the barrel of the gun at the clerk's forehead.

"Lord have mercy," the assistant quaked. "Gone. He left on the evening boat."

"If you are lying, you are dead!" Headley threatened.

"I'm not lying!" The man shook. "He's gone. I'm to stay overnight and then return to Nashville."

Martin ransacked the bedroom, pulling the mattress to reveal a dust-covered floor. He rifled through a carpetbag, finding dirty clothes.

"Shit! Shit!" Martin repeated as he returned to the sitting room. "So close!"

"What about this one?" Headley held the clerk.

"Don't hurt me." The words were cut off as Martin shoved the clerk from the suite and down the stairs. Two other Confederates met them at the carriage and lifted the prisoner inside.

"Go!" Martin called and the driver lashed the horses.

"That ain't Johnson," one of the waiting Confederates announced.

"No, it sure isn't!" His companion confirmed it.

"Aw, shit, John!" Martin slapped Headley's shoulder. "How could you make a mistake like that?"

"Light was bad." Headley began to laugh.

The clerk was found tied to a tree the following morning. He told rescuers that the kidnappers had talked of going to Richmond.

* * *

WASHINGTON: FEBRUARY 9, 1865

Martin Delaney tossed the army great coat to a chair and fired his hat on top of it.

"Pack your bags, Private. Orders are coming from the secretary of war at the behest of the president."

The drops of the winter rain ran from the hat to form a small puddle.

"Clean that later," Delaney ordered. "Get your notepad. I want Abraham Shadd brought to me. It's Captain Shadd now. I knew him in Chatham. He knows how to deal with black folk and how to handle the white man. He'll take over as my aide."

Cyrus Edwards had tried to be indispensable but the order for Shadd meant the private's work was finished.

"Fill it out for my signature and designate the orders from the 104th United States Colored Regiment." Delaney paused momentarily. "That's a god-awful name for a fighting force. I wanted the Corps d'Africque."

Delaney sank into a chair and for a moment was silent.

"You met the president and the secretary of war?" Edwards asked.

"I had time with the president and Secretary Stanton. Stanton is a man with energy. The president appears very tired. If I were his doctor, I would order a full examination."

"But you are a doctor," Edwards reminded him.

"Not the president's doctor and not a white man and both carry weight in the capital of the United States. Colored people aren't allowed to ride in a streetcar with whites. Do you think a black doctor could treat the president?"

"Not much you can do if they don't want you." Edwards lifted the coat and hung it to dry.

"Lincoln is under pressure," Delaney continued. "I heard the conversation while waiting in the outer office. The War Department wants him to approve execution orders. The associates of Beall of the lakes, the fellow behind the raid on Lake Erie, are seeking a reprieve. Another spy is at Johnson's Island. The attorney general wants Lincoln to sign off on the death sentences but he's wavering."

"It's a lot to deal with," Edwards suggested.

"And he has personal problems," Delaney told him. "The wife's family doesn't help. A parcel of brothers and half brothers serve with the Confederates and the sisters-in-law have been to the White House. One of them smuggled medicine when she returned south. No one wanted to search the president's relative. And there's Mrs. Lincoln's spending. Large bills came due last fall and threatened to be an election issue. So he has worries beyond government."

"I never heard of any of that," the private told him.

"Few people have. Washington is full of secrets, as I suppose Richmond or London or Paris is full of secrets."

"These things are above a poor black man or a poor buck private."

"We have to elevate the black people!" Delaney suddenly turned to a familiar theme. "It's up to us...men whose blood has not been polluted by the white stream."

He paused before he repeated, "It's up to us. Sergeant."

Edwards spun, silently cursing for not hearing the arrival of a guest.

"No, Cyrus." Delaney seldom used his first name. "There's no one else. You are getting a promotion, Sergeant Edwards."

First shock and then a wide smile beamed from the new sergeant's face.

"Thank you, sir!"

Delaney smiled. "Quite a day. Our troops will assemble at Charleston and when all is in place, drive into Confederate territory. If the war ends before we attack, we'll help the freed men. We'll get them food, shelter, supplies, and best of all, their own land. We'll be in the right place."

* * *

RICHMOND, VIRGINIA: FEBRUARY 1865

Despite the chill, Mcgruder stripped to undershirt and drawers. He stank of smoke, stale beer, and dirt, and each night the smell grew worse. He and his men were fighting a losing battle to police the capital. "You wouldn't believe this city."

Sarah Slater lay on the bed, blankets pulled tight against her neck. A faded dress hung by a travelling bag, a sign she was ready to leave for the North.

"Gambling must be stopped," he told her, "every other house has a gambling den in the back. And every Confederate soldier is out to make a fortune. The booze may be free but it's cut with all kinds of concoctions and every hand that's dealt leads to an accusation of a cheating and a fight."

"But we've always gambled. More than one plantation has been won or lost in a hand of cards."

"This is different. The losers become angry and we have to step in and to send them back to the trenches. The winners buy a few minutes with a wretch in an alley and then we send them back. As we watch them go, we wonder if their luck will hold for another day or if the big payoff is a Yankee bullet. We even see senators and cabinet members. Judah Benjamin leaped through a back window and laughed about it the next morning. If we caught him it would have meant jail."

"Some men relax with the cards. Perhaps that's what keeps Benjamin going." Sarah tried to laugh. "Maybe Jeff Davis would be in a better mood if he played a few hands."

"I'm serious," Mcgruder scowled. "When night comes, reality sets in. Sections of the city are not safe even for my men. It gets worse with each day the war continues.

Mcgruder crushed the discarded clothes in a ball and heaved them across the room. "We had a chance with the Hampton Roads Conference but Davis and Lincoln scuttled the peace talks before they started. Davis demands recognition of the South. Lincoln is an adamant that we recognize the Union *and* accept abolition.

Sarah sat forward, balancing an elbow on one knee while she pulled the blanket around her shoulders. If he were in a mood to talk, she would listen.

"We're inconsistent," he continued. "The men in our delegation knew Lincoln before the war. Something might have been accomplished but instead, they float a half-baked idea of uniting Northern and Southern armies to take Mexico."

"I hadn't heard that part," she told him. "The British will be relieved. They worry about a Union army moving north."

"Our cabinet is still hoping the British will join with us. Davis sent Duncan Kenner to England last month with an offer to emancipate the slaves if the British recognize us."

"I hadn't heard that, either," she told him. "But with British recognition, the blockade could be broken—"

"A pipe dream!" He cut her off abruptly. "If the European nations haven't recognized the Confederacy by now, they're not going to. Besides, where would that leave us? A protectorate of the British, with about as much influence as British North America. A few of the gentry believe a British prince could lead Canada and another prince, of higher rank of course, could accede to a new throne in the Confederacy. Nonsense!"

"Is it so silly? The English in Montreal would accept a prince. Their new union may be called the Kingdom of Canada. Imagine how the great republic would feel with a kingdom on either side."

"You are forgetting the revolution. Sons and grandsons of men who fought the British are in the trenches at Petersburg. They couldn't accept it."

"You might be surprised," she told him. "Our Southern officer corps is close to an aristocracy now. It's people like you, without family connections, who end up with the dirty jobs."

"It's not about me!" His voice rose in anger and frustration. "I could care less who runs the government or the army, but in a few weeks it may be every man for himself."

He slumped on the edge of the bed and felt her hand rub his neck.

"Stay in Montreal," he said suddenly. "Don't come back after this trip."

"And do what?" she bristled. "Offer a safe house for couriers or escaped prisoners? I know the routes. I know what I'm doing."

"You should stay," he repeated quietly.

"And do what?" she repeated. "Go to one of the new indoor ice facilities and skate my life away? Or enter a nunnery?"

She pressed her chest against his back. "I wouldn't like a nunnery but I'd have my naughty memories."

"Sarah! It's serious." He turned to face her and clasped her shoulders. "Richmond may be abandoned. Listen," he shook her until fear stirred deep in her eyes. "If that happens, stay in Canada. Wait for me there."

CHAPTER 57

Quebec City, Canada East: February 1865

Paul Forsey pretended to be engrossed in the legal history of the province. He ran his hand along dusty books in the reading room as he edged closer to the meeting in the corner.

"I don't need a new nationality," Antoine Dorion, the opposition member, smiled. "I will tell them I am quite content to be British and propose a motion rejecting their new nation. Make them squirm."

Dorion led the French-speaking opposition to confederation. His Rouge party and a small group of English-speaking members from Canada East found common cause.

"Later, we'll attack the structure," Dorion continued. "Their central government has too much power. It will collect all the revenue and dole it out to the local levels. Will the new parliament back Montreal over Toronto when dominated by the interests of Canada West? A fat chance."

"But Cartier will argue that the local or the Quebec legislature will give us more control," Luther Holton suggested. The Montreal businessman had once supported a bid for annexation by the Americans. "Cartier will say he has won protection for Quebec laws, religion, and language. We'll be separate, a nation within a nation."

"Leave the silver fox to spout his rhetoric," Dorion laughed. "When the election comes, we'll question whether he speaks for the people or his employers at the Grand Trunk railway."

"But what do we suggest in place of the confederation?" another member asked.

"We don't!" Dorion shrugged. "Defeat their plan! The world will go on. Let them come back with better ideas."

Forsey pulled a book from the shelf and made a show of studying a page. The group paid no attention.

"Ordinary people don't care about the changes," another member complained.

"Stir them up," Dorion urged. "Talk about the potential abuse in the new system. Make them see the danger of a Senate appointed by the central government and question the costs. Circulate petitions. We can press for an election. Macdonald and Brown fear defeat and want their scheme carved in stone before any vote."

"The resolutions were put together in a hurry," Christopher Dunkin spoke for the first time. "I'll use my speech to tear it apart, clause by clause."

"Good! Do it! But now I have to prepare for my time in the legislature," Dorion said, rising. "I would like to speak in French but my words will be in English. Perhaps I can change the opinion of the *Anglais*."

Holton hesitated before leaving the room and circled to where Forsey shelved a book.

"A clerk must always be silent," Holton said. "A clerk who keeps silent is a valuable asset; one who doesn't is easily replaced."

* * *

"Mr. Speaker, I could continue for hours but I must draw to a close," George Brown addressed the legislature with his final arguments. "Shall we rise to the occasion?"

Only a dozen members watched from the opposition benches, and an equal number on the government side. Interest in the debate was waning.

"Mr. Speaker, the American side of our lines bristles with works of defense and we must put our country in a state of preparation. Our country is coming to be regarded as undefended and indefensible..."

"A good speech," John A. Macdonald leaned and whispered to D'Arcy McGee. "Although I fear he softened the argument by admitting he doubted the Americans would attack."

"I'll pick up the subject," McGee assured him. "You'll hear more."

"It must be union." Brown's voice echoed through the chamber. "Some of us will live to see the day when one united government under the British flag shall extend from coast to coast."

The speaker called for order and waited for the cheers to subside. "The Honorable member for Montreal West."

The opposition members delivered friendly hoots and jeers as D'Arcy McGee rose.

"What a fine performance from members who will soon represent a grand new nation." He paused to lift a glass and make a mock toast to Macdonald. "Pay attention now," he said softly before turning to face the house.

"Now, the Americans." his voice rose. "The policy of our neighbor to the south has always been aggressive with the desire for new territory. They coveted Florida and seized it. They coveted Louisiana and purchased it. They coveted Texas and stole it. They sometimes pretend to despise our colonies as prizes beneath their ambition, but if we didn't have the strong arm of England over us, we would not have had a separate existence."

Antoine Dorion and Sandfield Macdonald watched from the opposition benches.

"We can pick holes in their arguments," the Cornwall Macdonald plotted strategy. "The whole defense issue is overblown. But we'll have more luck with the costs. The national parliament and the local legislatures are huge expenses. We're spending money to reward Tories with patronage appointments."

"Yes," Dorion smiled, "and our supporters won't be at the trough."

"I hope Christopher Dunkin is up to this," Macdonald continued. "The man knows his stuff. He can tear the proposals to shreds. But he is so dull. The members may drift away or nod off while he speaks."

"Are you preparing for failure?" Dorion asked.

"Oh, we'll continue to debate. This can go on for weeks. I'd like to think that London will force changes but the British are preoccupied with defense. The American war frightens them. They want united colonies for a united defense and they want united colonies to shoulder the costs."

CHAPTER 58

Johnson's Island, Ohio: February 17, 1865

"Are you going to tell him?"

"And what should I tell him?" Col. Bennet Hill snarled at the telegrapher. "Should I admit that the president of the United States has passed judgement but we don't know what the president means?"

He stared again at the telegram from Washington and read aloud the phrase, '*whose sentence has been commuted, if not, let it not be done.*' Does he mean hang him or the sentence is commuted? I've had to wire for clarification."

Across the square, the gallows stood ready, the rope in place, and the measurements taken to ensure the trap door would send Sam Davis to his death.

The sun broke through a layer of thin cloud. It was a rare day, with no wind whipping across the ice and the sun had a hint of spring.

The telegraph clattered to life and the attendant leaned by the key to copy the message before he passed the pad to Hill.

In the cell block, Davis heard the doors open and the conversation stop. He stood and glanced about the cell. His last letters rested on the bunk along with a list of where his few possessions should be sent. Hill would surely agree to that. The door to the cell opened and he saw the Union colonel.

"Samuel Boyer Davis," Hill began the formalities, "captain of the rebel forces engaged in rebellion against the United States of America. The president has reviewed your case. The sentence of death is commuted. You won't swing, but you'll spend the rest of the war—and probably your life—in prison."

* * *

TORONTO, CANADA WEST: FEBRUARY 1865

"They hanged him!" William Cleary choked on the words. He turned to the window to stare into the street and to hide tears.

"No, no it's a mistake." George Sanders plucked a paper from his desk and read. "Sam Davis was given clemency by Lincoln."

"Not Davis!" Cleary sobbed. "Beall. John Yates Beall."

Sanders's face sagged as he too fought for composure.

"Are you sure? Beall was just moved to another prison."

"Where they hanged him," Cleary told him. "He stood on the scaffold while they read the complete court martial findings. A soldier like Beall deserved a firing squad, not some stage performance for Union bureaucrats."

"What else do you know? Beall knew all of our operations. It wouldn't be like him to talk but perhaps under torture…and we know the Yankees use torture."

"No. Beall wasn't the type to talk."

"Brave men," Sanders reflected. "Kennedy gone, too, facing the South as the bastards fitted the noose."

The room was quiet until Cleary cleared his throat. "The lawyers believe Bennet Burleigh will be turned over to the Americans for trial on a piracy charge. They'll hang him, too."

Beall and Burleigh, as the leaders of the Lake Erie raid, had become special targets. Bennet Young, another target after St. Albans, remained under the dubious protection of the Canadian courts.

"What I don't understand is the haste with Beall. There was no time to get his orders from Richmond. No time for his family or friends to win a reprieve. And they did try. Several American congressmen went to Lincoln. Even the actor, John Wilkes Booth, was trying to help. He has connections to a senator," Sanders suddenly laughed. "Or to be more precise, a senator's daughter."

"How can you think of something like that?" Cleary exploded. "A brave man is dead and you joke about an actor and lovesick teenage girl."

"Easy, William," Sanders advised. "We all feel bad. Beall was a brave soldier but the fight goes on and Booth will play a major role."

"Booth will never equal a Beall. The actor is just a talker."

"Don't be so harsh, Booth has big plans."

"What sort of plans?" Cleary found himself drawn into Sanders's drama.

Sanders walked to the door and suddenly pulled it open. Satisfied that no one was outside, he closed it and returned to center of the room.

"He's going to kidnap Lincoln."

"What kind of nonsense is this?" Cleary burst out.

"It's not nonsense. It's a well-conceived expedition to capture Lincoln. Let's see how the American government functions without a president."

Cleary was shocked to silence.

"Booth and his associates will snatch Lincoln from under the very noses of the enemy. We should hear of his success any day."

"How will he do it?" Cleary managed to ask.

"Where there is a will there is a way. Booth will find it. Perhaps he'll use the lovesick teenager in some way."

"And then what?"

"Our government may exchange him for our prisoners in the North. That would be a fitting bargain. Or he'll be put on trial for crimes against the South. There will be a new and inexperienced vice president in Washington and there's no clear case for what happens when a president is…well…unavailable. Stanton, Seward, maybe the whole cabinet will wrestle for power."

Sanders smiled and rocked on his feet. "We may win independence in exchange for the release of the president."

"And Mr. Thompson knows about all this?"

"The broad outline, but the nuts and bolts are up to Booth, and I coordinate with him."

"Why bring me in on the secret?"

"Because when I ask for a special courier or extra funds, I won't have to explain. I can deal with you and take pressure off Thompson."

* * *

WASHINGTON: MARCH 6, 1865

John Surratt swore and dabbed at the mud. The suit was new and if not for the actions of a carriage driver, it would be clean. A slight turn and the carriage would have missed the sloppy hole but instead the wheels threw dirty spray onto the walkway. The black man on the carriage seat had ignored his shout of anger. To Surratt, it was more evidence the black population was out of control.

A Negro woman carrying a laundry basket moved slowly toward him. Surratt blocked her path and watched with satisfaction as she stepped into the muddy street. He considered following her to keep her in the muck but Booth was waiting.

Booth had missed a chance at the inauguration. The actor had had a special pass and reached the area set aside for dignitaries, but he'd done nothing. Then today, a summons for another meeting.

* * *

"You are late, John," Booth chided him as he entered the room at the National Hotel.

Surratt looked for a seat far from George Atzerodt and Lewis Payne, fearing body odor would migrate to his new suit. He took an empty chair by David Herold, who at least was clean. Booth, as usual, was immaculate.

"We'll move soon," Booth began. He saw the nervous anticipation in Herold and Surratt. The other two offered no response.

"Lincoln enjoys the theater. We can seize him there. Another option is to seize him on the road. He often rides alone or travels by carriage to the Soldiers Home."

"Davey," Booth said to Herold, "you and John must guide us along the back routes to the Potomac. George must have a boat ready."

Atzerodt shifted under the attention.

"We can't hurt the big ape, in fact my orders are emphatic about that, but he'll be roped and cuffed," Booth continued. "Lewis will be at my right hand to provide any extra muscle."

"What about a pursuit?" Surratt asked. "The Federals aren't completely dumb."

"We'll move at night if at the theater and late in the day if on the road." Booth was nonchalant. "I have other distractions planned. So, no, John, I'm not worried about pursuit."

Booth turned again to Atzerodt. "The boat is ready?"

The voice was low, the German accent thick. "Ya, der boot ist reedy."

"Lewis, did you have any questions?" Booth asked. Lewis Payne or Lewis Powell, depending on the day, was devoted to Booth and unlike the others, could use brute force.

"No."

"I could find more men," Surratt offered. "One fellow lives at my mother's boarding house. Lou Weichmann works for the Federal government but he sympathizes with the South."

Booth immediately rejected the offer. "I'll decide who is involved and who is not."

"When do we go?" Surratt ignored the snub.

"I'll decide that, too."

"I'm running low on cash," Surratt explained. "I left a job at Adams Express for this and now I have no income. I might make another courier run to Montreal."

"I need you close for the next couple of weeks. After that a Southern hero won't need to worry about money."

"It's time," Surratt told them. "Time to put the Yankees in their place!"

As he spoke, he again noticed the dirt on his coat. "And a Negro bastard splashed me on the street. We have to bring the colored under control."

"Damn right!" The deep voice of Lewis Payne surprised them. "A Negro bitch got uppity at my boarding house in Baltimore, so I slapped her, but the owner calls the police—and just for teaching the woman her place!"

"And did the police come?" Booth showed sudden interest.

"They came but I was out," Payne smirked.

"Just the same, Lewis," Booth continued smoothly. "Stay in Washington for a few days."

"I don't have money, either."

"I'll take care of that. I'll take care of all of you."

CHAPTER 59

Quebec City, Canada East: March 11, 1865

For a second day, a blizzard slammed the old city. Only one cab driver agreed to face the elements for the short trip from the hotel to the legislature. John Macdonald and George Brown shared the sleigh and a heavy buffalo blanket.

"As cold and miserable as Quebec City can be," Macdonald announced. He slumped low in the seat, hoping the body of the driver would break the wind. Brown's taller frame made any escape from the wind impossible.

"At least we can talk privately."

"And quietly, in English," Macdonald said, throwing a glance at the driver.

"I think we have it," Brown sighed. "Provided, of course, Cartier can keep the French in line. We'd have done better if Tilley hadn't called an election and lost in New Brunswick. We all have to face the electors eventually, but why hurry?"

"The opposition thinks we're finished," Macdonald said, shifting to pull the blanket around his shoulders. "They are in for a surprise."

Brown sniffed the air. Despite the wind, he could smell alcohol.

"Should we leave for London immediately?" he asked.

"By all means," Macdonald answered. "We should handle British questions in face-to-face meetings. I'll let the dust settle from the vote and prorogue the House.

"Surely, a simply adjournment would do."

"It would," Macdonald agreed. "But we can start fresh with a new session when we return from the old country. Besides, a new session means another six hundred dollar stipend for the members and the promise of extra money appears to be swinging votes in our favor.

He smiled as the sleigh reached the door of the legislature. "Consider it insurance."

* * *

The bells finally called the members for the vote at four a.m. A few were roused from sleep while others had finished the liquor hidden around the building.

Paul Forsey watched as Cartier had final words with a few reluctant French-speaking members. Cartier had won a tepid endorsement from the Roman Catholic Church and the hints of lucrative railway construction contracts overcame more reservations.

At last the speaker rose. "The results of the vote: yeas, ninety-one; nays, thirty-three. The accord is approved."

The legislature erupted in cheers and boos. Canada West had given strong approval while Cartier swung twenty-six of the forty-seven votes in Canada East to deliver the majority.

From the government benches, someone began a chorus of "God Save the Queen" but another voice on the opposition side bellowed a *voyageur* paddling song. More well-lubricated voices joined in English.

"Row, brothers, row, the stream runs fast.
The rapids are near, and the daylight is past."

Macdonald and Cartier linked arms to lead the way from the chamber and slowly the house emptied.

Forsey gathered his private papers. The official records of the debate would soon be read across the provinces but someday his journal would show the world how a country was really created.

* * *

PETERSBURG, VIRGINIA: MARCH 1865

The first light revealed a land scarred by lines of trenches, broken trees and stumps. The fortifications spread for miles around Petersburg, where the two armies met stalemate.

"Good morning, Mr. Rebel," a booming New England voice greeted the day. "We had another good run of Johnnies last night. Why don't you come over, too? Special bounties paid in cash. Bring a gun and get a few dollars more. Give it up, Johnny Reb?"

In the Confederate line, a sharpshooter tucked a rifle to his shoulder.

"See him?" Col. Eugene Waggaman asked.

"Thought I saw a hat," the sniper replied, and folded his head behind the sight.

"Yes, sir, a very good run of Johnnies last night," the voice repeated. "They're having breakfast—bacon, eggs, and real coffee."

The bark of the rifle interrupted the speech.

"Now, that was a nasty," the voice sang out.

For the second time, a rifle shot delivered the reply and the sniper leaned back with satisfaction.

"Got him. They pop their heads up after they hear a shot. It gives me a better chance to see 'em. I put the bullet just below the hat."

"Well done!" The colonel offered congratulations. He raised field glasses to the top of the trench, sweeping the field before focusing on the crude, Federal-controlled Fort Stedman. A bullet slammed into the ground nearby but the colonel did not flinch. Instead, he sharpened the focus of the glasses.

"Might want to step back, Colonel. Yankee's seem riled. They got enough ammunition to shoot all day."

Instead, the colonel shifted to brace the glasses. The ground between the trench and Fort Stedman was scarred by shell holes, rifle pits, and makeshift barriers but he could see a route his men might follow.

"Get down!" the sharpshooter warned as artillery fire plowed the ground around them.

The colonel brushed away dirt before returning the glasses to a case. "You must have nicked someone they were fond of." Waggaman studied the sharpshooter. The blue overcoat was dirty but showed no excessive wear. Beneath the open coat was a jacket of faded gray and in the belt was a long, gleaming knife. The boots were caked with mud. The rifle, clasped in his thin hands, was clean, recently oiled, and well polished.

"What's your name, soldier?" he asked.

"Wilbur Dirks. A private and I like it that way."

"Got new clothes?" The officer shouted over the roar of the cannons. "Fresh supplies must have come up."

"No, sir. I do midnight foraging. Yankee that wore this coat doesn't need it anymore." He shifted to display a hole in the back where a jagged tear suggested a slash from a knife. "He was going the wrong way." The sniper reversed to face the colonel with a wide grin. "A soldier should never run away. His back is exposed."

"Supplies are coming in," Waggaman said, letting the sad joke pass. "You don't need them but tell the others."

"I'll do that, sir, or tell the ones that are left. The Yankees are right," Dirks observed, "men are slipping across the line every night."

He decided the colonel was willing to listen. "One fella got a letter from his wife asking him to desert. Said she couldn't keep the farm going without him, and sure enough, he's gone. He didn't give up to the Yankees, he went home. It's not like the jackasses who surrender. What becomes of them?" he asked.

Waggaman wearily slumped against the trench, forced to stay until the Yankees tired of throwing shells.

"Our former compatriots are sent to prison camps. If they take an oath of allegiance, they go west to fight Indians. Galvanized Yankees, is what they call them. The Federals don't trust deserters anymore than we do. But deserters run both ways. Last fall, we had Negroes sneaking to our side. They felt they'd be better treated by the Confederacy."

"You seem to know a fair bit about this." Dirks stepped to the top of the trench to survey the field.

"I worked in the Conscription Bureau in Louisiana," the colonel told him. "It was my business to know."

"Are there many men left to call up?" Dirks brought the rifle back into position and peered down the sights for a likely target.

"There are men by the hundreds, probably thousands," Waggaman explained, "and every one has an excuse. I can understand the plantation owners. Someone has to oversee the slaves. But there's another whole class that rely on exemptions. Thousands of men hiding away in government offices, drawing pay, and claiming their work is essential."

The rifle barked again. "Hope I don't interrupt their breakfast," the sniper snickered as he slid lower in the trench.

"There were some I didn't take," Waggaman continued. "A man that lost an arm or a leg. An officer can work around those injuries. A disabled soldier, on the other hand, is a hindrance."

The colonel lifted his slouch hat to shake off the dirt as another shower fell on their position. "Shite!" He slapped the hat and returned it to his head.

"You've been in it from the start, colonel?" the soldier asked.

"Right from the start," Eugene Waggaman replied. "I was captured at Malvern Hill and I learned about Yankee prison camps."

"You escape or were you exchanged?" the sniper asked.

"I was exchanged."

The colonel found a strange sort of comfort in talking with this private. Neither man had any place to go. "My sister was married to the Canadian premier Sandfield Macdonald. He's out of office now but used his influence back in '62."

"You could have been out of the fighting," Dirks said.

"Oh, I could picture myself sitting at Ivy Hall, that's his home at Cornwall. It's close to the St. Lawrence, near Montreal, and I know my sister, Christine, would have royally entertained me, and the thought of that mix of Scottish and Cajun culture was inviting, but I would have been haunted by the idea of other men doing my fighting."

Another round of cannon fire interrupted the conversation. The sniper glanced at the colonel, who sat coolly unperturbed. When the fire slowed, the field glasses reappeared along with a scrap of paper as he studied Fort Stedman. After a few minutes, he folded the paper and dusted the latest debris from his uniform.

"You think we'll be here much longer?" the sniper asked.

Waggaman considered the question for a long minute. "No, I don't believe so. Something must happen soon."

* * *

CENTRAL KENTUCKY: MARCH 1865

The farmhouse stood a half mile from the nearest road. A weak oil lamp burned in a second-floor window, a sign all was well. A small fire near the barn was large enough to provide warmth but not large enough to attract attention.

Tom Hines stood watch. James Crawford snored loudly, a damp horse blanket covering his tall frame. Beside him, Michael Harnes stirred and rolled onto his side. Crawford, from Morgan's Cavalry, had a reputation as a fighter. Harnes knew every local road and cow path.

Hines moved beyond the small circle of light and waited ten minutes before he heard the snort of a horse. "Pompeii," he whispered and fingered a revolver until he heard, "Vesuvius," the countersign, and Theo Schultz led his horse from the darkness.

Schultz pointed to the two sleeping men. "I could have killed both of them and I knew you were here. Three mugs by the fire and only two people."

"I'll remember that," Hines told him, extending his hand to an old friend.

Schultz moved slowly to prevent noise. He lifted two mugs with one hand and pulled a flask from his pocket with the other.

"May as well take advantage of the utensils." He poured a splash in each cup and handed one to Hines. "You wouldn't have anything to eat?" Schultz asked hopefully.

"Sorry, no. The few who have supplies hide them."

"Same in Virginia," Schultz told him.

"Did you find Duke?" Hines asked.

"General Duke is hard up for food, supplies, ammunition, horses, and men, but still there. The men are on foot. The horses are spread around so they get some feed. The animals will be thin but still able to carry men come spring."

"It's a far cry from what we were."

"He's hoping for more Kentucky men, but judging from what I see," he pointed again to the sleeping men, "the pickings are slim."

"I haven't given up," Hines assured him. "Colonel Jessop has men."

"But what kind?" Schultz asked. "Jessop likes to call himself a guerrilla, an irregular, or a partisan, but he's like Champ Ferguson. Just plain bad news."

"Any other suggestions?" Hines's tone was angry. "I didn't think so. I take what I can get."

Schultz tried to steer the conversation to safer territory. "Where's Breck?"

"A prisoner in Fortress Munroe. His family got to Lincoln. He won't hang and might be banished to Canada. Grenfell is a different story. We have a Chicago lawyer but it's a stacked deck, another military tribunal picked by Judge Holt."

"Any chance of getting him out?" Schultz asked.

"Slim. The jail is well guarded but if they move him again, we might have a chance."

"Seems to be a lot of 'mights' around the Confederacy."

"Had enough, Theo?" Hines asked.

"I suppose I have. A lady in Nashville has agreed to come with me and make a fresh start in California."

"Long way to go," Hines commented.

"There's nothing to hold us."

"You won't leave until it's over?"

"No, but that day is close. I see it in Virginia and I see it here. It doesn't matter who wins, everyone has lost, except maybe the Negro and he didn't win much. So I'm going to drift to Nashville. You can reach me at Blocker's Tavern for the next few weeks."

Schultz reached again for his flask.

"I'll take one!" James Crawford interrupted, shaking off his blanket. "Man can't sleep with all the talking."

Crawford slipped a revolver back into his holster. "Wasn't sure what was happening," he explained sheepishly. "But I came to realize Captain Hines was in no danger."

He picked up the third mug and glanced at his snoring companion. "Let Mike sleep. Things have been tough on him. He found three of his family hung and don't know who did it or why. The country has become a sorry place."

"We're not alone," Hines hissed and kicked sand to douse the fire. He shook the sleeping Confederate, placing his hand across the mouth to stifle any yell.

"Light has gone out at the house. It may be a Yankee patrol."

"Lead on Michael," Hines ordered. "We'll take those walking paths you were telling us about."

Schultz was already mounted but held out a hand. Hines gripped it one last time.

"I'm going west," Schultz explained. "They'll have to track in two directions. Good-bye, Captain Hines."

"Take care, Theo."

CHAPTER 60

Virginia: March 14, 1865

The confidence was growing in the North. Sarah felt it in the capital with the troops swarming the streets. It was a swagger, a sense the powerful Federal forces would soon overwhelm the faltering rebels.

Still George Sanders had been exuberant when she left Montreal assuring her that the dispatches would change the course of the war. She touched her side, below the breast, and felt the strength of the herringbone corset. Inside the bone was the coded message.

"That is a very pretty outfit, Mrs. Slater." John Surratt tried again to make conversation.

"Thank you, John."

"Did you get it in Montreal or New York?"

Surratt was more annoying when persistent and she ignored him.

"I don't think ladies in Washington are wearing that shade of green."

The two women were dressed in their best. The clothing would be sold for a handsome profit.

"The pickets are acting different of late," Surratt resumed. "Hope everything is hid away." He stared into the low cut of her gown. Despite the warmth of the early spring, she pulled the cloak tighter and fastened the top buttons.

The checkpoint was as Surratt predicted. The questions were more direct and probing until a tiny, officious lieutenant ordered them from the wagon.

"Over there," he said, pointing to where several blankets hung from ropes to form a rough square.

"Go in there and disrobe. Place your clothing over the top of the line for inspection."

"I will not!" Sarah summoned her best haughty voice. "I am a lady and I will be treated as a lady."

"Disrobe or we'll disrobe you," the lieutenant told her. From the corner of her eye, she saw Surratt chuckling.

"Why not check the men?" she blurted out and instantly regretted the words. Surratt might be hiding something.

"Because we'd rather check women," the lieutenant persisted. "Women have more places to hide things."

The cloak, dress, petticoats, and pantaloons soon hung on the ropes to be probed by the dirty fingers of the guards.

"The rest of them."

The lieutenant wasn't tall enough to see over the blankets but Sarah could feel the leer on his face.

"Corsets, under things have to be checked."

"I will not!" Her anger mounted.

"You will or we will remove them."

"No!"

The lieutenant swore and called, "Marcie! Get over here. We have two reluctant belles."

"I's coming."

The blanket was pulled aside and held open long enough to offer a view for those beyond the enclosure. A series of whoops sounded from the guards.

A tall black woman stood before them. She wore a Union army blouse and pants.

"You can take them off, I can take them off, or I can bring a couple of the soldiers in to remove them."

Sarah was speechless.

"Do it now!" The woman drew closer. "I been putting up with white trash all my life and the bottom is now on top."

She motioned to Sillery. "You too, missy. You too close to white for my liking."

Sillery made the first move, going to Sarah, her shaky fingers fumbling with the ties on the corset until it fell away.

The black woman flung it on top of the rope.

"Might have to use the axe and break those bones," she called. "Check it all through. You next, missy! Everything!"

"No!"

"Don't sass me. Those soldiers would like to run their hands over you."

"No!"

The black woman moved quickly to grab the thin shift and pull. The cloth split and a small package fell to the ground.

"What we got, missy?" She scowled as Sillery backed away and covered herself with her hands.

The guard tore at the package, exposing a stack of card-sized photographs.

"Mistress know about these? Well she's going to now."

Her hand framed the images of a man and woman in the throes of passion.

"Look here." She forced the pictures into Sarah's face.

"Lieutenant! You got to see this. It's what's called French postcards!"

She opened the blanket curtain again to pass the cards. The officer began to laugh and the other guards joined in. Sillery cowered in a corner.

"You bitch! You whore!" Sarah exploded. "What kind of vile thing are you!"

"I sell them in Richmond," Sillery cried. "Men will pay."

"Tramp! I should have you whipped!" Sarah slapped hard, striking Sillery on the cheek. She moved to swing again but her arm was stopped by an iron grip.

"Ain't going to be no more whipping," the guard said, thrusting her face close to Sarah's. "Servants learn bad habits from white folks. Besides, if she don't want to go south, she don't have to."

Sillery rubbed her bruised face. "No, I'll go. I got a man in Richmond. I want to go."

"You a damn fool, girl!" the guard snapped. "But if you don't know any better, just go." She raised her voice. "Nothing else, Lieutenant, just a set of pale asses exposed to the wind."

The laughter from outside showed the guards were engrossed in the cards.

"OK Marcie, button them up and send them on their way."

Marcie glanced at the corset that hung forgotten on the rope, grabbed it and shook it before throwing it at Sarah's feet. "Little dust and dirt will make a nice pattern on that white skin. Get dressed!"

* * *

They were an hour beyond the checkpoint before anyone spoke aloud.

"Stop it, John!" Sarah demanded. "I am sick on your demented chuckling! A real man would have come to our defense."

"Like how?" He faced her. "I travel this route more than you do. I have myself and other couriers to protect."

He smiled as he thought of how to describe the scene. "Nearly naked," he'd say, "And one starts hitting the other. Soldiers didn't know what to do."

"I need an assurance of silence," Sarah pleaded. "A true gentleman would not discuss an incident of this nature."

"An incident of this nature," Surratt mimicked her words.

He pulled the horse to a stop and, still laughing, stepped down to check the harness.

"Can we hurry along?" Sarah asked.

"We'll go when I'm ready and not a moment before."

Sarah heard muffled sniffles coming from where Sillery sat on the wagon floor. "I'll deal with you later," she snapped. "Let's go!" she called to Surratt.

Instead, he lifted the horse's hind foot and picked at the hoof. Sarah stamped her foot in frustration.

"John, we must go!"

"John ain't going nowhere!" With a low growl, a soldier emerged from the brush. A faded blue tunic was ripped to expose the stump of an arm. In his one hand was an army revolver.

"Come out, Fred," he called.

Another scarecrow rose from the opposite side of the road and teetered for balance.

"We'll be taking the wagon, John. We'd take the women, too, but I can't abide by bitchy Southern types. You got your hands full, sonny."

Surratt stood speechless as the one-armed man advanced.

"Fred and me have had enough Southern hospitality."

Fred tried to speak but a harsh cough wracked his body and left him fighting for breath.

"He caught a prison disease and is feeling poorly," the one-armed man told them. He kicked at the back of Surratt's legs to send him tumbling to the ground.

"You know what's good for you, you'll stay down." Another kick in the middle of the back left Surratt flat on the road.

"You women, get out of there! Fred, get on the wagon. We'll ride in style."

Sarah and Sillery sat frozen.

"I ain't shot a woman yet but I can start," he warned. "Get down."

Sarah began to lift the long dress and swing over the side when she saw Surratt's gun on the wagon floor. She bent grabbed the gun, aimed at the one-armed man and fired. His face erupted in a bloody mass.

She spun to face the one called Fred, praying there was another bullet in the chamber. Fred stared through the horse's legs at his writhing companion before he crumpled from the second shot. Sarah dropped the gun as her arm began to shake.

Surratt pulled himself to a sitting position to comprehend what he had seen. Sillery covered her eyes with her hands.

"Come on," Sarah ordered. "Drag them into the bush."

She grabbed the foot of the one-armed man, trying not to look at what was left of his face. She felt rather than saw Sillery grasp the other leg and pull.

"Not too far," she gasped. "Get him behind the bushes."

"This one's still alive." Surratt stood above the wounded man.

"Drag him away," Sarah called, struggling with the body. Sillery lost her grip but Sarah wrenched the leg so the corpse could be moved.

Surratt still stood above Fred. The chest heaved as he fought for breath.

"Drag him." She pointed to the trees. "Leave him in there!"

Surratt continued to stare.

"Now, damn it!" she screamed.

He gingerly grasped the arms, stumbled, but regained momentum to drag the soldier from the road. Over the rasping wheeze, Sarah heard a sharp thunk as the head struck a rock, and then merciful silence.

"He was breathing," Surratt said, returning to the road. "But he can't last long." He bent to retrieve the Union revolvers.

"Give me one and throw the other away," Sarah ordered. "Don't go through the checkpoint with extra weapons. Heave it into the woods."

Surratt obeyed, flinging the gun into the brush.

She walked to where he stood, her expression full of loathing. He placed the other revolver in her hand.

"The safe house ahead. Gus Howell's, right?" she demanded.

He stepped back and nodded.

"We can walk," she told him. "And John, know this! I never want to see you again."

She turned her back and called to Sillery, "Let's go."

Surratt watched as the two women walked toward the South.

"I don't want this mentioned to anyone!" Sarah was cold and calm. "If I hear one word, I'll raise the French postcards. You say anything and I'll see that your child is taken away for good!"

"I don't collect them," Sillery tried to explain. "I sell them to make money. Men, especially soldiers, will buy anything."

"Just raise your skirt and make real money!" Sarah regretted the words as soon as she spoke. "I'm sorry. We've always been so lucky in our travels but all of this today. I'm not sure how much more I can handle."

* * *

WASHINGTON: MARCH 1865

Annie Cole chose a seat where she could see the front entrance. She wanted to see the surprise on Johnny's face. The desk clerk at the National had been reluctant to say anything beyond, "Mr. Booth has gone riding."

His last letter asked for money and said he missed her and that was reason enough for the hurried trip from Toronto.

"We should go to the theater," Annie heard a man say, one of two young civilian men in conversation.

"Nothing to see," his companion replied crisply. "None of the major players are in the city."

"But John Wilkes Booth is here," the first man replied. "I saw him this morning but I understand he doesn't perform regularly."

Annie shifted to better hear the conversation

"He's too busy with other…" the second man left a suggestive pause, "affairs."

"Quite a hand with the ladies, is he?"

Annie felt a blush. The things she could tell these boys.

"Certainly is." The first man dropped his voice. "He was in his cups earlier this week and I sat with him. The stories he told!"

"Well, go on," the second man prompted.

"He likes them young. He told me about a fifteen-year-old he was with last summer and surprise, surprise, her father didn't approve."

"Senator Hale isn't in rapture over Booth seeing his young daughter, either," the second man volunteered. "The girl can't be more than seventeen but she and Booth make a pretty picture."

Annie fought to control her emotions.

"Well, Hale's daughter isn't the only one," the first man snickered. "Booth was praising the skills of someone named Ella...uh, Ella Tasker. She's in a brothel in Hooker's Division."

Hooker's Division, the Washington red-light district, had grown with the war. General Joe Hooker's name graced the streets after he failed in an attempt to police prostitution and crime.

"Booth showed me a picture," the man continued. "He carries it in his pocket." He made a show of slurring his words, "So she's always close to his heart."

The two men began to laugh but Annie had heard enough. She rose only to see Booth stride through the entrance. Despite the anger, she felt the familiar surge of emotion. But his face was red, curled into a tight smile, a sure sign that an explosion was near.

"Annie!" He grasped her arm, no warm greeting, only a firm hand guiding her forward.

"My cousin has arrived," he told the desk clerk. "She needs to rest."

The clerk winked at Booth as the couple climbed the stairs.

"What are you doing?" he demanded in the privacy of the room. "Especially today?"

She reached for his hand but he pulled away.

"It's not a good day, Annie. I have to leave quickly."

He opened a suitcase. Shirts flew from a drawer but he didn't notice the small card falling to the floor.

Annie stared at the photograph of a smiling young woman with long, dark hair and an open blouse.

"Another cousin?" She tossed the card on his clothes.

Booth didn't hear or understand but began to ramble. "We were so close. We were going to grab him on the road to the Soldiers Home. I was so sure we'd have Lincoln today. The boat was ready, but it was all for nothing."

Booth slammed the case without noticing the card was half in and half out.

"The Federals may be on to us. Everyone got away, but that young pup Surratt insulted me. He said he'd seen women do braver things and that I wasn't equipped to lead and two other men want proof that Richmond approves."

He appeared to regain control as he paced. "But it's not over. I have men hidden around the city."

"Johnny!" She wanted to talk, to confront him over the women, but also to hold him.

"I have to go," he announced. "To New York."

"I'll come with you!" The thoughts of other women vanished. "I brought the money. We can go away together."

"The money," he spoke as if suddenly realizing that someone else was in the room. "Yes, I'll need funds."

"Then let's go," she urged.

"No! I have to go alone. Did you bring cash?"

Tears were close as she extracted an envelope. He thumbed through the greenbacks before stuffing it inside his jacket.

"Wait here!" he ordered. "Wait for an hour or so. If I'm being watched, they'll follow me."

"And when will I see you?" Tears blurred her vision.

"Soon. In Toronto. Or better yet, New York. Maybe the end of the month."

She waited for the embrace that never came. Instead, he snatched the suitcase from the bed and strode to the door.

The picture card was half out of the bag and she grabbed and tore at it. Booth didn't notice but as the door closed, she crunched the half girl to a tight ball.

Her eyes roamed the room as she sat on the bed. Booth had left a large trunk and a long coat hung from a peg. She toyed with her handbag and withdrew a second envelope. She wasn't sure why she had split the cash. Perhaps she expected him to say that half was hers, but more likely, she decided, it was habit, born from long experience with men and money.

CHAPTER 61

Richmond, Virginia: April 1, 1865

Dan Mcgruder delivered a light tap on the door and when a second, harder knock brought no response, he returned to the lobby of the Spotswood. The counter was bedlam with men lined four deep shouting instructions and questions.

"A carriage," one called, "Five thousand Confederate dollars for a carriage."

"I'll pay in greenbacks," another called, pushing the first aside. "I'll rent or buy as long as I get it now."

Mcgruder stepped on a chair to catch the eye of the harried manager and signal for the passkey. A black porter began to work through the crowd. Richmond was in turmoil but a colonel from the War Department could get action.

"Room 220," Mcgruder said, shoving the man up the stairs.

"Everyone is in an uproar over them Yankees," the porter told him. 'They say General Lee will abandon Richmond. What you think, Mr. Colonel, sir?"

"Never mind. Open the door!"

The porter shrugged and fumbled through a ring of keys.

"Lady must be feeling poorly."

He tried one key and when it didn't fit, tried another. "She used to be seen all the time, always well dressed, sparkling, a real Southern lady. But these past two weeks she stays in the room. Don't even come out for meals."

The fourth key turned the lock but before the porter could open the door, Mcgruder stepped forward.

"That's all—go!"

He waited for the porter to start down the stairs before entering the suite. The room was stuffy and dark and he opened the curtains to allow the daylight to penetrate.

Sarah lay as he left her, a small form covered by blankets, a bottle of laudanum half empty on the bedside table. At his insistence, Sillery had reduced the daily treatment.

"Vapors," a doctor had diagnosed. "Women's nerves aren't strong. Let her rest and keep her quiet."

Two weeks earlier, he'd found her perched on the side of the bed. She had thrown the corset at him.

"Take it to Judah Benjamin!" Her voice was coarse. "And tell him I'm done!"

She would say no more.

The corset had produced the opposite reaction at the War Department. The bones were opened to reveal coded messages and a flurry of couriers were dispatched with special orders. Mosby's men went on high alert; the railway superintendent prepared a special train; and a section of the Libby Prison was cleared. Bunks for twenty men were removed to leave a single iron bed. But as the days passed, there was no word from the North.

Lee tried to break the stalemate at Petersburg, driving a force into the American line at Fort Stedman but the attack failed.

Varina Davis, the president's wife, and her children had already joined the stream of refugees fleeing Richmond. Mcgruder suspected that her husband, the cabinet, and the rest of the Confederate administration would soon join the exodus. He considered his own plan as he sat beside Sarah.

Her blonde hair was matted and tangled and her usually bright eyes opened in rings of dark shadows.

"What daze sit?" The words were forced.

"Saturday, April 1."

She pushed to a sitting position. "Did they come?" she asked.

"No, we're waiting."

She tried to focus.

"No word?"

"Nothing."

"But you are still waiting?"

"We'll wait as long as we can," Mcgruder told her. "But conditions are changing fast. I need you ready to leave tomorrow."

"Then they won't come," she reasoned. "They were to bring him to Richmond. If there's no one here, why would they come?"

"That's what I think, too," he told her and gently took her hand. "The doctor thinks your nerves were acting up but Sillery and I believe you picked up some kind of disease. The fever affected your mind."

Sarah sank back on the bed.

"I have a vehicle." Mcgruder began to outline the escape plan. "Tomorrow night, I'll come for you. We'll move toward Jetersville. There's a farmhouse off the main roads. It's well supplied and safe."

"Sillery?" she asked.

"She'll come, too. Her daughter is there."

"She kept secrets," Sarah told him. "There were things I didn't know."

"What kind of things?" he asked.

"It's not important, at least not now. It doesn't concern us."

He continued to stroke her hand. "Rest. You'll need all of your strength."

"And you?" she asked.

"I have papers to destroy."

"The Canadian operations?" she asked.

"Yes. Sanders's message, the instructions on the raids, the incendiary attacks, the Northwest confederacy, everything. I'm not sure whom Benjamin is protecting but he wants them destroyed. He's sent word to Montreal that all records are to be guarded and if the worst happens, destroyed."

"And what is the worst?" she wanted to know.

"The worst is the failure to join the two armies. If either Lee or Johnston is beaten, Jeff Davis will face a tough decision. He refuses to consider surrender but if the armies are gone, there's nothing left. The men might take their guns and scatter into the woods and the mountains. Yankees would have to pacify the South."

"I've seen what happens when men take their own action." She turned to avoid his gaze. "I don't want to see any more."

* * *

COLLINGWOOD, CANADA WEST: APRIL 1, 1865

Great slabs of ice dotted the waters of Georgian Bay after the wind broke the main ice sheet. The harbor was open. True spring was weeks away but one day was all they had. The engineers confirmed that the boilers on the *Georgian* were serviceable and the ship showed no evidence of winter damage.

In the wheelhouse, Eramosa Willis called for power. The ship shuddered before breaking a thin layer of ice and moving slowly forward.

"Take her beyond sight of land," George Denison ordered. The dock was crowded with men and Denison suspected several were detectives.

"Thank you for coming so fast," Denison said, raising his voice over the thump of the boilers and the breaking ice. "This may be the last chance to finish."

Erin had exploded when the summons arrived a few days earlier, but a month's pay for a few hours work was too good to pass up.

"You sailed with Beall last fall?" Denison moved closer so there was no need to yell.

"It's strange without him," Willis nodded. "The ship is a pig, very slow in the water, but Beall made her work. We'll miss him."

"That we will," Denison agreed.

"So you know, this is a legal voyage. The province is trying to overturn my purchase and seize the ship, but judges take their time. She's mine at the moment and I'll decide where she goes."

"Don't count on privacy." Willis pointed to a small boat raising a sail to follow the channel through the broken ice.

"Damn!" Denison snorted. "McMicken has men everywhere."

"McMicken?" Willis asked.

"John A.'s spy. Macdonald has secret funds at his disposal as attorney general. And he thinks we bear watching."

He shaded his eyes to peer at the sailboat. "Can you out run them?"

"Not with the *Georgian*," Willis told him. "Not a chance."

"Damn!" Denison swore again. "We just need a few minutes."

"Well, you may get lucky." Willis pointed ahead. "There's a small fog bank. A brisk wind will break it up but if the wind stays calm, we'd have a few minutes before that sailboat arrives.

"That's all we need. Steer for it," Denison ordered. "I'll bring your man on deck and tell the rest of the crew to stay below."

Denison was back by the time the *Georgian* reached the fog bank.

"Stay here," Willis told Denison and pointed to the compass. "Keep her aimed due north. It won't take long."

He bounded from the wheelhouse and down the short flight of stairs to the deck where a figure shrouded in a overcoat and fur hat waited.

"If this is spring, I don't want to see winter," Amos Baker greeted him.

"This way." He guided Baker through the maze of lumber to two large wooden boxes. Willis lifted an axe from where he'd placed it earlier.

"There's one for you, as well. Let's see those black muscles work."

The axes soon shattered the wood and Baker whistled in surprise.

"Cannons! What are we going to do with cannons?"

"Put your back into it!" Willis ordered, pushing the first carriage and the black snout toward a loading gate on the ship. He pulled the pins to swing the gate open.

The two men bent and heaved to send the gun over the side. Minutes later, the second gun followed.

"Easiest money you will ever make," Willis told his helper. "Close and lock the gate."

Willis had returned to the wheelhouse by the time the fog cleared. The sailboat was a hundred yards off and moved toward them as the breeze filled the sails.

"Just in time," he told Denison, reaching up to blow the whistle as the *Georgian* changed course to return to the harbor.

"She feels fine to me," he told the owner. "In fact, she feels a little lighter."

"Thank you, Mr. Willis. I'll see you and your friend are well paid. I hate to lose the cannon but the Confederates have no more appetite for adventures in the North. Best to destroy the evidence."

QUEBEC CITY, CANADA EAST: APRIL 4, 1865

Geoffrey Ralston resembled a prehistoric beast. The great coat covered a tunic and vest; the pants topped woolen under drawers that emerged at the top of his socks. The boots were warming by the fireplace and his feet pointed to the flames.

"I caught a chill on the Niagara while training the militia and can't shake it." He blew his nose and glanced at the result before pushing the dirty linen back into his pocket.

"I've been laid up in barracks. This is my first time out and I do feel better."

"Good of you to share your misfortune." Forsey was testy. Despite the coughs and sneezes that dominated the legislative offices in the winter months, he was remarkably healthy.

"Surgeons say it's not contagious," Ralston reassured him. "It's a result of the climate on the Niagara with the freeze and thaw, freeze and thaw. The brisk cold of Quebec City is healthier."

"Well everyone will feel better when the spring comes," Forsey told him. "Especially your superiors at the Citadel."

"What's that supposed to mean?" Ralston demanded. "We don't get much news in the sick wards."

"When the river is open, reinforcements can come easily from England," Forsey explained. "The Confederation plan includes a railroad and year-round access to the East coast but until it's built, we depend on one bad road. And that's why we'll feel better when the river is open and the troop ships can reach Quebec."

"Do I detect a new level of anxiety?" Ralston asked. "A little fear picked up through association with the high and the mighty, perhaps? Are Macdonald and Cartier hearing something through the grapevine?"

"Well, it's common sense," Forsey told him. "When the Americans are fighting among themselves, we're no more than a distraction. But everything indicates a Northern victory in the next few months. They may not want to dismantle the war machine."

"So what's changed? We've know this for the last three years," Ralston replied.

"It's what they're hearing from the peace talks."

"The peace talks?" Ralston was incredulous. "The famous Hampton Roads Conference! It failed."

"Oh, you read the papers," Forsey shot back. "A few paragraphs to cover hours of meetings. It's what the papers don't report that's worrying."

"Go on," Ralston urged.

"Well, for a start, at Hampton Roads, the South suggested an armistice, time to settle the differences and re-arm, and then combine the armies and take Mexico."

"That's a problem for the Spanish and the Frenchies," Ralston told him.

"And do you think they would stop there?" Forsey asked. "They want the continent."

"But the talks failed," Ralston repeated.

"Oh, there's more. Have you heard of Chandler, Zach Chandler?"

Ralston considered for a moment. "Yes, politician from their Michigan territory, isn't he?"

"An American senator," Forsey replied. "A powerful senator. Chandler wants a two hundred thousand-man army of Confederate and Union troops. If he can win over a few more senators and President Lincoln, that army would be aimed at us."

"Two hundred thousand," Ralston repeated. "A powerful force."

"How can you be so nonchalant?" Forsey demanded. "It's like this happened every day."

"In my world it does," Ralston told him. "That's why we have the British army. That's why we train the militia. The army and the militia weren't created to parade on the Queen's birthday."

Ralston lifted his boots from beside the fire and slowly pulled them on.

"You've tapped into a deep pool of information. What's the best guess on when it would happen?"

"Macdonald believes the greatest danger is in the next year or so, perhaps next spring."

"And in the meantime?" Ralston asked.

"He'll push forward with the confederation scheme. One big country will be harder to conquer than four little ones."

CHAPTER 62

Richmond, Virginia: April 2, 1865

"Colonel, these horses are mighty fidgety just standing. Better if they're working."

"Not long now, soldier." Mcgruder dumped the contents of another crate on the bonfire.

One more box and he would be away. Another sharp explosion pulsed through the air. He had given up trying to determine the origin of each blast. The Tredegar munitions factory contained a mountain of ammunition, or it might be gunboats exploding from the river defenses on the James. Anything of value was being destroyed, from cotton and tobacco to food. Lee's army of Northern Virginia was in retreat and the Grant's army of the Potomac was not far behind.

Mcgruder poked the fire with a bayonet attached to a broken rifle. Light from the flames allowed him to read a label on the last of Judah Benjamin's files.

"Canada, Sanders, Booth." He froze for a moment and then with a quick motion pulled the file from the fire and stamped out the flame. The thick envelope was barely singed. In another moment, it was inside his jacket.

"Let's go!" Mcgruder had commandeered the services of a soldier, a team of horses, and an army ambulance. The canvas sides were unrolled and no would be able to see who was inside. The extra springs designed to soften the ride for the wounded would ease Sarah's journey.

"Spotswood," he told the soldier, noticing the crutch for the first time. "Can you walk?"

"Not very fast," the soldier replied. "Not fast enough to keep up with the army. I was in the Chimborazo Hospital, but this morning anyone that could move was called to duty and they put me on this ambulance. First thing I had to do was pick up a body…General Hill. A. P. Hill."

"Hill is dead?"

"Yes. Killed this morning. Mighty tough on the wife. She was General Morgan's sister."

Mcgruder wondered if Lee would find officers to replace men like Hill but concentrated on his primary mission.

Half an hour later, with Sillery on one side, and Mcgruder on the other, they lifted Sarah to the stretcher in the ambulance.

"Our bags." Sillery turned to return to the hotel.

"Leave them," he said.

"No. They're too valuable."

"Go then, but hurry!"

The crowds had begun to loot the stores and each pedestrian carried extra clothing or other booty. The order to destroy the army supply of alcohol was thwarted by the thirst of the mob.

An aging black man lurched against him. "Jubilee," he sang. "The whiskey is flowing in the streets. You catch it with your hat." He proudly displayed a sodden top hat.

His exhibition was interrupted by a regiment of Confederate soldiers. "Clear away! Clear away damn it!" A sergeant jumped to the boardwalk, drawn by Mcgruder's uniform.

"Still fight in 'em, sir. We've double timed from Petersburg and they're good for a few miles more."

"Well done, Sergeant, keep them moving."

"We'll be back," he yelled as he fell in at the rear of the column. "We'll be back."

John Breckinridge, the secretary of war, was the single cabinet member to stay in the city to supervise the evacuation. Eventually, the mayor would take control. The flames spreading across the sky suggested there was little time left for the transfer of power.

Sillery returned with a heavy carpetbag in each hand. The jingle of coins was lost in the noise from the street as Mcgruder lifted the bags to the ambulance. He pulled a revolver from his belt and thrust it into her hands.

"If anyone tries to climb in, pull the trigger."

The fear in her eyes was visible in the light from the burning city.

"I'll ride up front," he told her. "If there's trouble, I'll come back quickly."

As he turned an envelope fell from his coat. Sillery bent and retrieved it as a drunken soldier staggered toward the ambulance.

"Hey, I need a ride, too."

The appearance of a revolver changed his mind.

"Sillery, get in," Mcgruder ordered. His gun was trained on the soldier until she was on board.

The fires, drunken crowds, carriages, men on horseback, and bands of soldiers slowed the pace but at last, the ambulance bumped onto the bridge to the neighboring countryside. Only a few stragglers from Lee's force were still making their way over the river.

Mcgruder ordered the driver to lash the horses. Over the thump of the wheels on wood, he heard a shouted conversation between the engineers on the bridge guard.

"That ambulance will be the last. Blow her to hell."

* * *   ————

JETERSVILLE, VIRGINIA: APRIL 3, 1865

The shrill scream of the whistle signalled the approach of another train. John Headley and Robert Martin took a tighter grip on nervous horses as the engine and cars lumbered past the depot.

"That's the fourth train in the past hour. I didn't think the railroads would be that busy," Headley observed.

"Maybe we should take a train into Richmond. It would give the horses a rest and give us time to report to the War Department."

"Yes, do it the easy way," Headley agreed and began to tie his mount to a post. "The stationmaster can probably recommend a stable."

"I won't recommend a damn thing." The stationmaster's head appeared in the open window of the depot. "Far as I can see, the whole South is going to hell in a handbasket."

The man bolted at the sound of another train whistle. "Come around front. I can talk there."

Yet another engine lumbered across the greening Virginia countryside. The stationmaster waved a small flag until there was an answering whistle. The train inched forward, pulling the swaying cars.

"Pretty busy today," Martin noted as the train drew closer.

"Where in hell have you been?" the stationmaster demanded.

"Kentucky, Tennessee," Martin replied brightly. "Just back to Virginia."

"Well, everybody is leaving—at least everyone that can."

Martin tried to speak but the noise of the passing train drowned his words. Armed guards rode in the engine and in the vestibules between the carriages. The blinds were drawn on the final passenger car and more guards on the rear platform completed the show of force.

"Must be an important passenger," Martin said, watching as the train rattled off.

"We used to think so." The stationmaster cleared his throat and spit on the track. "That train is carrying Jeff Davis and the Confederate cabinet. Richmond has fallen, boys. Yankees moved in this morning."

His words were met with silence.

"Special trains have been coming out of the city for a week. First, it was well-to-do passengers and now this. Word is the Yankees have set the city on fire."

"Where's Lee?" Martin was thinking of the next move.

"Pulled out, I guess. Army supplies have been placed along the tracks in the last few weeks so we figured something was coming."

A train whistle drew his attention back to the line and in the distance, a dark smudge of smoke.

"This should be the last one. Last train out of Confederate Richmond! They could have moved faster on foot or on a wagon. Look there!" An army ambulance stirred the dust on the nearby road. "That could have come from Richmond as fast as these trains."

"Morgan's men," Martin asked. "Have you heard any word on Morgan's cavalry?"

"No, sir. If you want to know more, follow the path of our esteemed president."

The engine had picked up speed and churned toward the station.

"Damn fool!" the stationmaster swore and grabbed another signal flag. He waved frantically until the engineer responded with the whistle and the train slowed.

"Last thing we need is for the treasure train to rear-end the president."

Young men, cadets in uniform, looked down as the cars passed the depot.

"A sorry site," the stationmaster summed it up. "The president of the Confederate States of America rolling off into the sunset and a bunch of kids guard the treasury. There she goes, boys. I think I've seen the last of the Confederacy."

* * *

NEAR JETERSVILLE, VIRGINIA: APRIL 5, 1865

Sarah woke to the sound of songbirds. She eased slowly from the bed and staggered before grasping support on the windowsill. Below, an apple tree was ready to blossom and the grass had turned a bright, vibrant green. Her mind was clouded. She remembered a covered wagon and strange shadows that danced across the canvas, and voices, the throaty roar of mob mixed with exploding fireworks.

She saw Sillery in the yard below, pushing a black child who exploded with joy as a swing rose higher. Another black woman watched and smiled.

"It's the daughter." Dan Mcgruder's voice startled her but she relaxed at his hand on her back.

"I kept my promise to her," he began. "The only commitment I have left is to you."

Sarah braced against the window frame.

"You are getting stronger," he told her. "But we'll rest for a few days."

"Where will we go?"

"To Montreal and to Europe and as far away from war as we can get."

She had a sudden thought. "The bags! Gold coins were in my bags!"

"Sillery brought them. With the gold and what we have on deposit in Montreal, we can start fresh."

Money would be no problem. His only regret was the loss of the file salvaged from the fires. It had disappeared in the confusion of the escape.

"Where are we?" Sarah's question interrupted his thoughts.

"We're a few miles from Jetersville. Grant's army is close but we're off the beaten path."

"Sillery." She pointed to the scene below. "I have to thank her but she isn't what I thought."

"She saved you from a Yankee prison."

"She told you!"

"It was part of the plan from the start. She carried those pictures on every trip. We never knew when you would need a distraction. It was safer than arming both of you."

"And the Yankee prisoners?"

"There are escaped prisoners and deserters from both sides all across the South. There's no one left to maintain law and order."

CHAPTER 63

Near Appomattox, Virginia: April 10, 1865

The private's tone showed that he expected respect from a surrendered foe, even a ranking officer.

"Orders from General Grant. He said to bring these wagons of rations and you could distribute them."

"Thank you, private. That's very kind." Col. Eugene Waggaman forced himself to stand and walk to a wagon.

"In all honesty, it's your supplies," the private confessed, "seized just before the surrender. If you got there first, we'd still be fighting."

Waggaman ran his hands across the bags. If the men had had the rations at Petersburg; if they'd had time to eat and sleep instead of fighting at Saylers Creek; if they had been a few hours faster in the march; if they had been able to convince Lee to fight on...too many ifs. "It's welcome. We thank General Grant."

He studied the Union private and found something familiar. "I watched the Mclean house through my spy glasses yesterday," Waggaman said. "Were you there when the surrender was signed?"

His eyes had misted when General Lee slipped down from his horse, Traveller, to enter the house and he had looked at his handful of men and remembered the hundreds who had joined in New Orleans in 1861. He didn't say he considered joining those slipping off to fight on. Instead, he asked, "Are you on Grant's staff?"

"I'm part of the headquarters guard. Billy Caldwell is at your service."

"I'm Col. Eugene Waggaman." He put a special emphasis on the "colonel." The dirt on the uniform would make it difficult to distinguish rank.

"Then, Private Billy Caldwell at your service."

"Where are you from?" Waggaman needed to practice conversation for the coming days among the former enemy.

"I'm a foreigner," Caldwell smiled. "My family lives near London in Canada West. The Federal army bounties were too good to pass up."

"And did you earn the bonus?" Waggaman asked sharply. Thousands of enlisted men from many countries had turned the tide for the Union.

"I guess I did, Colonel. My regiment was pretty much wiped out at Cold Harbor. The few of us left became Grant's guard."

Waggaman's mind raced to the slaughter at Cold Harbor, the seven thousand Federals dead in less than an hour. He could have explained that Cold Harbor was one of the Grant's few blunders but instead he said, "Then you earned the bounty."

Waggaman saw his men watching. The scarecrows were hungry and he gave orders to unload the food.

"Was there something else?"

Caldwell had waited as the hungry men began to eat. "Well," the private appeared embarrassed, "the fellows say with the war ending it's important to have a souvenir."

Waggaman put his hand to his sword. He would not surrender the weapon to a mere private.

"Go on." His voice was icy.

"Well," Caldwell stammered, "a rebel button will impress the ladies."

Waggaman drew the sword and sliced a button from his sleeve. He picked it off the ground, polished it against his uniform, and handed it to the Canadian.

Caldwell drew himself to his full height. "Thank you, Colonel. You are a true Southern gentleman."

"And thank you, Private."

"And…uh…Colonel, if you ever travel to Canada West, come see me. But…uh…at London ask for Ira Kilbourne. People back home wouldn't know me as Billy Caldwell. He's a relic from another war."

* * *

WASHINGTON: APRIL 12, 1865

The crowd cheered and shouted for more but the secretary of war bowed politely and retreated from his second-floor balcony. "That should hold them." Edwin Stanton removed his glasses and began to polish. "Good to see you, Peter. How are you feeling?"

"I still tire easily. The doctors say to rest but I've been resting for months, and I couldn't miss this."

Washington was in the midst of a giant celebration set off by the fall of Richmond and Lee's surrender. Happy crowds filled the streets. Military bands paraded and virtually every building was lit by gaslights or by candles and torches.

"The illumination is a grand sight," Stanton confessed.

"And a chance to show loyalty," Peter Watson added. "The houses that are dark harbor rebel sympathizers."

"We'll soon deal with them," Stanton said. "But the President wants to let the South off easy—even allow Jeff Davis to escape. I'm betting he'll pardon most of their leaders."

"Like Lee?" Watson asked.

"Just one example. Grant's generous surrender terms were based on what he thought the president wanted. It's a little too generous for my liking. The vice president, on the other hand, smells blood. He believes those guilty of treason should be hanged."

"And the Negroes? What becomes of the freed slaves?" Watson asked.

"Ah, more divisive issues," Stanton replied. "If we allow rebels to regain local control, the Negro will suffer. The new labor agreements are already stacked in favor of the planter. Mr Lincoln suggests the intelligent Negro or those in the army might be allowed to vote. We both know military and intelligence don't always fit.

But those are issues for the future. The rebel fighters are just about played out."

"So will you begin to disband the army?" Watson asked.

"We'll take our time. A few Confederate diehards could take to the hills. I also want to send a message to our European friends. A few divisions on the Mexican border will put the fear of the Lord into the French and their puppet regime."

"And to the north, a message for Great Britain?" Watson asked.

"We'll be subtle with the Canadians. The Confederates are still there but the Canadians did surrender another of the Lake Erie pirates. There's still a legal fight over the St. Albans bunch but the northern border appears secure.

* * *

RALEIGH, NORTH CAROLINA: APRIL 13, 1865

"Where in hell is Wilson?" Lieutenant Carswell wheeled his horse beside a wagon loaded with barrels of gunpowder. "Is he drunk again?"

"Don't know," a soldier replied. "He was here a few minutes ago. He may have had a drink but he wasn't soused."

"I want that wagon moved..." The lieutenant stopped in mid sentence as Owen Wilson stepped from behind a stack of crates and buttoned his pants.

"Shake a leg, Wilson. That powder is needed at the front. General Sherman isn't going to accept any delay in capturing Raleigh."

Owen checked the harness on the team before walking to where the lieutenant waited.

"The powder will be delivered...sir."

Carswell could only shake his head. Wilson, once a dedicated soldier, had become a problem. If he wasn't drunk he was insubordinate.

Wilson pulled a cigar butt from a pocket and whipped a match against the iron rim on a wheel. He puffed deliberately before tossing the burning match aside.

"Stamp it out and now," Carswell ordered. "And put that damn cigar out, too. We're too close to the end to be blown to pieces."

"Yes, sir!" Wilson slowly stamped the lighted match and drew on the cigar before rubbing the butt against the wagon. A few sparks flew into the air before the embers died.

"You really don't care," the lieutenant said, shaking his head. "Lee's surrendered. When we finish off Joe Johnston, the war is all but over, and you don't care."

"Can't say as I do." Wilson stepped onto the wagon seat and grasped the reins of the team.

"Powder shipment goes straight up this road?" he asked.

"Right up to the outskirts of Raleigh." Carswell began to edge his horse forward but stopped.

"I know you've been through hell," he said softly, "but we can soon go home."

"Nothing to go home to, Lieutenant. I'm not sure where home is anymore. And I don't really care."

Carswell gave up. "Just go."

Wilson waited until he was out of site of the supply depot before reining in the team. He reached under the seat for another match and cigar before he urged the horses toward Raleigh.

CHAPTER 64

Charleston, South Carolina: April 14, 1865

"Close the door, Sergeant. Captain Shadd and I want to catch up before the ceremony."

Sgt. Cyrus Edwards delivered a crisp salute, stamped his foot, and marched from the room. Martin Delaney began to laugh.

"A few weeks ago, that man acted like a field hand who had never seen the big house. Now he's a man, right down to the boots, shined, so you could see a face. But what news from Chatham? Is the family well?"

"Everyone is fine," Shadd told him. "My father's last letter spoke of Mary Ann feeling lowly—not really sick but drained emotionally. Those recruiting trips took a lot out of her. But she'll recover, she always does."

"A fine woman," Delaney nodded. "But she needs a man's direction. She has some very progressive ideas—women's rights and that sort of thing."

"Well, that's Mary Ann. We won't change her. My father is watching the Canadian political scene and this business of uniting the provinces. He'd like to be one of the members in the new Parliament but knows the odds of electing a black man are pretty long."

"Vote in a block," Delaney began, but stopped abruptly as Shadd held up a hand.

"The black community around Chatham is shrinking. First, a few men left to join the American army. Now others are drifting south.

Father will stay. Kent County is home. But there won't be enough men at the county level to elect a black man. The rest of us have cast our lot with the USA."

"And in the USA, we must organize the black vote." Delaney lifted a thick document from a bookcase. "This shows Southern counties where the black population is larger than the white. You might want to study that."

"It will be a struggle," Shadd told him.

"But we have the power and the right to speak," Delaney countered. "Last night I spoke to an Episcopalian minister, a man all sanctimonious. He used to offer a weekly prayer for Jefferson Davis but won't do it again. And he won't be using his favorite texts. No more sermons on, 'Servant, obey thy master'. I stopped that too."

"Ministers don't take kindly to that," Shadd told him.

"And ministers don't have a black army to back them. The people must decide how to worship. The other morning, I went to the shore before dawn to watch the sunrise. Two men were there before me. As the sun rose, they bowed toward the east. I've seen it before, among the followers of Mohammed in Africa. The tradition came on the slave boats with their ancestors and no white logic or whips could beat it out. It makes me wonder what other memories are locked in our hearts. And—"

A crisp knock on the door interrupted him.

"Come in," he called.

Sergeant Edwards marched into the room, stamped his foot on the floor, and stood at attention. "Toussiant Delaney of the 54th Massachusetts. I'm sorry, I forget his rank, but he's waiting at the carriage."

"Would you wait with him, please?"

The boot stamped the floor and the sergeant marched away.

"So your son is safe?"

"He's safe and will help us as we make history. Four years to the day since the rebels opened fire on Fort Sumter, and we'll see the very flag that was lowered rise again."

"There's not much there but a pile of rubble."

"But the ceremony is a symbol. And when black men like us stand proudly and salute the flag, it will show how the world has changed."

"You are sure the world has changed?"

"Oh, it's changed," Delaney asserted. "I met the president of the United States. The changes may take time but Lincoln will support us."

* * *

WASHINGTON: APRIL 14, 1865

"Mr. Booth is a guest but he is out and that is all I will tell you." The desk clerk at the National Hotel was in no mood for polite chatter.

"Could you check to see if he left word of where he was going?" Annie Cole demanded.

Booth had failed to arrive for a rendezvous in New York City but Annie was determined to give the actor one last chance. The clerk scowled but reluctantly checked the mail slots.

"Nothing," he said smugly. "You'll have to move on."

"The theaters?" she asked. "Johnny has friends at Ford's. Where is that?"

"Go up Pennsylvania to Tenth. It's not far."

The Good Friday crowds swarmed the sidewalks as she made her way.

She hadn't decided what to say. The war was ending. She wondered if he would return to the stage or perhaps when he saw her dedication, the two of them would be together.

"Out of the way!" someone shouted an alarm.

A well dressed rider was hunched over a horse, whipping it to a full gallop.

Annie was jostled and struggled for balance.

"That fellow is either drunk or a complete asshole," a man concluded. "He rode out of the alley behind the theater and didn't care who was in his way. Are you all right?" He extended a hand to steady her.

"Oh, I'm fine."

He shook his fist at the departing rider. "He should be arrested for carrying on that way."

"Ford's Theater?" she asked. "Is it far?"

"No, just ahead there, where the people are coming into the street. That's Ford's but the show must be over. Everyone is leaving."

"Someone's been shot!" a man yelled from ahead. "We need a doctor at Ford's!"

"It's the president!" a woman screamed from the theater door. "President Lincoln has been shot!"

Annie felt the weakness spread through her body. She pushed across the sidewalk and leaned against a wall.

"It was one of the actors," said a woman rushing by. "An actor shot him."

"I saw him!" another witness called. "It was John Wilkes Booth!"

"Get out of the way!" A squad of soldiers arrived to clear a path. "They're bringing him out."

Annie forced herself to the edge of the cordon.

A group of men carried a silent form. Strong hands gently cradled the head while soldiers lifted his arms and legs. "Take him to that boarding house across the street, the building that Peterson owns."

A bloodstained man walked backwards, scraping at Lincoln's head. Gore dripped onto the street with each step.

"It's real bad," she heard someone say. "He won't survive the ride to the White House."

The press of the crowd carried Annie within steps of the procession.

"He won't make it," a man sobbed. "And the son of a bitch that shot him won't get far. I'll cheer when John Wilkes Booth is hanged."

The procession entered the house as more soldiers arrived to ring the building.

"Oh, no!" She heard another scream. "Seward has been attacked too! Mr. Seward, the president, and maybe more. It's the rebels, as sure as you live! A rebel plot!"

She thought of Booth's associates, the plans for abduction, and felt sick but stayed in place through the night. She was in the silent throng as dawn broke and a coffin arrived, and when a military guard surrounded a wagon to walk the dead president to the White House.

And then it was time to go. To search for a place where no one would ever find her.

* * *

CINCINNATI, OHIO: APRIL 15, 1865

The glass in the store window smashed but the shower of rocks and stones continued.

"All of Cincinnati must show respect!" a high-pitched female voice sang from the crowd. "Loyal storekeepers are putting up crepe and pictures of our beloved Mr. Lincoln but these Southerners are going on with business. There's another store with no remembrance. Smash it! Break it open!" And the mob surged to the next target.

Tom Hines joined the chants for retribution.

Outside the Western Union office, someone had chalked the latest headlines.

"President Lincoln murdered; Search continues for Assassins, Great Confederate Conspiracy."

The mob surged forward but Hines slipped into the telegraph office to find a single operator at work.

"Be with you in a minute," the operator called. He finished the message and strode to the counter.

"Sending a telegram?" he asked brusquely.

"No, George. I wanted to see you."

The full beard and moustache matched the gray over the customer's ears. He wore a battered Union army cap but the blue eyes were familiar.

"Tom." He took a breath. "Tom Hines."

"I was hoping you would be on duty, George."

"Not for long," Ellsworth told him. "I'm waiting for my relief. After that, I'm gone. Things are a little hot for my liking."

"I can help with money," Hines told him, opening his coat to withdraw an envelope. "I wish it could be more. You've served us well."

"Didn't do much but take messages," Ellsworth responded, but he snatched the envelope.

414

"You heard Grenfell was convicted?"

"No, but I expected as much."

"Death but no execution date. The newspapers described him as 'a merciless mercenary'. Grenfell was shackled and so weak that a soldier had to carry the ball when they took him to the cells."

"Is the lawyer still in town?" Hines asked.

"No, but he was in the other day. The message to his family in Chicago said he was going to Washington. He wants a stay of execution. Maybe he'll approach the British. After all, Grenfell is English."

"If I leave another envelope, can you get it through? It might buy Grenfell an easier time and show him he's not abandoned."

"I can do that." Ellsworth pocketed the second envelope. "Grenfell and I had our differences when we rode with General Morgan but we patched things up."

"Thank you, George." Hines turned to leave but then asked, "What about you? Where will you go?"

"South," Ellsworth smiled. "Maybe deeper south than I've ever been."

"Always work for a good telegrapher," Hines prompted.

"No, that's changing, too. Pennsylvania Railroad has been training women for the last few years, and they work cheaper. But some South American country wants to hire fighting men. I'll see what they have to offer. And you? Where can Tom Hines find shelter?"

The street door swung open and teenage boy entered the office.

"Evening, George." He stepped behind the counter. "Not safe on the streets tonight. People are crying and scrapping over the death of the president when a few days ago they were all railing against him."

"That's my relief, Tom Edison," Ellsworth explained. "The boy is young but smart as a whip when it comes to electricity and making gadgets." He dropped his voice. "And he's hard of hearing. So where will you go?"

"Canada." Hines spoke softly. "A couple of friends have a house on Lake Erie. I'll look for refuge there."

"I thought of going home," Ellsworth told him. "I talked about it with the boy, here. He worked the railroad in the southern part of

Canada West and has family there. But we both decided it was too quiet."

Hines smiled. "Quiet may be what I need."

"George? Have you forwarded these messages to Detroit?" Edison called from across the room.

"Yeah, but there's another set over on the supervisor's desk." Ellsworth turned and pointed to the table in the corner. He dropped his voice again when he saw Edison reach the stack. "It was an honor to serve with Captain Hines."

But the Confederate agent was gone.

Through the glass in the office door, he watched Hines dart past Union soldiers and disappear in the night.

EPILOGUE

Tom Hines did find refuge in Canada but later returned to Kentucky, where he became a judge.

Thomas Edison included George Ellsworth in his autobiography, suggesting the telegrapher came "to a bad end," but other evidence suggests "lightning" was drifting through the South into the 1890s.

Sarah Slater and Annie Cole appear to have vanished with the end of the war.

John Surratt escaped to Montreal and was in hiding when his mother was hanged as an accomplice of John Wilkes Booth.

Bennet Young was active in the Confederate Veteran movement. He also wrote a book on the Battle of the Thames.

Bennet Burleigh returned to England to become a famous war correspondent but apparently wrote nothing of the raid on Johnson's Island.

The death sentence imposed on Georges St. Leger Grenfell was commuted to life in prison. He was confined at Fort Jefferson on the Dry Tortuga's, escaped in a violent storm and disappeared without a trace.

John A. Macdonald became Canada's first prime minister when Confederation was implemented in 1867. He continued to employ Gilbert McMicken as a special detective. McMicken's men infiltrated the Fenian movement but were unable to prevent the assassination of Thomas D'Arcy McGee.

George Denison remained active in the Canadian military. Toronto's Denison Armoury bears his name.

Dr Solomon Secord became a family doctor in Kincardine, Ontario.

Mary Ann Shadd Carey returned to the classroom before playing a role in both the Civil Rights and Women's movements.

Martin Delaney remained active in Reconstruction and with the Freedmen's Bureau.

To learn more and see a list of sources visit www.almcgregor.com.

———

ACKNOWLEDGEMENTS

My thanks to all of the historians and history buffs who patiently answered my questions over the years. For the Civil War period, a salute to the Buxton National Historical Site where I was introduced to the rich stream of Black History and to the members of the South Western Ontario Civil War Roundtable, who educated and entertained me.

Matthew Godden at Thames Valley Wordworks provided early editorial suggestions, while K.C Steffani through CreateSpace helped bring the manuscript to completion. Deborah Phibbs at Quantum Communications created the cover.

Shannon, Sean, Chris and Staci, suffered through the monologues at family gatherings through the years but continued to offer valuable help and encouragement.

And, Suzanne. For everything!

Al McGregor
Canada West, 2012.

Stephen Dayle 44   London, Ca 406
Gen Ulysses Grant 68
Chatham 79
Shadd 117
Josiah Henson 176
Irish or negroes 138
Horace Greeley 142
George Sanders 144
Booth 161
PCI 188
Jeff Davis 199
Mann Bars Island 202
Will can't trust The Canadians
Blacks in army 8 corp 237
Learn from US mistakes 242
Darcy McGee (good) 242
Class distinction 244
Rush Bagot Agreement 248
Forsay ? Ralston Fenwick ?256   wms
Fen ½ ein 2 win Vic
If wishes were horses then beggars would rede 257
War 261
Germans oppose slavery 264
Lynched an African 334
War may end for whites not for blacks 344
Savannah ? 356
Andrew Johnson 357
Yankees use torture 369
Three of in family hung 381
Marcie 385

Made in the USA
Charleston, SC
14 April 2013

Headly #1